PROGENY

WARRIOR SERIES

Also by Melanie P. Smith

Warrior Series

> Dusk
> After Dark
> Serendipity (Novella)
> Dawn
> Shadows
> Intrepid (Novella)
> Chaos
> Exposed

Thin Blue Line Series

> Mount Haven

Novels

> Hidden Lakes

PROGENY

Warrior Series
Book Seven

---

by:
Melanie P. Smith

MPSmith Publishing

0 9 8 7 6 5 4 3 2 1

www.melaniepsmith.com

Dedication:

Progeny is the 7th and final book in my Warrior Series. Therefore, I thought it only fitting to dedicate this story to the 7th and final member of my family...my youngest brother, Josh. Here's to superheroes, mayhem, dancing before you could walk and all the "lasts" out there who make life a little more interesting.

Chapter One

Dante sat in the overcrowded room, wishing someone would turn the bloody music off. The stereo was turned up so loud the speakers were vibrating profusely. A small speaker perched on a nearby bookshelf caught his eye. He waited patiently, knowing the thing would tumble to the floor any minute. Each boom from the bass brought it closer to the edge. Just a couple more bounces and the speaker would be toast. Dante sighed, it wouldn't be so bad if the sound vibrating throughout the room was tolerable, but rap music? Now, wasn't that an oxymoron? He never did understand the draw. Okay so it had a beat, but that didn't make it music. Listening to a guy yelling gibberish as fast as he could while music played in the background was not singing. Dante let out a short laugh. He was starting to sound like his grandfather. Pops incessant complaining about rock music had always

Progeny

amused Dante. Hard rock wasn't singing either, but he enjoyed the classics every once in a while. There's nothing like a little Axel Rose, Def Leppard, or AC/DC to get the blood pumping. He continued to grin remembering those long days on the yacht, waxing the deck and listening to album after album while Pops mumbled under his breath about the state of the world today. His grandfather attributed every catastrophe imaginable to the younger generation and their obnoxious music. That was different he assured himself, deep down knowing it was exactly the same. Dante was getting old.

His mind continued to wander, remembering the last time he'd seen his Grams and Pops. He'd tracked them down outside Australia, then flown out and surprised them for the weekend. The time they'd spent on the open water had been heaven. He wished he could do that again. He hadn't seen them in over a year now and he missed them terribly. They rarely sailed into New York and with this annoying vampire war, it would be months before he'd have a free weekend to travel again. A relaxing weekend on the yacht was definitely in the distant future. But, it was exactly what he needed right now.

Dante grunted in annoyance and jumped to his feet just in time to avoid a lap full of redhead. She was beyond drunk but he wasn't sure the loss of balance was an accident. In fact, he was pretty sure it had been deliberate. The woman had been eyeing him all night. Not so long ago, he would have been game for a little action but not tonight and never with a redhead. He was losing his appetite for casual flings. To be honest, he'd lost his appetite a long time ago. Wouldn't his fellow warriors be

2

stunned to hear that? They were so sure he still loved to party. Dante walked to the large cooler and pulled out another beer. This whole scene was getting to him. He casually leaned against the wall and glanced around the room in disgust. Why had he ever believed this was fun? There was a small group in the corner getting high. He'd always hated the smell of marijuana and never understood why humans used drugs in the first place. The smell threatened to take him back to another time, another place, a time he didn't want to think about, so he continued to scan the darkened room.

There was a couple sprawled in the corner, a corner that wasn't nearly dark enough for their current state of undress. In another minute or two, they'd be in the throes of passion, right there in the open. At least he always found a room, or at the very least a closet. Along the far wall was a large group downing shots then cheering themselves like they'd achieved something spectacular. The rest of the crowd was dancing, drinking or yelling at each other in an attempt to converse over the loud music. He was sick of this scene. He was sick of himself. This wasn't fun. It was degrading. Dante found himself wondering once again why he was here. He downed the last of his beer and stumbled for the door. He had to get out of here. He couldn't take one more minute of the absurdity these people called fun. It just wasn't the same without Nick and Thomas. Just when he thought he'd make his escape, a curvy blond blocked his exit.

"Hello Dante," she crooned. "I was hoping you'd be here tonight." The woman took his arm and led him toward the couch. "Don't tell me you're leaving already." Her

Progeny

face shifted into a pout to match her tone. "I haven't had a chance to talk to you yet," she paused, then fluttered her eyes. "Do you like my dress? I wore it just for you." She was wearing a very short, very tight skirt and a skimpy tank that barely covered anything.

Dante let the girl pull him back onto the couch. He'd humor her, for a minute. Then he'd escape. She'd just have to deal with the disappointment. He knew he had a rep and usually he didn't mind. It made things a lot less complicated when he needed that escape. Tonight, he did mind. Tonight he just wanted to be left alone. So he'd talk to the girl until she pressed for more, then he'd try to let her down easy. This one would pout. He was sure of it. She'd pout and try to manipulate, then she'd leave angry and hit on someone else. He'd seen it a million times before. That was another thing he'd grown to hate about this scene, the people here were all so shallow. Dante settled against the back of the couch. He was stuck for now but the instant he got an opening, he was heading home.

Cornelia exited the alley and continued along the sidewalk. Tonight had been a bust. She'd been restless since the New Year's battle. She knew she should have left town but every time she decided to go, Dante convinced her to stay. It was infuriating really. The man was just too sexy and adorable for his own good. Well, for her own good anyway. She'd promised him, numerous times, she wouldn't leave without talking to him first. And for some reason, she couldn't tell him no. It had been over a month and she was still here. She was worried that man could talk her into anything. That was dangerous, very dangerous, but unavoidable. Next time she talked to him she would

4

tell him no. She would ignore her libido and insist she had to leave. Yeah, right. As if that was going to happen.

Her days were easy enough to occupy. The job Dante had asked her to take on was proving a bit more challenging than she would have believed. Lillie's ex wasn't a financial wiz, but the guy paying him had talent. She'd finally tracked the money to the Cayman's but then it got tricky. Whoever was funneling those funds was no amateur that was for sure. She thought she'd caught a lead this morning, but was stonewalled the minute she called the bank. If she couldn't find someone willing to talk over the phone, she might have to fly out there and deal with the problem in person. Dante would argue of course. But either he wanted her to find the culprit, or he didn't. It was really that simple, she told herself with a defiant nod. It had nothing to do with her desire to bolt, not really. Cornelia frowned, she never could lie to herself. It had everything to do with the need to escape and she knew it.

She sighed, her mood getting worse by the minute. She was becoming an insomniac and wondered if she could actually die of the boredom. She had nothing to do. Once normal business hours were over, everything had to be put on hold until the following morning. That was the downside of handling an investigation from miles away. Twice, she'd attempted to pass the time by stopping in at night clubs, but that had only depressed her. She blamed Dante for that too. The man did things to her emotions. Things she'd never experienced before. Just his touch sent electricity jolting through her system. Something as simple as his sexy grin sent her stomach muscles into a frenzy. How was she supposed to enjoy another man's company

Progeny

when she couldn't get Dante out of her head? Needless to say, both attempts had failed. She'd sat in the dark alone, watching the door all night, wishing the sexy warrior would miraculously walk in and join her. She knew it was ridiculous, but she just couldn't stop herself. Both nights she'd left even more depressed and lonely than she'd been when she arrived. After the second time she gave up, what was the point? She was destined to be alone and fantasies about sexy warriors made it harder to accept that fate.

Then there was the other thing. The vampire thing. It was keeping her up nights worrying. The night of the battle had shaken her more than she liked to admit. She was sure Radek had sensed her. The vampire king's pull was persistent in the beginning, but she'd been able to ignore it without much effort. Then it grew stronger and more intense. The more she ignored it, the stronger it became. If she had just a little more vamp in her, she would have been doomed. Knowing that terrified her. But the thing she feared even more was the possibility that her father might try to imprison her or worse, convert her and use her against her friends. She would not join the vampires. She would die before she hooked up with those blood sucking monsters.

And what about Alex? So far she'd been able to avoid the Fae Queen, but that wouldn't last. Now that Alex knew about her genetics, Cornelia would be shunned for sure. Or worse, shackled and turned over to Radek. Cornelia was still angry with herself. She'd made such a stupid mistake and it had cost her. If she hadn't been injured in that New Year's battle, Alex wouldn't have healed her wounds. Now the queen knew she was part vampire, there were too many differences to overlook. Dante was convinced Alex and Dimitri would accept her regardless of her DNA, but Cornelia wasn't so sure.

She turned a corner and stopped abruptly when she spotted a man. Was that Dante coming out of such a dilapidated building? What was he doing in there, alone? She glanced at her watch, then back to Dante. It was after one in the morning. She got as close as she dared, then moved into the shadows and watched.

Dante was drunk, which was fine with him. Unfortunately, his body was already fighting off the toxins in his bloodstream. That wasn't okay, before long he'd be sober. The downside, he'd be in desperate need of blood. He exited the old building, reached back to pull the door shut, tripped and stumbled to the ground. He let out a short laugh then forced himself to stand. He needed to get home. Once there, he could drink a bag of blood and fall into bed. Maybe there would be just enough of a buzz left to help him forget his past and get a couple hours rest. The fiasco he'd just left hadn't helped. He should never have let that blond pull him back into the room.

He had to admit at first, the catfight between the two women was entertaining. But, by the time they were finished, Dante was bolting for the door. He wasn't a slab of meat. Sure, both the blond and the redhead were hot, but they acted as if he didn't have a choice in the matter. To the victor goes the spoils. Well, no thank you. And were all redheads that vicious? No, they weren't, he reminded himself. He knew that. Sam was a beautiful, sweet redhead and nothing like that woman, nothing like

Progeny

his ex-wife, Shannon. He used to love Shannon's hair, Dante mused. The vibrant color almost glowed in the sunlight making her seem ethereal somehow. The various colors of red that made her seem so soft and angelic at first, reminded him of the fiery depths of hell in the end. Shannon had been vicious, selfish and spoiled, just like the redhead he rejected moments ago. He closed his eyes and took a deep breath, trying to push the memories away and failing.

Dante reached his car and fumbled in his pocket for his keys. He allowed himself an instant to savor the moment one last time. It had felt so good to shoot that red headed vixen down cold. He only wished he'd done the same thing to Shannon thirty-five years ago. But he wouldn't go there, not tonight. He fumbled again with his keys, trying to find the right one and watched as they slipped from his fingers and collided with the asphalt. Dante swore under his breath, reached for the keys, lost his balance and ended up on the ground again. This time he didn't move, he just closed his eyes and groaned. He was beginning to wonder if he'd ever get home. His head was pounding and the alcohol was rapidly wearing off. Anyone that saw him would think he was drunk. Not so much, not anymore. In the short space of time between the catfight and leaving the building, his blood had already consumed most of the alcohol, leaving only pain behind. Now he was suffering from the aftermath. Once again, he pulled himself upright and began fumbling through his keys. If he could just find the right one, this night would be over soon and his head would stop pounding.

Cornelia approached the car, grabbed Dante's keys then pushed him out of the way impatiently. The man was drunk. She didn't know that was possible for a warrior, but she'd encountered her share of drunk humans before. Dante had all the signs. She pressed the button on the remote to unlock the doors then took Dante's arm and began leading him toward the passenger side.

"Hey," Dante said planting his feet. Cornelia gave his arm a tug but when she felt resistance, she let go. Dante hadn't expected that. The instant release caused him to lose his balance. He stumbled and landed flat on his behind...again. He groaned as pain shot through his head.

Cornelia crouched down immediately. "I'm so sorry. Are you okay?" she asked, concern radiating in her voice. If the man kept falling down, he would eventually get seriously hurt.

"I'm fine," he grumbled, standing again. "Look, I'm on my way home. If you're looking for a good time I recommend you go to a club or something. The party up there is a bust."

"I'm not looking for a party, Dante." She took his arm again and led him toward the car.

Cornelia reached down and pulled the passengers' door open then tried to push Dante inside.

"Did you hear me?" he asked impatiently. "I said I'm going home. And this is America. We steer from the left." He jabbed his finger at the other side of the car.

Progeny

"Get in the car," Cornelia said just as impatiently. "You're drunk. I'm driving."

Dante looked at Cornelia in surprise, one eyebrow rose in challenge. "My car, I drive."

"Not tonight," Cornelia said, giving him a more forceful push. Dante stumbled, then fell onto the seat. Cornelia didn't hesitate, she shut the door then rushed around and slid behind the wheel. "I could see you were drunk from a mile away. If you were stopped by a cop, he'd draw blood for sure. Then what? How would you explain the anomaly? I'm not risking exposure to satisfy your ego."

Dante laughed. "Points for you," he said, amused. He'd never been stopped by a cop before and didn't intend to start tonight, but if Cornelia wanted to drive him home he'd let her. The effects of the alcohol were gone now. He'd need some blood soon or the cramping would begin. Not a good combination with the headache.

"Now that we're on the same page, where am I going?" Cornelia asked as she started the engine. Of course, the sleek sports car had to have a manual transmission. She could drive a stick shift, but it had been years. She knew she'd be rusty and hoped she didn't embarrass herself.

Dante rattled off his address then let his head rest against the side window. He was tired, but worse he was fighting the pain and fatigue that always accompanied his partying. Severe cramping would come next. That was the downside of a good drunk. His body or more to the point his blood, would rush to the alcohol and consume it. Unfortunately, that would also break down and consume the warrior blood. If he didn't replace it quickly, his body would have to run short causing pain, fatigue and ultimately cramping. Dante frowned, he was weaker than he should be. Nick had warned him about too much drinking, but Dante had blown off his friend's concern for decades. Now he was beginning to wonder if Nick was right. The more Dante drank, the longer it took for him to heal and the more blood he was having to consume to feel whole again. Dante closed his eyes and tried to force everything from his mind. He didn't want to think about Nick's lectures. He didn't want to think about the intense loneliness that had become a constant companion now that his two best friends had found the women of their dreams. He didn't want to think about anything. He was just going to sit here and enjoy the silence and the cold window on his throbbing temple.

Cornelia pulled into Dante's garage and shut down the car. She glanced at the muscular man next to her and wondered what she was going to do now. He was leaning against the window, eyes closed and perfectly still. She was pretty sure he had passed out on the way home. If she opened the door, he'd fall to the floor. She was strong, but she didn't think she was strong enough to carry a warrior to his bed. She jerked in surprise when she realized Dante was watching her.

Dante felt the car stop and opened his eyes. They were parked in his garage and Cornelia was concentrating. He wasn't sure what was going through that pretty little head of hers, but he thought she looked adorable. He grinned when she jerked out of her thoughts and struggled for something to say. Dante reached for the door knob and slowly stepped from the car. "You're welcome to come in if you want. Otherwise, I'm going to need my keys. I keep the door locked when I'm out."

Cornelia jumped from the car and ran for the door. She glanced at the keys and isolated the one that looked like a house key, hoping she was right. Once she'd dealt with the lock, she placed a hand on Dante's arm and guided him into the house. Dante reached for the light, but Cornelia stopped him. She didn't need it. She could see just as well in the dark as she could in the daytime, one of the actual benefits of being part vampire. She paused long enough for Dante to shut off the alarm, then guided him through the kitchen and into a large foyer. "Where to cowboy?" she asked, trying to sound casual.

"Upstairs and to the right," Dante answered. Did he want Cornelia in his bedroom? He couldn't answer that right now. He didn't need her help. His buzz was completely gone now. What he needed was blood. Then he could decide what he wanted to do with, or maybe to, the sweet but sexy PI.

Cornelia helped Dante up the stairs and into the master bedroom. She released his arm the instant they reached the enormous bed. "Restless sleeper?" she joked, trying to push away the image of Dante's gorgeous body sprawled in that big bed.

"Huh?" Dante asked confused as he pushed off his left boot with his right foot.

"The bed," Cornelia waved her hand. "I think that's probably the biggest bed I've ever seen. I was just wondering if you were a restless sleeper," she paused, a little impressed that he'd gotten his boots off so quickly. "Do you roll around a lot and need the room so you don't fall off?"

"No," Dante said, forcing himself against the headboard. "Would you please grab a bag of blood out of that small refrigerator in the closet?" His head was pounding so hard it felt like it was going to explode. Just the thought of leaning over to retrieve the blood himself was agonizing.

"Oh," Cornelia said in surprise. "Are you injured?"

"No," Dante assured her. "But alcohol depletes my blood. I need a bag to replenish what my body has used up trying to kill the toxins," he paused. "If you need some, there's plenty. There are glasses in the small cupboard next to the fridge."

Cornelia returned with a bag of blood and two glasses. "I thought I'd share yours then if you need more I'll get you a fresh one." It was still strange for her to sit down and have a glass of blood with Dante as if they were sipping fine wine or something. She'd never been comfortable drinking blood in front of anyone before, not even her mother. She glanced at Dante and somehow knew she'd never be this comfortable around anyone else. Knowing that made her a little sad. She was going to miss him so much when she finally moved on.

Progeny

"Thanks," Dante said as she handed him a glass. He took a sip and studied Cornelia. She seemed nervous and maybe a little melancholy. That was a drastic change. She'd had such a take charge attitude when she thought he was drunk and planning to drive. Well, he had been a little drunk but that condition was very temporary once he stopped consuming the alcohol. He forced down the blood then handed her the glass for a refill. The two of them silently went through two bags of blood. Once he finished his last glass, Dante stood, stripped to his underwear and crawled into bed. He was so tired.

Cornelia studied Dante and sighed. Now that she got the man home safely, what was she supposed to do? He was obviously still sloshed. Otherwise, he would have offered to take her home. She wished she knew more about a warrior's metabolism, but she'd been sheltered all her life. Maybe Dante had a guest room. Or...maybe she could just sleep in here, with him. Cornelia hesitated only an instant then stripped down and climbed into bed. She'd get a few hours' sleep, then work on tracking Lillie's ex again. When Dante got up he could drive her home. There was no reason to search the house for a guest room when there was such a large inviting bed right here. Dante had probably passed out again anyway. She could snuggle against him tonight and he would never know. There was no harm in indulging herself just this once. She may never get the chance again.

Cornelia slid closer, pushing her body against Dante's as a soft sigh escaped her lips. She was content for the first time in her life and she planned to enjoy the moment as long as she could. Her eyes grew wide and she practically jumped in shock when Dante turned and pressed his lips to hers in a soft tantalizing kiss.

Cornelia was even more surprised when his hands slid casually behind her back maneuvering her even closer. Dante's hard body was now pressed tightly against hers. She knew she should stop him. He wasn't himself tonight. He didn't know what he was doing. But she couldn't. She was melting inside from the contact and she just wanted more. A tiny voice in the back of her mind told her this was wrong, but she silently told that voice to shut up. How could something that felt this good be wrong? They were both adults and it wasn't like she was forcing herself on him. Dante was drunk, but they were only kissing. There was no harm in kissing. She should indulge him, or more accurately indulge herself, just this once. He wouldn't remember it in the morning anyway. She felt another slight tinge of guilt at that thought but ignored it. She'd fantasized about Dante since the instant she'd met him. Being this close to him, actually lying next to him in his bed, was a dream come true. Cornelia stopped thinking when Dante's kiss deepened and his hands got even busier.

Cornelia awoke to the smell of coffee. She slowly opened her eyes then bolted upright. The sheet that had been covering her body immediately dropped to her waist. Cornelia fumbled for the thin cloth then quickly pulled it to her chin and stared into Dante's eyes, mortified at the amusement she saw dancing there. Her situation was anything but funny, she groaned inwardly. What an idiot, she'd fallen asleep last night before she could hide the evidence. Now here she was, naked in Dante's bed while he lounged in a comfortable chair fully dressed.

Progeny

"I thought that might do it," Dante said casually. He stood, reached across the bed and handed Cornelia a cup of coffee. "I don't have any food here. I planned to go shopping today. If you're in the mood for breakfast there's a small café just up the road."

Cornelia sipped her coffee considering the situation. Dante didn't seem upset. He didn't seem to have any reaction at all to waking up next to a naked woman. Well, of course he didn't, everyone knew the man was a womanizer. This was probably a typical morning after for him. Well, she'd just pretend it was normal for her, too. *And how was she supposed to do that?* Last night had been the best night of her life. And that was saying something, she'd had a long life. In all her one hundred and seventy-three years she had never experienced anything that came close to the intimacy she shared with Dante last night. It was more amazing than her best fantasy. More earth shattering than all the extreme sports she'd tried combined.

Living in solitude with her mother for her first hundred and twenty-six years had given her plenty of time to fantasize about finding a mate. She knew it could never happen. She was part vampire. No fae would want her and she'd never hook up with a human permanently. Once a man realized what she was, he'd run for sure. She had accepted that fact as a teen and shortly afterward the fantasies began. Her eyes darted to Dante then quickly moved back to focus on her coffee. He didn't seem to mind her vampire lineage, but he also wasn't looking for anything permanent. Cornelia knew that. That's the only reason last night had happened. She was sure of it. Dante knew Cornelia was only in town until she testified at

Kahn's trial. Everyone agreed that vicious serial killer had to be locked away for good. That fact made her a safe bet for Dante. She was just a quick fling, with no possibility of strings. Plus, he had been drunk.

"I can practically hear the wheels turning in that head of yours," Dante said casually taking another sip of his coffee. "So, let me guess. We're going to have yet another conversation outlining the reasons you need to bolt." He continued to study her as he set his cup on the small table and leaned forward. "What are you running from this time Cornelia, me or Alex?"

Both, Cornelia thought inwardly. "Neither," she said, hoping she sounded as casual as Dante. She really wished he'd stop looking at her that way. It was impossible to look into those deep blue eyes and conjure a coherent thought. But if she looked away, he would know he was right. "I caught a lead I need to follow up on," she blurted. "I've done all I can do from here. I've hit a wall. I need to fly out west and track this one down in person." She was proud of herself. Dante couldn't argue with that. It was a solid excuse.

"So," he pondered. "You want me to believe you're not running this time. You are simply tracking down a lead. On Lillie's case, I presume?"

"That's what I am doing," she said more forcefully.

"And once you track down this lead, you plan to return to New York?" He asked, picking up his cup and taking another long sip of the hot liquid as he settled back into the comfortable chair.

"Probably," Cornelia said, evasively.

"I see," Dante said unconvinced. "I'll take that as a no."

"It's not a no," she disagreed. "It's a maybe...eventually," she mumbled.

Dante's mind was racing. He had to keep Cornelia in New York. She couldn't leave, not now. He needed more time. Somehow he had to convince her to stay in New York permanently. If she left now, he'd lose her for good. And after last night, he was even more convinced he needed her to stay. "You didn't answer my question," he began. "You might come back, but you might not. Is that because of me or Alex?"

"You know why, Dante," Cornelia said impatiently. "I've told you before, I won't risk being turned over to the vampires."

"And I told you that would never happen," Dante said flatly. "It's been over a month since Alex healed you. She knows what you are and she doesn't care. I realize you've been avoiding her, but don't you think she would have tracked you down by now if it was a problem? She knows you've been staying at the apartment."

"Maybe," Cornelia said softly. At this point, she really didn't know where she stood with the queen. "But even if you're right and Alex won't banish me to live with the vampires, that doesn't protect me from my father. What if he comes after me? I have to protect myself from him."

Dante studied Cornelia for a long time. "I think you really are worried about that," he finally conceded. "But if he hasn't found you by now, what makes you think he's going to?"

Cornelia shifted uncomfortably. She wasn't sure she should trust Dante with what had happened on the battlefield. Somehow she was sure that made her an even bigger risk. But she couldn't lie to him and for some reason, she didn't want to keep any secrets from him either.

"You're over thinking again," Dante said impatiently. "Just tell me what's going on in that head of yours so we can deal with it. What are you hiding now?"

Cornelia wanted to pace. She dealt with pressure better when she was pacing. But she couldn't. She wasn't comfortable enough with Dante to expose herself that way. He'd enjoyed her body last night, but he was also drunk at the time. In the light of day, she didn't know how he would react. He might not even remember all the wonderful things they had done together. She wouldn't go there. She couldn't think about that now. Instead, she pushed her back against the headboard and stared out the window. "I felt Radek's pull," she finally said. "When he called his vampires back on New Year's, I felt him. I'm pretty sure I saw him. He was in the shadows of the orchard, watching the battle."

Dante immediately moved to the bed and took Cornelia's hand in his. "Tell me about it," he said softly. No wonder she was scared. If she felt Radek, had Radek felt her? Logic said yes and Cornelia would know that.

Progeny

Cornelia turned back to Dante and took a deep breath. "At first, it was very faint. Just a nagging feeling I needed to go. I needed to head north to the caves."

Dante began circling his thumb over Cornelia's palm in an attempt to sooth her. "Go on," he pressed.

"I don't know what caves. That's all I got, just head to the caves. I assume that's the order he was giving his men. Retreat and head for the caves. The vampires clearly knew which caves he was talking about because they immediately started to retreat. That must be where they're housed, in a cave somewhere close by."

"I agree," Dante said. He shifted his body and started to rub her back, hoping the contact would soothe her enough to finish her story. "Then what happened?"

"I was thinking that if I had more vampire blood in me, it would have been impossible to ignore the command," Cornelia admitted. "I got scared. I wondered if I could feel him, hear his orders, could he feel me, too?" She took another deep breath. "That's when I began searching for him. I was looking of course, but I was also searching with my mind I guess. It's kind of hard to explain. Anyway, that's when I felt him. I actually felt Radek's presence. I spotted a shadow in the trees and when the shadow moved, I knew it was him. The more I ignored the command, the stronger it got. I had to concentrate to withstand the pull. I cleared my mind and thought of happy memories. It helped. It gave me the strength I needed to ignore the pull. But the more I ignored it, the stronger it got. At the end it was...dark, I guess. It's hard to describe but dark and violent."

"So you're afraid next time you won't be able to ignore it?" Dante asked, wanting her to be specific. He didn't blame her for being afraid, he just needed her to open up and tell him exactly what had spooked her so he could help her overcome her fears and stay. Stay with him. Then they could address the rest. There were so many implications that would need to be looked at, but Cornelia's concerns came first.

"No," Cornelia said, she'd thought about that and knew she could withstand a command in the future. "I think Radek used all the force he had and I was still able to resist him."

"Then what has you so worried?" Dante asked. He knew what worried him; Cornelia's safety.

"I'm afraid my father can use that connection to find me. I'm afraid if he finds me, he can capture me. Mostly I'm afraid of what he would do if he got me. I don't know if he would kill me, imprison me, or try to use me to get at you guys. I'd never betray you, but the idea of being tortured terrifies me. I've heard the rumors of what Lilith can and will do. I heard what happened to Dahl. I'm not strong like a warrior. I guess mostly I fear the pain, or more specifically cracking under the pain, I know too much about all of you."

"How would your father know?" Dante asked. "I mean, did your mother say your father was close to Radek? Was he one of the organization's top men? Someone Radek would confide in?" Dante didn't know of anyone Radek confided in these days. From what they heard, Hector and Lilith were the only ones that had Radek's ear.

Progeny

And there were rumors Radek no longer trusted Lilith. Although that was doubtful since Lilith was intimately involved in every attack they'd had since Hector's death.

Cornelia was quiet for a very long time. She trusted Dante. She really did. But she wasn't sure how he would take the rest of her secret. She didn't want to lose the connection she was starting to develop with him. It was too important to her, especially after the closeness they had shared last night. Even if Dante didn't remember that, she did.

Dante reached up and brushed the hair from Cornelia's face. "You can trust me," he soothed. "Whatever it is, you can trust me." He pressed a light kiss to her forehead.

"Radek is my father," Cornelia finally whispered. She was looking at her hands now. She just couldn't bear to look into Dante's eyes. She was so afraid of what she'd find there. Disgust for sure, hatred maybe, betrayal, she wasn't sure what else. But surely not the compassion she'd grown to love so much.

Dante studied Cornelia. She looked so fragile and vulnerable. He wanted to pull her against him, hold her close and promise her she'd be safe because he would protect her. He wanted to make love to her all over again. But he knew that would only scare her away. He had to convince her that being Radek's daughter didn't change anything. He already knew she was part vampire. Being the daughter of a powerful and sadistic vampire king didn't change how he felt about her. They'd have to take more serious precautions to protect her, but he didn't care about the rest. He reached out and cradled her cheek with his hand, then palmed her chin and forced her to lift her head. Her hands were still covering her eyes. "Look at me, Cornelia," he said softly.

Cornelia shook her head.

Dante laughed a little. "Please?" He asked again.

Cornelia sighed then raised her head and looked directly into Dante's beautiful blue eyes. She didn't see anything she'd been dreading. The look she saw was gentle and caring. Why didn't he hate her? Why didn't he despise her? He should find her disgusting, but he didn't. If she didn't already love the man, she would have fallen for him in that instant.

Dante saw the raw desperation and surprise in Cornelia's eyes. He slowly leaned forward and pressed his lips to hers. When he straightened, she was still staring at him in amazement. "You should have told me Radek was your father before now." He shifted and pulled her into his arms, pressing a soft kiss to the top of her head. He'd deal with the consequences later, right now he needed to hold her. "If Radek knows you're here, that puts you in danger. You need a safer place to stay," he decided. "You can't stay in that apartment any longer. Victor hasn't fortified that place for trouble."

"That's why I need to leave," Cornelia said into Dante's chest. She knew she should pull away, but being in his arms felt too good. "I still need to leave for me. I won't deny that. Like I said, I'm not brave and strong like you. The idea of being tortured or killed terrifies me. But

Progeny

I also need to protect this community, the warriors and the queen. Now that Radek knows I'm here and I'm in your inner circle, he will try to use me against you." Mostly she needed to leave because she would never put Dante in danger.

Dante considered the situation for a long moment. "You said this lead, the money trail, leads out west. Where out west?"

"Las Vegas," Cornelia told him.

Dante cringed. He had avoided Vegas for more than thirty years. He didn't want to go there now, but he also didn't like sending Cornelia away alone. "If you tracked down this lead, would you return?" He finally asked.

"I don't know," she admitted. "I would keep in touch. Convicting Kahn is just as important to me as it is to you, and the rest of the community. I'm just not sure I should come back here. We'll see how long it takes and if the trail ends in Vegas or leads me in another direction. I think I could talk to the DA. I could tell him I have another case that needs immediate attention but assure him that I'll make myself available at a moment's notice. As much as he might like to, he can't jeopardize my livelihood for his case. He won't like it, but he'll have to agree to let me leave. He can't keep me here forever and Rand said the defense has filed another motion. This could go on for months."

"How about a compromise?" Dante asked, wanting to do just that. He knew he couldn't keep her here forever, but some instinct deep inside told him that keeping Cornelia close was of vital importance somehow.

"What kind of compromise?" Cornelia asked reluctantly.

"It's going to be impossible to find a room in Vegas right now. From what I hear, the place is completely sold out around Valentines," Dante began.

"I hadn't thought of that. I might have to stay in St. George and rent a car," she considered.

"Here's the compromise," Dante continued. "Give me a day. Take the rest of today and try to track down leads from New York. In the meantime, I'll talk to Thomas. He'll probably have a suite in his Vegas Casino you can use. I'll arrange for your flight and hotel and you stay in Vegas while I look into things here," he paused. "I still have a few contacts. Nick and I will generate others. Let's figure out what Radek knows and what he plans to do about it while you're away. Once you finish the work on Lillie's ex, stay in Vegas until I tell you it's safe to come back. You can think of it as a paid vacation."

"I don't know," Cornelia hesitated. She didn't like the Deveraux's being in charge of her plans.

"Did Radek try to find your mother? When she escaped with you and went into hiding, did he try to track her down? Was he upset that she left with his child?" Dante asked.

Progeny

"No, he didn't try to track mom," Cornelia said, evasively.

"What are you not telling me now?" Dante scowled. Surely she knew she could tell him anything. What did he have to do to earn her trust?

Cornelia only hesitated a minute. She'd already told him more than she should have. It was just so hard to confide in anyone. Her mother had drilled into her, probably from the second she was born, the need for complete secrecy. Coming clean felt like a betrayal somehow. "Mom said Radek didn't know about me," she admitted. "Mom left during the early stages of pregnancy. He didn't even know she was pregnant. The instant she recognized the symptoms, she started planning. I know the ordeal was horrific, and I believe her escape was harrowing but she's never given me details. She did say that from the instant she realized she was pregnant she knew she had to escape before Radek found out. She told me she was willing to do anything to get me out of there. She was prepared to die before she allowed me to be born and raised by vampires. She fled during the day and left the area immediately. She didn't have any family in New York. They were all still in Ireland. So her disappearance went unnoticed for the most part."

"That's good," Dante decided. "If Radek knows you're his daughter that jeopardizes your safety. But maybe he doesn't know."

"But I felt him, I'm sure he felt me," Cornelia argued. "I've thought about this for the last month Dante. In fact, I've thought of little else. I think the reason the command got stronger was because he felt me and was angry that I disobeyed."

"I agree," Dante told her. "However, that doesn't mean he recognized you as his daughter. It only means he was angry that you had the nerve to disobey his command. It would have enraged him. That vampire has an ego and doesn't like being defied."

"I hadn't thought of that," Cornelia admitted. "So you think there's a chance he still doesn't know he has a daughter." *That would be nice*, Cornelia thought. She would still be in danger. Radek wouldn't allow a vampire to defy him or to take up with the fae. But if she could hide her relationship from him, her mother might be safe. Maybe if she kept her distance Radek would never know about the connection.

"So, back to the compromise," Dante said. "Give me a day. See what you can do from here and let me make arrangements for you in Vegas."

"I'll give you a day, but I'm not going to get anywhere from here. I already tried. I need to head to the bank and seek out a man I can deal with in person," Cornelia said absently.

"Why a man?" Dante said, not liking the direction this conversation was headed.

Cornelia smiled. "Because men are easily manipulated by a woman's charms," she told him. "With the proper attire, I'll get everything I need in one visit."

Progeny

Dante frowned. "You plan to find a male employee and seduce him into giving you information?"

"No," Cornelia said, offended. "I plan to put on a sexy outfit," she paused, considering. "Maybe a little black skirt...and head to the bank. Hopefully the manager will be a male, if not I'll know which guy to approach. It's a piece of cake from there. I'll flirt a little, show a little leg, maybe leave a button or two open to reveal the slightest bit of cleavage and walk away with everything I need. I don't have to seduce a mark to get information, just give him a glimpse of the goods."

Dante grinned. "Those long legs and beautiful breasts certainly worked for me last night." His grin widened as memories flooded his mind. "I'm certainly hoping for another glimpse of the goods."

Cornelia blushed. At the time she'd thought Dante was too drunk to remember their night together. Clearly, the blood had cleaned out his system and he remembered everything. Would she have let herself go so completely if she'd known he was going to remember everything so clearly? She didn't know the answer to that, but it was too late to go back now. "I'll give you a day, but that's it. Whether you can make arrangements with Thomas or not, I'm leaving tomorrow," she blurted, still embarrassed.

"Deal," Dante said, standing. "I'll let you get dressed so I can take you home. I'd like to catch Thomas this morning. Feel free to use the shower. There are clean towels in the cabinet." Dante slipped into the hallway and silently shut the door behind him. He had to get out of that room. Thoughts of Cornelia the night before were leading

28

him in a dangerous direction. Sitting next to her on his bed, knowing she was completely naked under that thin sheet, was a temptation he couldn't indulge right now. He shouldn't have indulged himself last night. But he couldn't stop himself. The instant she slipped into bed next to him, he'd lost his self-control. It just wasn't possible to lie next to that sexy vamp and not touch her. Especially after she'd pressed her gorgeous body against his. He'd only meant to kiss her, but she'd responded so enthusiastically he couldn't stop himself. Maybe he should regret their night together but he didn't. He just hoped the feeling was mutual. She was already so afraid. He couldn't bear the thought she might fear him now, too.

Dante slipped into the guest room and climbed into the shower. He needed a long cold one this morning. He was going to take Cornelia out for an early breakfast then drop her at the apartment so she could prepare for her trip. Afterward, he would head over to Thomas'. An image of Cornelia's sexy body popped into his head. He groaned and shifted so the cold spray pummeled his body. He had to stop thinking about her. Getting her out of his house was a great first step.

Dante closed his eyes and began washing his hair. That was a mistake, the image of Cornelia instantly clarified. She was so beautiful. He loved the way her honeycomb hair draped across her shoulders, not to mention that curvy body of hers. She was adorable and classy. He was completely taken by surprise last night. She'd been so uninhibited. The experience was refreshing and a little shocking. He'd been with so many women over the past two hundred years, intimacy had lost its appeal.

Progeny

He would never have believed one night could make him feel so much. He hadn't had sex for over a year now. Maybe that's why it was so potent. Nobody knew that but him. The warriors were constantly giving him a hard time about his partying. They assumed he used casual intimacy to mask his pain. Maybe that was true in the beginning but not now, not for years. He didn't correct them. It was easier that way. He'd learned that from Victor. Once the rumors got started, they were impossible to stop. The human women still made their moves, like the blond had last night. But they were easy to resist. He wanted something real, something permanent, something like all his friends had found. But deep down, Dante knew that would never happen for him. Whatever this thing was with Cornelia, it wasn't permanent. She was itching to get away and he was realistic enough to know in the end, he wouldn't be enough to stop her.

Once he was dressed, he headed for the bedroom. The first thing he needed to do was get Cornelia out of town to safety, then they could start gathering information. Getting vamps to talk these days was more difficult, but not impossible. He needed to know what they were dealing with. He was determined to protect Cornelia at any cost. That knowledge was a little unsettling. He wasn't ready to evaluate his feelings for the woman right now. He had feelings for her, strong feelings, but that was as far as he was willing to go. For now, his priority was keeping her safe. His second priority was convincing her to return to New York. He had to find a way to keep her here as long as possible. Beyond that, only time would tell.

Chapter Two

Radek prowled the small room, ignoring the screams coming from the corner. The man wasn't telling him anything. How was he supposed to win this war if he had to constantly stop strategizing to deal with incompetence? He was sick of the constant delays. The New Year's battle had taken place over a month ago. Lilith was too slow. She'd spent two full weeks on Zorak. After all that wasted time, the unit leader didn't know anything. Then, she insisted on questioning all the vampire soldiers that fought in Zorak's sector that night. None of them had much to say about the mysterious woman either. They hadn't even noticed she was a vampire. How could anyone be that stupid? The only worthwhile lead Zorak had given them pertained to the vampire suffering in the corner. He arrived in town around the same time the woman had. Radek assumed the two were working together. He put Lilith on it immediately, but that had also taken way too long. She'd scoured the streets for almost three weeks before she caught the wily scoundrel.

Radek's eyes shifted back to the corner. Slow roasting the nomad over hot coals should have been effective and quick. So far, they hadn't gotten anything from him. Radek growled in frustration, would this war have no end? Normally he would have enjoyed torturing and interrogating the drifter himself, but not tonight. This war was taking away all his great pleasures. He hadn't had sex in months and now this. Radek felt frustrated and restless. That rogue vampire was up to something, he was sure of it. There was no other explanation. The woman had to be a traitor, trying to take over his kingdom. Why else would a vampire join ranks with the fae and kill their own kind? That told Radek, whoever she was, she was ruthless and would stop at nothing to get what she wanted. He was worried about her ability to ignore his command. The only explanation he could come up with was the fact that she hadn't actually joined his nest. Maybe she was still loyal to another king so Radek's commands were ineffective. He'd need to keep that little secret to himself. He couldn't have his vampires using a loophole to disobey him.

He wished he still had Hector. Radek scowled. He never thought there would come a day he'd wish that scoundrel was still around. Hector was disrespectful and impossible to control, but the guy was a good strategist. Far better than Lilith. A year ago, Radek was well on his way to power thanks to Hector's abilities. Marlena had been killed and Hector was laying a trap for that menace,

Luke Deveraux. Radek had been sure once the parents were taken out, the children would fall into line. He'd been wrong about that, but if Hector were still alive it wouldn't have mattered. If Hector were still alive, this blasted war would be over and Radek would be living the good life. He'd be living the life he was entitled to as King. But Hector was dead and here Radek stood with yet another obstacle to overcome. He had to know who that woman was. Radek picked up a small table and flung it angrily against the wall, then stalked out of the room. Lilith could finish this tonight. He needed to relax. He couldn't think when he was this angry and uptight. The moment he entered his chambers, Sammael was standing in the doorway.

"Your majesty?" Sammael said weakly. "Is there anything I can get for you?"

"Yes," Radek decided. "Get me one of the drunks. I need to relax." Then he lumbered across the room and settled into his large chair next to the fire.

"Of course," Sammael said, smiling inwardly. The king was losing it. His request would only take a minute, nowadays they always kept a few drunks on hand for this very reason. The king was too impatient to wait for someone to go out and catch a fresh one. Once Radek was settled for the night, Sammael could sneak out and make a phone call. There should be just enough time before dawn to fill Ammit in on the new developments.

"Has Lilith returned?" Radek asked.

Progeny

"Yes, sir," Sammael assured him. "I saw her about ten minutes ago, I think she was headed for her chambers."

"Good," Radek said gruffly. "Tell her to deal with the prisoner. I want him to roast at least ten more minutes, then she can try to interrogate him again," he paused. "I expect her to learn something this time," he added for effect. "He's not going to last much longer."

"I'll tell her immediately," Sammael assured him. "Then I'll bring your nightcap."

Radek felt his tension ease slightly. At least he had Sammael. The kid was proving useful. He was too weak to fight, but he was so loyal. Radek smiled. Lilith had been furious when Radek announced Sammael would be joining her while she interrogated Zorak. But Radek didn't trust her and she knew it. She also knew that with Sammael in the room, she couldn't hide anything. Sammael wasn't happy with him either, but the guy needed to toughen up. Forcing Sammael to watch while Lilith tortured and interrogated a strong, vibrant vampire was good for the kid. And anyway, his decision had ultimately saved Zorak's life. Sammael should be grateful for that.

After he'd calmed down, Radek knew allowing the man to live had been the right thing to do. At the time, he was letting his temper make his decisions for him. Lilith had pushed him to save Zorak's life. She assured him the man didn't know anything else and wasn't associated with the mysterious woman in any way. Radek believed her. He may not trust Lilith, but she was the best interrogator he'd ever come in contact with. If Zorak knew anything, he would have told Lilith and Sammael would have told

Radek. But he didn't like the alliance Zorak and Lilith appeared to be forming. The deciding factor had been Sammael. The kid stepped up and meekly pointed out that morale among the men was low after the incident with Proctor. His soldiers didn't understand why Proctor had to die simply because he couldn't locate Radek's troops. If Radek kept killing men, especially someone as well respected as Zorak for reasons his men didn't understand, the vampires would begin to desert his army. Radek was trying to build an army. He couldn't afford to lose any men when the tides were finally turning in his favor. Radek had to admit the kid was intelligent. By the time Sammael had finished his soft plea, Radek was calm enough to realize Sammael and Lilith were right. Allowing Zorak to live would do more good than killing him. His men would know they'd be held accountable for their mistakes, but if they cooperated, they would live. Zorak's torture would be viewed as punishment for failure.

Radek looked up as Sammael escorted a drunk man into the room. The guy could barely walk. The instant Sammael released him, the human fell to the floor laughing. He wouldn't be laughing for long. "Thank you Sammael," Radek said in dismissal and began to drink. He immediately felt better. After only five minutes he felt good enough to enjoy the images his mind was conjuring. Lilith would be inflicting horrendous pain on the nomad by now, maybe he would finally get some answers. He inhaled deeply, savoring the aroma. The smell of roasting vampire and the knowledge that Lilith was torturing the traitor finally made him smile.

Progeny

Sammael left the kings chambers and headed for the exit. He needed to slip out unnoticed. That should be easy enough. This group believed he was harmless and never paid much attention to his movement. The only exception was Lilith and she was tied up at the moment. Sammael cleared the ridge line and paused to survey the area. Once he selected his spot, he settled onto a large rock and waited. If Lilith had noticed him leaving, she'd send someone to follow. He couldn't take any chances. Not with Lilith, she was jealous of the trust Radek had in him and would stop at nothing to undermine it.

Once Sammael was confident he hadn't been followed, he pulled the phone from his pocket and made the call. Ammit answered after the first ring.

"Yes," Ammit said cautiously.

"I have news," Sammael told him. "Is this a good time?"

"Give me a minute," Ammit told him.

Sammael waited while Ammit excused someone. His king was always careful to ensure complete privacy when speaking to Sammael. Moments later Ammit was back on the line. Sammael outlined what he had learned. He told Ammit about Zorak, the mysterious part vampire woman that had fought in the New Year's battle with the fae, and how Radek was drinking more these days. "He's on the edge," Sammael finished.

"I think it's time," Ammit finally said. "Is the cave prepared?"

"Yes," Sammael assured him. "But I don't think I'll be able to get away to greet you. Radek is getting paranoid. He doesn't trust anyone these days. Plus, Lilith is watching me more closely. It's hard enough to sneak away to get you information."

"That's not a problem," Ammit said, still pondering. "We'll be there within the week. I'll find a way to get word to you once we arrive," he paused. "Typhon will be bringing a new vampire named Martinez. If he shows up and tries to insert himself into Radek's army, do what you can to help him."

"If this Martinez is new, can we trust him?" Sammael asked hesitantly.

"Keep an eye on him," Ammit said cautiously. "Typhon seems to trust him and he did provide us with some valuable information. But, you know me. I don't trust lightly. You shouldn't either. Help him get established, but watch your back for now."

"I'll watch for him," Sammael promised. "I better get back. I've been gone too long already. Is there anything else I need to know?"

"No," Ammit said, still preoccupied with his thoughts. "I'll be in touch." He disconnected the phone and turned to Gallo. "It's time," he said forcefully. "We leave at nightfall," then he dialed Typhon to set things in motion.

Progeny

Dante needed to talk to Thomas. He was the only one Dante could trust with this. Thomas would know how to handle things with Alex, which would take care of things with Dimitri. Dante was sure the connection with Radek wouldn't matter to anyone. They all hated the monster, but no one would hold that against Cornelia. He just wasn't sure how Alex would react to learning she had another living relative. Eventually she'd be happy, but the link was with Radek this time, not her human father, not someone she loved. The situation was delicate. Alex had only recently learned the details of Marlena's time in captivity which resulted in the birth of Radek. Dante wasn't sure how Alex would deal with the news that she had a niece. A niece that was connected to a violent family history. Thomas was the only one that could help him with this. Thomas would know what to say to Alex and how to keep her focused on the positive, not the ugliness of the past.

He was still lost in thought as he left the highway and pulled into the long drive that led to the Deveraux mansion. It took him a minute after spotting the car for things to register. He was a little surprised the man still kept a car in the city, but the ostentatious sports car was unmistakable. Anger instantly swelled deep inside. What was he doing here? They had a deal. Carlo was going to regret reneging on that particular promise. Dante pressed the gas and closed the gap between himself and the mansion a little too fast. The car came to a screeching stop, barely missing a planter full of flowers. Dante jumped from the car and slammed the door behind him. He didn't bother knocking when he reached the porch, he just opened the door and let himself in.

Once inside Dante moved to the study and stood in the doorway, glaring at his father. He took several long, deep breaths trying to control his temper. So far it wasn't working that well.

Thomas noticed his friend first. He rose from his chair and walked to the entrance of the large room. "I'm glad you're here," Thomas said casually. "I was just about to call you." He put a hand on Dante's shoulder in support. "Please, join us."

Dante gave a slight nod and strolled into the room. It still amazed him, the bond he shared with Thomas. They'd known each other for such a short time, in the whole scheme, and yet that small gesture from his friend had loosened something inside. His muscles relaxed a little. They were in this one together. Dante continued across the room and plopped casually into a chair. His father looked...what? Haggard? That was it. Clearly, he'd lost sleep and had some sort of problem. Did he seriously think he could bring his troubles to Thomas Deveraux? Of course, he did. Carlo Santora firmly believed the world revolved around him. He actually thought he was in the same league as Thomas and Alex. The man's arrogance was infuriating.

Thomas studied Dante. So far, he was handling this well. Thomas was proud of his friend. He was certainly a better man than Thomas was. He grinned a little, remembering his own reaction to seeing Carlo Santora. Thomas didn't know the man, but the instant he opened the

Progeny

door he knew it was Dante's father and it was all he could do to hold himself back. His first instinct was to punch the man in the face, then keep on going until the rotten scoundrel was huddled on the ground begging for mercy. But Thomas had constrained himself, barely. Yes, Dante was a far better man than he was. Thomas had only heard about the family history. Dante had actually lived through it. "Your father was just about to tell me why he believes I should help him with his problem." He turned a stony gaze toward the older man. "Do continue."

Carlo glanced wearily toward his son. He didn't want him here. He didn't want to deal with Dante Santora, but now he didn't have a choice. The spoiled brat was going to have the final say in this. His job was going to be much more difficult now. "I believe vampires are involved," Carlo said trying to add a little panic to his tone. "You and your sister have raged war on the vampires and my family is paying the price for that dispute. I feel you have an obligation to rectify this immediately. It's only fair. Marlena and Luke could always be counted on to do the fair and equitable thing. I came to you in hopes that you take after your father enough to handle this quickly and efficiently."

Thomas struggled all over again. He knew he had a temper and he couldn't let it loose right now. He thought of his father. How would Luke handle this man, this problem? "Why?" Thomas asked coldly.

Carlo furrowed his brow in confusion. "Why what?" He finally asked.

"Why do you think vampires are involved in the abduction of your wife?" Thomas asked flatly. "What evidence do you have that points to vampire involvement?"

Dante was surprised. So the fool had gotten Shannon abducted. No wonder he looked haggard. But he wasn't kidding anyone. Vampires weren't involved in this and Carlo knew it. The man was in over his head and needed help and he thought Thomas had the power or the resources to fix it. He was trying to manipulate the situation as always. Dante looked at Thomas and realized his friend was fighting for control. He grinned a little. Thomas was on the verge of losing his temper. As enjoyable as that might be to watch, Dante would have to step in. He was about to speak when Carlo beat him to it.

"Well, I think it's obvious," Carlo said defensively. "My wife and I have lived in Vegas, in peace, for decades without the slightest problem until your family waged this war. Now, all of a sudden someone sneaks into my home and takes my sweet, helpless Shannon by force. Any idiot can see it has to be vampires... and it has to be linked to this war," Carlo finished.

Dante saw the look on Thomas' face. The man was about to fly across the desk and strangle the obnoxious fool. Leave it to Carlo to call a Deveraux an idiot. Dante didn't move. He continued to sit casually in the lounge chair with his legs crossed, one ankle resting on his knee. "I'd watch myself if I were you old man," he said softly, the tone made his threat even more menacing. "It's rude to come into a man's house and insult him, especially when you're here asking for help. Whatever you've gotten yourself into this time, it has nothing to do with vampires and everyone in the room knows it."

"Don't tell me..." Carlo began, his face was red, eyes hard.

"Quiet," Thomas interrupted.

Carlo's mouth shut instantly. He studied Thomas and realized Dante was right. Thomas was pissed and offended. Okay, so he'd played that one wrong. But he had to get Shannon back. He knew the warriors were his only hope, and he wanted Thomas. He wanted the Deveraux connection. Once his competitors heard Thomas Deveraux had personally come to his rescue, nobody would ever mess with him again. "I apologize if you took that the wrong way. I meant no disrespect. I'm just so worried about Shannon."

Thomas continued to glare at the man. He was thinking about Carlo's problem. Someone had kidnaped his wife, someone other than vampires. That meant humans had a warrior in captivity. Not that the spoiled, pampered woman really counted as a warrior. Not in any way that mattered. Considering the type of man Carlo Santora was, the humans were probably ruthless and evil. If, or more to the point when, they began to torture Shannon they were going to figure out she wasn't human. Santora's recklessness had put them all in danger. "I'm going to give you one more opportunity to explain why I should care about your . . . situation," Thomas finally said. "This time, I want the truth."

Carlo glared at Thomas. Did this... child think he could intimidate him? Carlo Santora was not intimidated by anyone. He was as good as... no, he was better than this spoiled, entitled idiot. Nobody called him a liar, not even a Deveraux. "I can see you disagree with my interpretation of the situation," Carlo began. "You have that right, of course. I, on the other hand, am confident I'm right. This is connected to you and your sister. I realize you've both had to step in and try to get your footing during a difficult time. So, I'm willing to make allowances. However, the bottom line is that my wife is missing. Someone broke into my home and kidnapped her. I have no doubt her life is in danger. If I'm right, if they are vampires..." Carlo took a deep breath in desperation. He didn't have to fake that, he was desperate. If they didn't agree to help him, he would never see Shannon again. "She may already be dead."

Thomas rolled his eyes. Did this tactic really work in the human world? The one where Carlo had been living. Apparently. "I guess honesty is more than I can hope for with you," Thomas began, not caring that the man was about to explode with fury. "So let me help you understand the situation from my point of view," Thomas paused, giving Carlo the opportunity to speak. One more insult and the man would find himself flat on his back, out in the cold.

Carlo wisely remained silent.

"You have gotten yourself into a jam, a human jam, not a supernatural one." Thomas watched as Carlo opened his mouth to speak then shut it immediately. "That does make this our problem. Not because vampires are involved, but because your ineptness is now threatening our entire world. If we do not step in and take care of this, the fae, the warriors, everyone is in danger of being discovered. That's on you, Carlo. You don't get to push your mistakes off on me or my sister."

Carlo continued to sit silently. His hatred for this boy grew exponentially with each passing second.

"I will not travel to Vegas to fix this for you," Thomas told him flatly. "Yes, I know that's what you were hoping for. You want to use my name, my status and my reputation to fix whatever underhanded deal that's gone bad. I'm not nearly as stupid as you think I am. You thought you could maneuver me. Get me to Vegas then brag to your friends, your colleagues, your enemies that I was there as your personal guest. More to the point your personal lackey. Deveraux's do not allow themselves to be used by garbage like you," Thomas said, disgust burning in his eyes. "However," Thomas said taking a deep breath, "As unfortunate as it is, I can't just throw you out and tell you to handle it yourself. You have endangered us all and something has to be done to fix your mistake."

Carlo didn't understand where this was leading. "What does that mean, exactly? What do you plan to do? If you won't go find my Shannon, who will help me?"

"I don't know," Thomas said honestly. "I need to call Dimitri."

"What does he have to do with this?" Carlo asked angrily. He didn't want Dimitri involved. Once Dimitri Montgomery knew about this, Oberon would know. Carlo didn't want to answer to Oberon. He had to admit he had underestimated Thomas Deveraux. He'd believed the kid was in over his head and would be easy to manipulate. Well, he couldn't do anything about that right now. He had to accept whatever he was offered. The most important thing was to get Shannon back. He could deal with the rest later.

Dante answered. "Dimitri is the warrior leader, but you already knew that. You should have gone to him yourself, not to Thomas. Dimitri will decide if we will help you. And, if so, who he will send to handle the job."

"Why can't you two just make that decision on your own?" Carlo asked turning to Dante. "Maybe Nick would be willing to..."

Dante laughed out loud. "You so don't want to come within a hundred miles of Nicholas Moretti. You wouldn't survive a full minute with him. I sincerely doubt you've forgotten your last encounter with my good friend Nick."

Thomas grinned. Dante was right. Carlo Santora had no idea how passionately Nick hated the man. Nick and Dante were closer than brothers and Carlo Santora had hurt Dante. No one hurt Dante and got away with it. The only reason Nick hadn't already gone after the man was because he'd promised Dante he'd leave him alone. Thomas continued to watch the two men, father and son, while he waited for Dimitri to answer his phone. The hatred and resentment were so strong between them you could actually feel it in the air.

"Yes, Thomas?" Dimitri said a little impatiently. "This better be good or you'll be answering to your sister."

Progeny

"I just thought you might like to know I'm sitting here, in my study, with Dante and Carlo Santora," Thomas paused for effect.

"I'll be right there," Dimitri said without hesitation. "Is Dante okay?"

"Yeah, we're fine here but we need you to make a decision on something. Actually, you might want to bring Alex with you. It's probably more appropriate for her to make the final decision," Thomas said grinning.

"We'll be there in five. Take care of Dante," Dimitri ordered. "I couldn't care less what happens to that no good piece of..."

"Got it," Thomas cut him off, amused. "We'll be here, waiting patiently. Tell Alex I'm sorry for the interruption." He clicked off and focused on Dante. "I'm going to make some coffee," he declared. "You two want anything?"

"I'd prefer brandy if you have it," Carlo said immediately. He needed the alcohol to calm his nerves. The boy should have offered it twenty minutes ago.

"Coffee, thanks," Dante said, not taking his eyes off his father for a second. He was going to have to take care of this himself and wanted all his wits intact when Dimitri arrived. Somehow, he was going to have to convince Dimitri to send him to Vegas to find Shannon. It was the only option. He wouldn't pawn this off on another warrior. It was a family problem and Dante knew he needed to be the one to take care of it. Then he'd make sure his father was clear on his boundaries. His dear old dad didn't know that with one stroke of a pen, the monthly allowance he'd grown so accustomed to could be gone forever. The only reason Dante hadn't done it before, hadn't cut his father off completely, was because it kept him away. The money kept Carlo out of his life. Carlo and his pathetic excuse for a wife. But he would know, as soon as this was all over, Carlo would know the consequence he would suffer if he ever stepped foot in New York again.

Alex watched Dimitri frantically take a corner too fast. The car fishtailed, then the tires caught and Dimitri regained control. "I assume when this is all over you're going to fill me in on the details." It was more of a mandate than a question. She would demand an explanation right now but Dimitri needed to concentrate on his driving. They'd be lucky to get to the mansion alive as it was.

Dimitri glanced at Alex briefly then refocused on the road. "I promise. I don't know why Carlo is here, but whatever the reason, its trouble."

Alex sat silently, waiting for as much information as she could get before she met Dante's father.

"Thomas said we needed to make a decision on something regarding Carlo," Dimitri supplied. "He specifically asked me to bring you and said you might have to be the one to make the final decision. Please follow my lead, sweetheart. Carlo can be charming and cunning, but he's as slippery as a snake. He has no integrity, no ethics. I don't know why he's here, but I'm sure it has something to do with a shady dealing of some kind. Please don't feel sorry for that man. He doesn't deserve an ounce of sympathy. I promise you, I will tell you everything I know when we get home. All you need to know right now is that Carlo and his equally manipulative wife, Shannon, hurt Dante very deeply," Dimitri paused. Thomas hadn't mentioned Shannon. He was surprised at that. Carlo wouldn't leave Shannon out of this, especially if they intended to meet with Dante while they were in town.

"What is it?" Alex asked curiously. Dimitri's demeanor had changed slightly.

"I was just wondering why Thomas didn't mention Shannon. I would have expected her to be in the middle of this, whatever this is. It's odd, that's all." Dimitri slammed on the brakes and shoved the car into park. They had reached the Deveraux Mansion. He didn't waste a moment. He flung open his door and was grateful Alex hadn't waited for him to open hers. The couple walked hand in hand into the foyer and headed purposefully to the study.

Alex surveyed the room intently. Thomas was on edge, no he was furious, and looked as though he was ready to pounce given the slightest opportunity. Dante was sitting in a chair sipping coffee, eyes focused on the stranger in the room. The stranger, which now that she got a good look was obviously Dante's father, looked up at them wearily. Alex continued to hold Dimitri's hand. She didn't understand the situation here but it was crystal clear that if Mr. Santora made one wrong move, he'd have three warriors on him in an instant. She'd never seen so much emotion in Dante's eyes. There was anger and hatred sure, but Alex also saw just a hint of sorrow and something else. She just couldn't put a finger on it. Normally she'd hold out her hand in greeting, manners again, her mother's fault. But she decided to take Dimitri's lead on this one. The hatred she could feel in the room was only one reason she hesitated. As she studied the stranger, she instantly knew she didn't like him. She didn't trust him. He had a dark, sinister look about him. To be honest, she was surprised Thomas had invited the man into their home. Luke and Marlena were very cautious about who came to the house and who was directed to the office out back for a meeting. A thought struck her and she turned to Thomas, the question showing in her eyes.

"She's at her parents' house," he said in understanding. "I didn't want her here. I don't like the company and didn't want Abby exposed to him. In truth, I don't like you being exposed to the likes of Carlo Santora either, but I didn't have a choice."

Alex was shocked. Thomas was never rude and that was just plain rude. She needed to know the history here. She needed the whole story. How could she make any kind of decision if she didn't have the background? But then she remembered what Dimitri had said in the car. This man and his wife had hurt Dante very deeply. Well, that combined with her unsettling feelings toward the man was all she needed to know. She let Dimitri guide her to the couch and sat beside him. She'd just sit here quietly and try to keep up.

"So," Dimitri said giving Carlo a hard, unfriendly glare. "What is it that I need to decide? What could be so important to make you leave Las Vegas and travel all the way to New York when you know you're not welcome here?"

"Shannon has been abducted," he said ignoring Dimitri and focusing on the woman. This had to be Alex, their queen. Women were easy to manipulate. All he had to do was play on her sympathies. She'd send someone to Vegas to rescue his precious Shannon. He was sure of it. If he did this right, it still might be Thomas or maybe Alex would go herself.

"I'm asking the questions, not Alex," Dimitri growled. "I know you, Carlo. You think if you focus on Alex, play this up, she'll feel sorry for you and give you whatever you want. Well, you're wrong. Now, tell me what this has to do with us. Why do you think we care if your wife has been kidnaped?"

Wow! Alex thought. She'd never seen Dimitri like this before, either. Whatever this guy did, it was a whopper. She continued to sit silently, trying to keep her face from showing any emotion at all.

Carlo looked to Thomas. He was the one that called Dimitri, shouldn't he be the one to explain why they needed to help him?

"Carlo wants us to believe Shannon was kidnaped by vampires," Thomas said without emotion. "He initially claimed this was our fault. Apparently, Alex and I started this war with Radek because he killed our parents and it's leaked over onto him. His family is suffering because of our actions," Thomas said with disdain. "We all know that's bullshit, but he's sticking to that story. I guess he just can't admit he's a worthless piece of crap and can't protect his own wife from his underhanded dealings with the human race."

"I see," Dimitri said still scowling. "Well, no I don't. I still don't see how that's my problem or your problem and I certainly don't see how it could possibly be Dante's problem. Somehow I doubt any of us care if Carlo's family suffers."

"I agree with you, on the surface," Thomas continued. "My first instinct was to tell Nancy Boy to grow a pair and deal with the problem himself. But then I remembered who we were dealing with." Thomas paused to shift his attention from Carlo to Dimitri. "It suddenly hit me that Carlo only deals with the shady criminal type. Men that would abduct his wife and eventually torture her to get whatever it is that they wanted."

"I see," Dimitri said in understanding. "You're right. I guess that does make it our problem." He turned to Alex wanting to make sure she was following their logic. She was.

"Just so I'm clear," Alex said, trying to hold back her own anger as she glared at Carlo. "You entered into some kind of shady deal with the humans in Vegas. As a result, your wife was abducted from your home. At which point you decided to travel to New York, to my brother's home, and request his assistance?" Alex paused to take a deep breath. "Rather than throwing yourself on his mercy and begging for help, you blamed the Deveraux family for your bad deeds. I suppose you thought Thomas would jump on a plane and head out to help you himself. You thought,

51

Progeny

Luke's dead, the kid has to be a pushover. I'll just blame him for this mess and he'll use his name, his power and his connections in Vegas to boost my name, my status and my connections a little. Does that about cover it? Am I up to speed on this so far or is there something I've missed?" She was almost shouting now. She was so angry.

Thomas burst out laughing as he leaned back in his chair. He loved Alex. He especially loved watching her deal with men like Carlo Santora. "I'd say you pretty much pegged that one sis." He continued to grin at her, then turned to Carlo and sobered. "Guess you misjudged her, too. She's not the pushover you were hoping for is she?"

Carlo sighed in defeat. He had misjudged the girl as much as he misjudged the boy. He didn't know what to do. For the first time in his life, he didn't know how to maneuver the situation to ensure his desired outcome. This trip really hadn't gone the way he had planned. It was a disaster and on top of everything, if Dante called his grandparents, the Waterson's would stop the monthly payments. He needed that money. He couldn't support Shannon the way she expected if he lost it. Shannon, a feeling of terror and desperation filled him again. He couldn't lose her. If they lost the money, he'd find a way to make up the difference. He just couldn't lose her.

Alex turned to Dimitri. "Thomas was right. This is my problem to solve," she paused to consider. "We have to get involved whether I like it or not. We have to send someone out there and let them handle the situation any way they see fit. I can talk to Tony and see if he and Megan can go," she said reluctantly. She didn't want to keep using Megan that way.

"That's not necessary," Dante said immediately. "I'll take care of this. It's my problem, my family, I'll handle it myself."

Dimitri studied Dante. He understood the man's position and honestly wasn't surprised by it. But did Dante really think they would make him go out and rescue that imp? The emotional toll Dante would pay was far too high to even consider. "No," he said with finality.

"Dimitri, I need a minute alone," Dante said standing and walking to the door. He didn't even wait to see if Dimitri followed. He wasn't going to give him the chance to object.

Dimitri watched Dante leave the room then glanced at Thomas.

Thomas shook his head, adamantly. "You can't let him do this. You know that, right?"

"I'll listen to his argument," Dimitri said soberly. "But it's going to have to be a good one for me to change my mind and allow his participation." He glanced at Carlo then at Alex. "Are you okay here?" He asked quietly. "Will you be okay if I leave you here with Thomas?"

"I'm fine," she said still glaring at the man that was so unlike his son. She didn't like him, not even a little. And that was before she knew his history. He had come to New York and insulted her family, in their family home no less. Before this was finished, the man would know just how big of a mistake he had made.

"Thomas, please don't let her eat him for breakfast," Dimitri grinned when he saw Carlo's frown deepen. "She's grown on me. I'd hate to see her spend time at the island for murder."

"I got it," Thomas assured Dimitri. "I'm kind of fond of her myself. Don't worry about our girl, she'll behave."

"Oh, just go," Alex told Dimitri. "He's not the first of his kind I've had to deal with in my life." She rolled her eyes at the two men she loved more than anything. "And I'm sure he won't be the last."

Dimitri found Dante in the kitchen. He'd switched from coffee to coke. "So?" Dimitri finally asked. "Convince me this is the right thing for you because from where I'm sitting right now there's no way in hell I'd ever ask you to go rescue that woman."

"You're not asking," Dante said flatly. "That piece of shit in there that calls himself my father is. I don't have to like it, but he is my family. That makes him my problem. He's screwed up. This time his selfish, ineptness has put our entire species in danger. It's my responsibility to fix it. I'm asking you not to stand in my way. I'm asking you not to pawn this off on someone else and force me to sit back idly while another warrior deals with my baggage."

Dimitri took a deep breath. He hadn't thought of it that way. But he would have, if he were sitting where Dante was sitting. And he'd be arguing just as vehemently to handle this himself. "I'm not saying I agree with you, but if I let you get involved who are you going to take with you? You know I won't let you deal with this alone. You're going to need help, who? Normally I'd say Nick but under the circumstances, I don't think that's a good idea. And we all know Thomas isn't going."

Dante smiled. "Alex would so kick your butt if you offered up Thomas. She was good in there. You are definitely a lucky man. Hold on to that one, she's one of a kind."

"She is," Dimitri said smiling a little himself. He'd seen the slight flicker of sadness in Dante's eyes and decided to ignore it this time. "I'm sure Thomas already put Carlo in his place before we arrived."

"He did," Dante confirmed. "Dear old dad didn't like the idea of Thomas calling you in. He's worried about Oberon."

"Rightfully so," Dimitri said sobering again. "Oberon's not going to like this at all. I have no doubt he's going to take this to the council when he hears about it. Your father will certainly be sanctioned for this one."

"He should be. His greed and selfish exploits have put our entire race in danger this time. It's past time Carlo paid for something." Dante paused and took a deep breath. He wasn't going to rant about his father tonight. He had a decision to make. He knew Dimitri was right, he couldn't go out there alone and he couldn't take Thomas or Nick. Alex and Dimitri were out, too. Dimitri couldn't go without Alex and bringing her in would have the same impact as

Progeny

Thomas. Then it hit him. "I'll take Cornelia with me," he finally said, the plan falling into place. "We'll head out tomorrow. If we need more help I'll let you decide who you want to send. Victor comes to mind, but I don't know about that. He's dealt with family trouble before, but that also makes him a little less tolerant. It takes a lot of patience to deal with Carlo, unless of course you don't mind if he ends up dead in a ditch somewhere." Dante smiled at the conflicted look on Dimitri's face. "In that case, I'll let you decide who. Initially just me and Cornelia though. I'll let you know if I need help."

Dimitri didn't answer immediately. He hated the whole situation. He wanted to pound Carlo Santora into the ground for this. The emotional toll rescuing that evil woman was going to have on Dante infuriated him. But forcing him to stay back, to sit here in New York while someone else handled this problem, would take an even bigger toll on Dante. Dimitri wouldn't do that to his friend, his brother, he had to let him go. The first chance he got, he'd be filling the rest of the warriors in on this. Dante might have to stand up and take out the garbage, but the warriors were going to be there for him when he returned. "Okay," Dimitri finally agreed. "I don't like it, but I understand and I won't stand in your way. But the instant there's trouble, I expect a call."

"Thank you," Dante said. He would have gone anyway, but it would have strained things with Dimitri and that was the last thing he wanted. He was grateful he had Dimitri's blessing and didn't have to force that rift between them. "I appreciate your concern Dimitri, but I can handle this. It's been a long time and I've accepted the past and moved on. Stop worrying about me. I'm fine."

"No, you're not," Dimitri said standing. "And don't thank me, I'm not sure I've done you any favors here. But, I also know you would have gone anyway." Dimitri paused when he saw the quick flash in Dante's eyes. "I know you, Dante. I also know I would have done the same thing, damn the consequences. I do understand and we'll all be here for you when you get back. I'm trusting you to tell me if it's worse than we think. I'm not sure who I'll send you, but I'm counting on you to be honest with me and keep in touch." He placed his hands on Dante's shoulders and forced eye contact. "Don't let me down. Don't try to be a hero. I expect a call immediately if you need more help. I'm going to know, anyway. I'll feel it."

"I'm crystal clear on that," Dante assured him. "I'll call you."

Dimitri turned to head back to the study.

"Uh..." Dante called. "I'd rather not go back in there if it's all right with you. I've had about all I can take of that man for one day."

"I understand," Dimitri said, giving Dante the reprieve he needed. Dimitri was proud of Dante. It took a tremendous amount of self-control for the man to sit in the same room as a father that had betrayed him the way Carlo had. Dimitri was having a hard time being that close and not decking the man himself.

"Are you finished with Thomas?" Dante asked trying to sound casual. "There was actually something I needed to talk to him about. That's how I ended up here in the first place. Something that has nothing to do with Carlo Santora."

Dimitri studied Dante for a minute, searching for a catch. "I'll send him back," he finally agreed, walking soberly back to the study.

"What's up?" Thomas asked the instant he stepped into the room. He wondered if Dimitri was just trying to get rid of him or if there really was something Dante wanted to discuss.

"I need to talk to you about something important and confidential," Dante paused, looking around to make sure they were alone. "It's about Cornelia and the reason I showed up in the first place."

Thomas was watching Dante. He was on edge, but the fact that his father was sitting just a few yards away could account for that. "What about her?" Thomas asked.

"It's about her father, the vampire," he began. "She's been extremely secretive about that since she arrived. Now I know why. She's terrified of him and worried he's going to find out she's here. I was actually headed over to see if you could swing a Vegas suite and a plane for her. Now, I guess we need accommodations for two. I assume Dimitri told you Cornelia and I will be heading to Vegas to handle this problem for the Great Santora in there?"

"He did and I personally think it's a terrible idea. You shouldn't do this anymore than I should," Thomas said in disgust.

"Be that as it may, I'm going," Dante softened. Thomas was just trying to protect him. "And you know if the tables were turned, you'd do the same."

"I would," Thomas agreed. "That's why I'm not giving you more grief about it. But let's get back to Cornelia. That man's taken more than enough of our time today."

"Right," Dante said, unsure of how to proceed. "Well, she's terrified and was already planning to head to Vegas to follow a lead she found on Lillie's case. Basically, it was just an excuse to get out of town. Now that she told me who her father is, I don't blame her. But, I can't keep it a secret either," he paused, but when Thomas didn't push he continued. "It's Radek." Now he got a reaction. Thomas was outwardly surprised.

"No wonder she's scared. He's so obsessed with his heir being a son, and a shifter son to boot, if he knew she was here, her life would be in serious danger," Thomas considered. "Does he know about her? Did he recognize her?"

"She doesn't think so," Dante assured him. "Radek abducted her mother years ago. He was following in his father's footsteps with that one I guess. He held her captive for some time and raped her regularly. Just like Balthazar and Marlena. Radek kept Shaylee, Cornelia's mother, weak and barely alive. Once Shaylee realized she was

Progeny

pregnant she knew she had to escape. An opportunity presented itself very early on in her pregnancy. Her family didn't even know she was pregnant. They were still in Ireland. She packed up and told them she couldn't cope in the city any longer. That's when she moved to Utah and began to live such a solitary life. Her parents eventually learned Shaylee had a child, but they assume Cornelia was part human. Shaylee never told them about the abduction."

"Why the big secret?" Thomas asked. "I mean other than the obvious. If Radek knew, Cornelia would be a huge target for sure."

"Shaylee believed that if anyone knew, she would be forced to turn her child over to the vampires," Dante began.

"What?" Thomas asked appalled. "She thinks my parents would have forced that? Why?"

"Yes," Dante confirmed. "She believes that your parents would have been intolerant of a fae raising a vampire child in their community. She also believes the community would have shunned her and Cornelia. She fled to give her child a chance at life."

"I still don't understand. My parents weren't like that. They were kind and understanding. They would never..." Thomas was offended.

"I know," Dante said cutting him off. "But Shaylee, well everyone, knew about Marlena and Radek. Shaylee just assumed that since Marlena left Radek to be raised by his vampire father, the queen had very strong opinions about it. That was the only explanation she had for why Marlena would abandon her own child that way."

Thomas almost began to argue again. The idea was utterly ridiculous. But he didn't because he'd heard some of the gossip himself. Everyone knew that Radek was Marlena's son. Most of the information surrounding Radek's existence was private, though. Very few people knew the details. *Well wasn't that the nature of the beast,* Thomas mused? People always came up with their own explanation when kept in the dark. "So, should I assume that Cornelia believes the same thing?" Thomas finally asked. "You've said all along that she doesn't want you to tell anyone. Is that because she thinks as soon as we learn who her father is, we're going to bind her and throw her to the wolves, or vampires I guess would be more accurate?"

"She is worried about that," Dante admitted. "I know that pisses you off and I can't say that I blame you. She's wrong, but I've tried to look at things from her perspective and I guess I understand how she got there. Look at her mother. Shaylee's a recluse. And, she's warned Cornelia since birth that Luke and Marlena would turn her over to Radek if they ever found out about her. I think it took a lot of guts to come here with Tala in the first place. She knew Radek was here. She believed if we knew her secret she'd be turned over to him immediately. He'd have free rein to do whatever he wanted with her. I don't think I would have done it," Dante admitted.

"Spoken from the moron that's going to Vegas to rescue that man's wife," Thomas countered. "Yes, you would have. So why are you telling me this? There's obviously something you need from me," he finally asked.

"Because I know I can trust you with it. We're leaving in the morning. I'm going to try to talk to her while we're gone. I'll continue to do my best to convince her that Alex would never turn her over to Radek. It doesn't matter that she has a small amount of vampire in her DNA. Alex won't care about that. I'd also like to talk to her about what happened with Marlena if you think that's okay. Maybe if she understood why Marlena left Radek, she'd realize she's not in any danger from us. The situation is completely different," Dante told him. "I've been working on her since the battle on New Years. I think I've already planted the seeds of doubt. Alex healed her but hasn't come after her yet. Cornelia is confused about that and I think she's starting to believe me, at least a little."

"Well, that's something at least. Go ahead and tell her what we know about Marlena. Alex won't care," Thomas paused, he could tell there was more. "And?"

"And," Dante continued. "Alex needs to know everything. So does Dimitri. I realize I'm betraying Cornelia's trust and she may never forgive me for that, but it's important that they understand the situation. Cornelia is in danger, but so are we. She believes, and I'm inclined to agree, that if she ever comes in close contact with Radek he will know immediately that she's his daughter. She said he would be able to smell it. Cornelia has been helping us with this war, she's killed vampires. Radek knows that. He saw her in our last battle. She defied his command to retreat. If he finds her, I'm positive he will try to have her assassinated. Her life is in danger. Alex and Dimitri need to know that. They need to decide what they want to do about it. Once Alex knows Cornelia is family I think she'll want her protected, if it's presented the right way."

"I agree," Thomas said, thinking. "Cornelia actually felt and rejected the vampire king's demand? That's huge," Thomas considered. He wasn't sure if he should be impressed or terrified. "I'll handle it with Alex and Dimitri. We'll have a plan by the time you get back. This doesn't have to be presented in the right way. Alex would protect her anyway," Thomas paused, "So what do I tell them about you."

"Me?" Dante asked, confused. "What about me?"

"Are you sleeping with Cornelia?" Thomas asked bluntly.

"I don't see how that is any of your business," Dante said defensively. "I didn't ask if you were sleeping with Abby and the two of you were basically living together."

Thomas smiled, he'd take that as a yes. "Fair enough. I just thought if Alex and Dimitri knew how much Cornelia meant to you it might add to the urgency of the situation."

"It shouldn't matter what Cornelia means to me. They should understand the urgency and protect her anyway. Cornelia was instrumental in the Kahn investigation. Our community owes her. She's made herself a target for us," Dante paused. "If Cornelia and I decide to sleep together to pass the time, that's our business. It has no bearing on the situation with Radek."

Thomas didn't believe for one minute that Dante was just passing time. The guy had feelings for Cornelia, strong feelings. He might try to hide it, or maybe he didn't realize it yet, but Dante was falling for the beautiful, sweet vampire. Thomas only hoped Cornelia was falling just as hard for his friend. He wasn't sure Dante could survive another hard blow in the relationship department. "You're right. It doesn't matter," he finally agreed, but it would make a difference. He'd wing it or maybe he'd talk to Nick and get his take before he took this to Alex. Regardless, they'd have a plan when Cornelia returned to New York. "Cornelia is family. That alone is going to fuel my sister's protective instincts," Thomas finally said. "That and the fact that she basically saved my butt from being thrown in the slammer for murder."

Dante smiled. Now he could leave, knowing the situation would be handled by the time they got back from Vegas. He had known coming to Thomas was the right thing to do. Thomas would talk to Alex and Dimitri and most likely Nick. He could trust them. Once he and Cornelia returned, a concrete plan would already be in place to ensure her safety.

Chapter Three

Cornelia watched as the plane touched down on the runway. She was breathing a lot easier now that she was out of New York. Being in Las Vegas almost felt like coming home. She hadn't lived there for years but for the past few decades, she'd spent all her time in the area. Sometimes she lived in Moab, sometimes in St. George, sometimes in Vegas. She never moved too far from Salt Lake since her mother insisted on living in that remote cabin in the Uintah's. She didn't want to be more than a day's drive away in case of an emergency.

The moment the plane came to a complete stop, Dante was out of his chair. He'd been tense the entire flight. Cornelia felt bad for him. She knew he hadn't told her the complete story. That hurt a little. She'd trusted him with so much. He should be able to trust her with an explanation of something so simple. The reason for the rift between him and his father couldn't be more personal than all the things she'd confided in him. She also got the distinct feeling Dante didn't care for his stepmother. None of that mattered to Dante though. In spite of the bad blood between them, Dante had hopped a plane and flown thousands of miles to rescue his father's wife. That's just the kind of guy he was, Cornelia supposed. She stood, collected her luggage and followed Dante to the now open door. She had expected to be sharing a plane with Dante's father but was immediately informed *he could find his own damn ride.* That too was telling.

"Thomas promised he'd have a car ready to take us to the casino," Dante called over his shoulder. Once he reached the bottom of the stairs, he paused to survey the area. Then he turned and took Cornelia's hand, pulling her toward a waiting limo.

Cornelia's heart did a little flip. Her step faltered as electricity shot through her arm and straight to her heart. But she didn't think Dante had noticed her slight pause. This was the first time he'd shown her any affection since he'd dropped her at the apartment yesterday morning. She knew he was preoccupied, but she'd been worried about the lack of contact the entire flight. She'd finally come to the conclusion their night together was just an opportunity for Dante, not the special intimate evening it had been for her. That made her self-conscious and unsure how to act around him. She took a deep breath and tried to relax. Dante taking her hand was a good sign. For now, she'd just play it by ear and let him take the lead for a while. She knew how she felt about him, but she was completely in the dark when it came to his feelings for her. Hopefully, Dante's actions over time would guide her on this one.

The two of them didn't speak as they rode to the large casino. Cornelia followed Dante to the check in area and waited silently for arrangements to be made. She had to admit, Thomas was efficient. He'd ensured smooth sailing all the way. Dante requested two keys, then turned and waited for the bell boy to collect their luggage and lead them to the elevators. Cornelia was expecting a nice suite, but the elevator opened into a luxurious penthouse. She tried to focus on what the man was telling them, but her eyes wouldn't stop wandering. The room was amazing. It was more like a large apartment than a hotel room. She didn't think she'd ever been in anything so plush and luxurious before. Cornelia barely noticed when Dante tipped their escort and silently closed the door behind him.

"I think you're drooling," Dante said, laughter in his voice.

"I'm sure you're right," Cornelia said, glancing his way. "Any idea where the napkins are? I think I might need one by the time I finish my tour."

Dante opened a large closet and hung his garment bag inside then turned to Cornelia again. "You hungry?" he asked casually.

"I'm starved," Cornelia admitted. "What did you have in mind?"

"I was thinking we could grab a bite to eat then head over to the bank. We should have plenty of time to dig into those financials this afternoon," he paused. "We're not going to have much time tomorrow. I've agreed to meet with my father in the morning, at ten. I'm afraid that investigation is going to take most of our time so if we can clear up the Brad Shepherd thing today, we won't be pulled in different directions while we're here."

"I agree," Cornelia said stepping to her luggage then glancing around. "I need to change if we're going to the bank. Any idea where the rooms are?"

Dante smiled. "Yeah, upstairs. Take the master. I'll crash in one of the guest rooms."

Cornelia didn't say anything, she collected her luggage and headed up the stairs. She wouldn't occupy the master suite. Thomas was Dante's friend and he should stay in the larger room. She was sure the guest rooms were more than adequate for her needs. She'd never been in a place as expensive but homey as this one. She glanced over her shoulder and saw Dante watching her. Cornelia turned away, hoping Dante hadn't caught the thrill in her eye or the blush on her face. The man was so distracting and dangerous. So why did the knowledge that he was riveted as she ascended the stairs give her such a thrill? She was still smiling when she opened the door to a pretty blue room.

Dante watched Cornelia as she headed up the short flight of stairs. The woman was hot. She didn't need to change, the shorts and tight shirt she was wearing would have gotten her more information than she needed at the bank. He was curious to see what she'd be wearing when she returned. *That little black skirt she talked about?*

Maybe. He smiled at the thought. He did love to look at those long, sexy legs of hers. Dante walked to the kitchen and checked the fridge. He was sure Bastian's men wouldn't put the blood in the main refrigerator, but he had to be sure. Once he determined there was only food inside, he headed upstairs himself. Cornelia would be in the master bedroom, but he could check the small units in each of the closets and see what kind of supplies had been left.

Once Dante reached the top of the stairs he realized Cornelia had taken one of the guest rooms instead of the master. He'd rectify that later. He was just exiting the bedroom when Cornelia stepped into the hallway. She wore sleek black trousers, a thin silk shirt and sensible shoes. He was glad to see she wasn't wearing high heels with the outfit. He was a man, so those strappy little thing's women liked to teeter on always gave him a jolt, but today they were going to be doing a lot of walking. He didn't want to worry about Cornelia twisting an ankle in an attempt to keep up.

"You ready?" She asked with a smile. Cornelia realized Dante hadn't changed. It wasn't fair. How could the guy look like a million bucks with no effort? The moment she'd stepped in front of the mirror she'd groaned. Her hair was tasseled and her clothes were wrinkled from the long flight. She'd only had a few minutes to make herself presentable and here Dante was, standing there all GQ in his khaki slacks and golf shirt. The same shirt and pants he'd been wearing all day.

"Ready," he agreed. "I thought you were taking the master," he said casually.

Progeny

"I wanted you to have it," she told him as they started down the staircase. "I noticed the small refrigeration unit in my closet. It's stocked with plenty of blood if you need any."

"The master is stocked as well," Dante told her. "They also stocked the other guest room. That should be plenty but we can always order more if we need it. I hope we won't be here too long, but don't worry about blood. We're covered no matter how long it takes." They had reached the front door and Dante placed a hand on the small of her back as he pulled open the large door. "I'm not that familiar with the area, it's been years since I've been out this way. Any idea where we can get a good meal?"

Cornelia smiled. "How do you feel about BBQ?"

"If it's good, we get along just fine," Dante grinned.

"Good," Cornelia's smile widened. "I have a friend that owns a little out of the way place not too far from here. The food is great and we'll avoid all the tourists."

"Local secret, huh? Sounds perfect." They had reached the lobby. Dante pulled open the front door and stepped onto the sidewalk. "Do you know the address? The driver will need it before we leave. If not, he should be able to look it up."

"If the driver is local, I'd lay odds he knows the Mud Pit already," Cornelia said sliding into the backseat of the limo.

"Joe?" Dante called as he slid in next to her. "We're headed to lunch, Cornelia wants BBQ so we thought we'd head to the Mud Pit." He shot a look at Cornelia, a silent signal to fill in the information.

A huge smile spread across Joe's face before Cornelia could reply. "And here I was all disgruntled because you didn't give me enough time to grab a bite on my own. I take back all those errant thoughts about spoiled rich kids," Joe said happily. "Today turned out to be a stellar day after all. Ms. Amelia always hooks me up just right when I have a minute to stop in. I guess she feels sorry for me."

"Sorry for you?" Dante asked laughter in his tone. "Sorry for what?"

"On account of me having to drive all you Richie Rich types around in traffic all day," Joe teased. "Most of the suits I'm saddled with wouldn't recognize a sense of humor if it bit them in the you-know-what."

Dante laughed. "I can't argue with you on that one, Joe. Lucky for you, that you got stuck with us for the next week or so."

"So far, so good. I'm eating BBQ, ain't I?" Joe pulled into traffic and the conversation ended.

"I take it you and Joe are old pals," Cornelia surmised.

"Yeah," Dante said, still amused. "The old guy is one of a kind. I tried to talk him into dumping the

Progeny

Deveraux's and working for me in New York, but he wouldn't hear of it. They treat him too well and he loves it here in Vegas. Don't let him fool you. He's never going to move."

"I thought you said you haven't been to Vegas in years," Cornelia said, confused.

"I haven't," Dante agreed. "But when Thomas is shorthanded, Joe flies out to California and drives for us there." Dante wasn't going to finish his thought out loud. The truth was, the guy would never take a vacation. The only way Thomas, and before him Luke, could get Joe to take a break was to fly him out to California on the pretense that the guys needed a beach vacation. Joe rarely had to drive them anywhere but he was able to get away for a while. He, Thomas and Nick would hang at the beach for a week and Joe basically hung with them. They had a driver when they needed one and Joe got out of Vegas for a while. It was a win/win for everyone.

"I see," Cornelia said. "So Joe is familiar with California as well as Vegas?"

Dante shot a glance at Joe then back to Cornelia. "He is now."

Cornelia figured there was more to the story, but she let it drop for now. Joe was pulling to the curb, so it was time to exit the limo. "Thanks for the ride, Joe," she called as she opened the door and jumped onto the sidewalk.

Dante reached up and slipped Joe a hundred then followed Cornelia out the door. "Give us about an hour. Then we'll need to head to the bank."

"Will do," Joe said cheerfully. He was always surprised at how generous Thomas Deveraux and his closest friends were. He rarely got tips when driving the regular suits, but these guys were classy and generous. Too bad they insisted on living in the Big Apple.

It was over an hour later when Cornelia and Dante climbed into the limo and headed for the bank. The two sat in silence for several minutes. Finally, Cornelia spoke. "I'm so stuffed," she complained.

"Me too," Dante agreed, smiling. It was refreshing to eat with a woman that didn't just pick a little here and there. Cornelia's appetite had amused and delighted him.

Cornelia turned to Dante and smiled. "It must be nice to be you," she said, still grinning.

Dante smiled back at her. "Usually, but which parts are you referring to... specifically?"

"Oh, come on," Cornelia said knowingly. "You live a charmed life, Dante. Having everything you want when you want it must be nice." Cornelia was leaning back against the headrest, her eyes closed, legs stretched out, totally relaxed. "You only decided yesterday that you needed to go to Vegas and here we are being chauffeured around in this expensive limo. And that's after we hopped a private jet and checked into the penthouse of the most expensive casino in miles. If that's not enough, every time

Progeny

I turn around you're passing out hundred-dollar bills like they were candy or something. I'm just saying, it must be nice to be you." Cornelia opened her eyes and realized Dante was frowning.

"The jet's not mine, neither is the limo nor the penthouse. If our accommodations make you uncomfortable I'm sure Joe can track down a sleazy motel we could move to," Dante grumbled. He was looking out the side window, still frowning. He knew he had more money than most that's why he always made sure to tip well. He didn't pass out hundreds like it was candy. Sure, he'd slipped Joe a tip earlier today and he left a fifty for each of Cornelia's friends at lunch but that was only because they wouldn't allow him to pay his bill. He never flaunted his wealth, but Cornelia was acting as if he had done something wrong.

"That's not what I meant," Cornelia began. She wasn't sure what she had said that offended him, but clearly something had. "I'm perfectly happy at the penthouse and I know it belongs to Thomas. I'll have to find a way to thank him when I get back."

Dante continued to quietly stare out the window. His mind was wandering again. He wasn't sure why Cornelia's assessment hurt so much. Maybe because he'd been careful to slip the money to both Joe and Cornelia's friends discretely. Maybe because Cornelia was acting as if he was a spoiled child that never had any problems. Wasn't that the reason he was here in the first place? His problems. Problems with his father, problems with his father's wife, problems with his past. Dante closed his eyes and took a deep breath. All of his problems seemed to have a direct link back to his money. Maybe that was the rub. Cornelia thought having massive wealth was all rainbows and butterflies. It never had been for him. For Dante, having billions had caused more than his share of difficulties. But Cornelia wouldn't know that because he hadn't told her.

Joe pulled the limo to the curb in front of the bank and lowered the window. "You want me to stay here and wait?" he asked jovially.

"Yeah, thanks Joe," Dante said sincerely. "This shouldn't take long. I don't think anyone will bother you, but if the cops ask you to move just drive around the block until we get back."

"Will do," Joe agreed.

Dante pulled open the door and stepped onto the sidewalk. The two of them walked to the entrance in silence. Once they stepped inside the bank Dante turned to Cornelia. "Which one are you going to approach?"

Cornelia studied Dante for a minute but decided there was nothing she could do about his mood right now. They needed information. "I'll take that one." She motioned to a young man in his early thirties sitting behind a desk. "What are you going to do?"

Dante glanced around the room and focused on a young teller. The girl was obviously nervous and her unease was directed at him. She was trying to remain professional, but every few seconds her eyes would dart to Dante's then immediately move away. "I'll take her," he said motioning to the end of the counter. The girl's actions seemed strange and out of place.

Dante and Cornelia headed in opposite directions. There wasn't a line for the man so Cornelia sat down and immediately began her quest for information. Dante had to wait. Luckily it wasn't a long line. Once the girl finished with the two patrons in front of him, Dante plastered on his best smile and stepped forward.

"Good afternoon," the girl said nervously. She widened her smile in an attempt to hide her discomfort.

"Good afternoon," Dante said pleasantly. He studied the girl for a minute, making sure she noticed his interest. "You seem nervous, are you okay?"

"I'm sorry, Mr. Santora," she said immediately. "I didn't mean to offend you."

"Well," Dante said pausing for effect. "I am a Santora, but I honestly hate being called mister. Maybe you could call me Dante?" His father must use this bank. It was the only explanation for the strange behavior and the recognition. It was going to take all his charm to put this poor girl at ease.

"Oh," the girl said, a little surprised. "I thought..." she trailed off. "I mean, you look so much like Carlo Santora I thought..." she bit her bottom lip unsure what to say next.

"I understand," Dante said to soothe her. "We do look a lot alike."

"Yes," the girl said, relaxing a little. "You do. Are you brothers?"

Dante didn't answer that question. He couldn't tell the girl Carlo was his father. They looked too close in age for that. Going on instinct, he gave her his most winning smile and asked, "I'm glad you noticed the family resemblance, it will save time. I was wondering if you could give me the details of Carlo's accounts." He leaned in closer and practically whispered. "He's a little busy today and couldn't get down here himself. When I told him I was headed into the city, he asked me to stop by and get his account balances for him," he paused, smiling again. Trying to make her feel like she was a part of something important. While he was here, he might as well do a little investigating on their other problem. He certainly wouldn't count on Carlo to be completely honest and upfront when it came to finances. Anyway, Cornelia would probably get everything they needed from the love sick pup she was dealing with. "We're thinking about going in together on an investment and Carlo can't decide how much he wants to throw in," Dante laughed a little. "I don't mind, I practically fell into a sure thing and felt obligated to share... us being family and all. But to be honest, the less he invests, the more profit for me. You understand, don't you?" Dante asked, adding a bit of a conspiratorial tone to his voice as he gave her a friendly wink.

The girl smiled and relaxed a little more. "I understand." She hesitated only a minute then moved to her computer. "I can give you the balances but that's all I can do. If Mr. Santora wants you to have access to his accounts he will need to come into the bank and sign a waiver to add you in," she glanced up. "You'll have to come too. We need to have a signature card on all account holders." She was starting to get nervous again. Carlo Santora was so difficult to deal with, but his brother seemed a lot more relaxed and easy going. Still, she hated to give either one of them bad news or make them muddle through red tape. If they complained, she might lose her job.

"I don't think that will be necessary," Dante assured her. "For now, I just need the balances." He wondered how many accounts dear old dad had at this bank. "It's comforting to find you have such great security measures. I'm just visiting, but if I lived here, I'd definitely bank with you." He gave her another smile. "I hope Carlo appreciates the good job you do. I can tell his money is secure here."

"Oh, it is," the clerk assured him. "Here are the balances on Mr. Santora's checking and savings accounts," she paused to hand him a printout. "Those are his joint accounts with his wife, Shannon. The account numbers are in the corner so you can tell them apart. Did he also need the special account balance?"

Special account? Now wasn't that interesting? Carlo was hiding money from the love of his life? "I guess," Dante finally said. "Carlo just asked for his balances. He didn't specify how many so I guess I better get them all. He'll be able to keep them straight."

"Okay, here you go," the clerk said, handing Dante another printout. "It was a pleasure meeting you Mr., uh...

I mean Dante," she was serious. The guy was gorgeous and far more delightful than his brother.

"The pleasure was all mine," Dante said with a smile. He glanced around and saw that Cornelia was still busy with the male employee. He exited the bank and climbed into the limo. He lowered the partition and told Joe to wait for Cornelia then began to study the documents. The name on the account jumped out at him almost immediately. Carlo's special account was the Three Waters account they were trying to track. So, Carlo was the one that had lent Lillie's sleazy ex a boat load of money. Carlo was also the one extorting funds from the guy under the guise of interest payments. And the one sending Brad and then Lillie on those mysterious trips.

Dante lowered the documents, closed his eyes and pondered. He knew his dad was unscrupulous. He hadn't known Carlo was into smuggling. What would his father be bringing out of Mexico? The most obvious answer was drugs, just like Lillie had suspected. Was Carlo dealing, or using? Dante's head began to throb. It was almost impossible for a warrior to get a headache unless he was drunk of course, but Dante felt one developing. Was any of this tied to Shannon's disappearance? Was she the one using? Dante's mind began to wander to the past, but he stopped it. The past didn't matter, only the present. If Carlo was dealing, Shannon may have been abducted by a rival drug cartel. Someone that didn't like competition. He was still thinking about the possibilities when the door opened and Cornelia slid in.

"I didn't get much," she admitted, not really looking at Dante. "I was able to get a printout of all activity on the Three Waters account for the past three months." She paused as Joe lowered the window and patiently waited for instruction.

Dante didn't open his eyes. "We're finished for today, Joe. Just drop us back at the casino and then you can go home."

Joe nodded, concerned by the stressful look on Dante's face. Once he dropped the couple at the casino, he'd give Thomas a call. It was time for him to check in, anyway.

Cornelia waited for Joe to raise the barrier then continued. "That man was afraid," she said, lowering her voice to a mere whisper. "No matter what angle I tried, he wouldn't give me a name." She was clearly frustrated. "I can usually get through the fear, but not today. Whoever opened that account lives here in Vegas, I'm sure of it." Dante still hadn't said a word. He hadn't moved at all. Cornelia finally paused to study him more closely. "Dante?" she asked, worried now.

Dante opened his eyes and sighed. Then, he held out his paperwork and waited for Cornelia to reach for them. "The Three Waters account belongs to my father," he said flatly. "Looks like our two investigations just became one complex problem."

"Your father?" Cornelia said softly as she studied the top page. There was no mistake, the account number listed in the top right-hand corner was the same account number she'd been trying to track down for weeks. Three Waters Incorporated was clearly printed across the top, but Carlo Santora wasn't listed anywhere. Her mind was racing through possibilities but there were so many of them she forced herself to block them out. Her eyes shifted back to Dante and softened. "You okay?" she asked, knowing he wasn't.

"Sure," he said as he sat up and stared out the window. "I'm sorry I got you into this," he finally said, then turned to face her. "I'm afraid this is going to get a lot uglier than I originally believed and I'm sorry."

"Dante," Cornelia began but she didn't really know what to say.

"No," Dante said, covering her hand with his as he shook his head. "There's a lot you don't know," he paused. "A lot of family history that you probably need to know. When we get back to the room, I'll fill you in." He turned to look out the window again. "Once you know the whole story I'll let you decide if you want to stay or if you want out. Maybe you can head up and spend some time with your mother or something."

Cornelia turned her hand linking fingers with Dante, hoping the contact would give him some comfort. "You were there for me when I needed you," she paused. "More than once, in fact. I'm not going anywhere. We'll talk when we get back to the room because I need to know everything. If we're going to crack this case, find Shannon and fix the problem for Lillie, I need to know everything." She paused, waiting for Dante to look her way again. When he finally did, she looked into his eyes, unwavering.

"But I'm not going anywhere. We're going to deal with this together," she promised. "I have a few daddy issues myself, remember?" She smiled weakly trying to lighten the mood a little.

Dante sighed, forced a smile then lifted Cornelia's hand to his mouth and kissed it softly. "Thanks," he finally said. "I won't hold you to that until you have all the facts, but thanks just the same."

They traveled in silence the rest of the way. Cornelia's heart broke for Dante. She didn't know what skeletons lay hidden in his past, but they were obviously painful. It didn't really matter to her. There was nothing Dante could tell her that would change the way she felt about him. There was nothing he could reveal that would make her leave him to deal with this alone. She was in love with him and she would be there for him no matter what.

Chapter Four

Cornelia sat quietly on the large sofa. They were back in the penthouse now. Once Joe dropped them off, Dante wanted to go for a walk. They'd spent hours, walking in silence. Cornelia let Dante stew even though the silence had killed her. She knew he needed time to cope before he could share his thoughts... his story with her.

She took another sip of wine as she patiently waited for Dante to begin his story. He'd been so withdrawn since they left the bank. Cornelia alternated between wanting to shake the story out of him and wanting to pull him into her arms and silently comfort him. The sadness etched on his face was killing her, but she had to let him do this his way. She smiled a little. His way had to be better than the hysterical blubbering she'd forced Dante to endure when she told him she was part vampire. He'd been so patient

Progeny

and caring with her. She'd been terrified the night he'd caught her stealing from Bastian. But Dante had simply picked her up, walked to the couch and cradled her in his arms as she wept, uncontrollably. Dante wouldn't cry, but she knew he was in pain. Cornelia was determined to be there for him. Somehow she would help ease his pain the same way he had eased hers.

Dante finally turned and looked into Cornelia's eyes. He must have found whatever he was looking for because he set down his coke and walked toward her. He didn't sit next to her like she'd hoped. He slowly lowered himself into the large lounge chair across from her and began to tell his story.

"I've never had much of a relationship with my father," he began. "In fact, I didn't meet him until after I turned twenty-five."

Cornelia was surprised by that but remained silent.

"I'm told my mother was head over heels in love with the man, although I can't understand why," he paused, then shrugged. "But in all fairness, my information was filtered through my grandparents and Nick, who are all extremely biased." He grinned thinking about Nick and his grandparents. "They all hate his guts," he said without emotion. "Anyway, my mother got pregnant early on in their marriage. She was a petite woman and the pregnancy was difficult. You know how it is with the Fae. All pregnancies are difficult but some are more dangerous than others. Mom was bedridden almost from the start. As the months passed, she got weaker and even more fragile. My father was more interested in partying and rebel rousing than taking care of mom, so she moved back in with her parents. Mom died minutes after I was born. She lived long enough to hold me, name me and make her parents promise to watch out for me." Dante stood and began to pace in front of the large bank of windows. Cornelia didn't blame him. She had the same habit. For her, walking somehow helped her align her thoughts, especially when relaying something difficult.

"When my father finally showed up, mom had been gone for hours. My grandparents were so deep in grief they could barely function. Nick was the one that took care of everything." Deep emotion crossed Dante's face. "Nick has been there for me my entire life. He was there for my mother before I was even born and my grandparents after my mother's death," he paused to swallow the lump in his throat then continued. "I'm told my father was furious when he learned my grandparents had changed mom's trust. Grams and Pops believed that Carlo had married mom for her money. Richard and Jasmine Waterson, my grandparents, both came from extremely wealthy families. Their daughter, my mother Chelsea, was the sole heir of a fortune," Dante laughed without humor. "We're talking millions; the word fortune doesn't even begin to describe their wealth. Anyway when mom got sick and Carlo basically abandoned her to party and carry on as he had for years, my grandparents changed their trust."

"They prevented him from inheriting your mother's money," Cornelia said in understanding.

"Yes," Dante said picking up his coke and taking a sip. "They were completely devastated by mom's death, but they're smart. Carlo went through the motions, acting upset about mom. He even feigned outrage at Nick for not tracking him down earlier so he could say goodbye to his loving wife. But, true to form, he began scheming immediately. He told my grandparents he was worried about me. He didn't know the first thing about caring for an infant and wanted my grandmother to step in and take me until he had time to grieve. He begged them to do it for my sake, not his. He said he just needed help for a couple years until I didn't need a woman's care any longer. My grandparents took a hard stand. They told him it was all or nothing. They wouldn't help him unless he signed away all parental rights to his child...to me. He agreed almost instantly."

"Smart," Cornelia said impressed. "Otherwise, he could have used you to get anything he wanted from them, money, power, anything."

"Exactly," Dante agreed. "Like I said my grandparents are smart. They didn't only have my father sign away his rights, they involved the council. They did everything in such a way that Carlo couldn't break the contract. There was no going back once it was done."

"Sounds like they'd been planning things for some time," Cornelia mused.

"They could see how weak and fragile mom was. They also heard, regularly, what Carlo was up to all those months that mom lay fighting for her life and the life of her unborn child. They had never liked Carlo but by the time I was born, they despised him intently. They hoped for a miracle, but had a plan already in place just in case mom didn't make it. If she had survived they would have waited a few years then changed the trust back, giving her everything."

Cornelia thought it spoke volumes that Dante referred to a mother he had never met with the endearing label of mom while he never used the term dad. It was always Carlo or my father.

"My father had already signed away his rights when he learned the details of mom's trust. I'm told he erupted like a volcano. He even took the matter to the council. He claimed the changes were unlawful and wanted the council to reverse them immediately. His request was denied. The council ruled that the money belonged to the Waterson's and they could distribute it in any manner they saw fit. Carlo received a generous lump sum basically to get rid of him, but nothing further. I was the new heir to their fortune, but I didn't have any control until after I turned twenty-one."

"I see," Cornelia said disgustedly. Dante's father was a schemer. He waited a few additional years before he inserted himself back into Dante's life, thinking his motives wouldn't be as obvious. And really, what was a couple years to a man that would live several millennia?

"I had a good life," Dante assured her. "My grandparents loved me, probably more than I deserved sometimes," he paused. "We traveled until I was three then they moved back to the farm. I grew up being loved by Grams and Pops who indulged my every whim and by Nick and his parents, who taught me respect and responsibility." Dante stopped, remembering the carefree days of his youth.

Progeny

"Nick was like a father to me back then. I think he was the only one that ever told me no. Once I grew up we became friends, more like brothers I guess. He's always been protective of me, and he's always deeply despised my father. Sometimes I think Nick hates the man more than I do."

"That explains a lot," Cornelia said, thinking about the close relationship Nick had with Dante.

"Anyway, just after my twenty-fifth birthday Carlo Santora waltzed back into my life. At the time, I didn't think he knew my grandparents had altered the trust again, but now I'm not so sure. I had access to the funds, but there were limitations."

"What kind of limitations?" Cornelia asked. Dante's grandparents seemed like smart, intelligent people. Surely they realized Carlo Santora would try to take advantage of a young man just as he had their daughter.

"There were strict parameters. There was a limit on how much money I could give away to any one person or single organization. That included subsidiaries of any parent corporation. It also detailed how much I could invest in any one project, things like that. Basically, they made sure Carlo couldn't scam me for cash or manipulate me into investing for him. Of course, when Carlo found out the details, he was livid. That's when he decided to play the loving father. Hoping to get money that way, I suppose." Dante returned to the chair, sat, then immediately stood and once again began to pace.

Cornelia waited. She could see they were entering the difficult part. She was terrible at comforting people. Another downside of living in seclusion for most of her life. She just hoped she would know what to do when he needed her.

Dante took a deep breath then continued. "Surprisingly, Carlo had invested his money wisely. He'd taken his lump sum inheritance and basically doubled it. But Carlo is greedy. He wanted more. So, he thought he'd become part of my life. I guess he hoped I would be able to buy things for him, circumvent the trust somehow, or convince my grandparents to look the other way. Life went along okay for a while. Carlo would show up at the house, invite me out for a beer, that sort of thing. I'd grown up not knowing anything about my father. Like I said Nick, the Moretti's, my grandparents all despised Carlo but they were careful not to bad mouth him when I was around. None of them liked the time I spent with my father, but they didn't stand in my way either. I guess they wanted me to figure him out on my own." Dante returned to the chair and sat down with a sigh. "I didn't, not at first. Carlo was exciting, charismatic, sometimes he was even funny. If that's the only side of him my mother saw, I guess I can understand why she loved him," he paused to take a long drink. "Gradually Carlo realized the effort wasn't worth it. He couldn't squeeze more money out of me because the trust was air tight and I wouldn't betray my grandparents that way. I saw less and less of him. Gradually, he disappeared altogether."

"I'm sorry," Cornelia said. "That must have been hard on you."

Progeny

"A little," Dante agreed. "But not as hard as you might think. I was still living in Italy at the time and I had my grandparents and the Moretti's. Eventually, I talked Nick into coming to America and joining the warriors. As time passed, I learned more than I cared to about Carlo Santora. The warriors tried not to bad mouth him when I was around, but we spend a lot of time together. Things slipped out, I overheard conversations, you know how it is. Anyway, the warriors had no respect for my father. Most of them could barely tolerate being in the same room as him. He was a warrior, technically. But he was unreliable and only served for a short time. While he was active, he spent more time and energy trying to get out of work than it would have taken to just do the job. The warriors were glad to see him go, he made things more dangerous for them. I took the bits and pieces I'd stumbled across to Luke and asked him to fill in the blanks. Luke was honest with me, I always appreciated that," Dante paused. He still missed Luke Deveraux and realized he probably always would.

"Once we moved to America, I saw Carlo occasionally. I think he mainly dropped by to keep the channels open. He assumed that eventually my grandparents would turn the entire trust over to me. Once that happened, he planned to swoop in and pick up where he left off. He showed up and weaseled his way back into my life about forty years ago." Dante paused, but when Cornelia didn't say anything he continued. "Carlo is smooth. He pretended to be all humble and regretful. He said he was getting older and realized he'd messed up with me. He asked for another chance. He said he knew it was too late to be my father, but he wanted a chance to be friends. He'd let me determine the parameters of our relationship, but he needed his family back. I was skeptical but decided to give him another shot. I guess mostly because I remembered how it had been when I was twenty-five. I wanted to see the best in him and he was family.

By this time he owned a casino in Vegas. Somehow he'd gotten in on the ground floor and avoided getting tangled with the mob. Maybe because his casino was small and unthreatening to their organization. More likely, they'd worked out some sort of deal because of the Italian connection. Anyway, he'd become friends with the guy that owned an equally small casino next door, Eric Johnson. For the most part, the mob was gone now and wealthy businessmen were taking over the Strip. My father and Eric wanted to become partners. They would combine their two properties and build a new, more elaborate casino to compete with the big boys."

"Convenient," Cornelia said sarcastically.

Dante smiled grimly. "Eric Johnson is your typical sleazy, underhanded criminal. His family was loosely associated with the mob. Eric's great, great, I can't remember how many greats, grandfather was some kind of runner for Lucky Luciano's organization. Anyway, his family is and always has been dirty which is why he gets along so well with my father. Neither one of them have any scruples."

"Let me guess, your father approached you with a business deal," Cornelia asked.

Progeny

"Eventually," Dante agreed. "But first, he tried to re-establish the connection. He started coming to New York pretty regularly to visit and hang out. After a year or so, he started pressuring me to come to Vegas," Dante paused. "Actually, I guess I need to back up a little. Carlo has an informant here in New York. A mole that feeds him information on my trust. By this time my grandparents had altered the terms to give me more liberal control of the money. In fact, I have complete control and basically did back then. However, my grandparents talked me into leaving language in the official documents that limited financial interaction with Carlo Santora."

"I'm not sure I understand," Cornelia said.

"We left language in the trust that limits what I can give my father. It limits how much I can invest in any project controlled or run by him," Dante clarified.

"Your grandparents still didn't trust your judgment when it came to your father?" she asked.

"They trusted me completely," Dante assured her. "They just thought it would be easier on me if we left language in the trust that limits Carlo. They knew he would become a nuisance otherwise. It wasn't about trusting me, it was about protecting me from harassment."

"I see," Cornelia said, liking Dante's grandparents more and more by the minute. "So the informant notified your father when the trust was changed again?"

"She did," Dante agreed. "I know who the mole is and could have her sanctioned for violating confidentiality, but so far it's been more beneficial to leave her in place. She feeds Carlo what I want her to feed him. I have complete control over the trust. I want to make that clear to you because I intend to make it clear to my father tomorrow. That's something he still doesn't know."

"Why?" Cornelia asked. "It sounds like the two of you are estranged, I doubt he'll ask you for a loan anytime soon."

"No, he won't," Dante agreed. "But for the past thirty-five years he has received a monthly allowance, I guess you could call it. He and his wife depend on that money and they wouldn't want to lose it. I can take it away."

"Why on earth do you give them money every month?" Cornelia said in amazement.

"I'm leading up to that, but we're getting ahead of the story," Dante told her.

"Okay," Cornelia said, even more curious now. "So you have control of the trust but there was language that limits what you can give Carlo."

"Yes," Dante nodded. "So my father kept pressuring me to go to Vegas and meet the players. More specifically, he wanted me to meet Eric Johnson. I finally went and disliked the man instantly. I could see he was unethical. I didn't like the idea of investing in a company that would be run by my father, whom I still didn't trust, and Eric Johnson. I held out. My father tried every trick in the book to change my mind. It got to the point that every time I saw

Progeny

him, that's all we talked about. The casino was going to cost more than Carlo and Eric could come up with. They needed investors. I was family. Didn't I care about family? My father sacrificed his time and money to visit me in New York because family was so important to him. I on the other hand rarely visited Vegas and refused to invest in my own father's future. He wore me down. I started taking more trips to Vegas. It was a difficult time in my life. I was being pulled in one direction by my father and I felt like I needed to give it a good faith effort. Otherwise, I'd never have a relationship with him. Nick didn't like it, so he was pulling me in the other direction. We were constantly arguing. I knew how much he disliked my father, so I shut him out. I hated the rift that was growing between us. At the time, I blamed him. Now, I can see it was my fault. Nick was just trying to protect me."

Cornelia remained silent. Obviously, the two had worked things out. She wouldn't know what to say anyway. She'd never had anyone the way Nick and Dante had each other. She loved her mother, and they were close, but not like Dante was to Nick. She envied them that.

"I talked to Luke about the situation," Dante continued. "He was on Nick's side of course. He knew Carlo very well and didn't like how much time I was spending with him, but he understood. Luke would never get between a father and a son. We worked out a schedule so I could have several days off at a time. I spent three quarters of the week in New York handling warrior business and the rest of the time I spent in Vegas. I only saw Nick when we hunted together," Dante paused. "Are you hungry? It's dinner time, we could order room service."

"A little," Cornelia admitted. She could see that Dante was stressed and knew he was stalling. Maybe if she ate, he would at least pick at something. "I saw a menu in the kitchen, let me grab it." Cornelia figured Dante needed a short break and she was willing to give it to him.

Once the meal was ordered Dante excused himself to take a shower. When he came back down, he immediately settled in to finish the story. "So, I was spending more and more time in Vegas. One night I was having a business dinner with my father and Eric Johnson when a beautiful redhead approached the table. Eric introduced her as his daughter, Shannon, and asked her to join us. Talk of business ceased. Eric began bragging about his daughter. He kept talking her up like she was something special, even though she'd never accomplished a thing. I was supposed to believe Shannon showing up was purely coincidental, but I didn't fall for it. I knew it was a setup. At the time, I thought both of us were being set up, though. I was wrong, Shannon was in on it from the beginning." Dante moved to the window, looking out into the darkness. He stood there for a long time, watching the lights but not really seeing them.

There was a knock on the door, room service. Cornelia stood. "I've got this," she said softly and moved to the door. Once the food was left and the delivery guy sent on his way Cornelia moved in next to Dante. He hadn't moved. He was just standing there motionless, staring into the distance. Cornelia placed a hand on his arm and waited.

Dante felt Cornelia's touch. It was so warm, so gentle. He hated thinking about the past, but he really hated having to lay out all the sordid details for Cornelia. She was strong and independent. She knew what she wanted, but more importantly she knew what she didn't want. She had never had a father in her life, but she didn't care. He'd been weak back then. He'd been given so much, but he wanted more. To this day, he still didn't know why it had been so important to bond with his father. There was no void in his life. His grandparents, Nick, the Moretti's had all filled any void his father had left. And still he jumped in with both feet the instant Carlo Santora showed up on his doorstep. Dante turned to Cornelia and tried to give her a reassuring smile. "I'm going to apologize again for all of this," he began.

Cornelia placed a finger over his lips and shook her head. "No, you're not," she said softly. Then she took his hand and led him to the table. "You're going to join me for dinner, then we're going to come back in here and finish this. Then, when you're done, we're going to decide how to proceed." Cornelia gave him her most reassuring smile and pushed him into a chair. She started to turn, but Dante hadn't let go of her hand. He just sat there, looking at her, holding her hand. Cornelia turned back, moved in closer, then slowly leaned down and pressed her lips to his.

The kiss started out soft and casual, but Dante needed more. Almost instantly he deepened the kiss, holding onto Cornelia as if his life depended on it. Her touch was rejuvenating. Kissing Cornelia felt like a lifeline. His energy had been so depleted, but once she pressed those wonderful, soft lips to his he felt full again. He was turning into such a sap. He knew he should back away, but he couldn't...not yet. He held out one second, two...just a little longer. Then, he slowly pulled away. Cornelia straightened but didn't move back. She was standing in front of him, her fingers gently running through his hair. He didn't even think about it, the reaction was automatic. Dante slowly leaned forward, resting his forehead against her stomach and wrapped his arms around her waist. They sat there for a long time, Cornelia running soothing fingers through Dante's thick hair. Dante with his eyes closed, savoring the strength that Cornelia was giving him.

Finally, Dante sighed and straightened. "Thank you," he told her as he let go of her waist. He was embarrassing himself. He wasn't sure what was wrong with him. He'd never behaved this way in his life. Okay, so it was difficult to talk about his past. But he was acting like an idiot. Never in his life had he turned to a woman for comfort and certainly not for strength. He shot a quick glance at Cornelia then looked away. He'd expected to see amusement but instead, he saw compassion. Well he didn't want that either, did he? Dante shifted his chair and reached for his food. He'd just sit here and pick at whatever Cornelia had ordered. He wasn't hungry, but she probably was. He'd let her eat all she wanted, not rushing her. Then, when she was finished, they could return to the sitting area and finish the story. After that, like she said, they'd decide how to use the information to their advantage.

Progeny

Cornelia ate slowly, she wanted Dante to have plenty of time to bounce back. She didn't feel that hungry, they'd had a big lunch. But, Dante needed a break. She didn't like the direction the story was going. He was talking about being set up with Eric's daughter, Shannon. She also knew they were here to find Carlo's wife, Shannon. Had Dante fallen for the beautiful redhead and then lost her to his father? And she thought she had daddy issues. She jumped a little when Dante stood and took her plate. She'd been so deep in thought she hadn't noticed it was completely empty.

"I guess you were hungry," Dante said with a warm smile.

Cornelia glanced at Dante's plate and saw it was only half gone. Well, at least he'd eaten a little. She'd have to be content with that. "I guess I was hungrier than I thought," she admitted. "The guy said to put the plates back on the cart and move it just outside the door. They'll pick it up when they do their rounds."

"That's one good thing about hotels," he said, placing the dinner dishes on top of the cart. "No dishes to contend with. I just hate dishwater hands."

Cornelia watched as Dante opened the door, pushed the cart to the side then turned toward the living room. He seemed surprised to see her still sitting at the table. He immediately pivoted and was standing by her side. Dante reached down and pulled her to her feet, resting a hand on her shoulder. Cornelia smiled up at him trying to act normal as tingles spread through her body from the casual contact. Her stomach did a little flip when Dante reached out and ran a finger over her cheek, then tucked a strand of hair behind her ear. It took all the willpower she possessed but she didn't lean in and press her mouth to his. She was proud of her self-control and disappointed. But she knew they had to get through this and Dante might use that as an excuse to avoid what was coming.

"Let's finish this," he said giving her hand a little tug. The two of them returned to the living room but this time, Dante sat on the couch and stretched out his legs. One was still on the floor, the other was propped against the backrest. She was about to turn and move to the chair when he gave her arm a gentle tug, positioning her in front of his body.

Cornelia leaned back and relaxed against his hard chest. Dante's muscular arms instantly wrapped around her waist locking her in place. Cornelia shifted a little, turning so she could see his face then relaxed against his shoulder. She liked this much better. She was sure he would eventually push himself up and pace around the room again but in the meantime, she was going to enjoy every minute she had in his arms.

Once they were both comfortable Dante picked up where he had left off. "So, I met Shannon. I wasn't sure how I felt about her at first. She was beautiful, but she reminded me of a porcelain doll. You know, weak, fragile and delicate. She's very petite," Dante paused to consider. He thought of Cornelia as the beautiful, tiny vampire but he wouldn't describe her as delicate or fragile. Hot, sexy, tiny and a million other adjectives that turned him on, but not fragile or petite.

Progeny

Cornelia cringed. So, Dante liked his women petite. She'd never fall into that category. Just another strike against her. Another reason this was just a fling, nothing more. She needed to remember that. Just because she was in love with him, didn't mean the feeling was mutual. She was a vampire, she was strong and independent. Not weak and fragile. Dante liked fragile and petite.

Dante pressed a kiss to Cornelia's head then caught himself. He had to get through this. If he let his mind wander any further in the direction it was going, he'd cave. He knew himself. He'd use their attraction to delay finishing this humiliating story. "I continued to spend time in Vegas, and my father and Eric continued to push Shannon on me. At first, I resisted. I didn't like the two of them trying to set us up. But Shannon was kind and every once in a while she'd do something, just a small tentative flirtation, that softened me ever so slightly. She seemed so innocent and vulnerable back then," Dante paused to remember the past. "About six, maybe seven months after I'd met Shannon my father started talking about her needing protection."

"Protection from what?" Cornelia asked. "Other than her father and yours, I mean?"

Dante smiled, Cornelia couldn't be more wrong. If anything, the men needed protection from Shannon. "They explained to me that Vegas is more civilized now that the mob has moved out, but there are still criminals. There are drugs and guns and all kinds of mayhem down there. They pushed the tourist angle, too. There's a lot of international tourism here. Anyway, one day Eric came to pick me up at the airport. He wanted to have a talk, you see. It was all hush, hush. He was worried about his daughter. He'd always hoped she'd meet a big strong man like me that could take care of her, protect her, make her feel safe. I still didn't like Eric, so I didn't give it a lot of thought and basically blew him off. Then my father started in. Before long, talk about Shannon and pressure for me to marry her was all either of them talked about. I was grateful I wasn't getting pressure to invest anymore but the idea of marriage was even worse.

All the warriors were against it. Nick went ballistic. I was worried he would fly out and pulverize Carlo for the suggestion. I was being pulled apart. Nick pushing for me to take a step back, my father pushing for me to step up and marry Shannon. One day my father and I were over at Eric's casino. Shannon ran in, crying. She was acting hysterical. She said she'd been attacked and threatened by a local gang. This particular gang was known for their violence, I was told. They were also heavily involved in the distribution of drugs in the area. Shannon's shirt was torn and she had a scrape on her elbow. It took a long time to calm her down. The instant my father and I were alone he started in again. Shannon was human and needed protection. The streets were tough, but I was a warrior. I had the skills and the ability to take care of her like no one else could. Then he threw in a little family loyalty and I finally agreed to go through with it.

I thought we'd have a quick wedding and that would be that. Boy, was I wrong. Shannon wanted the works. That should have been a sign, I should have known we'd be on opposite ends of the spectrum throughout our marriage, but I ignored it. She cried, big crocodile tears, when I suggested we just get the license and head over to one of those fancy Vegas chapels. She wanted a nice big wedding with all her friends and family. Of course, I agreed. She got upset and cried again when she decided I wasn't participating enough in the planning. She told me if I didn't love her enough to start our union out the right way, maybe we should rethink the whole thing." Dante let out a deep breath.

"That woman missed her calling. She's quite the actress. If I hadn't experienced it myself, you'd never convince me someone that selfish and malicious could come across so sweet and innocent. Every time I turned around I was being played by one of them, my father, her father and Shannon. I fell for it all hook, line and sinker."

Cornelia snuggled in closer but remained silent.

"We had the big wedding in her father's casino. All the warriors came to the wedding, but none of them supported it. I could tell. I knew those guys well enough to know what they thought about my family sacrifice. At the time, I honestly thought I was doing the right thing. I knew I didn't love Shannon, but I thought I could come to love her. All I saw was this sweet innocent kid that needed someone to protect her. I figured marrying Shannon would prove I was a standup guy. My father wouldn't doubt my family loyalty anymore, Shannon would be protected and in the end, it would only cost me fifty or sixty years. Shannon was human, so it wasn't like the whole thing was permanent. And deep down, I honestly thought I could come to love her. I knew we'd never have wild passion in our marriage. No explosive intimacy that rocks you down to your toes. But I was okay with that. I figured I could live with sweet and tender for a while." He hesitated then lowered his head and gave her a quick hard kiss. "I was wrong. Chemistry is important." He kissed her again, long and deep this time. "Now that's what I call chemistry, baby. You definitely rocked my world the other night."

Cornelia smiled, she agreed. It was probably the vampire in them. She'd heard that vampires were sensual creatures. Warriors had some vampire blood in them too and were rumored to be excellent lovers. She had as much or more vampire blood than they did. Her night with Dante had been explosive. Off the charts, mind blowing. So, she understood what he was talking about. It was nice to hear she'd affected him just as profoundly as he had impacted her. Well, in the bedroom at least. "You're getting off track," she finally said. "Talking about the other night is only going to lead to trouble. Finish your story."

Dante smiled, "I'd rather investigate the trouble." He sighed when she just looked at him with those gorgeous blue eyes of hers and sobered. "Okay, you're right. We've gotten this far, I need to finish." He shifted her slightly then continued with his story. "We got through the wedding, although I hated it. Luke and I worked out a new schedule so I could be in New York for several days then Vegas for several days. I was worn out all the time and so tired of flying back and forth across the country. Eventually, I purchased a jet and hired my own pilot. Shannon wanted to see the world, so I did my best to show her. I'd work for a week, then have a week off to take her shopping in Paris or Italy. Anywhere she wanted to go, we

Progeny

went. She was going crazy with the spending, but I didn't care as long as Shannon was happy and safe.

At first, Nick would fly out at least once a month to spend his off days with me. He usually brought one of the other warriors with him, but Shannon started to complain. It was very subtle and very calculating. She was still playing the naive, innocent girl so she couldn't demand I break off contact completely. No, she was more subtle than that. I'm sure she knew if she made demands I would resist. Instead, she said they made her feel uncomfortable. She felt like they didn't like her. They gave her intimidating looks. Nick threatened her. Which, of course, he did. He saw right through her and promised that if she hurt me, she would pay dearly. Things got worse. I was constantly fighting with Nick or Luke, sometimes both. It was always tense when Nick came to Vegas. I saw him less and less, then eventually he stopped coming all together. Three months after my wedding, my grandparents arrived. They were disappointed and frustrated. We fought too. I was still angry with them when they left. That's never happened before or since. I had to take it out on someone, so I blamed Nick. I knew he was the one that contacted them in the first place. For a while, I still saw Nick when I worked, but eventually he asked Luke to schedule us on different shifts. He couldn't stand seeing me so angry and miserable.

Within a year I was isolated from everyone. My life was a mess. I think that's why the three of them got away with the scheme for so long. Once they got everyone else out of my life, they started to push. I finally gave in and helped fund the new casino. It was hard to say no when I was being hit from three sides. Plus, I didn't care about the money, I had plenty of it and giving it to them got them off my back. Once they had what they wanted, things changed at home. Shannon didn't want to take vacations with me anymore, she just wanted access to the jet so she could shop on her own. She fired my pilot and hired some friend of her father's. I was miserable, I hated flying so much and being in New York without Nick was making me depressed. One night I finally got fed up with everything and told Shannon I was going to quit the warriors. She overreacted big time. If I hadn't been so out of it I would have figured everything out right then. But I was tired and stressed. Shannon did a one-eighty and became timid and soothing. She begged me not to quit. She said she'd feel too guilty if I gave up something I loved so much just to stay in Vegas with her. She had a way of coming across so self-sacrificing and innocent.

Anyway, we continued on this way for a couple years. The casino was finished by then and bringing in good money. My father and Eric Johnson were thrilled. Shannon and I, however, drifted further and further apart. She was gone more than she was home. Then I caught her smoking marijuana in the house. I wasn't happy about the drugs, but I was extremely pissed she was doing it in my house. I was lonely and fed up. We fought for weeks and I came close to ending it right then. Shannon promised she'd stop the drugs, but begged me to build her a sanctuary. She said she needed the drugs to escape. She could give them up if she had her own place somewhere that she could relax. That's when we started construction on the cabin, the one in Colorado. I had already put the brakes on her spending. In the beginning, she basically had free rein to buy or do whatever she wanted. After the first year, I gave her a budget. She wasn't happy about that. She pouted for months, but I wouldn't budge. Eventually, she accepted my decision but started the manipulation tactics. Thus, the cabin. I don't think I've ever had a bigger headache than that stupid cabin. I sank more money into that thing than it was worth but I figured if it helped her stop the drugs, it was worth it.

I ended up working a shift with Nick one night. Victor had an emergency with his dad and Nick reluctantly agreed to fill in. It was tense at first but after a couple hours, we were back on track. Having Nick back in my life saved me. It didn't take long for me to confide in him. Nick, of course, was pissed. He never liked Shannon and saw the arrangement for what it was. He told me to divorce her, immediately. I was starting to warm up to the idea but wasn't quite there. For some reason, the idea of divorce made me feel like a failure. Then, one night I was going through some bills and realized my wife was cheating. She didn't even try to hide the expenses. I went back six months, then gave up. I didn't really want to know how long it had been going on. Every time she went on one of her shopping sprees, she charged thousands of dollars to my card...men's suits, shoes, watches, jewelry. I called a couple shops and got them to send me itemized lists. They were all tacky items that I wouldn't have been caught dead wearing. You saw the cabin, so I don't have to explain Shannon's lack of taste to you."

Cornelia smiled. "I saw the aftermath. It was bad enough. I'm thankful I didn't see the place before you redecorated. The artwork was hideous," she paused.

"What made you think it was a lover? Couldn't she have been buying those things for her father? From what you've told me, they were pretty close."

"The suits and jewelry could have been, but there was more. She took the guy on vacation with her. She paid for a week at the spa, his and hers. There were expensive dinners at romantic restaurants, things like that. Then I found the sex toys, perverted stuff."

"I'm sorry, Dante," Cornelia said, knowing it was inadequate. She felt so bad for him but didn't know what to say.

"Don't pity me," he barked. "I don't need your pity. It happened, it's in the past and it's over. I was a fool. Now I'm not, it won't happen again."

Cornelia sat up and studied Dante's face. "I feel bad for you, yes. But I wouldn't call you a fool. None of this was your fault. They took advantage of you." She was angry now and she was worried. He said it wouldn't happen again. Did that mean he would never get married again? Did it mean he would never trust a woman again? She wanted to know, but it was too soon. *Too soon?* What was she thinking? She knew this was temporary. It was just getting so hard to remember that. She kept finding herself hoping for more, hoping for something permanent.

"Anyway, I had proof she was cheating," he continued. "I waited. It was the hardest thing I ever did. I wanted to track her down and beat the guy into a bloody pulp, but I waited. The next day I flew to New York and confided in Nick. He talked me into going to Jake. He was

Progeny

great. Jake's a very good attorney, he started working on my case immediately. A couple days later I was headed back to Vegas, divorce papers in hand, Nick by my side. He insisted on coming in case there was trouble. I arrived at the house and found a note from Shannon telling me she was at the cabin and would be back in a week. That's when it hit me. She wasn't looking for a sanctuary, she was looking for a place she could spend time with her boyfriend. I lost it. I'd tolerated her tantrums, her ridiculous demands and sank far too much money into that sanctuary of hers to make the place perfect for her and her lover.

I wanted to head to Vail immediately but Nick talked me into making preparations. A few hours later we had a plan. Both of us thought it was a good plan. We packed our bags and headed out. When I got to the airport the first thing I did was fire the pilot. He was shocked of course. Apparently, he'd worked for Eric most of his life. My plane was locked down and put into storage. Then we rented a car and drove to the cabin. I remember climbing out of the car just in time to see a spectacular sunset. The place was beautiful and seemed so peaceful. It was an illusion of course, but I'll never forget those few seconds of peace before my life changed forever.

We were so sure of ourselves that night. Nick and I swung open the door, confident our plan was perfect. Unfortunately, it had one fatal flaw. We planned to confront Shannon, give her the divorce papers, throw her and the sleazy boyfriend out on their butt, then head back to Vegas and explain everything to Carlo and Eric. I was sure the divorce wouldn't be a problem. My father and I

108

held the majority interest in the casino. If Eric couldn't do business with us any longer, I'd simply buy him out. Things would continue on, minus Shannon. That was before I knew my wife's lover was my father. I remember walking into that awful bedroom and seeing the two of them naked, on the bed just as clearly as I remember that sunset.

Cornelia closed her eyes. She had known what was coming of course, but somehow hearing it out loud made it so much worse. "And yet, they live," she said coolly.

Dante paused, a little surprised by that. "Barely. It was all I could do to stop Nick from attacking."

"That's too bad. I'll have to express my disappointment the next time I see him," Cornelia said flatly.

"Anyway," Dante continued. "I didn't serve Shannon the divorce papers. I decided I wasn't feeling that generous any longer. The original papers gave Shannon the cabin among other things she loved. I didn't care about them. I figured if I gave them to her maybe she'd just go away." He was feeling restless and couldn't sit any longer. He gently pushed Cornelia into a sitting position, stood and walked back to the window. "I decided she didn't deserve the place. I know it was petty, but I insisted on keeping it for the sole purpose of taking it away from her. I knew how much the cabin meant to her and my father."

"Good," Cornelia said. "But not perfect. It would be far more satisfying to gut the place and turn it into a livable vacation spot, then enjoy the hell out of it," she hesitated, wishing she could throw Carlo Santora and his tacky wife out a window, a very high window.

Dante laughed. He couldn't help himself. She looked so angry and defiant. He hadn't been prepared for this kind of reaction. He'd expected pity, but not righteous indignation on his behalf. He'd heard so many women brag about taking their husbands to the cleaners. Most women seemed to stick together and enjoyed hearing the sordid details. He adored Cornelia, she was definitely one of a kind. He walked back to the couch, pressing a soft kiss to her temple as he sat down next to her.

Cornelia shifted and pressed her lips to his. "Carlo Santora hasn't met me yet," she told him, her face void of emotion. "I'd be happy to drive over and give him a little payback." She smiled a slightly scary, malicious smile. "No charge. Call it a freebie among friends." She was so enraged by Dante's story she wanted to punch something. She wanted to pulverize Carlo Santora then move on to his petite little wife.

"Thanks, but I'll pass," he said pulling her into his arms.

"I only have one question," Cornelia scowled. "For now. I'm sure I'll have more later."

"What?" Dante asked, enjoying the feel of Cornelia's body.

"Why do we care what happens to Shannon?" She pushed back a little to look him in the eye. "Why are we here? I for one couldn't care less if Shannon is tortured and murdered and her low life husband suffers miserably for the rest of his worthless life." She inhaled, trying to calm down but never taking her eyes off Dante.

"We care because if a human tries to torture Shannon, they will instantly realize she's not human. It's a danger for us all," Dante pointed out. "I guess I'm not quite finished with the story," he admitted, his emotions were very mixed right now.

"Not even close," she agreed. "You still haven't explained the money. Why do you give your father a monthly allowance?" That, she realized was the cherry on top of the shit sundae Dante had been gagging down for the past thirty years. It infuriated her.

Dante took her hand, studying it carefully. Then he sighed deeply and told her the rest. "Like I said, Nick was out of control. I thought he was going to kill Carlo. I'm confident he would have. He stopped for me. He stopped because I basically begged him to walk away and leave the two of them unharmed." He smiled at the sour look on her gorgeous face. He thought she was the most beautiful woman he'd ever met. Not just outward beauty, though. She was beautiful on the inside. Her character, strength, sense of fairness all drew him in somehow. The entire package was what made her so beautiful, not just those sapphire blue eyes or that curvy, sensual body of hers. Eyes that were currently burning hot as coal, threatening to spontaneously combust at any minute. He knew she wanted to say more, but she didn't. He liked that about her, too. She just patiently sat there, smoldering, waiting for him to finish his story. Letting him set the pace.

Progeny

"I realize you don't understand that any more than Nick did. Or Thomas does now. But if Nick had killed my father, there would have been consequences. It would have killed me to see Nick punished over a situation I had caused." He smiled and placed a finger on her lips before she could argue. "I did create it. I was the one that agreed to let my father back into my life when I knew better. I knew what he was forty years ago. I knew he couldn't be trusted, that he was selfish and manipulative. I chose to overlook it. I decided I wanted my father in my life regardless of his shortcomings. As a result, I got hurt. But, I refused to let them hurt Nick. I love him and respect him far too much for that."

"I understand," she nodded for him to continue.

"There was a scene before we left that night. Shannon was furious. The gig was up so there was no need to act any longer. She let loose with all the sordid details. Screaming them at the top of her lungs. I'll spare you the particulars and give you the cliff note version," Dante said. "Her and my father were intimate before I ever met Shannon. In fact, they'd been together for almost four years by then. They wanted my money and figured if Shannon married me, they would have access to it all. Once I put Shannon on a budget, she started plans for divorce. The only reason she stuck it out as long as she had was for the money. She believed the longer we were married, the more substantial the payoff would be in the divorce.

Nick and I flew back to New York that night. I couldn't stand to spend another minute in Vegas. The casino, the house, everything was a constant reminder that the last several years of my life was all a lie. Nick called Jake and he came right over. We worked all night altering the terms of the divorce. I knew she was going to ask for money, alimony, and a lot of it. She'd become quite accustomed to the good life by then. She didn't get it. I was pretty stubborn about that. Jake was frustrated with me. He was so sure the Vegas courts would award her something outrageous. He wanted to attack first with a reasonable offer. I wouldn't even consider it. I knew my father would step in and he did. It was probably petty, but I just couldn't bring myself to pay that woman one dime when our entire marriage was a sham from the start."

"I'm glad to hear it," Cornelia told him.

"We hashed things out all night. The following day, Nick and I returned to Vegas," Dante told her. "I wanted to go alone. I didn't want Nick any more involved than he already was. The whole situation was embarrassing. I couldn't believe I'd fallen for that woman's tricks. Anyway, Nick calmly explained that I could let him go with me or he would simply fly out on his own and handle things his way. That scared me. Nick is quiet and respectful at most times, but he is also very loyal and protective of his family. Cross someone he loves and his temper takes over. Nick in a temper is an ugly, scary, unpredictable thing."

"I'm liking him more and more by the minute," Cornelia said softly.

Dante studied Cornelia. "Somehow, I think you might have that same silent cobra inside you that Nick does. A silent predator, coiled patient and deep, waiting to deploy its deadly strike when the enemy least expects it."

"I'm glad we understand each other," she said flatly.

She'd said it in such a matter-of-fact way, a shiver ran through his spine. "Then I'll tell you the same thing I told Nick," Dante said seriously. "This is my problem, leave it be."

"For now," she said coyly and shrugged.

"Cornelia," he said more forcefully. "Promise me you will not hurt Carlo or Shannon in any way. Otherwise, you're going back to New York...no, to Salt Lake. Finding her is going to be hard enough. I don't need to worry about you going off halfcocked while I'm trying to do the job."

"I never go off half-cocked," she answered calmly. "I'm an overachiever." Several moments passed in silence, then she sighed at the worried look on his face. "I won't go after either one of them, but I will defend myself if I need to." *Or you*, she thought inwardly. He wouldn't get more of a concession than that from her. She hoped he'd accept it and move on.

"I guess that will do for now," he decided. "So, Nick and I flew back to Vegas and had a little meeting with dear old dad. I was more on edge having Nick in the same room with Carlo than I was about dealing with the details. But I knew it was better to have Nick with me, where I could keep an eye on him, than to have him out there on his own."

"Wise choice," she said under her breath. She'd never seen that side of Nick, but knowing he had it in him made her respect the guy even more.

Dante didn't respond to that, Cornelia's mood was making him uneasy. "I'd spoken to my grandparents. That was even worse than confiding in Nick and Jake. I knew I'd disappointed them. They convinced me to keep up the bluff. They wanted Carlo to think they were still in charge of the money. If he had to go to them for changes, that would be the end of it. I reluctantly agreed. Like I said, I control the money. We have billions now, more than the three of us could ever spend. I take care of the books, manage investments, basically control the money but my grandparents have unlimited access to the funds. It works for us."

"But Carlo still doesn't know that?" she asked.

"No, but he will after our meeting tomorrow," Dante supplied.

"Why open yourself up to those problems again?" she asked, concerned. The last thing Dante needed was his father showing up on his doorstep on a regular basis trying to con him into the next investment.

Dante smiled. "Your lack of faith in me hurts, darling," he paused, then sobered. "I'm not opening myself up for anything. Carlo won't come to me for money any more than he would approach my grandparents. In fact, I think he'd be more likely to ask them in a bind."

Progeny

"I take it you haven't finished the story," she inquired.

"Let's just say Nick and I made sure Carlo understood the consequences of his actions. I told him the trust had been changed to provide a monthly allowance, but only if he talked Shannon into accepting the divorce settlement I planned to file without contesting anything... including forfeiting her right to alimony. He knew any money Shannon received would be short lived, we were only married three years. I also explained that this allowance was contingent on certain behavior. Technically, this thing with Shannon violates those provisions. He's got to be sweating it. I think that's why he went to Thomas. He wanted the Deveraux name and reputation for sure, but he also worried that if he asked me, my grandparents would find out and cut him off."

"So, why don't you cut him off?" She asked curiously.

"Because I want him to stay away," Dante explained. "He gets a few thousand each month, minus the cost of blood," Dante smiled. "Bastian supplies all our people with blood, free of charge. He won't accept a penny for the stuff, other than Carlo that is. Bastian's company delivers a couple cases of blood to Vegas every other month for a nice fee. The fee is taken off the top and a check is mailed to Carlo for the balance."

"I'm sorry, but that just doesn't seem like enough," Cornelia frowned.

"In exchange for the money, Carlo agreed never to step foot in New York again. He also agreed to keep Shannon, her father and all other Johnson family members far away from me and my friends. In addition, Eric and Carlo signed over 30% ownership in the casino to me. They kept 35% each," Dante smiled again. "A couple years ago the casino got into a little trouble. The two of them needed money. They each agreed to sell a portion of their interest in the casino. They figured if they each sold ten percent, they'd jointly retain fifty percent of the business and continue to have full control."

"You bought their twenty percent?" Cornelia exclaimed.

"No, Nick did," Dante corrected. "Now, between the two of us we also control fifty percent of the business."

Cornelia smiled. "They don't know, do they?"

"Nope," Dante said, grinning. "Mostly I try to ignore them. I rarely think about Carlo and Eric these days. But occasionally Nick or I will catch wind of some new scheme they want to try and we step in. It has caused them a substantial amount of aggravation over the years. I know, that too sounds petty, but it's necessary."

"So if I'm understanding this correctly, you basically pay your father to stay out of your life," Cornelia asked.

"In a nutshell, yes," Dante agreed. "He knew I wasn't happy about his recent visit to New York. I guess in his way, he must love Shannon. She's the only thing that could make him risk losing the money."

Progeny

"But you said she was human," Cornelia said, realizing the contradiction. "You also said the reason we are here is to protect the races secret. Does that mean your father turned her?"

"Yes, almost immediately," Dante said. "Our divorce was finalized and the next day Shannon and my father went to one of those little Vegas chapels that were too tacky for our wedding and got hitched. A couple days later, he changed her. I guess that's another reason dad accepted my terms. They couldn't have gotten married if they were depending on alimony. Now the world is blessed with those two miscreants for eternity."

"Lucky us," she said sarcastically. "Is there anything else I should know before we confront the monster?"

"No," Dante gave a half chuckle. "Isn't that enough?"

Cornelia studied him intently. "Dante, that is a horrible story. It makes me despise your father, your ex-wife and her father. I know that bothers you, but you'll just have to deal with it. I've despised clients before and it didn't interfere with my ability to do my job. It won't interfere this time. However, I will be sending Carlo Santora a bill. A bill I expect him to pay for himself. Thomas is providing lodging and transportation, Dimitri and Alex are prepared to send reinforcements or anything else we could possibly ask for at the snap of a finger. You and I have been providing our meals and any miscellaneous charges. I'm not okay with that. Carlo will receive a bill from me, just like every other client I've ever had. If you want to deduct the expense from his allowance, go ahead."

"Okay," Dante agreed. "We'll break the news tomorrow." He shifted her body and began massaging her shoulders. "Relax, Cornelia. This all happened a long time ago. I've had years to come to terms with that time in my life. Let it go, I have." *But had he?* Not completely, that's why his life had been full of one-night stands and too many gallons of liquor to count. So why did he feel like a huge weight had been lifted tonight? Why did talking to Cornelia, sharing his worst secrets, relax him? Because she was such a phenomenal woman, that's why. He let his hands drift down her back, then slowly back to her shoulders. He wanted her, which is why he moved his hands down her arms, gave them a little squeeze, then released her. He would not have sex with Cornelia tonight. If he did, he'd never know if she agreed out of pity or desire.

Cornelia took one look at Dante and knew he needed an escape. "I need some fresh air," she told him. "Would you mind going for a walk with me?"

"Okay," Dante agreed. The air might do him good. He needed to get out of this penthouse. He needed a crowd. Being alone with Cornelia was too much of a temptation.

"Just give me five minutes to change. I want to put on some jeans, then we can go." She jumped to her feet and rushed up the stairs. Moments later she returned, clean shirt, stone-washed jeans and comfortable shoes. "Ready?" she asked as she reached the foyer.

"Ready," Dante said, giving her an appreciative look as he opened the door.

Progeny

The instant they stepped onto the elevator Cornelia slid her tiny hand into his. She knew she was playing with fire but she couldn't help it. Just for tonight, she was going to throw caution to the wind and do her best to show Dante a good time.

Chapter Five

The large group of vampires entered the damp cave and began to settle in. After a quick tour, the four kings were satisfied. Sammael had done well. There were four sections that had been made into private rooms off to one side. The kings would take those. Then on the other side, there were smaller sections that Sammael had set up as living space for the rest of the convoy. Each king had brought several vampires with them. Ammit never went anywhere without Gallo. He also brought two vampire servants and a couple bodyguards. The others brought similar contingents with them.

A few hours later the group sat in the main section of the cave discussing their plans. Typhon turned to Martinez. "We all agree you are our best bet to infiltrate Radek's army. Sammael is the only spy we still have in his ranks. He has regular access to Radek, but limited power to manipulate his actions."

"Sammael is Ammit's man, the one playing servant to Radek?" Martinez asked.

"That's correct," Ammit said soberly. "He's important to me," he warned. "Think twice before you do anything that will blow his cover. I'll hold you personally responsible if he's harmed in any way."

Martinez looked at Ammit. He knew the Egyptian king didn't trust him, but he didn't mind. He'd be disappointed in the group if they had just welcomed him with open arms. He had earned his place in Typhon's kingdom, given enough time he would earn respect among this group as well. He glanced at Trumak then back to Ammit. "Is he expecting me?"

"Yes," Ammit said soberly. "Sammael has been spying on Radek and Lilith for over two years now. It's become more difficult since the death of Maedoc's spy, Hector. But he still has access to the basics. We need you to take Hector's place. We need the details. We need to know when he's going to attack and how. We need someone that can manipulate the situation to our advantage."

"You don't ask much, do you?" Martinez asked sarcastically. Typhon put a hand on his shoulder to silence him.

"Hector got lucky," Maedoc explained. "He was a good strategist and Radek was the one that changed him.

Radek pulled him into his inner circle almost immediately. After a fairly short amount of time, Hector was running his army. As much as possible anyway. Hector did his best to delay the attacks, but Radek is unstable. Hector knew he could only push so far, otherwise Radek would kill him. Having him get intimately involved with Lilith was a calculated risk. Hector was all for it initially, the rest of us worried it was too risky. Hector pulled it off, though. Unfortunately, he was growing bored with her at the end," Maedoc paused, remembering the talented vampire he'd sent to his death. "Don't follow in his footsteps. Don't do anything too risky and be careful around Lilith. We're getting close to something big. The time for recklessness has passed."

"I don't get why you think Radek will just let me in," Martinez told them. "You already said he's paranoid. He doesn't even trust Sammael, not completely. Why do you think Radek will trust me in time to help your cause?"

"Because you were part of the Mexican contingent. You already belong to Radek and you can bring him valuable information regarding Felix and the others," Ammit explained. "You already have an in, we don't have to create one for you."

"Don't think for a minute it's going to be easy," Maedoc warned. "Hector was smart. He was good at strategy and now he's dead. Somehow Hector's cover was compromised. We still don't know how. His situation was precarious. We took a calculated risk to save his life. A risk that eventually killed him," Maedoc paused, they had made a mistake that ultimately got his friend killed.

Knowing that always brought him so much pain. "Hector came across some dangerous information at a very opportune time. He learned the fae are allergic to lemon juice, fatally so. We didn't want someone as crazy as Radek to have that information, but decided Hector needed to use it to save his own life."

"Makes sense," Martinez nodded.

"Radek was ecstatic," Maedoc continued. "He immediately put a couple of his best men on the project. He wanted a projectile that could fatally wound the Fae Queen from a distance. That's when we realized he was serious about assassinating the queen. Hector did his best to slow the development, but ultimately his efforts made things worse. Radek ordered them to make a formula that was so concentrated there was no way a fae could survive. Minimal contact would be fatal. Radek insisted Hector had to be the one to kill her. We didn't like it, but it was necessary. The following night Hector killed the queen. He missed the mark, but the solution was so strong it killed Marlena anyway. Hector's position in Radek's organization made him the obvious target. Word of his intelligence and strategic abilities had become well known among the vampires by then. He had risen to power so quickly and was now Radek's first lieutenant. That always brings jealousy and betrayal. When Marlena was killed, the warriors immediately knew Hector was responsible. We think someone fed them information to make sure the warriors knew Hector was the assassin. Again, we don't know who."

"We knew Hector was in danger, but we thought we had time," Typhon supplied. "We were finalizing our plans to stage his death and get him out. It was going to be tricky. If Radek suspected Hector was still alive, he would be able to find him. All vampires have an unbreakable tie to the vampire that turns them. Radek had to believe Hector was dead. If he was certain, he wouldn't try to use that connection to find him. Everyone had to believe it. That was essential. Otherwise, it would create a ripple effect throughout the rest of the world. We would all be at war if a vampire assassinated one of their queens and we helped him escape."

"But we were too late," Maedoc said with regret. "He was sent out into the wilderness which limited his access to cell phone service. He finally slipped away and got word out that Radek had forced him to kidnap a couple shifter women. They were hiding in the wilderness and Hector was ordered to stay with them. We planned to use this isolation to our advantage. Unfortunately, Hector's brilliance didn't carry over when it came to women. I have no doubt Hector played with the women a little too much."

"Played?" Martinez asked, stiffening. They were trying to paint Hector as a hero or something, but Martinez wondered what they were leaving out. He didn't like men that abused women. If this Hector had harmed those girls as far as Martinez was concerned, he got what he deserved.

"Hector liked women," Maedoc said soberly. "All women. There's no way to know what he did to them while they were under his care. We can't ask him, he's dead. Obviously, we can't ask the women. We assume the shifters caught up to them and killed Hector to send a clear message to the vampires who took their women. The girls were both daughters of local pack leaders."

"So, when Hector died he was being hunted by the warriors because he had killed their queen and the shifters because he had their women?" Martinez asked. "Not to mention a mysterious vampire causing problems behind the scenes?"

"Yes," Typhon agreed. "The queen was married to the warrior leader. The man was ruthless in his pursuit of Hector." He glanced at Maedoc then continued. "Hector was forced to take him out. Not personally, but he was the one that came up with the trap that ultimately killed the warrior leader."

"And you left him in?" Martinez asked in amazement. "You couldn't see his death coming a mile away? The guy had killed the queen, her husband the warrior leader and he had two daughters of a couple pack leaders imprisoned. He was being attacked from so many sides the guy didn't have a chance."

"We know," Maedoc said, sadness radiating in his voice. "We failed Hector. We all know that. We knew he needed an escape, but we just didn't have enough time to get him out. He didn't tell us about the shifters soon enough."

"No offense but your man wasn't only reckless, he was foolhardy and rash. He gambled his life and lost. On top of everything else, he was sleeping with Lilith. If Radek knew about that, he could have had the guy killed himself. Nobody seems to know for sure who killed him," Martinez pointed out.

"That's true," Ammit agreed. "We don't know and we never will."

"If you think I'm going to be as reckless as this Hector fellow, you've picked the wrong man for the job," Martinez told them flatly. "I won't go in and create a situation where the whole world is out for my blood."

"Good," Typhon said instantly. "We don't want you to be reckless. We've learned our lesson with Hector. We lost a good man because of mistakes. We don't want to lose you, too." He glanced at Maedoc, then Ammit and finally DeMarco. "We have plans for you."

"What plans?" Martinez asked hesitantly.

"We'll talk about that later," Ammit interrupted. "Time will tell. Now, it's getting late. Let's finish this so we can all get to bed. Everything will be set into motion tomorrow night at sunset. Try to get plenty of rest, the first few nights under Radek may be tense."

The group began to review the plan again. They wanted to make sure Martinez was clear on what they needed. He had a lot of questions, so the planning session went on for several hours.

Progeny

Cornelia slowly opened her eyes then immediately buried her head in the pillow and groaned. Her head was killing her and her mouth was so dry her tongue stuck to the roof like glue. No matter how hard she tried, she couldn't generate an ounce of moisture. She hesitantly peeked out from under the pillow when she felt the mattress shift next to her.

"Here," Dante said gently as he handed her two aspirin and a cup of coffee. "If you tell me where you packed the tea, I'll get some started for you. After last night, I know you're going to need it."

"Actually, blood will help faster." She knew she should be uncomfortable admitting that, but right now she'd tell Dante her deepest, darkest secrets if it would stop the pounding in her head. The coffee was good, though. She took another sip.

"Really?" Dante said a little surprised. "I guess I just assumed that since you have more fae than vampire you'd need the tea."

"Tea helps relax me," she explained as she continued to sip her coffee. "It has other benefits, too. I'll be sure to fill you in some time. But like you, blood heals my injuries faster than anything."

"Blood it is," Dante said pushing himself off the bed and moving to the small fridge. "Is one bag enough?"

Cornelia forced herself to sit up. She tried to open her eyes, but the light was too bright so she closed them again and rested her head against the wall. "I'll start with one, then go from there," she squinted at Dante with one eye when she felt him settle back onto the bed. He poured her glass after glass until the entire bag was gone. Cornelia studied him, then narrowed her eyes. "Why do I have the hangover from hell and you look like you've just spent a week at the spa?"

Dante smiled, wondering how he was going to answer that question. "Just lucky I guess," he said as he stood and deposited the empty bag in the trash. "I think you should eat something." Dante walked to a table and brought back a slice of toast.

Cornelia studied it for a long time before she agreed. That was a mistake. The instant the smell hit her nostrils, her stomach began to churn. Cornelia jumped from the bed and darted to the bathroom. She barely reached the toilet before bright red blood filled the clean white bowl.

Dante entered the room so quietly, Cornelia didn't know he was there until he placed the soft blanket over her shoulders. That's when she realized she was naked. She tried to remember something from the night before, but so much was missing. The last thing she remembered was sitting in the noisy club, drinking margaritas. Well, that wasn't exactly true. There were flashes of something. Things that didn't make sense. For some reason, a picture of a man and a woman kept pushing its way into her head. The woman was bubbly and annoying. The man a fashion train wreck, but friendly.

Progeny

Dante crouched next to Cornelia and pulled her hair back from her face. She was so pale and unsteady, it worried him. He placed his lips to her temple and kissed her softly. Cornelia started to turn in shock, lost her balance and fell forward. Dante immediately placed a hand on her hip and steadied her. "Do you think you're finished?" he asked softly.

Cornelia tried to swallow the lump in her throat. She was so embarrassed. "Please leave me alone. Just go and close the door on your way out." She wanted to die.

"Sorry, but I can't do that," Dante said as he stood, cradling her in his arms. He walked to the bed and placed her on the edge. Then he returned to the bathroom.

Cornelia sat motionless. She could hear water running but it didn't register until he walked back to the bed, pushed her onto her back and placed a damp cloth on her forehead. He used another damp cloth to wipe her face and neck. Even with her eyes close, she could feel him walk away. She was just about to open her eyes when he placed a hand behind her neck and lifted her head slightly.

"Let's try this again," he said pressing a glass to her lips. "We'll forget the food for now. If you can keep this down for a half hour or so I'll order you something from room service."

Cornelia moaned but forced herself to drink the whole bag of blood. Dante settled onto the bed and pulled her into his arms. Within minutes, Cornelia had drifted off to sleep.

Dante brushed Cornelia's hair away from her face. Sleep would help her recover. Until he filled her in on the details of their wild, drunken exploits that is. Then what? He had no idea how she was going to react. He shifted, pulling her a little closer then closed his eyes and did his best to relax.

An hour later Cornelia woke to find herself wrapped tightly around Dante's perfect body. She smiled and started to shift, then remembered her bathroom episode. She'd humiliated herself. How could Dante ever take her seriously again? She closed her eyes, wishing she could crawl into a hole and hide.

Dante watched Cornelia as emotion flittered across her face. She started out relaxed and content, then upset and finally embarrassed. He ran his knuckles across her cheek then gently trailed a finger over her chin and down her neck. "I don't know why you're embarrassed. You had a natural reaction to excessive alcohol consumption. You know how hard I've partied the past few years. Do you honestly think I haven't suffered the same fate myself?"

"Have you?" Cornelia asked in disbelief. "I mean, before I took you home that night, I didn't even know a warrior could get drunk."

"We can get drunk and we suffer the consequences just like everyone else." She didn't need to know his consequences were far less drastic than hers.

Progeny

Cornelia pushed herself into a sitting position and ran her hand through her hair. She frowned when a ring got caught in the strands.

Dante casually reached out and disentangled her. "Do you think you can handle some food now?" He asked, ignoring the fact that she was wearing a cheap ring on her left hand.

Cornelia's mind raced, disjointed images flashing through her mind. The strange couple, a quaint little chapel, a beautiful bouquet of flowers. Her head shot up and she stared, wide-eyed at Dante in shock. "We didn't..." She paused and looked at her hand again. "I mean, I didn't..." She pressed her face into her hands, horrified at herself. "Tell me I didn't do what I think I did last night," she groaned. Her voice came out muffled, she still had her face pressed hard against the palms of her hands. She finally peeked through her fingers when Dante didn't answer. He was watching her intently. She saw a faint twitch at the corner of his mouth, but couldn't tell if he was amused or upset.

Dante watched several emotions cross Cornelia's face before he spoke. "If you're talking about that wet t-shirt contest, I'm afraid you did," he paused to run a finger across her collar bone. "I still say we should file an appeal. Miss Double D didn't have a thing on you." His finger gently trailed across one breast.

Cornelia slapped his hand away. "Not funny, Dante," she scowled, waiting for a serious answer.

"Oh, you meant running through the Bellagio fountains naked." He sobered. "We're lucky the audience thought you were part of the show. It was a narrow escape; I admit I was worried there for a minute. Cops in this town don't seem to have a sense of humor when it comes to public nudity." He gave her that cocky grin of his. "I, on the other hand, thought you were spectacular. It was rather stimulating the way the lights danced over that gorgeous body of yours."

"Would you please be serious?" Cornelia said, unamused. "I did not participate in a wet t-shirt contest and I know I didn't dance through the fountains naked. We need to talk about what happened last night."

Dante wiped the grin from his face, pretending to look confused. "I guess that could have been a dream." He looked at her, wide-eyed. "What about the wild monkey sex? Was that just a dream too? No, that part was real. You will never convince me it wasn't." He sighed, then shook his head. "I was afraid you might be upset about that. You seemed to be enjoying yourself at the time, but that thing we did on the table..."

"Dante," Cornelia interrupted angrily. "Please tell me we didn't get married last night."

"Oh, that," Dante said, feigning relief. "Well, I could tell you we didn't get married..." He paused to play with her ring. "But, the papers I found on the table this morning would be pretty damning evidence that I lied. Especially combined with this awful ring." He looked her in the eye and casually added, "I just don't think it's a good idea to start our marriage off with deceit. We should always tell each other the truth. Let's make a pact. A blood pact with a girl just doesn't seem right. What could we do?"

Cornelia shot out of bed and pulled on a robe. She was too distracted to wonder where it had come from. "This isn't a joke, Dante." She grabbed the papers from the table and studied them. What had she done? He must hate her for sure. She moved to the large window and stared out at the city. How was she going to fix this?

Dante stood and moved in behind Cornelia. He wrapped his arms around her waist and pulled her against him. "Cornelia, sweetheart," he whispered softly. "This isn't the end of the world," he sobered. "Well, not for me anyway. I guess the idea of being my wife might seem like it for you?"

She looked at Dante, confused. Why was he so nonchalant about this? She twisted in his arms so they were facing each other. "Why aren't you upset?"

"Why are you so upset about it?" He asked moving in to press his lips to hers.

She was surprised when Dante's mouth covered hers in a soft, gentle kiss. This kiss was different than his other kisses. He was so gentle and, if she didn't know better, she'd call it loving. But Dante didn't love her. Which brought her back to her original concern. She had to find a way to fix this predicament before anyone found out about it. How had she let this happen? Especially after everything he'd told her last night.

Dante felt Cornelia's body stiffen. He relaxed his hold and straightened. "What now?" He asked, not liking the determined look on her face. There was also a hint of grief in there.

"I am so sorry, Dante," she finally said. "You just finished telling me all the horrible details surrounding your first marriage less than twenty-four hours ago. And what do I do? I take you out on the town and trick you into marrying me." She walked to the couch and plopped down in disgust.

Dante followed and sat down next to her, taking her hand in his. "Cornelia, you didn't trick me into anything. Why are you taking all the responsibility for this on yourself? I'm pretty sure we both had to be there to say I do. I hold just as much blame as you do." He watched her then sighed inwardly. "It's not a big deal, we can get a divorce." He hated that idea, but he didn't want her to worry about this.

Cornelia shook her head. "No," she said forcefully. "We have to get this annulled. I won't let you suffer another blow by getting divorced a second time."

Dante smiled. "I'm pretty sure last night's monkey sex disqualifies us," he paused, still grinning. "The marriage has now been consummated."

Cornelia looked at Dante, confused. "Why aren't you upset about this?" She asked again, really wanting to know. He was acting so casual and unconcerned.

Progeny

"I can see why you might be upset at the prospect of being my wife." He was serious now. "I mean, I'm not exactly the best catch. You deserve so much better. I have a reputation that is going to tarnish you. It might even make you socially unacceptable with some of our people."

Cornelia was frowning now. "Dante, I'm part vampire. My family history already makes me socially unacceptable. I hardly think your reputation for partying is a factor in all of this. I can't even begin to imagine what people would say if they found out you married someone like me. And I won't have it. I won't make things worse for you," Cornelia continued to frown. Was the man serious? How could any aspect of being his wife come close to being horrible? If she thought he was serious about this, if he just loved her, she'd be doing a happy dance on the table right now. But she couldn't trap him the way Shannon had. She couldn't let him ruin his life for her.

"Well, we're not getting this marriage annulled," he said with finality. "In fact, I've been thinking about this all morning," he smiled at her. "I had plenty of time. You really should watch your alcohol intake, babe. You might be strong and mighty on the battlefield, but slip you a couple margaritas and you're down for the count."

Cornelia gave him a weak smile. "I know. I can handle a small glass of wine on occasion, but other than that, I really don't drink. I guess I'm what they call a cheap drunk."

"Anyway," Dante continued. "After the initial shock, I realized this marriage could work to our advantage."

"How so?" she asked skeptically.

"Well, for one thing, it resolves any problems you might have with Alex and the council." Dante knew there weren't any problems, but Cornelia's insistence they'd force her out of New York was going to benefit him today. He needed more time. If they were married that might just give him the time he needed to persuade her to stay.

"I'm not following you," Cornelia admitted. She didn't see how being Dante's wife resolved anything. In fact, she was sure they would just banish him along with her when they found out.

"The institution of marriage is sacred among our people," Dante began. "You are now my wife. Nobody, even someone with strong feelings about vampires, will reject you. I'm a warrior, Cornelia. Normally that would be enough to stifle any objections, but we are at war. I'm needed more now than ever before. When we go back to New York and announce to everyone we got married out here, you are going to be instantly accepted. In fact, only Alex and a few others know you are part vampire. They wouldn't announce that anyway, I keep telling you they don't care. But now that you're my wife, they will guard that secret as closely as you have. More importantly, if you are my wife, Alex will protect us. Even if someone finds out and a request is made to banish us, Alex wouldn't allow it. I'm not sure you understand how close the warriors are. Dimitri wouldn't allow it, we're friends. We watch out for each other. We protect each other no matter what."

Cornelia allowed herself just a moment to think about the possibilities. She could be welcomed as a member of the community instead of shunned as a freak. The idea was exciting, and oh so enticing, but wrong. "I won't use you to make my place in society, Dante. You already entered into one marriage for protection. I won't let you do it again."

Dante ignored her. "In addition, as my wife you will have the protection of all the warriors, not just me. When we return to New York, the threat of Radek coming after you will be drastically reduced. It will also prevent any negative talk about your character when you move into my home," he smiled. "Our home, that is."

"Dante, I can't..." Cornelia began.

"You can and you will," Dante said forcefully. "If you don't want to share my bed, that's fine. But, you will move into my home and at least give the appearance we have a traditional marriage. I won't even try to explain why my wife is staying in one of Victor's apartments. You will stay with me for the length of our marriage."

"That's just it," Cornelia said stubbornly. "This marriage has to end before anyone finds out about it."

"Tell me why," he said flatly. "Why are you so anxious to throw away such a perfect solution to both of our problems?" He had to convince her to give this a chance. How else could he make her fall in love with him? He was starting to feel desperate, but he wouldn't allow her to see that.

"I can see how this benefits me," Cornelia began. "I think you're right, Alex and the others will accept me completely if we are married. They are all so in love, the idea of taking your wife away would be inconceivable to them."

"Exactly," Dante allowed himself to relax a little. "I'm glad we agree on something."

"But I don't see the benefit for you and I won't use you that way. I won't be like Shannon and your father. I won't let you sacrifice your own happiness and well-being to fix my problems," Cornelia had to stop this.

"The very closeness that will protect you has become a problem for me," Dante began. "The warriors are more than business associates. We are like brothers, Thomas and Nick are even more than that to me. Because of that bond, the six of them are putting a lot of pressure on me to find my mate. I know they mean well, but add in their wives and it all gets a little old. This marriage will benefit us both. The longer I can convince you to stay with me, the less pressure I'll have from all of them. We can both just relax and enjoy each other for a while," he smiled. "If we add sex to the mix, I come out ahead. I realize you are contractually obligated now, but under the circumstances it's negotiable."

Cornelia studied Dante for a long time. She wasn't sure she was buying it. But on the other hand, she had personally witnessed the pressure Dante got from the others. Abby and Thomas were constantly dragging him to Victor's club and other activities where he was bound to meet more people. More to the point, female prospects.

Progeny

"You would be doing me a favor, Cornelia," Dante pushed. "I need a break and I think we get along fairly well. I know we're compatible in the bedroom. It's a win/win for both of us. You get to stay in New York as long as you want, and I get a break from all the do-gooders," he smiled. "And we both get smoking hot monkey sex. I just can't see a downside."

Cornelia continued to study Dante. She knew she should say no. He was just being noble and self-sacrificing again. But she didn't have the strength. She wanted this. She wanted to stay married to Dante Santora for the rest of her life. She knew it was going to kill her when they finally ended it, but she wanted whatever she could get in the meantime. She wanted the memories they could create together. She wanted the fantasy, even if her happily ever after couldn't last. "Okay," she finally agreed. "I just hope you know what you're doing." Because she didn't.

Dante couldn't stop the smile from spreading across his face. He pulled her against him and kissed her hard. Then jumped to his feet and lifted her into his arms. "Come on. We have a lot to do today. But first, we need a shower."

Cornelia glanced at the clock in confusion. They had plenty of time before their meeting with Carlo. An uneasy feeling crept in, but she pushed it aside. For now, she'd just play it by ear. Her time with Dante was going to be spontaneous and memorable. If she was going to do this, she was going to do it right. Dante was going to be loved. That was something she could give him. Nobody would ever love Dante the way she loved him.

Dante pushed Cornelia into the limo and handed Joe an address. He was so excited for his surprise. She'd protest and argue, but he was determined to win this battle.

Cornelia frowned when the limo stopped in front of a jewelry store. She narrowed her eyes when Dante pulled her from the car and approached the front door. "What do you think you're doing?" She said, planting her feet just inside the building.

Dante took her left hand and removed the cheap ring. "I may have settled for this drunk, but there is no way my wife is going to wear something that tacky." He gave her a gentle kiss, took her hand and walked to the display case.

There was a young girl at the counter, watching them. "Can I help you?" she asked, not nearly as enthusiastic as most sales people.

Dante smiled. "Yes," he said, walking forward. "I was lucky enough to convince this beautiful woman to marry me last night but I didn't have a ring. We bought this one at the church," Dante placed the cheap ring on the counter. "But my wife needs something more appropriate. I was hoping you might have something a little more...unique."

"Uncle Chen will have to help you with that," she said, pushing herself from the small stool and heading for the back room. "Give me just a minute, someone will be out to help you."

An older gentleman appeared from the back room. He didn't look happy to see them. Dante took a step

Progeny

forward. The men at the club last night had been right. This man despised Carlo Santora it was clearly written all over his face. Well, that was nothing new. He'd just have to be charming and smart. The man standing before him had that look of intelligence in his eyes. Dante casually moved forward but didn't hold out his hand. He knew the man wouldn't accept it anyway. "Hello," he paused. "My name is Dante Santora." He thought he should get that out of the way immediately. "I can't hide the family resemblance, so I'm forced to accept it."

The man narrowed his eyes but didn't respond.

"I'm going to be up front with you Chen Lu," Dante continued. "I have two reasons for being here today." He pulled Cornelia in next to him. "I married this wonderful woman last night and need to buy her a ring." He glanced around the room. "I'm sure you have some elegant pieces out here, but I want something more unique for my wife. Price is not an issue. I'd like to look at your other items. The higher priced stuff."

Chen still didn't respond.

"I'm also interested in information," Dante continued. "I'm willing to pay for that as well. I'm told you are the info man here in town. I've also been told you won't sugarcoat it. Some of the information I'm looking for is on Carlo Santora. He seems to intimidate most people around here. I can't trust the information I get from someone that fears Carlo. I need the truth. Are my contacts correct? Are you the man I should talk to?"

"I don't think I can help you," Chen finally said. "Go talk to someone else."

"That's your choice, of course," Dante said. He wasn't deterred. He had known this was going to be difficult. "I have to admit, I am surprised. I guess my first impression was wrong. I thought you were a smart business man."

Chen didn't take the bait, but he did look intrigued.

"I'm looking for an expensive wedding set for my wife. Are you seriously turning me away?" Dante asked. "I know you get wealthy customers in here on occasion, but there's also a lot of competition. You've been presented with an opportunity to make thousands of dollars today and you're turning your back on it," Dante paused. "I understand disliking Carlo, I feel the same way. But I'm not sure I understand harming yourself because of it."

"You dislike Carlo Santora?" Chen asked skeptically. "A smart businessman isn't fooled that easily," he paused. "I'm not interested in selling precious gems for the price of cheap costume jewels. Go, find a ring elsewhere."

Dante smiled. He was making progress. "So, Carlo tried to con you into giving him a deal I see. Typical," Dante sighed. "I'll pay whatever price you ask for my wife's wedding ring," he waited. "I know jewelry, though. Don't try to scam me and I won't insult you by asking for a deal. If that business goes well, we can work on the other."

Progeny

Chen still didn't trust this guy, but he was a good judge of character. This man was nothing like Carlo Santora and he was right, it was stupid to miss out on a profit because of a grudge. "I don't care for Carlo. I don't trust him and I despise him," Chen finally admitted. "He knows that. It won't make any difference if you tell him."

Dante smiled. "The feeling is mutual."

"If Carlo is your enemy, why are you here?" Chen asked. "You're not local, so you must be visiting from out of town."

"I wouldn't say Carlo is my enemy," Dante disagreed. "Enemy assigns too much importance to that man. I dislike Carlo. To say I don't trust him would be a monumental understatement. I'd trust a sleazy politician before I trusted Carlo Santora with anything. You also said you despise him. My feelings go much deeper. They are difficult to explain, so I think I'll just leave it at that. As for why I am here, obligation. Carlo has misplaced his wife. My family has an obligation to help. We may not approve of Carlo. We may not even like Carlo, but he's family." Dante hoped that would be enough.

Chen gave a quick nod, accepting the explanation. "Tell me what you are looking for and I will bring out some pieces that fit your requirements," he suggested.

Cornelia listened as Dante described jewelry that must cost a fortune to the small, but powerful man. Chen Lu asked a couple brief questions, then rushed to the back. Dante had introduced her as his wife. She was starting to get used to it already. That surprised her, after a couple hours, she was already comfortable being Cornelia Santora. It must be the way Dante said it. He had that low, husky voice that could make something disgusting sound sexy. He could have called her anything and she probably would have agreed. He just had that effect on her. She needed to get a grip. If they were going to be married, she couldn't be a pushover. Dante would happily take advantage of any weakness he discovered.

The strange old man returned with a tray covered in felt. It held several sparkling wedding sets. They were huge and all so beautiful. She couldn't let Dante spend that kind of fortune on a temporary ring. "Dante, let's look at some of these."

Dante ignored her protests, again. She was getting tired of that. It was another thing she was going to have to put a stop to. Dante simply took her hand and led her forward. Then he began systematically studying each ring. He set two of the rings aside and told the jeweler he was finished with them. He then turned to Cornelia and asked for her opinion.

"I think they are all too expensive. I would be happy with something less," Cornelia began.

"You can stop right there," Dante said, unamused. "Don't ever start a sentence with I'd be happy with something less. You're my wife now. You don't settle for less." He pulled her closer to the counter, encouraging her to check out the merchandise. Dante was watching Cornelia. She was impressed by the selection, but nothing seemed to be catching her attention. He turned to Chen Lu. "Do you have something else we could look at?"

Progeny

Chen Lu considered. "I have a fancy red that just came in last week."

Dante raised an eyebrow. "Really?" He glanced at Cornelia then smiled. "We'd like to see that one."

Cornelia turned to Dante, confused. "A red diamond?" She finally asked.

"They're rare. Fancy reds are completely untreated. I kind of like the idea of a red wedding set. I think it suits us. We'll see if it meets my requirements, but be honest. I really want to know what you like." Dante was anxious to see the red. He hoped it was a good sized ring and good quality. He'd been serious. Cornelia was not settling for anything less as long as he was around. As much as he wanted to study the ring, he kept his eyes on Cornelia. He had to see her initial reaction. She could mask her feelings after the fact, but he wanted to see her face when she first saw the ring."

Cornelia watched as Chen Lu gently placed the felt covered tray on the counter. The ring was beautiful. She'd never seen anything like it before. She wished she could accept it, but there was no way she would allow Dante to buy something like that for her. She turned to face him, prepared to protest again but didn't get the chance.

"I'd like to look at it more closely, but I think this might be the one," Dante grinned at Chen Lu as he lifted the jewelers' loupe and began his assessment. A few minutes later Dante was ready to talk price. "Cornelia, why don't you peruse the cases and see if there's anything else you would like. Chen Lu and I need to talk business."

"No way," Cornelia protested. "I need to know the price before I agree to this."

"Sorry, sweetheart," Dante said giving her a little push. "You don't have a say in this. If I had done things right, I would have bought the thing alone then surprised you with it and asked you to marry me. We're doing this backward, but I still want to buy my special woman the perfect ring."

Cornelia walked around the shop. It was beyond ridiculous for Dante to think she was going to buy something else. But if pretending to shop would allow him to get information on Shannon from Chen Lu, she could accommodate him."

Dante walked up behind Cornelia and wrapped his arms around her waist. He gently kissed the side of her neck and whispered softly. "We'll have to come back in an hour or so. Chen Lu is going to size it for you."

"Did you get what you wanted from him?" she turned to ask. "Did he know anything about Shannon?"

"Not much, but a little," Dante said taking her hand and pulling her towards the door. "Let's talk about it on the way to my father's. After we meet with him, we'll come back for your ring."

"I can't believe you bought that thing." Cornelia tried to protest again but Dante just pushed her into the limo. "Dante, you can't waste money on me like that."

Progeny

Dante frowned but didn't answer her right away. He lowered the partition and directed Joe to his father's house. Once the partition was securely in place he turned back to Cornelia and sighed. "We are married now. You agreed to keep it that way. If this is going to work, you have to trust me. I told you I'm rich. I could spend recklessly for the rest of my life and barely put a dent in my family's money. My friends know that. They are aware of my wealth. If you show up with that cheap excuse for a wedding ring, the gig is up. Nobody will take our marriage seriously. Now they will." He kissed her softly then relaxed into the seat. "I also plan to give you other things. Get used to expensive gifts, I plan to buy them for you frequently."

"But..." She had to stop the nonsense.

"But nothing," Dante said casually. "I told you, I gave Shannon unlimited access to my money for the first year of our marriage. I bought a new plane and let her shop in Paris and Italy. Do you honestly believe I'd do less for you?"

"That's different," Cornelia persisted.

"I don't see how," Dante replied, closing his eyes. He wanted to relax before his encounter with his father, not argue with Cornelia over a wedding ring. "Well, that's not entirely true. I actually care about you. Shannon was just an obligation. So you are right, this is different."

That stopped her. Was it true? Did Dante really care about her? She wanted to grab onto that little bit of hope and cherish it, expand on it. But, she couldn't. She had to be realistic. Dante was right. They'd need to convince his friends they were in love, or what was the point of remaining married. If Dante were truly in love, he'd give his wife the world. She'd have to give it all back when she left, but she wasn't going to argue now. "Fine," she relented. "So what did Chen Lu tell you about Shannon?"

Dante opened his eyes, suspicious now. Cornelia was planning something. Something he wouldn't like. But they could deal with that later. "It turns out my dear ex-wife slash stepmother is a drug addict."

Cornelia mulled over the new information, then suddenly lowered the partition and called out. "Joe, can you please find a parking lot to pull into? I need a minute with Dante before we decide on a destination."

Joe glanced at Dante, then agreed once he saw Dante's subtle nod.

Cornelia tried not to be annoyed but failed. She was used to being the one in charge, the one that gave the orders, the one that gave the subtle nod of approval. She took a deep breath and raised the partition. "Can you call your father and postpone our appointment?"

"I can," Dante said slowly, "But first I need to know why."

"You need to fill me in on everything Chen Lu told you," she began. "Did he know what drugs she used, how did she get them, everything."

Progeny

Dante paused then pulled out his phone and dialed Carlo. Once he relayed the message that they would be late to his father's butler he ended the call and focused on Cornelia. He didn't mind rescheduling the meeting, in fact, he thought it was a great idea. He should have thought of it himself. Carlo had now been put on notice that he wasn't running the show here, Dante was. It was a good lesson for the egomaniac.

"So, what did Chen Lu tell you?" Cornelia pressed.

"I shouldn't have been surprised, but I was. Remember I told you I caught Shannon smoking marijuana in the house?" Dante said.

"Yes," Cornelia hadn't exactly missed that, but she hadn't really placed any importance on that fact either. Apparently, she should have.

"Apparently, she's graduated from smoking a little weed to snorting cocaine," Dante said with disgust.

"I see," Cornelia said, sitting back while she pondered the situation. "Did Chen Lu know where she gets it?"

"He gave me the name of a guy," Dante admitted. "He spends a lot of time at the Bellagio, gambling." He smiled when he looked her way. "I thought we'd check it out later, maybe I can see that naked dancing after all."

"Funny," she said, not amused. "Would he be there now?"

"Probably," Dante said, curiously. "Why?"

"Because I think we should meet up with this guy before we talk to Carlo," she said absently, still deep in thought. "Shannon's disappearance might be connected to drugs, I don't know. But I do believe the connection with Brad Shepard is. I suspect this guy is a middle man. Shannon contacts him, then he somehow contacts his man in Mexico. Once they arrange a time and place for the pickup, Brad Shepard flies down and picks up the merchandise. He brings it back here, then goes home. He makes enough money to pay a portion of the debt he owes, but Carlo makes sure the guy never pays him off completely. It's just too handy to have access to your own drug smuggling plane."

"Makes sense," Dante agreed. "And if you're right, it's easy to correct."

"Oh?" Cornelia said furrowing her brows. "How so?"

"There's that little matter of the monthly allowance," Dante said flatly. "Let's go talk to the contact. If you're right, he can give us a better idea of how it all works. Then, when we talk to Carlo we'll know enough to shut him down."

Chapter Six

Dante sat in the limo, fuming. Cornelia had been right. They had a tidy little drug smuggling operation going on here. Nothing too big that would catch the attention of the locals or the DEA. No, Carlo was smuggling in just enough for consumption and a little business on the side. His contact, Tuck and what kind of name was Tuck, told them everything Dante needed to know about things on this end. Apparently, he was more afraid of Dante than he was of Shannon. He should have known Shannon would be the contact. Carlo was too good for something so trivial. But Tuck wouldn't say a word about the operation in Mexico. Dante didn't really blame him. Vegas wasn't that far away, and the Mexican Drug Cartel wasn't a group to be crossed.

He glanced up as they approached the house. Cornelia was watching him. He knew she was worried, but he could handle this. Dante inhaled two deep breaths then took Cornelia's hand. "It's been a long time," he finally told her. "I'm glad you're here. I always hated this house. It's so big and... modern, I guess. It just doesn't seem to fit with the neighborhood."

Cornelia gave Dante's hand a squeeze then stepped from the car. She paused for only a moment before heading for the front porch. "Shannon's doing, I suppose?" She asked, staring at a freaky gnome set that flanked both sides of the porch.

Dante laughed and nodded once. The door swung open and a stuffy looking man stood in the opening. "Carson," Dante said coldly, then pushed passed the man pulling Cornelia in behind him. "Where is he?"

Carson cleared his throat in disgust then motioned to a large room to the right. Cornelia knew immediately she wouldn't like Carlo's butler. He was stuffy and pretentious. The man looked to be in his late sixties, with a long pointy nose and glasses. He was looking down that nose of his as Dante turned and headed for his father. "Wait," Carson called after him. "I haven't announced you."

Dante snorted but kept walking. Cornelia followed close behind. She already hated the house. It was nothing like Dante's. She'd only been in Dante's home that one night but she loved it. This place was cold and badly decorated. Honestly, had the woman never heard of a color wheel? She glanced up to see a man sitting in front of a large fireplace. No wonder Dante was getting such a reaction from the locals. The resemblance between father and son was impossible to miss. Well, the outward resemblance anyway. They were nothing alike on the inside. Carlo suddenly looked their way and Cornelia stopped. She hadn't meant to and the action made Dante pause and look at her in confusion. Cornelia shrugged and followed him to the couch. She hadn't been prepared for Carlo's eyes. They were nearly black and so cold. If she had to describe them, she'd probably use the word dead. Cornelia instantly knew she was not going to get along with Carlo Santora.

"I see you still haven't learned proper manners," Carlo said, raising a hand in dismissal to Carson who had followed them into the room.

Carson backed away, pulling the large doors closed behind him.

Dante didn't respond. He sat on the couch, legs outstretched, one ankle crossing the other. He looked perfectly relaxed and right at home.

Cornelia knew better. She could feel Dante's tension radiating from every pore. She decided to take the lead on this one. Dante could switch off when they brought up Shannon's kidnapping but the two of them had agreed to hit Carlo with the drug smuggling right off the bat. "Mr. Santora," she began.

"Who is this woman?" Carlo asked Dante, not even sparing her a glance.

"My wife, Cornelia," Dante answered flatly. "She's also my partner. She's a private investigator. I brought her here to help work on the case. Actually, she was already headed this way. Following a lead on another case she'd been working on for Nick."

The news that Dante was married clearly shocked his father. He was now studying Cornelia with interest. He was looking for weakness. He wouldn't find any, but the fact that he was looking was infuriating. "You can stop right there," Dante warned. "Cornelia is a good judge of character. She's a lot like Nick that way. Since you don't have any..." he shrugged.

Carlo was up on his feet, face red, hands clenched to his sides. "I won't tolerate your disrespect in my home, Dante. I know we've had some problems in the past. I had hoped this crisis might bring us closer together again." He sighed, trying to portray sadness and regret. "You're my son. If I can't have your love, the least you could give me is respect."

"Uh, Mr. Santora," Cornelia interrupted. She could see where this was leading and she wouldn't stand for it. The guy had no conscience. After everything he'd done to Dante, he was actually trying to make his son feel guilty.

"Yes, Cornelia," Carlo said a little too sweetly.

Dante growled.

Cornelia stood. She knew how to take control of a situation and sitting on the sofa while Carlo Santora hovered above them was not in the plan. She smiled at the annoyance that spread across Carlo's face. He didn't like working on a level playing field. *Well, too bad.* "As Dante told you, I've been working on a case for Nick Moretti. Well, it has more to do with his fiancé than with Nick, but that's just semantics," she gave a little wave. "It's important to me that I take care of that business before I begin working on your case."

Carlo mumbled something under his breath, then returned to his chair. Apparently, he realized Cornelia wasn't going to back down. The conversation would occur on their feet if he didn't relent. The instant he was seated, he turned back to Dante. "I have Dimitri's word that Shannon takes priority. He promised me you wouldn't work on anything else until she's found. I don't care what your wife does with her free time, but you're mine."

"I've never been yours," Dante said placing his arm around Cornelia's shoulder when she returned to the couch. "Cornelia's almost finished with Nick's case but she has some questions for you."

"Me?" Carlo asked, surprised. He was starting to get an uneasy feeling about all of this and he didn't like it. "I have no idea what you mean. How could you have questions for me? I haven't seen or spoken to Nick Moretti in decades."

"I'm aware of that," Dante assured him. "Otherwise, I would have received a request for more money. Knowing you, I'd be expected to pay your doctor bills... or funeral expenses."

"I don't see why that man's temper amuses you," Carlo spat out. "He's vile and completely out of control. I can't believe his parents tolerate such..."

"If you have any sense at all, you'll stop right there," Dante interrupted coldly. "I'm the only reason Nick has allowed you to live. One word from me and you might just disappear one day," Dante shrugged. "People disappear all the time. Many of them are never seen or heard from again, especially around here. So much desert terrain to choose from."

"I intend to report you to Oberon," Carlo bellowed. "You may have manipulated your grandparents into giving you access to their money, but you don't fool me. You are a spoiled brat who thinks he can go around threatening anyone that stands in his way."

Dante didn't say a word. He just sat there, silently watching his father. Carlo glared at his son, defiant and full of hatred. Moments later, Carlo lowered his head in defeat. "Cornelia, do you want to fill him in or would you like me to?" Dante asked.

"I will," Cornelia said cheerfully. "I think I'll just start at the beginning if that's okay with you," she said watching Dante.

Dante smiled and gave her a nod.

"Lillie, Nick's fiancé, is a pilot," Cornelia began. She could see that got Carlo's attention. "Prior to meeting Nick, she was married to a man that forced her to make monthly runs to Mexico," Cornelia paused to let that sink in. She could see it was working, she now had Carlo's undivided attention. "For one reason or another, Lillie became suspicious. She stopped making the runs. Her husband didn't like it, but apparently he didn't have a choice. He once again started making the runs himself. Now, fast forward a few years. Lillie and her husband have divorced and she meets our charming friend, Nick Moretti. They fall in love and Nick learns of the illegal activity Lillie was forced to participate in by her evil ex-husband. Dante, being an expert on evil ex's, came to me. He was concerned for Lillie and wanted to make sure her past couldn't come back to hurt her in the future."

"That's a nice story, but I still don't see what it has to do with me," Carlo said, regaining some of his composure. They couldn't know about his drug running.

"Well, coincidentally," Cornelia glanced at Dante then looked back to Carlo. "It has a great deal to do with you," she said flatly. "After all, you own the company that is paying Brad Shepard for those runs to Mexico. Three Water's Incorporated also gave him a rather large loan about fifteen years ago. A loan he will never be able to pay off, thanks to some fancy bookkeeping and an outrageous interest rate."

Carlo's eyes grew wide, but he immediately regained composure. "I think it's time for you to leave Ms. Cornelia, we're finished here and I need my son to find my wife."

"Oh, that's Mrs. Santora to you," she beamed. "And I'm not quite finished."

"I'm afraid you are." Carlo started to stand again, but glanced at Dante and froze.

"If she goes, I go," Dante assured him. "We can either clear this up now, or I will spend the next several days helping Cornelia gather enough evidence to lock you up for years," he paused. "Of course, Shannon will be dead by then but you'll be preoccupied with your own problems. I don't think you'd like life on the island. You know the council would send you there. We can't have warriors sentenced to several years in a regular prison. Too many secrets to protect."

Carlo slumped in defeat. "What do you want?"

"The truth," Cornelia answered. "I'm told that is fairly difficult for you," she glanced at Dante again. She needed to make sure she didn't upset him. "It's my understanding that Thomas Deveraux asked you for the same thing, but you didn't quite manage it."

Carlo inhaled, he had to breathe. He couldn't lose his temper. He hated this woman. Not only for her condescending cocky attitude but because another plan to access Dante's money had just gone up in flames. Why hadn't his son married a weak, naïve woman instead of this head hunting pariah? He wished he could just throw them both out of his house, but he couldn't. Shannon needed him. He could endure their torture for a few more days. Once he had Shannon back, he'd tell them what they could do with their investigation.

Progeny

"So," Cornelia continued. "We know Shannon is addicted to cocaine. Is she the only one that indulges in that habit or are you an addict as well?"

"What we really want to know is if you took advantage of Shannon's fondness for marijuana and turned it into a drug habit for your own pleasure or if she accelerated to cocaine on her own," Dante corrected. "After you turned Shannon, every time she got high, you would feel high as well. I understand that whole shared emotion's thing." He paused to take in the daggers his father was shooting his way. "I knew about it before, but I've actually witnessed the connection between Sam and Ty over the past few months. It's really quite potent, isn't it?"

Carlo was surprised that his son's accusations actually hurt him. He thought he was beyond feeling anything for Dante Santora. But knowing his own son believed him capable of turning his wife into a drug addict for his own pleasure damaged something deep inside. "I may not be an honorable man, but even you should know I would never do anything to harm Shannon," he paused to swallow the lump that was forming in his throat. "I love that woman more than life itself. Why do you think I risked going to New York? Without Shannon, life just isn't worth living."

Dante almost felt sorry for his father. Almost, but not quite. The man was a manipulator, but for once Dante thought he was telling the truth. "Okay, you love Shannon. I get it. I've always gotten that part. So Shannon had a marijuana habit to support. When did she escalate to cocaine?"

"A few years ago. Five, maybe six. I don't know for sure," Carlo admitted. "She hid the marijuana from me while she was human. She couldn't hide it once I changed her. I didn't like it, but I figured it was harmless," Carlo stared out the window and sighed. "Then she started to snort the coke. I begged her to stop. I told her I'd buy all the weed she wanted. She just laughed and said that didn't do it for her anymore."

"So you gave in," Dante supplied. "You always gave her everything she wanted."

"I didn't know how the drugs would impact our system. Some human drugs are harmful to us. I was able to talk her into letting me do the drugs. I'd snort the coke and she could benefit from the high without the risk. She only let me do that once. She said the high wasn't as potent that way. She needed the hit, not just the euphoria."

"So you started buying the drugs for her," Cornelia pressed.

"Yes," Carlo admitted. "I was worried about her. Shannon can be reckless. I didn't want her out on the streets buying drugs from some criminal."

"How did you hook up with Brad Shepherd?" Dante asked.

"He came to the casino a few years before all this happened," Carlo sighed. "He scammed his way into a private poker game without the funds to back his losses. When the rest of the players found out, they were ready to kill him. I gave him a loan. He's slowly paying it back but at my interest rate, he'll die before he ever comes close."

"So you contacted him with your brilliant business deal," Dante supplied.

"Yes, I contacted him," Carlo barked. "I manipulated him. I threatened him and I made sure he would do what I wanted. Is that what you need me to say? Is that honest enough for you? Shannon needed drugs. I need Shannon. I did what I had to do to protect her," Carlo glanced at Cornelia. "If she's really your wife, you just might understand how it feels to love someone so much you're willing to do anything to make her happy." He put his head in his hands. "Are you going to take this away, too?" he finally asked.

"Yes," Dante said coolly. "But not for the reason you think." He looked at Cornelia then continued. "It's just your bad luck that Brad decided to pawn the dirty work off on his wife. Nick is going to marry Lillie. Brad forced her to do the runs for over a year. That makes her vulnerable. I won't leave Lillie exposed that way. If you continue to use Brad to smuggle drugs, he's eventually going to get caught. Any investigation into his finances will lead to Lillie. I don't care if you smuggle drugs for the next millennia, just find another pilot."

"Brad Shepard owes me money," Carlo protested.

"No, he doesn't," Dante corrected. "His debt has been paid in full. I've seen the account. You're bleeding him dry. You already admitted that he could never repay the loan at the interest rate you gave him," Dante glared at his father. "You've made enough money off that man. He's stupid and he'll get himself into trouble again. But it won't involve Lillie and it won't involve my family."

"I guess I should be flattered that you still acknowledge our family connection," Carlo said dryly.

"Keep it up and that might change," Dante countered. "You don't want to fight me on this old man. You won't like the outcome."

Carlo sighed. "If I agree to find another pilot, is this over? If I agree, will you stop this ridiculous investigation into Shannon's drug habits and start working on getting her back for me?"

"Basically," Dante agreed. "I'll need to make sure all records of your transactions are destroyed. We've already done that on Brad's end. This is about protecting Lillie, not you, not Shannon. If the two of you want to destroy your lives with drugs, be my guest."

"I don't need your permission," Carlo said through clenched teeth.

"No, you don't," Dante agreed. "The only other thing I need to know is if Shannon's drug use has anything to do with her disappearance."

Carlo's face went white. "How would that be connected?"

Progeny

"That's what I'm asking you," Dante pushed. "Are the drugs strictly for consumption or have you been selling? And don't lie to me. I'm going to find out. You might have some people in this town running scared, but not everyone. I admit our family resemblance is an obstacle I have to overcome, but I will find the truth. And, if I find out you kept information from me, I guarantee you will pay."

"You sound like a broken record," Carlo grumbled. "Do this or you'll pay, do that, don't do that. My son, the control freak. I'm so proud," Carlo said dryly. "The power is the same for you as the cocaine is for Shannon. I get it already. If I don't comply with all your wishes, you're going to have your grandparents cut off my money."

"You're wrong," Dante said watching his father. "This isn't about control. It's not about revenge or bad blood either. If you want me to find Shannon, I need to know the truth. If you lie to me, it's going to delay my investigation. That means it's going to take longer to find your wife," Dante sighed. "Just start from the beginning and tell me everything. I need to know about business dealings, the drugs, your enemies, everything. If I didn't want you to have the money, I wouldn't have started the payments in the first place," he paused. "Try to act like a normal human being for a change and tell me what I need to know."

Cornelia was watching Carlo Santora. He was upset and on the edge. One wrong word and she was sure he would erupt. "Mr. Santora," she said softly. "This is what I do for a living. Trust me and Dante to do our job. I'm confident we can get your wife back as long as you are honest with us," she paused but when the two men remained silent she continued. "I have some standard questions. Some I ask in every investigation, some that are specific to this type of situation. Can we start there?"

Carlo turned and stared out the large window for several minutes. "Go ahead." he finally capitulated. "Ask me anything. Like I said, I would do anything for Shannon. That includes sharing my deepest, darkest secrets with the only man alive that can hurt me."

"Thank you," Cornelia said softly. Then she pulled out a notebook and began to work.

Chapter Seven

Dante and Cornelia stepped into the elevator and waited for the door to close. Neither one had said much on the ride back from Carlo Santora's house. They were each deep in thought, trying to put together the information Carlo had given them. Carlo had so many enemies. Anyone could have snatched Shannon. The only thing they knew for sure was that she hadn't run off with a new boyfriend. The warrior connection prevented that possibility. If Shannon had been cheating on Carlo, he would know about it. That was something she couldn't hide.

The doors opened and the two stepped into the penthouse. Dante took Cornelia's hand and prevented her from entering further. "Thank you," he said softly. "I swore to myself that, if I was ever lucky enough to get married again, my wife would never meet my father. I'm sorry I had to break that promise."

Cornelia smiled. "I never thought I'd get married, too many complications, you know what they are. Anyway, I knew if I did miraculously find someone that would have me anyway, I never wanted my husband to meet my father either. Chances are you've already met him. If not, I'm sure it's just a matter of time before you do. Let's just call it even." She wasn't sure what to think about Dante's words. Did he really think he was lucky to find himself married to her? Her thoughts were abruptly brought to an end when she saw movement in the lounge area.

"Wife!" Nick asked in surprise.

"Husband?" Lillie asked, rushing to Cornelia's side. She frowned when she saw Cornelia's cheap ring.

Dante closed his eyes in defeat. Could this situation get any worse? "What are you doing here?" he asked.

Nick smiled. "Did you honestly think anyone could stop me?"

"Hope springs eternal," Dante grumbled. He put an arm around Cornelia and pulled her close. "Stop frowning, Lillie. I plan on picking up Cornelia's real ring this afternoon. It had to be sized. Our marriage was..," he paused, "Unexpected," he finally decided. "We had to make due with a cheap substitute to get us through the ceremony."

Progeny

"Oh," Lillie said, clearly relieved. "That makes sense." She studied the couple for a long moment. "But how could you get married without me and Nick? I mean really, Nick is supposed to be your best friend. How could you get married without him?"

Dante glanced at Nick. His friend was unusually quiet. Nick didn't say anything, he just raised an eyebrow and waited. Dante took a deep breath then led Cornelia to the large couch. "Look, it's nothing personal," Dante began when Lillie and Nick joined them. "Cornelia and I have been attracted to each other for a long time. Since the two of you got together, we've become closer. I had more time on my hands and so did she." He glanced at Nick, then at Cornelia. "Neither one of us planned on getting hitched, it just happened, but now that we're married we both agree it was the right decision."

Cornelia smiled at Dante. She didn't like deceiving her friends or forcing Dante to deceive Nick. Those two were very close, but she'd agreed to let this play out so they didn't really have a choice.

"So why the rush?" Nick asked softly.

"We were a little drunk," Cornelia admitted. "So drunk in fact, neither of us knew what we had done until the next morning."

Dante studied Nick, trying to gauge his friend's thoughts. Nick was hiding them pretty well. "But once we sobered up and talked about it, we both knew it was what we wanted," Dante added. He linked his fingers through Cornelia's and continued to watch Nick.

168

"I see," Nick finally said. "Then congratulations."

Dante knew Nick wasn't buying it. His friend was too controlled, too subdued. Dante knew the instant he and Nick were alone, there would be an interrogation. Well, he'd just have to handle it. "So, tell me how you convinced Dimitri to send you here," Dante said, changing the subject. "Or are you AWOL?"

Lillie laughed. "We didn't give him a choice," she answered, grinning from ear to ear.

Dante gave Nick a questioning look.

"We threatened to run off and get married," Nick finally said grinning. "I thought it was an original idea, but apparently not."

Dante frowned. "You are getting married."

"True," Nick conceded. "Lillie and I went to Dimitri and Alex hoping they would give us permission to come out here and help. Dimitri was adamantly opposed to the idea," Nick paused. "You know it's a little insulting that none of you guys trust me to maintain control when it comes to Carlo Santora," he scowled. "Except for Bastian, I'm the most level-headed warrior of the entire group."

Dante laughed. "Most of the time that's true. However, when it comes to my father, you are a loose cannon. Nobody knows what you're going to do. In fact, I think Dimitri is more afraid of what you might do than he is me."

Progeny

"Maybe, but I'm not just being reckless," Nick said defensively. "The man deserves a wake-up call and I think I'm just the man to give it."

"Which is why I'm still wondering how you got here," Dante persisted.

"After Dimitri lectured me on my lack of self-control and said not only no, but hell no, Lillie explained her position on the matter," Nick said, grinning at the woman he loved.

"Which is?" Dante asked slowly.

Lillie was the one who answered. "I told Alex and Dimitri that Nick and I would be getting married, immediately. After careful thought, we had decided not to get married in Italy. We would be heading to Vegas where we would tie the knot and then take our week vacation out here in sin city." She was practically gloating. "I did have to remind them that it would be unfair to treat Nick and me differently than he'd treated all the other warriors that were recently married. Ty and Sam spent a week at the ranch, Bastian took Kylee to Ireland and Victor took Ariel to France for almost two weeks once things settled down after the ball."

"And he bought it?" Dante asked skeptically.

"He didn't have a choice," Nick shrugged. "We weren't kidding. Plus, Lillie reminded him how important it is for mom to have her dream wedding at the vineyard. That dream was going to be shattered, but it couldn't be helped. She was sure Zarah would eventually get over it."

Dante laughed. "No, she wouldn't," he paused. "But you two played that one well. Dimitri would not want Zarah as an enemy for life, which might happen if she doesn't get the wedding she's always wanted for her precious boy."

"Exactly," Nick agreed. "Which is why Lillie and I are here to help deal with this Carlo fiasco and get the two of you back to New York where you belong," he sobered. "We all need to get back. Radek has something cooking, I can feel it."

"What happened?" Dante asked, concerned.

"Nothing," Nick admitted. "But that's the problem. We had that big battle on New Year's, then nothing. No follow-up. No more attacks. Things are eerily quiet. I think it's the calm before the storm."

"I do have some good news," Cornelia said, uncomfortable with the topic of her father.

"Better than getting married?" Lillie asked sarcastically.

"No," she said, trying to stop a smile from spreading but failing. "But it's still good news," she studied Lillie. "I've tracked down the money and the connection."

Lillie looked confused for only a second. "The illegal flights to Mexico," she finally said with understanding.

"Yes," Cornelia agreed. "I told you we tracked them to the Cayman Islands, but I didn't have a chance to tell you from there the trail led here, to Vegas. I discovered it the day before Dante and I flew out. We went to the bank yesterday and between the two of us we were able to trace the account to the source."

"Now what?" Lillie asked. "Now that you know who Brad was flying for, what are we going to do about it?"

Nick wrapped an arm around Lillie in comfort. He didn't like the look on Dante's face and was pretty sure where this conversation was headed.

"It's taken care of," Dante finally said.

Lillie jerked her head toward Dante and frowned. "How?" she paused. "I mean, I guess the details don't matter but are you sure? Can you be sure I can never be linked to that operation?" Her mind was reeling. "Was it drugs?" she asked softly, not sure she really wanted to know. "Or something else?"

Dante gave Cornelia a slight nod, encouraging her to continue.

"It was drugs," Cornelia said. "And we know it's over because we talked to the source."

"You confronted him?" Lillie asked, worried. "But wasn't that dangerous?"

"Not so much," Dante grumbled.

Cornelia glanced at Dante, then to Nick. "Lillie," she said moving slightly so she could take Lillie's hand. "Dante's father owns Three Waters, Inc." She ignored the anger that crossed Nick's face and continued. "Your ex-husband came to Vegas one weekend and gambled out of his league. In other words, he joined a high-stakes game that he couldn't afford. When he lost, the men demanded instant payment. Brad couldn't pay. According to Carlo, the men threatened Brad and were about to teach him a lesson. Carlo was afraid the guy was going to end up dead and didn't want the hassle. He was mostly worried the gamblers would move to another casino and he'd be out the cover charge for the back room. They didn't like that Carlo had allowed a novice to play with the big boys. He stepped in and covered the debt, mostly to protect his own interests."

"I figured it was something like that," Lillie said. Her eyes were downcast, she was studying her hands, embarrassed about the whole mess. "I guessed that Brad's huge debt had something to do with gambling or something else illegal. Nobody pays that kind of interest on a loan unless it's on the shady side."

"This has nothing to do with you, Lillie," Cornelia said gently. "It happened before you were involved with Brad. It's in the past, and Dante and I have taken care of it. Nothing will come back on you, ever."

Lillie looked up then, her eyes filled with moisture. "I don't see how that's possible," she finally said. "I still smuggled drugs from Mexico."

"Is Carlo dealing?" Nick asked, gritting his teeth in an attempt to control his hatred.

"No," Dante answered. "Well, we don't think so at least. It's possible that Shannon was selling a little here and there, but I don't think Carlo is."

"Is that what got her kidnapped?" Nick asked, disliking their mission even more.

Dante sighed. "That's something we still need to determine," he turned to Lillie. "I was able to convince my father that continuing to use Brad to smuggle his drugs was a bad idea. He has also agreed to forgive the rest of the debt Brad owes him. The man has already paid for his mistake at least four times by now."

"Why would he do that?" Lillie asked, perplexed. "I mean he had such a sweet deal. With the interest Carlo was charging Brad, the debt could never be paid in full."

Dante smiled, "I gave him the incentive he needed to break all ties with Brad Shepard."

Nick understood. Dante had threatened to take away the money. "I assume you destroyed the records."

"We did," Cornelia answered. "I've double checked. Everything is gone. Even I couldn't locate a trace once we were finished. I'm good at what I do. If I couldn't find a lead to follow, the police won't either."

"Good," Nick said with relief, locking eyes with Lillie. "Dante and I took care of everything back in New

York with Brad. So, that part of your life is in the past now. You can stop worrying."

"Plus," Dante added. "In a few years, you're going to have to change your name and reinvent yourself anyway. There is no chance those few flights will ever cause you problems. We won't let it," he assured her.

Lillie sat in silence for a long moment. It was hard to believe that something that had caused her so much stress for so long was completely resolved. She took a deep breath and turned to Dante. "Thank you," she said sincerely. "And Cornelia, thank you. Without the three of you, I think that time in my life would have haunted me forever."

Nick pressed a kiss to Lillie's temple then turned to Dante. "So, back to the main reason we are all here. Clearly, you met with Carlo. Did he give you anything we can use to find that bimbo he's married to so we can get out of Dodge?"

"You're right Nick, I just can't imagine why anyone would doubt you and your control when it comes to Carlo and Shannon Santora. I for one owe you an apology." Dante laughed, he couldn't help it. The only person Nick despised more than Dante's father was his ex-wife.

"I just tell it like I see it," Nick shrugged. "Go ahead, try to convince me that two-timing, back-stabbing woman isn't a bimbo. I dare you." He smiled, knowing Dante wouldn't take the bait.

Progeny

"Dante and I planned to grab a bite to eat and then start checking into the places Shannon liked to frequent," Cornelia said, ending that conversation. "Now that you and Lillie are here, I think that's going to be easier."

"How so?" Nick asked.

"Well," Cornelia said, considering. "Shannon spent a lot of time at the spa. Of course, Dante cringed at the idea of spending the day with women in mud wraps and cucumber eyes." She smiled as she glanced his way then continued. "Now that you and Lillie are here we can split up. I'll take Lillie with me to the spa and you and Dante can head over to the more seedy part of town and rough up the street people."

Dante immediately approved. "Great idea!"

Cornelia laughed. "Isn't he adorable?" She gave his hand a squeeze. "Dante wanted to protect me from intermingling with the riffraff but he was having a hard time coming up with an excuse to leave me home. It's so cute, the way he wants to protect me. Like he thinks I've been sheltered from all that. Especially since he knows I've been a private investigator for years."

Lillie laughed at the scowls Nick and Dante were giving Cornelia. "It's a warrior thing," she assured her friend. "Our men think they have to protect us from everything." She turned to Nick and smiled warmly then turned back to Cornelia. "Spending some time with you in public will be a nice change. Nick has conveniently forgotten I'm a warrior now, too. He thinks I'm still fragile and breakable. I'd love to take on a human, for the practice of course. Maybe we'll get attacked on the street tonight," Lillie added enthusiastically.

"Very funny," Nick said without a hint of humor. "Let's get something to eat then you and Cornelia can head to the spa. Dante and I will head up north."

"Sounds like we're on the same page," Dante told Nick. "I think if Shannon started dealing some of her drugs, she would have taken them toward North Vegas. The danger would have thrilled her, plus there was no chance she'd encounter one of her high-class debutantes out there."

"Before we go I'd like to change," Lillie interjected. "We didn't know you guys would be newlyweds so Thomas said we could just stay here," she cringed. "That's not a problem now, is it? I guess we could find somewhere else to stay and give you two some privacy."

"Its fine," Dante said immediately. "We're in the master. The next best room is to the right and I already checked the fridge. Bastian's people stocked it well."

"Thanks," Lillie said, obviously relieved. "Otherwise, I think we would have to drive all the way to St. George for a room. It's busy here this time of year."

"Valentine's Day," Dante told her.

Chapter Eight

An hour later Nick and Dante dropped the women at the spa. As the limo pulled away Nick turned to Dante. "What's the story with this Chen Lu guy?"

"On our first night here," Dante began. "Cornelia and I went clubbing. I asked around and everyone told me Chen Lu is the go-to guy for information around here. He didn't like me at first, apparently he's had a couple run-ins with Carlo and Shannon. Near as I can tell, they wanted expensive jewelry for costume prices."

Nick grunted. "Sounds like Carlo."

"Anyway," Dante continued. "It took some doing, but he's given me a couple leads already. One panned out immediately. Chen Lu told me about Tuck, the middleman that Carlo used to arrange for everything in Mexico. I got

178

as much as we're going to get from him. Tuck is terrified of his contact in Mexico. He did mention a guy named The Pooch and said Shannon was afraid of the man. I checked with Chen Lu but he couldn't tell me much about this Pooch guy. Apparently, the man got his name because he has hangdog eyes and one side of his face droops like a hound dog. He seems to be new to the area, but Chen Lu was going to do some checking for me. I thought we'd head over to the jewelry shop first thing. If Chen Lu has discovered anything, we can follow up on that first. I also want to pick up Cornelia's ring. I can't wait for you to see it. It's an original and the red diamond fits her perfectly."

Nick smiled. He knew given enough time Dante would bring up Cornelia. It was a nice segue into the topic of their wedding. "While we have a little time and privacy, you want to tell me the real story behind your marriage to Cornelia?"

Dante cringed inwardly. He knew this was coming, but he'd hoped he would have more time to come up with something that would satisfy Nick. "I already told you," he said flatly. "We've been spending more time together lately and realized we were made for each other."

"Yeah," Nick said impatiently. "I got that part. What I'd like you to explain is the part about you getting so drunk you didn't know what you were doing, then you woke up and decided it was all meant to be."

Dante watched Nick. He knew that part of Cornelia's story had a huge hole in it. Unfortunately, Cornelia didn't know that. "It sounds like you understand just fine," he finally said, unwilling to explain any further.

Progeny

"Dante," Nick said, trying to force patience into his voice. "We both know you can't get that drunk. Sure you can get drunk, but you know exactly what you're doing the entire time. Your warrior blood expels the toxins in your system before you experience memory loss."

Dante sighed. "Cornelia doesn't know that," he admitted. "But the rest of the story is true. We were both drunk. Only I remember everything and she doesn't."

"Tell me the real story, from the beginning," Nick requested.

"We got into town and dealt with the stuff at the bank. It was a blow to find out my father was responsible for Lillie's dilemma, too. I realized I needed to fill Cornelia in on the entire story," Dante said, staring out the window.

"You told her everything?" Nick asked a little surprised, but relieved. He and Thomas had recognized weeks ago that Dante and Cornelia had feelings for each other. To them, it seemed like Cornelia was open with Dante but Dante was still holding back.

"I did," Dante said, turning to face Nick. "She was great about it," he gave a little laugh. "Actually, she reminded me of you. She wanted to know why Carlo and Shannon are still alive."

"I knew I liked that girl," Nick said happily.

"You do realize that doesn't help, don't you?" Dante asked.

"How's that?" Nick asked, confused.

"Now I have two of you to worry about," Dante said, turning back to stare out the window. "I know how intensely you hate my father and Shannon. Cornelia seems to be right there with you on that one. It scares me. I couldn't live with myself if you did something, if you got yourself into trouble, because of my family."

Nick sighed. "Dante, I told you years ago that I would back off. I'm not going to do anything that will send me to the island. I have too much to lose. I always have but now that I found Lillie, I would never risk that. I can't live without her."

"I'm counting on that," Dante said softly. He could never vocalize the feelings he had for Nick, they ran too deep. But if anything bad happened to his friend because of him, it would kill Dante. Now, Cornelia was exhibiting the same rage and indignation against Carlo that Nick had shown for years.

"You're getting off subject," Nick said, breaking into Dante's thoughts. "You were going to tell me how you ended up married."

"After I told Cornelia the sordid details of my past, we decided to go out. We went clubbing. That's where I got the information about Chen Lu. One drink turned into another and pretty soon Cornelia was drunk. That woman cannot hold her liquor. I don't really remember how the topic came up in the first place, I was pretty bombed myself. One minute we were dancing, the next we were walking into a quaint little chapel. I didn't plan on going through with it, but she seemed so happy and I just couldn't say no. So, we got married and I took her back to the penthouse."

"I know you care about her, but do you love her?" Nick asked seriously. "Well, I guess I should ask another question first. Do you two plan on staying married?"

Dante didn't answer immediately. He wasn't sure he knew what to say. Finally, he turned to Nick and tried to explain. "The first time I got married, I did it out of obligation. I married Shannon to please my father and because I thought she needed protection. I hoped I would grow to love her eventually, but I knew it was temporary so that part didn't really matter. Unfortunately, I did come to care about her. I was never truly in love with Shannon, thank goodness," Dante sighed. "This time, with Cornelia I already love her. It's taken me some time to figure that out, but I do. It's ironic really, I married Cornelia for love but she thinks it was for protection and obligation. If I don't let her believe that, she's going to leave me. I need more time. I don't know how long Cornelia and I will be together, but I know I'd like it to last forever."

Nick considered Dante's words. "You said you loved Shannon, but you were never in love with her. Are you in love with Cornelia?"

"I love her," Dante said again. "Is it the same kind of love you have for Lillie, or the intense love Thomas has for Abby? I really don't know. I know I can't stand the thought of losing her. I know the attraction we share is more intense than anything I've ever felt before. But I've watched how you and Thomas are with your women and

I'm just not there, maybe I never will be. Maybe that's not possible for me."

"You do realize we didn't get here overnight don't you?" Nick asked. "The bond I have with Lillie and the bond Thomas shares with Abby developed over time. We each had our own struggles to overcome. We overcame our obstacles, you can overcome yours."

"I guess that's my point. I need time," Dante said seriously. "All I know right now is I don't want to lose her. As Cornelia puts it we both have daddy issues. On top of that, I have ex-wife issues. I know you always thought I would find someone to love Nick, but I honestly never believed it would happen for me. I don't have the best track record and I just hope I don't mess this up. I guess that's why it took me so long to realize I wanted more than friendship with her. I didn't even begin to understand what I wanted until we were standing there, in that tiny little chapel in front of strangers. I knew Cornelia was drunk and didn't know what she was doing, but I couldn't stop it. No matter how wrong it was, I just couldn't stop it. I think if I have enough time, I can make her happy. I don't deserve her but with time, she might come to love me, too."

"Well, as an outsider looking in I think she might already be there," Nick said honestly. "It's obvious to me that she cares for you a great deal. That's a good start. And, I'll do whatever I can to help you get the time you need to figure this out."

"Thanks," Dante said. "Now, let's go meet Chen Lu."

Progeny

Nick had been so involved in the conversation he hadn't realized the car was parked on the curb. "Anything else I need to know about the man before we go in?"

"Just that he has some amazing items in the back room," Dante said with a smile. "In fact, I think he might have just what you've been looking for."

"Really?" Nick asked, getting a little excited. He'd been searching everywhere for the perfect ring for Lillie. Once he covered the stores in New York he started scouring the outlying areas. If he could find the right ring on this trip, he would be amazed.

Chen Lu was sitting behind the counter when the two men walked in. He glanced around then quietly told them to change the open sign to closed. He obviously didn't want company. Dante flipped the sign then approached the counter. "I'd like you to meet my good friend, Nick Moretti."

Chen Lu gave Nick a quick nod then focused on Dante. "Sit," he ordered.

Dante smiled and pulled out a bench. "Before you get too comfortable, my friend here is in the market for a wedding set for his lovely woman. She's really too good for him, but its true love and all that."

Chen Lu studied Nick then turned and stepped through the door.

Melanie P. Smith

"You're right, you know. Lillie is too good for me, but for some reason she loves me and I'm going to take advantage of that," Nick said, taking a seat beside Dante.

Dante sat in silence, considering Nick's words. He knew Lillie wasn't too good for his friend. They were perfect for each other. If Nick underestimated himself when it came to Lillie was it possible he was doing the same with Cornelia? Could he be perfect for his new wife? It seemed like too much to hope for.

Chen Lu stepped back into the room with the same felt tray he had used for Dante and a small ring box. He handed the box to Dante then set down the tray. It had some items on it Dante hadn't seen on his previous trip. He was happy to see Chen Lu had brought back the large diamond accented with sapphires. Dante knew it was just the right ring for Lillie. It matched her eyes perfectly.

Nick studied the selection then grinned at Dante. "You nailed it," he said confidently. "It's exactly what I was looking for."

Chen Lu waited silently. He had no idea which ring the man wanted but obviously, the decision was unanimous.

"I'll take this one," Nick said indicating the diamonds and sapphires. The two men talked price for a short time then Nick provided Chen Lu Lillie's size for alteration. Chen Lu told Nick he could return the following day and the ring would be ready. Nick tried to hand Chen Lu his credit card but the jeweler refused. He insisted on waiting for payment until the ring was ready for delivery.

Progeny

"Now," Chen Lu said placing the rings in the locked case. "We have other business to discuss."

"Were you able to learn anything about The Pooch?" Dante asked.

"Hai," Chen Lu nodded. "He hasn't been here long. Information is limited," he admitted. "He spends a lot of time on the streets in North Vegas."

Dante nodded, Chen Lu was confirming his instincts had been right.

"He's unstable and many say unpredictable," Chen Lu continued. "Use caution," he warned. "Some say he got his name from his looks, others describe him as a junkyard dog. Easy to rile and hard to shake."

Dante frowned. If this guy was a live wire, chances were good that their secret had already been discovered. He wasn't sure what they were supposed to do about that. Could they eliminate the threat or would they have to get creative? "Thank you, Chen Lu," he finally said. "I appreciate all you've done." He handed over an envelope full of cash.

"No charge this time," Chen Lu said, rejecting the envelope. "One more thing."

Dante frowned. He wanted Chen Lu to be paid for his efforts. "What's that?" he asked, sliding the envelope back into his pocket. He'd make sure Chen Lu got the money one way or another. If nothing else, he'd just add it to the next payment.

"He's been seen with another man lately. A large man," Chen Lu added. "I haven't discovered who, but I'm working on it," he paused. "Be very careful. The Pooch is always armed. It sounds like the other man might be something like a bodyguard."

Nick and Dante stood. "Thanks again for everything."

"Man that buzz like fly eventually gets squashed like bug," Chen Lu said in warning.

"I'll be back tomorrow afternoon to pick up the ring," Nick added, smiling. "It was a pleasure to meet you. And don't worry about Dante here. I've got his back, no bug stew on this trip."

Chen Lu gave a little bow as the two men exited the building. Once they were back in the limo they began debating their next move. One thing was obvious, they needed to ditch the driver.

"Joe," Dante called through the open partition. "Looks like you get the rest of the night off."

Joe glanced at the men through the rearview mirror. "You sure you won't need me later?"

"Yeah," they both said in unison. "We're sure."

Joe smiled then pulled into traffic. It was rare for him to have a full night off. He wasn't going to argue.

Cornelia waited for the door to shut then turned to Lillie. "I don't think we're going to get anything from here," she said resigned. "Nothing we didn't already know. Shannon was pompous and arrogant. Nobody seems to like her, but I'm not getting the impression anyone hated her enough to kidnap her. Just petty women stuff."

"I agree," Lillie said, completely relaxed. "So, are you going to put all the treatments on Carlo's bill?"

"Probably, why?" Cornelia asked.

"Because I signed us up for a pedicure," Lillie admitted. "Several women I spoke to said Shannon always had one when she visited the spa. Everyone says Shannon insisted Mattie Gable perform her pedicures. I made sure we got in with her," Lillie glanced at Cornelia. "I know it's a long shot, but I thought it was worth a try. I'm just feeling a little guilty about sticking Carlo with the bill. I haven't felt this relaxed in my life."

Cornelia smiled. "Let's see if Mattie the foot doctor gives us anything. Then we'll decide who pays the bill." Cornelia thought that was a good compromise. Sure, Nick could afford to pay for Lillie to have a pedicure but Cornelia still found it annoying that Dante had to pay his own father to leave him alone. The bigger her bill, the happier she would be.

"Okay," Lillie agreed. "I think I can live with that."

Two hours later the women settled in at Carlo and Eric's casino. Mattie had actually given them a lead. They were both a little surprised that Shannon had started selling at the spa. They had located two women who had bought cocaine from Shannon. Cornelia had to threaten them to get them to confess, but once they started talking, they couldn't seem to stop. Neither woman thought they had gleaned any information Chen Lu hadn't already provided, but it was good to have proof to back up the claims.

Lillie watched Cornelia for several minutes before she decided to plunge in. "Cornelia?"

"Yeah," Cornelia answered absently. She was watching the floor, hoping to see something suspicious they could check out.

"This whole marriage thing with Dante," Lillie began.

Cornelia refocused her attention on Lillie. She didn't know what the woman was going to ask, but she knew her answer would be important.

"It all seemed to happen so fast," Lillie continued.

"It did," Cornelia admitted. Where was Lillie going with this?

"I was just hoping..." Lillie broke off. She didn't know exactly how to find out what she wanted to know.

"What is it you really want to ask Lillie?" Cornelia finally said, watching Lillie closely.

"You know that Nick and Dante are close...very close," she corrected. "But you may not know I've come to care about Dante as well. I never had any siblings, but Dante is like a big brother to me. I just want him to be happy. He's had so much sadness in his life," Lillie paused.

Cornelia continued to wait, Lillie would get to the point eventually. Was Lillie going to tell her she didn't think Cornelia was good enough for Dante? Well, she would be right about that but Cornelia didn't think she could take it from Lillie. Cornelia thought they had become friends since they'd gotten to know each other at the cabin.

"I just need to know that you love him," Lillie blurted. "I can see you care about him but are you in love with him?"

Cornelia was surprised by the question. She let out the breath she'd been holding. "I do love Dante," Cornelia said honestly. "I don't feel like our relationship has developed any faster than you and Nick. In fact, I feel like I've known Dante...well all the warriors actually, a lot longer than you have. Why are you doubting my love for the man I just married?"

Lillie sat back and studied Cornelia. The woman was right. Lillie and Nick hadn't known each other that long, but Cornelia just didn't seem that happy to be married. "I am madly in love with Nick. Right now, I'm sitting here anxiously waiting for him to walk through that door. I miss him when he's not near me. I know that sounds needy and pathetic, but I think it's natural. We are so in love being apart is difficult," she paused, not knowing how to explain her feelings. "Every time I talk to Zarah about our wedding I feel so happy, so blessed and extremely nervous. I want everything to be perfect for Nick and his mom. I guess you just don't seem that happy to be married. You seem more resigned to the fact. If Nick and I just got married, I'd be itching to dance on the table and announce it to the world."

Cornelia understood where Lillie was coming from. If this was a real marriage, if Dante actually loved her too, Cornelia would be bubbling over with happiness. How could she explain that to Lillie without giving away their secret?

"I'm sorry," Lillie said, a little ashamed. "I know it's different for everyone. Just tell me to mind my own business."

"No, it's not that," Cornelia said reluctantly. "I am thrilled to be married to Dante. I do love him. Don't ever doubt that. It's just, I don't know. I wonder if he's happy. We were both drunk when we said I do. I can't help wondering if he's just staying married to protect me." She glanced at Lillie then continued. "I know Dante told Nick what I am, so I assume Nick's talked to you about it, too. That's one thing I do know. Two people that love each other the way you do, wouldn't keep secrets."

"I know," Lillie admitted. "I hope you know it doesn't matter. I'd never judge you based on where you came from. It would be rather hypocritical don't you think? I mean, you know all my dirty little secrets. My father was wonderful, but I don't know much about my mother. Then there were all the foster homes and to top it off, there was Brad. We all have skeletons in our closets," she took Cornelia's hand.

Progeny

"Mine are just a little darker than everyone else's," Cornelia supplied.

"I don't think so," Lillie said sincerely. "As far as I'm concerned you are just a sweet woman that helped me to feel welcome in a new world," she paused, then smiled. "I do hate you a little for being so gorgeous and sophisticated, but I'm getting over that little by little."

Cornelia was surprised by that. Lillie was a dark haired beauty. She couldn't honestly believe that. "Right back at you," Cornelia said lightly. "I'm okay, but you Lillie are a knockout. Haven't you noticed the hordes of men checking you out since we arrived?"

"No," Lillie disagreed. "They're checking you out. Chances are they'll stop to talk to me just to get a little closer to the beautiful woman I'm sitting with. They're probably hoping for an introduction."

"I guess we'll just have to disagree on that one. Maybe we could call a truce, call it a mutual concession. I'll forgive you for being beautiful if you will forgive me," Cornelia suggested.

"Deal," Lillie agreed, touching her glass to Cornelia's. "So, I've noticed you are scoping out the joint. See anything interesting?"

Cornelia smiled, "Not yet, but our men should be here soon. That will be interesting. I always love to watch Dante enter a room. He seems so oblivious to the attention he draws without effort."

Lillie laughed. "You've noticed that, huh? Nick's the same way," she relaxed a little. Hadn't she been apprehensive about her relationship with Nick in the beginning? Public displays of affection had made her almost hyperventilate. Maybe Cornelia had the same problem. Lillie grinned. "Tonight we're in for double the pleasure. The women in this place won't know what hit them."

Cornelia nodded. "And they are all ours," she added, wishing that were true. But the casual exchange had broken the ice. The two women shifted to everyday girl talk while they waited for their men to arrive.

* * * *

Sam pulled a file from her briefcase and settled in for a long night of boring paperwork. She was falling behind. This particular project was the most pressing. She'd been so excited when Alex promoted her to Director. John's job had looked so easy from the outside. Now that D-Tech was her responsibility, her viewpoint had changed drastically. They were trying to get a new contract, but the police department wanted some alterations. Since they were paying for the changes, she needed to get the programming figured out and quick. She was finally getting somewhere when the doorbell rang.

Sam waited, hoping Ty would take care of it. No luck. She pushed back from her desk and strolled to the door. Her annoyance immediately changed to concern when she saw the family standing on her front porch.

Progeny

Vivian was crying, but trying to be strong. Sam assumed the hysterical woman by her side was her mother. There was also a small boy of around ten holding the woman's hand. He was covered in blood. She glanced back at Vivian and realized she was also covered in blood.

"Bring her inside," Sam said, guiding the woman through the door. Sam led them to the family room and helped the woman onto the couch. "What happened?" She said, turning to Vivian.

"We were attacked," Vivian said soberly. She sat next to her mother and pulled the weeping woman into her arms.

"Let me get her some tea," Sam said, worried. She rushed to the intercom and pressed a button. "Ty, I need you in the family room." Then she hurried to the kitchen to prepare some tea, anxious to hear the rest of the story.

Ty glanced at the intercom and considered ignoring it. He was deep in the middle of code and didn't want to start over later. After another second he sighed and gave in. There was a tone in Sam's voice that worried him. As he entered the room, he knew something was terribly wrong. Sam wasn't there, but Vivian was with her mother and a boy that Ty assumed was her brother. "Vivian, what's going on?"

"Sam went to get my mother some tea. I think she'll be back any minute," Vivian began. She was doing her best to maintain control, but a sob escaped anyway.

Ty was on his way to find Sam when she stepped through the door.

"Vivian," Sam called. "I assume this is your family, but we've never met. Can you introduce us?"

"Oh, sorry," Vivian said shaking her head. "This is my mother, Virginia and my brother Jeffrey."

"It's very nice to meet you, Jeffrey," Ty said taking the young boys hand. He was extremely curious. Obviously, something terrible had happened. They were all covered in blood.

"Virginia, try to drink some tea. It will help settle your nerves," Sam said handing the woman a small cup. Sam turned to Vivian. "Tell us what happened."

Vivian swallowed the lump in her throat and began to relay the events of the evening. "We heard a noise outside then our neighbor, Cody Stewart pounded on the door. He was frantic and told dad we were being invaded. The two of them rushed outside to try to protect the neighborhood." Another tear ran down Vivian's cheek, but she brushed it away impatiently. "I rushed to the window and saw how many vampires were outside. I knew two men couldn't hold them off alone. I hurried to my room and got the bow and arrows Sam gave me." She glanced at Samantha then closed her eyes. "Thank you for that. It saved the three of us tonight."

"Where is your father, Vivian?" Ty asked soberly.

"My father is dead," Jeffrey told Ty almost defiantly.

Progeny

Ty looked to Vivian for confirmation. She nodded once, then continued her story. "I was able to get into a tree and began killing the vampires. Dad and Mr. Stewart continued to fight in the street. I knew the moment dad was killed. Mr. Stewart was injured and dad moved in to try and protect him. Once dad died, they swarmed my neighbor and he was killed as well. I continued shooting the vampires one after the other. Finally, they began to retreat. I don't know if they left the neighborhood or just moved to a spot where they could find easier prey."

Ty stood and moved toward the door. "I'll call you," he said over his shoulder then rushed to his car. As he pulled out of the driveway he was dialing Victor.

"This better be important," Victor said, sounding a little breathless.

"Where are you?" Ty asked.

"Fira's," Victor shouted. "And I'm a little busy, what do you want?"

"Are you fighting?" Ty asked, surprised.

"Yeah," Victor got out before the phone went dead.

Ty didn't hesitate. He needed to help Victor. Then they'd continue on to the Moore's neighborhood. He pulled up with a screech and jumped out of his truck. Victor was in trouble and he was alone. Where was Bastian? Ty jumped in and the two of them dealt with the large group surrounding Fira's house.

Once the vampires were dead, Ty turned to Victor. "Dahl was abducted from this house. We should have thought of that. Of course, the vampires would know another Fae would live here now that it's occupied again."

Fira slung the door open and studied the warriors. "You two okay?" She asked, worried.

"We're fine. Go back inside and lock the doors," Victor told her. "If they return, call Orin immediately. He knows how to reach us," then he turned to Ty. "We need to go check on Bastian."

"How did you two get separated?" Ty asked.

"Orin called and said Fira was in trouble," Victor frowned. "We were on our way over when Bastian noticed another neighborhood under attack. He broke off to help and I continued on to Fira's. I need to get back. He may be in trouble," Victor froze, "Wait, why are you here?"

"Vivian's father has been killed," Ty said soberly. "She said their neighbor, Cody Stewart was also killed. She was able to get her mother and brother away. They're at my house with Sam."

"Let's check on Bastian then we can head north and check on the Moore's neighbors," Victor decided.

As Ty and Victor came around the corner they spotted Bastian. He was headed their way. "Looks like you survived old man, barely," Victor called out. Once they reached Bastian, Victor studied his friend. "Are you hurt?"

"They're all superficial," Bastian grumbled. "Is Fira alright?"

"For now," Victor assured him. "She was definitely in trouble, though."

"So was your partner when I arrived," Ty joked. "Once again I saved the day."

Bastian turned his attention to Ty. "What are you doing here anyway?"

"If you're okay, we need to head over to the Moore's neighborhood," Victor said soberly. "Vivian's father has been killed."

Ty, Victor and Bastian pulled into Ty's driveway. They climbed from the car, exhausted. The moment they stepped through the door Sam was by Ty's side.

"I've been so worried," Sam scolded. "I thought you were going to call."

"Sorry," Ty said, pulling Sam close. "Things got hectic and I didn't have a chance."

"Dimitri and Alex are here," Sam informed them. "I called them shortly after you left. Virginia has been so hysterical and I realized both Vivian and Jeffrey had wounds. I thought Alex should take a look at the kids."

The warriors continued into the family room to discuss the situation.

Chapter Nine

Dante and Nick stepped from the cab and studied the area. They were so used to battling vamps, dealing with humans was going to be a challenge. They didn't want to hurt anyone. "Let's just wander a bit," Dante suggested.

"Good idea," Nick agreed.

Twenty minutes later they were approaching a grungy alley when a man jumped from behind a dumpster. Nick pivoted, easily avoiding the knife aimed at his ribs. The attacker lost his balance and almost stumbled to the ground. Dante stepped in, knocked the knife from his hand, and shoved him against the brick wall, holding him in place by the back of his neck.

Nick casually reached down and picked up the knife. "If that's the best you got, I'd say you need a new hobby, kid." He stepped forward to crowd the man. The guy couldn't be more than twenty. Nick assumed his attacker was homeless. His teeth were so yellow they were almost black and the man reeked something awful. He took a subtle step back then sighed. "We're looking for The Pooch."

"Don't know no Pooch," the kid croaked.

Dante tightened his grip. "We don't like repeating ourselves. Maybe you should try again." Both Nick and Dante had read the recognition in the man's eyes.

The alley was silent.

"Billy won't talk." A male voice came from the alley. "He's afraid of everyone. Let him go and I'll tell you what I know."

Nick turned, trying to adjust his vision to accommodate the shadows, he could barely make out a man half way down the narrow pathway. "And who might you be?" he finally asked.

"Look, Billy's an idiot but you have his knife. Let the man go and we'll talk," the voice came again.

Nick looked at Dante, who shrugged then leaned in and whispered something in Billy's ear. Once the kid was free he ran into the open and escaped down the sidewalk. Nick and Dante continued further into the dim alleyway. They hadn't gone far before they were standing in front of the man casually sitting next to a military tent.

The guy glanced back toward the roadway then studied the two warriors. "Mind telling me what you said to him?"

Dante smiled, "Yeah, as a matter of fact, I do." He studied the guy who hadn't moved an inch. His gaze moved slowly around the area, taking in his surroundings. "You offered information about The Pooch in exchange for the release of your friend. Was that a lie, or do you really know the man?"

"I'm familiar with the man," the guy admitted. These two punks were obviously used to getting information by intimidation.

Nick was watching the exchange and realized they were taking the wrong approach. "You have a name?" He asked, trying to sound friendly.

"Most people do," the man replied.

Dante laughed and held out a hand. "I'm Dante and this is my good friend, Nick."

The man hesitated then shook the warrior's hands. "Cameron, but most people call me Cam."

Dante shifted his gaze to the tent. "Just the tent or are you a military man?"

"Both," Cam said, not sure how he felt about these two yet.

"Please, slow down," Dante said holding up a hand. "I can't keep up with the constant jabber. The excessive information is confusing me," Dante grinned, amused. He was starting to like this guy.

Cam smiled.

"So, why are you living out here?" Nick asked, truly curious. "If you're a military man that seems odd."

Cam sobered. His injuries weren't a secret, but he didn't know these guys. Did he really want them to know he was vulnerable?

"Uncle Sam's disability check doesn't go far in the real world does it?" Dante asked knowingly. "Its cool man, we're not here to cause problems or rob you. We're just looking for someone," Dante smiled. "Although, I really dig the rainbow windsock. Very manly."

Cam laughed. "Garcia thought that would bruise my ego. It doesn't, but I'm definitely more cautious when I accept a bet with that man these days."

Nick and Dante laughed. It sounded like something the warriors would do.

"The Pooch hasn't been around for about a week now, maybe a little longer," Cam said, deciding to trust the men. He didn't know why, but they came across as honest. "Before that, he only dropped by to harass the locals."

"We heard he has a bodyguard, big guy that goes with him everywhere," Dante supplied.

"That would be Tiny," Cam said, sighing. "I tried to talk to Tiny about that, but for some reason he thinks he can trust that criminal."

"Tiny?" Nick asked.

"Yeah, the guy's about thirtyish but has the mentality of a nine-year-old. I suspect the Pooch bought him a Big Mac or something. Give Tiny food and he's loyal until you cross him. For now, Tiny's loyal to the Pooch," Cam told them. It was obvious he didn't approve of the friendship.

"I assume Tiny hasn't been around either?" Dante asked.

"Nope," Cam agreed. "I made it pretty clear to the Pooch that he's not welcome here. He pushed a little, but when I didn't back down and Tiny wouldn't get involved, he backed off. Tiny and I have an understanding. He likes me enough to avoid any problems. I assume they've moved on."

"Greener pastures?" Dante mused.

"What could be greener than this little island paradise?" Cam joked.

"You've got a point there," Dante grinned. "Doesn't it get a little hot and smelly in the summer?"

"Compared to Iraq?" Cam asked, "Naw. I suffered through 120 degree summers in a tent built just like this one with twenty other men. At least I don't have to deal with the dust storms," he paused. "Or Camel Spiders. Like I said, an island paradise."

"I guess it's all in the perspective," Dante agreed. "You ever heard of The Waterson House? I hear it's a great place for guys like you to get back on their feet."

Cam stiffened. "Yeah, I heard of it."

Nick and Dante exchanged looks. Something was wrong here. "I hear there's one here in Vegas. Maybe you should check it out," Nick added.

"No thanks," Cam said, annoyed. "Been there, done that. That weasel Cunningham is lucky he's still alive," Cam glanced at an elderly woman headed their way. "Now if you'll excuse me, business is booming, my customers need me."

Dante was about to object when his phone rang. He stepped to the side and answered it. "Yeah, Thomas. What can I do for you?"

"Have you found Shannon yet?" Thomas said, not wasting time.

"Working on it," Dante said a little annoyed.

"Well, work faster," Thomas pushed. "We've got a mess in New York. Expect a call from Dimitri ordering you back home. If you want another day, I'd shut off my phone. He'll think you're out of range if it goes directly to voicemail."

"What kind of mess?" Dante asked, worried. The warriors never shut off their phones.

"Vampires, what else," Thomas sighed. "They attacked in groups tonight. Somehow they located addresses for some of our people. There were a few fatalities and numerous casualties. Alex has been busy tonight. So have Ty, Victor and Bastian. With you and Nick in Vegas that leaves us extremely short handed. I'm still at the Fort with Abby, we were trying to sneak out to help you but changed our plans when I learned Nick conned his way into that assignment ahead of me. It's better this way, I really didn't want word to get out that I was in Vegas on behalf of your father. Anyway, Abby and I will be flying out tonight, which will help if there's another attack tomorrow. Dimitri has to stay with Alex. He's worried she'll overdo it again. That made things even worse tonight. It left three warriors to handle over a dozen attacks. They were spread thin, sometimes fighting alone. Like I said New York is a mess."

Dante ran a hand through his hair. "Thanks for the warning," Dante turned and kicked the dumpster. "I'll call you tonight. Don't try to call me, I'm taking your advice and shutting down the phone," he paused. "If all the warriors are in New York, who is going to protect the Fort?"

"Atticus and Tala are staying. So are Marta and Jake. Tony and Megan are heading back with me. Morrigan and Nadia are staying. Between the six of them, Atticus thinks they can handle it. Dusty and Nebi are back, too. So, I guess that makes eight. You know if there's trouble Dusty and Nebi will jump in and help."

"I don't like it," Dante admitted. "I'll tie things up here as soon as I can so we can return to New York. Keep your phone handy. I'll call you tonight when I'm back at the casino."

"Be careful out there," Thomas requested. "I know I told you to hurry, but don't get sloppy."

"Gotta go," Dante said, shutting down the call. He turned and saw Nick and Cam watching him.

Dante took a deep breath and strolled back over to the two men. He studied the human then turned to Nick. "Turn off your phone. We just entered a dead zone."

Nick looked at Dante in surprise. They never shut down their phones. The trouble must be big.

Dante turned back to Cam. "I just ran out of time and I need all the help you can give me. No more bullshit. We need to find The Pooch. A relative is missing, a woman. Her name is Shannon Santora. You may have seen her around these parts selling cocaine. Tiny redhead?"

Cam studied Dante, clearly the man just received bad news. He'd seen the woman. She was a complete snob. "Guess you can't pick your relatives."

"That's an understatement," Dante said without humor. "I take it you've met her."

"I have," Cam agreed. "I didn't like her either, but for different reasons. She's a snob and clearly an addict herself. Not much on patience as I recall."

"That's Shannon," Dante agreed. "Have you heard anything about her abduction?"

Cam studied the two men. "No, but if the Pooch is involved I might be able to help," he admitted.

"How?" Nick asked.

"Rumor has it the Pooch has been staying in a cabin just outside of town," Cam told them. "I've never been there, but I can give you rough directions. They should get you close enough to find the place. Unfortunately, I can't get you closer than that. There are several cabins out there, all of them vacant from what I hear. The Pooch decided to occupy one of them. I don't think he's been invited."

"Figures," Dante said. He handed Cam a pen and a small notebook. Then waited while the man drew out a rough map. Once Cam was finished, Dante thanked him then shifted topics. "Now, would you mind telling me about this Cunningham?"

Cam narrowed his eyes. "Why?" He finally asked. "What's it to you?" He glanced down at Dante's shoes. "Clearly, you're not in need of charity."

"Humor me," Dante pressed.

"There's not much to tell," Cam began, staring into the distance. "I returned from Iraq on a medical transport.

Progeny

After months of rehab, I was finally released. I tried to get a job but apparently didn't have the right skills. Manual labor was out. My back can't handle it. So, I went to visit one of my men. A Gunnery Sergeant of mine. I'd heard his girl left him, cheated on him then dumped him when she found out he had lost a leg. I needed to check on him to ensure he was coming through it all okay. I knew the last place he was living was in Denver. It took me some time to find Rick. His girlfriend had indeed dumped him for another man. When I finally found him, he was living in one of those homes. The Waterson Home, I mean."

Nick and Dante exchanged knowing looks. Cam had to be talking about Rick Simmons.

"He was so happy there," Cam continued. "He took me in for the night. We had a long talk. Rick had been so depressed when he returned from Iraq. He'd lost his leg, but he believed he still had his girl. When he got home and found her in bed with another man that broke what little spirit he had left. He was living on the streets barely surviving. He admitted he didn't really care if he survived. That's when a woman found him in the park. She took him back to The Waterson House and nursed him back to health. It wasn't easy. Rick had to be detoxified first. His wound was causing him a lot of trouble and he'd become addicted to the pain meds. Anyway, once he was clean a couple guys came to visit. Hardcore, arrogant pricks from the sound of it. They interrogated Gunny for hours. When they were finished Rick was escorted back to his room. He was sure he'd be thrown out, but a couple days later a doctor arrived and transported him to a clinic where he had a much needed operation. It seems some shrapnel from the bomb was still lodged in his leg. It was the reason Rick was still in so much pain. Once he recovered, he was hired on at Waterson. Within a few months, he was promoted. Last I heard he was happy again. I believe he fell for the girl who rescued him in that park," Cam sighed. "I eventually moved on. Denver was too cold. When I heard about the House here in town I decided to check it out," Cam scowled again. "That's when I met Cunningham. Rick had such a good experience in Denver I was shocked at the difference."

"So, what was different here?" Nick asked.

"Cunningham took me to a room, well a closet really. It was right next to the large central air unit. The place was noisy and cramped. There was a small cot, a tiny dresser and a card table with one chair. Cunningham informed me that I could stay at the house and this would be my room. In exchange for such lofty accommodations, I would need to work from sun up to sun down doing whatever he needed done that day. In addition, I would be required to cash my military check and turn over the cash each month. He was pretty shocked when I told him where he could shove his offer," Cam smiled. "Seriously, the man thought I would give up this private tent and complete freedom to be his slave. And, to top it all off I basically had to pay him for that ridiculous honor."

Nick and Dante were seething. "Excuse me," Dante said and moved away again. He switched his phone back on and dialed The Home. "Hello, Charlotte," Dante said when the woman answered.

Progeny

"Dante!" Charlotte said, excited to hear from her boss. "What can I do for you on this fine day?"

"Is Dave Cunningham around today?" Dante asked.

Charlotte sobered. "He was earlier. I think he'll be back this afternoon. He didn't say where he was going, but he's settled into a pretty regular routine. If we don't see him this afternoon he'll be here later tonight."

"Oh?" Dante asked. "What's the new schedule?" He wanted details.

"Well," Charlotte hesitated. She hated the man, but she wasn't in the habit of ratting on a co-worker.

"Tell me," Dante ordered.

"He typically comes in first thing in the morning then takes off until around noon. Then we don't see him until dinner time and then never more than twenty minutes. Sometimes he returns later in the evening, but mostly he stays away until the following morning."

"I see," Dante said, getting angrier by the minute. "I need a favor," he finally told her. "I need room 108 cleaned and prepared for a new tenant."

"Uh..." Charlotte stalled. "Cunningham said he already had someone moving into that room."

"You know I gave specific instructions to keep it vacant." Had they neglected things out here for so long all their employees were out of control?

"I know," Charlotte admitted. "I tried to tell him. Dave overruled me. He has some woman moving in tomorrow," she paused. "I think she might be a prostitute."

"Prepare the room," Dante ordered. "I believe I'm still in charge here and I say it's taken. I also need you to find someone to drive the van. I'll call you back in a few minutes."

"Okay," Charlotte said. She was worried about her job. What was she going to do if Dante was mad enough to fire her as well as Dave?

Dante walked back to Cam and studied the man. Then he glanced at Nick, waiting for approval. Once Nick gave him the nod, Dante began. "It seems Waterson has an opening with much better accommodations. Can I talk you into giving the place another chance?"

Cam looked from Dante to Nick. "No offense, but I think I'll just stay here."

"Did you know that Rick Simmons got engaged last month?" Nick asked casually.

"Of course he doesn't," Dante said before Cam could reply. "I guess there are no phones in paradise, huh?"

"So, Gunny's getting married. That's great," Cam said truly happy for his friend.

"Well, it would be except they haven't been able to set a date yet," Nick continued.

Progeny

"Why not?" Cam said, not understanding where this was headed.

"Because Rick refuses to get married without you. And, since he has no idea where you are, he can't set a date until he hires a Private Investigator to track you down," Nick said, annoyed.

"For someone that claims to be such a great friend, I'm surprised you haven't at least checked in to see how he's doing," Dante added.

Cam frowned. "I'll find a way to be at the wedding."

"Or you could just stop being stubborn and take the room we offered. The House comes with a phone," Nick told him.

Cam smiled. "Am I correct in assuming I just met the arrogant pricks?"

The warriors grinned. "You might say that," Dante said casually.

"Does Cunningham still have a job?" Cam asked.

"For the moment," Dante admitted. "However, it seems we have a management position opening up this afternoon. I heard you refer to your men a couple times during that story. What was your rank?"

"Lt. Colonel," Cam said, trying to decide what he would do if they continued to pressure him to move to the place.

"Sounds like you're qualified," Nick pointed out. "So, what do you say? If Cunningham is gone, you willing to give the place a shot?"

"Why?" Cam asked. "I'm sure there are plenty of candidates out there that could use a leg up. Why do you want me?"

"I've seen you in action," Nick replied. "This is your alley. These people rely on you. I saw you interact with that woman. You gave her some winter gloves with that sack of food. You take care of these people. You're a born leader and you clearly care about those in need. That's the kind of guy we need at Waterson. I knew there was something I didn't like about Cunningham, but we live in New York. We had no idea he was extorting money that way. He took advantage of the situation. Clearly, you wouldn't. We need someone we can trust to take care of those in need."

"But that's my point, what makes you think you can trust me?" Cam asked.

"Because you're doing it already and there's nothing in it for you," Dante provided. "You already take care of these people in your little paradise alley. We're giving you the opportunity to continue on a larger scale," Dante waited. "Don't worry, you can still take care of your people out here. If you have room, move them to the shelter. If not, bring the van out and continue on with business as usual."

"Can I think about it?" Cam asked.

"Sure," Dante told him. "You have fifteen minutes before the van arrives. How long does it take you to tear down that tent?"

"You are pushy, aren't you?" Cam asked. "I'm not taking the tent. Fred needs it. I'll get him to secure my spot for a week that should be enough time to try the place out and decide if I'm willing to stay."

"I can live with that," Nick said, relieved. He liked Cam and this was exactly the type of guy they had opened Waterson to help. Realistically, he didn't need much and to be honest Nick was sure within a few months, Cam would be helping them more than they ever helped him.

Nick watched as Cam moved to stand. He struggled a little then placed his hand on the brick wall for support. "What happened to the back?" He said leaning down to hand Cam his pack.

"Ruptured disc," he said casually. "The blast only threw me a few feet but the landing was harsh. I collided with a Hummer, the Hummer won. The disc combined with my spinal injury and my knee makes it a little hard to get around."

"How bad was the knee?" Nick pressed.

"Blew it out completely," Cam admitted. "The military docs did what they could, but it's never going to be the same."

Nick was making mental notes. The guy had devoted his life to his country. If there was anything that could be done to improve Cam's mobility, Nick would make sure it got done. Once they got back to the casino he'd be finding a local doctor to discuss the situation.

Dante finished making arrangements and turned to Nick. "We need to go," he turned to Cam. "The van is on the way. I trust you won't bolt before Charlotte arrives?"

"I gave my word, I plan to keep it," Cam scowled.

"Good," Dante grinned. "I'll see you later tonight. Right now we have a cabin to find."

Nick and Dante made their way out of the alley. Nick turned to Dante. "Who called?"

"Thomas," Dante sobered. "There's trouble in New York. We need to try to tie this up tonight and get back. They need our help."

"So, we turned off the phones to avoid Dimitri?" Nick asked.

"Yeah," Dante glanced at Nick. He knew his friend wasn't going to like that. "Thomas suggested it. He thought it would give us a little more time."

"What happened?" Nick pressed.

"They had several attacks tonight. Ty, Victor and Bastian tried to handle it but they were shorthanded. Thomas said they had to split up and fight alone," Dante told him.

"That won't happen again," Nick said with confidence.

"No, because Dimitri is going to call us back before we're done here," Dante scowled.

"No, because Sam, Ariel and Kylee are going to throw a fit. Their men won't dare leave the house without them," Nick corrected.

Dante smiled. Nick was right. The men would definitely be in hot water with their mates. "Good point," Dante paused. "Speaking of women, do you think we should go back and pick ours up before we head out to look for the cabin?"

Nick considered. "Probably," he decided. "We're dealing with humans. I think they can handle it. And I'd rather have them with me than leave them to fend for themselves at the casino."

"I agree," Dante said. "Let's find a cab."

Chapter Ten

Lillie and Cornelia remained in the casino, watching the door. They were both anxious for their men to return. Lillie spotted them first. She nudged Cornelia with a smile. "This is my favorite part," she said softly.

Cornelia looked up and spotted the men. Their entrance was already getting a reaction. Women were staring and starting to drool. She couldn't blame them. The men were off the charts, hot.

"Look at them. They're like Greek Gods." Lillie glanced at Cornelia and saw her friend was just as captivated as she was. "It still makes my stomach do cartwheels the instant he spots me. From that moment on, he only has eyes for me," Lillie sighed. "It still blows me away, the knowledge that the most gorgeous woman on earth could approach my man and he wouldn't even notice her."

Cornelia was taking in the room. "Double the pleasure," she said, amused. "Definitely double the fun."

The men spotted their women at almost the same time. Nick's face instantly lit up and shifted into a huge smile. Dante was more subtle, but his sexy half grin sent butterflies fluttering in Cornelia's stomach.

The moment Dante spotted Cornelia, his mood improved. She was so beautiful and she was his, for now anyway. With any luck, he might convince her to stay forever. He wasn't sure that was possible but he was going to work to keep her with him as long as he could. No matter how much time he had, he was going to enjoy every moment.

Lillie and Cornelia scowled when they spotted the two women approaching their men. Lillie actually growled. Cornelia would have laughed if she wasn't so annoyed. The women were both in their early twenties and clearly believed themselves irresistible. One was wearing the shortest mini-skirt Cornelia had ever seen. The other woman's hot pink pants were so tight she wondered how the girl could breathe. And those six inch heels had to be torture by the end of the night.

Nick didn't spot the trouble until it was too late. The pair moved into place, blocking both his and Dante's path. He'd been so focused on Lillie he hadn't even seen them coming. Definitely an occupational hazard. He glanced at Dante and saw his friend was just as annoyed as he was by the interruption. Their women awaited and they were stuck dealing with a couple of bar flies.

"Hey, boys." One of the women said, trying to sound seductive. Nick cringed, her voice and attitude grated on his last nerve.

"Excuse us," Nick said, trying to sound polite.

The women didn't budge. Nick took a sideways step, hoping to move around the obstacle. Dante took a step in the opposite direction. The move didn't work. The two women must have anticipated it, they both took a similar step and continued to block their path. The one standing in front of Dante reached out a finger and started to trail it down his chest. "I'm so thirsty," she crooned batting her eyes at him. "Do you want to buy me a drink?"

Dante grabbed the woman's hand, holding it away from him. "No," he said, dropping her wrist. "I don't."

The women were clearly surprised. They glanced at each other, which gave Nick and Dante the opportunity to step around them and continue toward the table.

Lillie elbowed Cornelia. "Told you," she said, smiling again. "That's my man. He only has eyes for me," she sighed, content again. "And that sleazy wench is lucky Dante didn't rip her finger off. That'll teach them to stand between a warrior and his woman."

Cornelia let out a little laugh. Watching Dante move toward her, eyes locked on hers, was a heady thing. She'd never experienced anything like it before. When the men finally reached the table, Lillie jumped from her chair and launched herself into Nick's arms. He caught her, laughing and instantly pressed his mouth to hers pulling her closer for a long, seductive kiss.

Dante settled into a chair, leaned in and pulled Cornelia close, shaking his head. "He's corrupted her," he grinned, then pressed his lips to hers.

Nick pulled out Lillie's chair, but instead of lowering her into it, he sat down and settled her onto his lap. He'd missed her while he was away scouring the streets for clues.

Dante's grin widened. "What happened to the shy, reserved woman I loved so dearly?"

Nick pulled her closer, wrapping his arms tighter around Lillie's waist. He was worried she'd become self-conscious and try to get up. He liked having her close and didn't want her to move.

"I fell in love," Lillie said with a shrug. "And my man is so getting lucky tonight." She turned and gave Nick a quick peck on the lips.

Dante watched, raising his eyebrows. "Who are you and what did you do with the pilot?"

"I don't think either of you knows how..." Lillie paused and looked at Cornelia. "What word am I looking for?"

"There are so many to choose from," Cornelia said, deciding to join in the fun. "Stimulating, breathtaking, orgasmic?" she supplied.

"All the above," Lillie agreed with a smile. "You have no idea what it feels like to watch a couple of Greek Gods walk into the room like that. Especially when the most handsome one ever only has eyes for me."

Nick leaned in and nuzzled Lillie's neck. Then noticed she was frowning. "What's wrong, baby?" He felt her body tense and because of their connection he could also feel her annoyance loud and clear.

"Some women just won't give up," she whispered, pressing her lips to Nick's temple.

Nick frowned as the two women who had blocked their path pulled up chairs and joined the small group. Clearly, they couldn't take a hint.

Dante placed an arm over Cornelia's chair and pulled it closer to his. "Ladies, this is a private party and I'm afraid you weren't invited." He knew he was being rude, but he didn't care. He wanted them to leave, now. He needed to talk to the others before they headed out to find the cabins.

The women laughed, assuming he was kidding. Their mouths literally dropped open when Nick stood, placing Lillie on the floor, then took her hand and led her toward the exit. Dante followed suit.

Progeny

Cornelia was shocked. Once they were outside she spoke. "I can't believe you just did that."

"What?" Dante asked casually.

"You know what," Cornelia said exasperated. "Those women thought they were going to get lucky tonight." Then she began to laugh, at first just a little giggle, then a full out belly laugh.

Lillie joined in. The women were almost in hysterics, they were doubled over trying to catch their breath.

Nick and Dante studied each other, clearly confused. Dante narrowed his eyes at Cornelia. "Have you been drinking again?" he finally asked.

"No," she said trying to catch her breath. "Did you see their faces?" Cornelia asked. The moment she looked at Lillie they lost it again. They were both laughing so hard, their eyes watered.

Nick studied Lillie. He had never seen her like this before. He opened up, concentrating on the connection they shared. Lillie was happy, truly happy and excited but underneath the joy, she was still a little annoyed. He shrugged at Dante and continued to watch the women with interest. "Lillie's not drunk, she's just in a good mood."

Dante folded his arms and waited. Cornelia regained her composure first. "I don't think we could explain things adequately, so I'm not even going to try."

Lillie slipped an arm through Nick's, sensing his confusion. He also seemed a little frustrated. "Neither one of you saw their faces," she began, stifling another laugh. "I mean those two were so confident, so sure they could lure you away from the two average specimens you were hanging with. I'm sure it never crossed their minds that you might leave with us instead of them."

Nick and Dante both frowned. "There's nothing average about either of you," Dante grumbled.

"You're so sweet," Lillie said with a smile. "But look at us. We're both wearing jeans, I'm in a sweatshirt, Cornelia a simple cotton T...average. Then look at them. The blond couldn't sit in that skirt without showing off her crotch. And don't get me started on those 'look at me' sex shoes."

"And I'm surprised the brunette didn't split her hot pink Pepto pants right down the middle," Cornelia added.

"Pepto pants?" Dante questioned, wondering how wise it was to ask.

"Yeah," Cornelia grinned. "They reminded me of Pepto Bismol in reverse. They're both bright pink, but instead of giving relief, they made me want to spew."

"Exactly," Lillie exclaimed with a laugh. "Those two were hot and sleazy and ready for a good time," she shrugged. "It never crossed their mind you might walk out on them. No, let me correct that because the two of you practically ran for the exit, ordinary blasé women in tow."

Progeny

Dante and Nick glanced at each other then back to their women. Neither man knew what to think about the female interpretation of events. "You think those two believed we would drop you for them?" Nick said slowly.

The women laughed. "Of course they did," Lillie exclaimed. "They had no doubt about it. That's why they are still sitting in there with their mouths dropped open wondering what happened."

"Then they're idiots," Dante grumbled.

"Cornelia and I took the gold tonight." Lillie leaned in and gave Nick a quick kiss. "It feels good, better than good, it's euphoric and energizing. Like I said before, my man is definitely getting lucky tonight."

Cornelia smiled. "The added bonus was the short trek to the door. Those two women hate us, but the others were green with envy. It's certainly a jolt to my ego, having the two of you around. Like Lillie said I'm pumped. That experience put me on a high."

Dante leaned in closer, trailing a finger down the side of Cornelia's neck. "How high?" Dante whispered softly next to her ear.

Cornelia's breath caught. "Pretty high," she whispered back. "It was euphoric and..."

"Orgasmic?" Dante asked softly, raising one eyebrow.

Cornelia noticed Dante's mouth twitch ever so slightly. He liked throwing her words back at her. She didn't mind, she was having too much fun and she felt a little bold. "Very," she whispered back. "My man's getting lucky tonight, too." She pressed her body a little closer to Dante's hard body and savored his reaction. His kiss was hard, intimate and implied promises she hoped he would keep.

Dante straightened and spotted Nick watching them. He should have felt self-conscious, but he didn't. He hadn't meant to put so much feeling into that kiss, but he couldn't stop himself. Cornelia made him feel, intense feelings he didn't even know he had. That surprised him a little. He experienced so many new emotions with her around. It was going to take time to get used to them all. He reached down and took Cornelia's hand in his. "We need to go. Fun time's over. Nick and I have business at The House then we have some cabins to check out."

"The house?" Cornelia asked.

At the same time, Lillie said, "Cabins?"

"You found something," Cornelia decided, watching Dante.

"Yeah, we got a lead," he admitted. "I think it might be a good one."

"Oh," Lillie said, remembering the message she was supposed to give them. "Dimitri called. He was a little annoyed he couldn't reach either one of you. I promised I'd tell you to call him."

Progeny

Nick and Dante exchanged glances then Dante pulled out his phone and turned it back on. "I also promised Thomas I'd call him." He scrolled through his contacts and selected Thomas' cell phone.

"Hey," Thomas said loudly. There was a lot of noise in the background. "We're just boarding for the city so I don't have much time."

"Anything new?" Dante asked checking his watch. It was late, after midnight in New York.

"I checked in with Alex about ten minutes ago. All the attacks happened early in the evening, right after dark. Once our guys got involved they pretty much died out. It sounds like it was chaos for a few hours, then nothing. The warriors are still out there and plan to stay out all night but it looks like the trouble might be over for now. I just hope we don't have a repeat tomorrow," Thomas paused. "Dimitri's not happy he couldn't reach you, but he thinks you were out of range. My advice, don't confess otherwise. I think you might have another day, two tops. Tomorrow night will be the deciding factor. I know you want to finish this, close the book and all that, but it's possible you might have to dump this back on Carlo and head home. Can you live with that?"

"If I have to," Dante admitted. "I think we got a pretty good lead today. If it pans out, we might be done tonight. Everything seems to be leading to a guy named The Pooch."

"Seriously?" Thomas said, amused. "On purpose?"

"Yeah, yeah. I know," Dante smiled. "Anyway, The Pooch is a small-time dealer that apparently had issues with Shannon. He sounds like the type that might try to use the situation to his advantage. I just can't figure out why my father hasn't heard from him yet. From the picture I'm getting, I'd expect the guy to want ransom. This has to be about money."

"You do realize she might already be dead, don't you?" Thomas asked hesitantly. "I mean, I never met the woman, but from what I hear a guy might lose it and just take her out for a little reprieve."

"I see you spend way too much time with Nick talking about my ex," Dante said, glancing at his friend. "But yeah, I've considered that. I just think Carlo would know, you know the connection and all that. I think he would know somehow if she were gone."

Thomas considered. "Probably," he finally agreed. "Well, gotta go. Call Dimitri, otherwise he's going to be pissed. I'll let you know when and if I know more."

"Later," Dante said, disconnecting the call.

"How much trouble are we in?" Nick asked hesitantly.

"None," Dante said, scrolling the entries. "He thinks we were out of range. I don't plan to tell him otherwise," he glanced at Nick. "Neither will you. We may not get to finish this. Let me check in, then I'll know more."

"Gee," Cornelia said sarcastically. "That would be a shame."

Nick smiled, Dante scowled.

"It's about time," Dimitri grumbled. "Where have you been? I've been calling for hours."

"Sorry," Dante said. "We've been following leads. My phone never rang, I guess the call couldn't get through. What's up?" Dante asked, hoping the concern in his voice sounded genuine. "I know you wouldn't have called Lillie unless there was trouble."

"We've been attacked," Dimitri began. Dante listened as his leader walked him through the events of the evening. Thomas had already filled him in on the basics, but he got a better picture of the situation from Dimitri. "I know you want to finish things out there, but if this continues I need you here."

"I understand," Dante said soberly. He proceeded to explain the situation to Dimitri, including Carlo's involvement in Lillie's past. "We don't know what's going to happen when we locate this Pooch character. Are we still okay if things turn bad?"

"Yes," Dimitri said soberly. "I've already talked to Oberon about the situation. Spare him if you can, but I trust you and Nick to deal with the problem. We don't want someone like that knowing our secret, no matter what the price. The security and wellbeing of our entire race are at stake. If you have to take him out, we'll deal with it. I'll back you and so will Alex and Oberon."

"Thanks," Dante said. "But hopefully, it won't come to that. I'll keep you posted."

"Check in with me tomorrow night," Dimitri ordered. "Everything hit just after five so I should know the situation here by around three or four Vegas time."

"How about I call you at five, eight your time? That way if the battle is raging I won't interrupt," Dante suggested.

"Sounds good," Dimitri said. "I know it might sound condescending and I hope you don't take it that way, but I'm proud of you. You are handling this better than I thought you would. Do what you can then get back home where you belong."

"Thanks," Dante said, his voice a little husky. He didn't feel like Dimitri was being condescending. It was nice to have such good friends. Men who truly cared about him and his well-being. "Oh, uh...there is something I guess you should probably know," Dante said hesitantly. He slowed his pace then covered the phone. "Nick, I need a minute alone, can you get the women back to the room? I'll be there in a sec."

"No problem," Nick said, sure he understood. Dante was going to talk to Dimitri about his marriage.

"What?" Dimitri asked, hoping there wasn't more trouble to deal with.

"Well, uh...Cornelia and I sort of got married while we were here," he confessed.

Progeny

Dimitri was silent. He wasn't sure what he thought about this new development. "I see," he finally said, still considering. "I didn't realize the two of you were that serious."

"I guess I didn't either," Dante finally said. "It just sort of happened."

"Well, then I guess congratulations are in order," Dimitri said cautiously. "We'll talk about it when you get back. For now, be careful and hurry home."

Dante slipped his phone back in his pocket, deep in thought. That wasn't exactly the reaction he'd expected. Dimitri was too reserved, not angry or happy. He wondered what that meant, but didn't have time for it now. They needed to head out to Waterson then get to the cabins and find Shannon. He'd never forgive himself if someone got hurt because they were wasting time on Shannon Santora.

Cornelia was captivated. It shouldn't have surprised her that Nick and Dante owned The Waterson House Foundation. They were both good, solid men. Men who cared about people. What had she ever done to help those in need? Sure, she cared for her mother and occasionally took a case for free when her clients obviously needed her, but couldn't afford her. But that seemed so small and insignificant compared to what these two had done. "It's huge, more like a large hotel than an apartment building." She commented as the group pulled up the long drive headed for the main building.

Dante gave Cornelia's hand a little squeeze. The closer they got to the building, the more irate he became. They had given Cunningham so much. Maybe too much. Too much power, too much trust, too much responsibility. If he'd been paying attention, or visited every once in a while, things wouldn't be so out of control. He took a deep breath and tried to shove his personal baggage back in the closet. It was his fault people had been victimized, but they knew about it now and it would be corrected immediately.

"Stop blaming yourself," Nick said softly. "It's just as much my fault as it is yours. I never came out here either. I didn't pay attention to the signs. I overlooked the fact that I never liked Cunningham from the beginning."

"If you guys didn't like him, why did you hire him?" Lillie wondered.

"He looked good on paper," Nick began. "And it was easy I guess. I had reservations, but nothing to back them up. He sounded good, looked good and we needed a director. Plus, at the time there wasn't really anyone else available. Nobody with enough experience to handle that kind of responsibility anyway."

"Then you made the right decision at the time," Cornelia put in. "Clearly, things have changed and you're dealing with those changes, but when you hired him, he was the best man for the job. You can't change it, so you should both stop worrying about it." She watched closely as the limo pulled up to a large apartment complex.

"So practical," Dante said as he stepped from the car then held his hand out to Cornelia.

Progeny

"Practical and smart," Lillie put in as she stood before the massive building in front of them. "Now the two of you should go in and kick a little butt. It will make you feel better," Nick had explained the situation to them on the ride out. Lillie hated men like Dave Cunningham. He reminded her of the numerous business associates Brad forced her to deal with while they were married.

The group walked through the large door and entered a massive foyer. Cornelia had never seen anything like it in traditional apartment complexes. She was curious and wished they had time for a tour. "I know we're pressed for time tonight, but someday I'd really like to walk through this place. I'd love to see how it all works."

"Maybe tomorrow," Dante said, taking Cornelia's hand. "We have to come back and meet with Cam. That's going to take a while so you and Lillie might be on your own for a couple hours."

Cornelia smiled. "What do you say, Lillie? You think you're up for the grand tour?"

"Absolutely," Lillie said enthusiastically. "And it's going to be so much better in daylight."

A woman in her mid to late thirties pushed through a door and walked purposefully toward the group. She was attractive in her way, not drop dead gorgeous, but not plain or homely either. She wore an air of professionalism and Cornelia found herself wondering why the men hadn't hired her as program director. She was about to ask when the woman reached them.

"Charlotte," Dante said in a friendly tone. "Did you get our guest settled?"

Charlotte looked from Dante to Nick then back to Dante. "Sort of, we have a bit of a problem."

"You look tired," Nick commented. "And I get the impression Dante and I have made a difficult day even more stressful for you. I'm sorry about that," he placed a hand on her shoulder and guided her to a large wooden bench. "Tell us what's going on."

Charlotte took a deep breath then plowed right in. "Dave is on his way back. He's livid with me. I kept your visit a secret, just like you asked. He has no idea the two of you are in town."

"Good," Dante nodded.

"I picked up Cameron just like you asked and brought him back here. We were still doing the walk through in the apartment when the woman arrived," Charlotte paused. "The woman Dave assigned to that room. She walked in like she already lived there. She wouldn't leave. When I told her there was a problem and that room was to remain vacant, she went off on me. Then she called Dave. Of course the instant he hung up with the woman, he called me. I went through the same thing with him, which is why he is on his way over. He implied I should start looking for a job."

"How did Cam take all this?" Dante asked, worried the man would get fed up and just leave.

Progeny

"Okay," Charlotte said taking another deep breath. "He said the room was fine and once I got it all sorted out he'd be back. In the meantime, he went for a walk. He said he wanted to familiarize himself with his surroundings."

"Okay," Dante said patting Charlotte's hand. "This is Cornelia Santora and Lillie Shepherd. Cornelia is my wife and Lillie belongs to Nick."

Charlotte rose and grasped Cornelia's hand in hers. "It's a pleasure to meet you." She dropped Cornelia's hand to take Lillie's. "Both of you."

"Nick promised me a glass of wine," Lillie smiled warmly at the woman. It was clear dealing with the unwanted guest had been stressful. "It looks to me like you could use one as well. What do you say us women head somewhere comfortable while the men take care of the problem?"

Charlotte glanced at Dante then Nick. "Oh, I don't want to dump this on you."

"Nonsense," Nick said, warmly. "Why don't you take Lillie and Cornelia into the lounge? The three of you can sit in front of the fire and relax with a nice glass of wine until we get back. If Dave shows up, don't try to stop him. In fact, do what you can to encourage him to come to the room."

"Well, if you're sure," Charlotte said hesitantly.

"Positive," Dante said giving her shoulder a little push. "Take good care of our women."

Once they had left Dante turned to Nick. "Charlotte told me she suspects this woman is a prostitute. Be prepared. After the stunt Dave pulled with Cam, I wouldn't be surprised at anything."

Nick and Dante entered the room and spotted the girl immediately. She wasn't what they had expected. Instead of a hardcore sassy woman, they found a young, distressed one standing in front of a large window. The door to the room was wide open but Nick knocked on the frame before walking inside.

The girl turned abruptly, expectantly. Then, her eyes grew weary and she sank into a nearby chair with a loud sigh. "Who are you?" She finally asked.

"Funny, I was about to ask you the same thing," Dante said taking a seat across from her. Nick opted for the large couch.

The woman sat silently studying the new arrivals. The silence sat heavy in the air, neither party willing to break. Finally, the girl stood and walked back to the window. "Lexie," she said in defeat. "My name is Lexie."

"Well, Lexie," Nick said without emotion. "Why don't you come back over here and sit down. We have some questions for you."

Lexie turned, watching for nearly a minute then she moved back to the chair and sat.

Progeny

"I understand you are a friend of Dave Cunningham's," Nick continued. "Is that correct?"

"No," Lexie said honestly. "We're not friends."

"Then how did he come to offer you a room at Waterson?" Dante asked.

"I met the guy, he said he had a room and we made arrangements for me to live here. I've already had the tour and agreed to his terms. As far as I'm concerned it's a done deal. I'm not leaving until Mr. Cunningham gets here. He said he was in charge, not that woman and he promised me this room." She folded her arms and glared at Nick.

"Mr. Cunningham is mistaken," Nick finally told her.

Lexie didn't budge. "Mistaken how? Are you saying he's not the director of this facility?"

"No," Dante answered. "At this precise moment, he is the director."

"Good," Lexie said, "Then I don't see the problem."

Dante wasn't sure what to make of the young girl. She was trying to stand firm, but underneath it all he sensed a scared, desperate woman. "Then you are also mistaken," he finally told her. "It's unfortunate that Dave overstepped his boundaries and offered you this room. He was told, in no uncertain terms, that this particular room was to be left vacant."

"Well," she said after a moment. "Since he's the director and that other woman is his assistant, his decision would hold more weight."

"I suppose that would be accurate if Charlotte was the one making that decision. As it happens, the decision was mine," Dante countered.

"And who are you?" she asked wearily.

"Nick and I jointly own Waterson House. I believe that trumps Director Cunningham," Dante said casually.

Dante saw the tears begin to form just before the woman stood and turned away. She walked back to the window, staring into the distance for several minutes. Then she took a deep breath, picked up her bag and turned to face the men. "I should have known this would somehow fall through, too. If you'll excuse me, I need to track down my daughter and find a place to stay tonight. The shelters will be full by now." A single tear trickled down her cheek. Lexie wiped it away and headed for the door.

"Wait," Dante said, more compassion in his voice than before.

"Why?" she asked. "You've made it clear I can't stay here and I don't have time to waste."

"Because we need some information from you, then we need to decide if we can help you," Nick supplied.

Progeny

Lexie studied the men then narrowed her eyes. "Look, the arrangement was for Cunningham. One guy. Sure, I'm desperate, but I'm not providing free sex to three of you just for a room. I'd do almost anything for my daughter, but I won't be taken advantage of that way."

Cornelia glanced at Lillie as she walked into the room. Then she headed straight for Dante. "I'm glad to hear that," she said casually. "I realize my marriage is new, but I simply can't imagine a day when I'd be willing to share this gorgeous man with anyone."

"Your...." Lexie began, eyes wide. "Oh! I'm sorry. I..."

Dante pulled Cornelia into his lap then smiled at Lexie. "That one over there belongs to Nick. I'd say your assumption is insulting, but considering who you've been dealing with I'll let it slide...once."

"Did that man actually expect you to have sex with him in exchange for a room?" Lillie asked, appalled.

"Well, yes," Lexie said hesitantly. "I mean, I don't have a regular job so I can't pay for the place. Otherwise, I wouldn't need to stay here. He said I didn't have anything else to offer so he'd settle for sex."

"How often?" Nick asked, barely controlling his anger.

"Huh?" Lexie asked, confused. "Oh, um...twice a week. Once for me and once for my daughter."

"Lexie, I got here as soon as I could." A male voice came from the doorway. "I don't know what's gotten into Charlotte. She's not typically insubordinate the way she was today." Cunningham stopped abruptly when he spotted the group. "Oh," he managed before his face went white.

"Hello, Dave," Dante said, menace in his voice. "We were just getting to know Lexie here. She was explaining the details of the arrangement you made. The arrangement for a room I specifically told you not to occupy."

"Arrangement?" Dave stuttered. "Uh, I'm afraid I don't understand."

"Funny," Nick broke in. "Neither do we. Lexie, why don't you outline the sordid details, now that we're all here and accounted for."

Lexie looked from the two large intimidating men, to the guy she'd dealt with before. Something wasn't right about all this. She wasn't sure she should get in the middle of it. "Um, I think I should just go find Bella Rose and get out of here."

"That's a good idea," Cunningham said with relief. "And I promise to contact you if we have a room open up in the future."

Lexie gave Cunningham such a look of disdain Lillie had to laugh. "Nonsense," Lillie said, standing. "Please, Lexie. My man needs to get to the bottom of this. I know it's embarrassing, but it's okay. I promise. Go ahead and tell them what they need to know."

Progeny

Lexie was surprised at the compassion the woman gave her. Nobody had ever talked to her that way before. She was considered a prostitute with a four-year-old after all. "There's really nothing to tell. I met Mr. Cunningham by accident. He mentioned he ran this shelter and they may have a room opening up. He brought me here, showed me this room and said it would be perfect for me and my little girl. He said it was unfortunate that I couldn't pay the rent, so he offered to let me stay here for free until I got back on my feet in exchange for sex."

"I never..." Cunningham said defensively.

"Shut up," Dante said then turned back to Lexie. "This is a family oriented establishment," he began. "A shelter for people willing to work for their keep."

"Mr. Cunningham told me that, but he also said I didn't have the skills. He said I really wasn't qualified to stay here, but he was willing to make an exception. He'd take care of me and my daughter if I would take care of him," Lexie said softly.

"What a despicable man," Lillie told Nick. "What kind of person takes advantage of a young, single mother that way? How do you look at yourself in the mirror?" She asked glaring at Dave Cunningham.

"And you agreed to the arrangement?" Dante asked.

"Yes," she admitted. "I know what that makes me. I know it's unsavory. But my daughter needs a roof over her head. I don't go out and stand on the corner, it's a little more civilized than that. If this man could provide a decent place for Bella to live, a place where she has her own room and a decent meal every day and I don't have to hook up with rich snobs anymore, it's worth it," she paused. "Even if I have to sell myself to him," she pointed at Cunningham.

"I assure you, I have no idea where this woman got such a notion," Cunningham began.

"She got it from you," Dante said coldly. He stood, took Cornelia by the hand then led her into the hallway. He silently shut the door behind them.

"Dante, please fire that man quickly. I only have so much control. One more minute in there and I'm afraid I might chuck him out the window," Cornelia was fuming.

"What is it with you and windows?" Dante smiled, then sobered. "We will. I need you and Lillie to take Lexie up to three. There's an apartment up there, it used to be Cunningham's. He will no longer be needing it. I sent Charlotte a text, she should be waiting for you. I have no idea what condition it's in, but I want to put Lexie and Bella Rose up there. I realize you aren't familiar with how we do things here, but the most important thing for her to know is there are no free rides."

"I think she got that already," Cornelia said flatly.

"And no riding the boss," he added with a smile. "She's going to have to work. Depending on the condition of that apartment, the work might be harder than she's used to. Then talk to her, find out what she can do other than the obvious. There are plenty of jobs around here, cooking, cleaning, gardening, I need to know what she's capable of. Can you and Lillie handle that for me?"

"Sure," Cornelia said, a little surprised Dante was trusting her with something so important. "And while we do that, you'll toss him out the window?"

"Figuratively speaking, yes," Dante assured her. "Don't worry, we'll handle it." He reached for the door and walked back into the room. "Lexie, could you please go with Lillie and Cornelia? We need a minute alone with Mr. Cunningham."

Lexie looked from Dante to Nick to the slime she'd been dealing with. She was a little surprised to feel the soft hand on her forearm. "Okay," she finally said, taking a breath. She liked the women. They seemed strong and classy. They'd have to be to attract such masculine and intimidating men.

Once the women were out of the room Dante turned on Cunningham.

"I assure you," he began.

"You're fired," Dante said without emotion. He'd like to toss the guy out the window like Cornelia suggested, but that would just complicate things.

"Are you seriously going to take the word of a prostitute over mine?" He asked in shock.

"We are," Nick told him. "You have five minutes to collect your things and get out. After that, we'll throw you out."

"I've devoted my life to you...to this place for the past seven years. I've sacrificed, I've...."

Dante tapped his watch. "Clock's started. You can waste time blabbering on or you can accept our cordial escort to your previous room and collect your things. It's your choice."

Cunningham took a deep breath then turned abruptly and took one step toward the door. He stopped mid-stride, spotting Cam in the doorway.

"Guess you haven't quite finished in here," Cam said casually leaning against the frame.

"You?" Cunningham spat in disgust. "What are you doing here?"

"Oh," Nick said jovially. "Dave, I'd like you to meet our new Director, Cameron Harris," he paused, waited then snapped his fingers. "Oh, that's right. You two already met. Back when you disobeyed another directive. I hear you wanted to cram him into that utility room next to the central air unit. And I was so clear on that one when you asked about it." Nick shook his head as if he were scolding a naughty child. He knew that would get to Cunningham more than anything.

"I guess you have an excuse for that as well?" Dante asked.

"What?" Cunningham asked.

"The scam you tried to pull on Cam," Dante said casually. "Make no mistake Dave, we will find out how many others you've victimized through the years. You're lucky Cam here didn't take you up on the offer to live in a closet, work himself to death then turn over his disability check each month for the honor. And if you've taken advantage of any other military hero's that way, you're not going to like the consequences."

"I haven't," Cunningham said immediately. "I wouldn't," he added belatedly. "I'll just get my things." He straightened his spine then walked out of the room.

"It's all yours," Dante said with a smile as he passed Cam in the doorway. "If you'll excuse us, Dave needs an escort while he's on the property."

Cam nodded, then slipped into the apartment and closed the door.

Chapter Eleven

"So, that was fun," Cornelia said as the limo pulled away from Waterson House. "What's next?"

The group laughed. They had come close to calling the cops on Dave Cunningham. He was beyond upset when he realized his cozy apartment was going to the woman he'd tried to con into free sex. If it wasn't for Cam's presence Cunningham might try to return, but with Cam around the guy wouldn't risk it. He wasn't quite as intimidating as the warriors, but he came pretty close.

"Now we head back to the casino and grab the car," Nick answered casually.

"Uh, we don't have a car," Lillie pointed out. "Thus the limo."

Progeny

"We do now," he said pulling out his phone. "I got the text letting me know it had been delivered about twenty minutes ago. It's in the lot and ready to go. The keys should be at the check-in desk."

"Great," Dante said, relieved. He was wondering how they were going to get out of town. There was no way he'd ask Joe to drive them out in the limo.

Nick composed a new text then hit send. He hoped Kylee set her phone to hold all texts until morning. He didn't want to wake her, but he needed the name of a good doctor out this way. None of his other contacts had been able to help and he was determined to find someone that could give a second opinion on Cam's condition.

The group piled into the car and headed out. They left Las Vegas, passed through Henderson and continued toward Lake Mead. When they got to the dirt road Cam had clearly marked on his hand written map Dante slowly pulled off the highway and stopped the car. "Cam said there are numerous cabins scattered throughout this wooded area. We all need to keep our eyes open. I want to drive further down this road before we head out on foot but help me watch for the first cabin," Dante maneuvered the car onto the dirt road. Their progress was slow and difficult. The car bounced over large rocks then settled, only to be jarred again when one of the tires slid into a deep rut. The thing had to be a foot deep.

"If this guy is a drug dealer I think he'd look for easy access. He's going to want a place out of the way, but convenient. I don't see someone like the guy you described taking a hike for an hour each day just to stay out of sight,"

Cornelia supplied. She was on alert, watching for clues, anything that would indicate people had been through here recently.

"I agree," Nick said. "From everything we've heard about this guy he's basically lazy. He didn't like Shannon selling in his area because it was competition and he would have to work harder to find clients. When Cam confronted him and didn't back down, he started to avoid that alleyway, he hooked up with this Tiny guy for protection so he didn't have to watch out for himself. I'm pretty sure he's not parking somewhere and hiking very far to reach the cabin."

Lillie spotted something a few yards from the road. "Stop," she told Dante. "I think there might be a cabin back there."

Dante pulled to the side of the road. "Okay, this is how we are going to do this. Nick you and Lillie stick together. Cornelia and I will partner up. Nick, you are the best at stealth so I think you should take the back. You and Lillie sneak around and see if you can peek through a window. You need to make sure you can see any exits on the left side of the cabin. Cornelia and I will hang out somewhere near the front. We'll find a place that keeps the right side in view. Does that work for everyone?"

"I want Lillie to hang back. If we both sneak up to the house to look through a window we're not going to be able to see the big picture. I have to get close to peek through an opening on the side, that's going to leave the back wide open. But if Lillie is stationed somewhere that she can watch my back as well as see any rear exit or escape route, it will be a lot safer for both of us."

"Bull, you just want me out of range in case there is danger," Lillie shot back. "But I actually agree with you. If I'm in a position to watch your back and see any other movement from windows or doors there's less of a chance they can sneak away."

"Then it's settled. Everyone stay on your toes. This isn't like fighting vamps. Humans carry guns. A strategically placed shot will kill us just as quickly as a human," Dante told them.

The cabin was vacant. The group continued moving through the area well into the night. At three o'clock in the morning, Dante finally called it quits. "Let's head back to the room. We all need sleep. Nick and I have a full day ahead of us at Waterson then we need to head back and finish this at nightfall. If there's trouble in New York again tomorrow, or I guess today, Dimitri is going to call us home. I'll leave without finding Shannon if I have to, but I'd rather get this resolved. We need to know how much Tiny and The Pooch have figured out."

"I agree," Nick said, settling in the backseat. "Home James." He smirked as he laid his head against the seat and pulled Lillie against him.

* * * *

Alex sat on the window seat, staring aimlessly out the window. Dimitri was out on a job, he had wanted to stay home but there was a problem with the system that belonged to a wealthy customer. If he didn't get it corrected, he could lose the contract. He was such a good, strong man. Unlike her. With each passing day, Alex felt more like a failure. She knew dwelling on the losses from New Year's wasn't healthy or productive. How many times had Dimitri and Ariel told her exactly that? But, she just couldn't stop. She knew those people. They were good, honest working members of her community and she couldn't save them. Then last night they lost the Moore's and Carl Stewart. Vivian's life had changed drastically because Alex had failed her people. She heard a sound in the doorway and jumped a little. When she turned her head, she spotted Thomas.

Thomas forced a smile and walked toward Alex. "You look so much like your mother sitting there, staring hopelessly out the window." He pushed her legs aside and sat down next to her. He studied her for a while then continued. "I'm having a déjà vu moment here, so bear with me."

"What do you mean?" Alex said shifting so she could lay her head on Thomas' shoulder. She missed this. The two of them had always been close. Their lives had changed so much since their father's death. She had Dimitri and Thomas had Abby, but she missed these quiet moments.

Progeny

"I walked in on Marlena one night," he paused to wrap his arm around Alex and pulled her close. "She was sitting on the window seat in her sunroom, exactly like you are now. Just staring out the window into the darkness," he smiled a little. "I walked in and sat next to her, just like I did you. She took my hand, the way she always did and rested her head on my shoulder." He closed his eyes, sorrow forcing him to stop for a minute. "It was a few months before she died." He absently began drawing little circles on Alex's arm. "She was so sad that night, just like you are this morning." He kissed the top of her head. "Are you still thinking about the ones we lost?"

Alex sighed. "Yes," she whispered, then took a deep breath. "I know; I should be grateful we didn't lose more. But I just can't. I feel like I failed them. I failed Margaret and her son when I couldn't save Donald. I finally got a hold of Peter. He said his mother will be moving to Chicago permanently. He also said she's still isn't eating. Losing the love of her life has devastated her. I'm not sure she'll ever recover. I wouldn't if I ever lost Dimitri. I failed Alveron by not saving his brother, Brok. Their sister, Nixie won't leave her house. Rhoslyn..."

"Alex," Thomas interrupted. "We both know how devastating it is to lose someone you love. We lost both our parents in a very short amount of time. Nobody understands loss better than we do. It's different than it was with mom and dad, but it's still natural to grieve for those that are lost. You wouldn't be the wonderful, special person you are if you didn't. We both saw what it did to dad when he lost Marlena. You escaped most of it because you fled to Italy to cope with the loss yourself, but dad stopped eating. He was more comatose than alive for months. It's natural to go a little crazy when someone you love is killed like that. Those families will suffer, grieve and then eventually start living again. Just like we did. I know I will always have a hole in my heart. I will always miss Marlena. I will always miss dad." He cleared the emotion from his throat. "I'll never stop longing for the talk's dad and I used to have. I'll never stop wishing for Marlena's hugs when I have a bad day. I took so much for granted, but I've learned to go on without them. Just like you've learned to go on without them. My parents will never meet my wife, my children. I know that you understand how sad and disappointing that is."

A tear rolled down Alex's cheek. "For me too," she whispered. They sat there for a long time thinking about the family they used to have and the journey they'd taken since Marlena had been killed. "But I should have been there to save them," Alex finally said, returning to the original point. "I'm the queen. It's my responsibility to protect my people and I failed. Then I failed again last night."

"Like I said, I'm having a déjà vu moment," Thomas said so softly, Alex almost couldn't make out the words.

"I don't understand," Alex said, wiping her cheek with the back of her hand.

"I walked in on Marlena a few months before she died. She was sitting in that little room she had off the master. The one she locked herself away in when she needed to wind down," Thomas said, lost in a thousand memories. Marlena had been the kind of mother he had

Progeny

always wanted. She'd loved him from the start, just like his father had loved Alex from the instant he laid eyes on her. Sometimes he felt guilty about the bond he had with Marlena. A bond he had never shared with his biological mother. "Anyway, the instant I stepped into the doorway my heart broke. Marlena looked so sad, just like you do right now."

"I don't remember mom being sad just before she died," Alex disagreed.

"You were preoccupied with Jenny at the time. She had just gotten that new job and the two of you were trying to spend as much time as possible together before she moved," Thomas remembered. "And, Marlena hid it from you. She tried to hide it from me and dad, but I know dad saw it too. They were so close, neither one of them could hide trouble from the other one. I'm lucky, I have that with Abby. I think you have it with Dimitri, too. He's worried about you."

"I know," Alex agreed. "But sometimes I think it might be a curse, something Dimitri has to tolerate rather than a blessing for him."

"I can assure you, Dimitri would disagree," Thomas gave her a little squeeze. "Anyway, I assume they talked and dad found a way to get through to her because Marlena was starting to come out of it by the time she passed away. She was still sad, but not so depressed and despondent," he looked at Alex. "She felt like she was failing her people, too," he finally told her.

Alex straightened so she could study Thomas. She had to know if he was just trying to make her feel better or if he was telling the truth. Thomas knew how much she idolized her mother. Especially now that she was trying to follow in her footsteps as queen. She studied him for a long time and realized the only thing she saw in his eyes was the truth. "Why did mom think she was failing her people?" Alex finally asked.

"Because a family died," he admitted. "A family Marlena had become close to. Then one night, they were all killed by vampires."

"Just like Sam's family," Alex whispered. "Like my father."

"Yes," Thomas agreed. "Although at the time I didn't know about them. The similarities would have added to Marlena's pain."

"Do you know the details?" Alex finally asked.

"Yes," he nodded. "She talked to me about it that night. The night I walked in and found her staring into the darkness. It was the only time I ever heard Marlena question her destiny."

"Really?" Alex asked, not sure she believed him. "I mean I question mine all the time, but I thought mom was comfortable being queen. Everyone keeps telling me how much she was loved and respected. I've also heard her described as confident. Plus, she was groomed for it since she was young."

Progeny

"Marlena was loved and respected, but so are you. That doesn't make you any more confident," Thomas pointed out. "Why do you think mom would be any different?"

"It is different," Alex argued. "I mean, her parents taught her everything she needed to know. They prepared her to take over as queen. I was kept in the dark all my life. I'm just stumbling through and I keep making so many mistakes."

"Marlena was prepared. She was also kidnapped, tortured and abused for over fifty years. She withdrew inside herself and only started to come out of it when she met your father. Then he was massacred by Radek, her own son. A short time later the family of the man she loved was slaughtered. Within a few years, the two of you were once again kidnapped and imprisoned. I don't see how anyone that went through what she did, could bounce back the way Marlena did. She was strong and beautiful and full of life, but she also had her moments of doubt. That's when dad stepped in and was strong enough for the both of them, and us," he added as an afterthought.

Alex thought about Thomas' words. He was right. Luke had been strong enough for all of them. Thinking back on their lives, Alex realized Luke and Marlena depended on each other. She could remember times when Marlena hadn't seemed herself, or Luke hadn't. But they always seemed to function as a single unit. When one was down, the other held them up. Her thoughts shifted to her relationship with Dimitri. They had the same kind of bond. It was still new and not fully developed, but he was always there for her and vice versa. "Tell me the story, Thomas. Tell me what happened just before mom's death."

"That's when the Naylor's were killed," Thomas said soberly. "It was a family of four," he began. "They were basically nomads. They moved in and took up residence without anyone knowing it. Later dad learned that the family had been treated poorly by their previous community. They'd been moving around, trying to find a place they could settle permanently," he stopped, wondering where to begin. "Things are different here, in New York. Remember when I first tried to explain things to you and I said the fae can't live together?"

"Yeah," Alex agreed. "I've been wondering about that," she admitted. "We all live here together. You said the fae are vicious and jealous. You said if they live too close, they fight and kill one another. I haven't seen any of that. I know you said our ancestors were different. That the group of brothers kept everyone together, but wouldn't that bond weaken with time?"

"It has, and there are reasons why we can function the way we do," Thomas began. "First, we are at war. Your people are afraid. They are looking to you, and to the warriors, to protect them. Because of that, they have forced themselves to be civil. It's not always like that. You've seen how the Jackson's and the Sander's behave. Status is important to them. They're jealous of you, they used to be jealous of mom. Don't even get me started on the Dillinger's."

Progeny

"Okay, but when you talked about our people you made it sound like they are volatile, not just petty and underhanded or crazy like Patricia Dillinger."

"They are," Thomas said flatly. "Another reason we don't have more problems is because we live in New York. Look around, do you have any idea how many people live here. We're spread out. That makes living in such close proximity tolerable for the fae. We've had a couple community events since you took over, but not that many. Compare the fae to the shifters. Mason's pack all live in a tight community. So tight, they don't allow outsiders in. Their neighbors are shifters and friends. Even a lot of the companies they work for are composed entirely of shifters. We don't do that. The only reason you haven't seen it is because the warriors are close. Warriors don't have the social problems the fae have. We get along, the seven of us spend a lot of time together. It's easy to believe the others are the same, but they're not. You've seen the dissension in the council. Avery and Oberon barely tolerate each other. Dahl didn't approve of Orin. He thought Orin was too young and too liberal in his thinking to be on the council. Warren gets along with Oberon, but he's jealous of Oberon's power and position. Warren believed he'd be appointed council chair after Durin died. We have problems and the way we deal with them is to fade into the crowd of New York. Time and space allow us to function as a community."

"I guess that makes sense," Alex finally said.

"Because we are spread out it took Luke and Marlena, even the council, awhile before they knew the

Naylor's had moved in," Thomas continued. "I think Rosa, that was the mother, stopped in at the Jackson's store. If I remember right, that's how word got out about them. They didn't live here, in downtown New York. They lived on the outskirts. They bought a small farm and grew most of their own food. Of course, the Sander's and the Jackson's immediately started in. Anyone that chose to live on a farm had to be lower class citizens.

Marlena, on the other hand, welcomed them instantly. She seemed to have an instant connection with Rosa. Now that I know about Sam's family, I suspect Rosa reminded Marlena of Sam's mother, Nicole. Marlena would sneak away for an afternoon whenever she could. Luke sent me out to retrieve her one day. The two of them were sitting on the front porch snapping beans and sipping ice tea. They both looked so happy and content. The kids were great. Parker was around twelve I think; his little sister Emily was maybe seven or eight. She was such a spunky kid and a tomboy through and through. Parker was more subdued, but that kid had an arm. I've never seen a kid that age so good at baseball."

"Sam said Michael was killed when he was twelve," Alex said quietly.

"There were a lot of similarities," Thomas agreed. "Marlena was happy, I know she was. But that night we talked, she told me she missed the simplicity of her old life. She missed the days she spent farming with your father. She missed quiet evenings on the front porch. She was elegant and sophisticated but simple. Her life with dad was anything but simple."

Progeny

"How were they killed?" Alex asked, not sure she really wanted to know.

"As far as we know, there was no connection to Marlena," Thomas sighed. "Marlena had a hard time believing that. At the time, I didn't understand her insistence that the Naylor's died because she had befriended them. I understand that conversation so much better now that I know about Sam and Michael and Sam's parents, Nicole and Troy. Marlena was reliving that horrible time in her life. She was losing her family all over again."

"And she blamed herself," Alex realized. Her mother would blame herself for all of it. She'd believe that it was her fault Radek, her own son, had killed James and Nicole and Michael and the rest. The similarities were too close to ignore. Alex knew her mother would have internalized the death of the Naylor's as well.

"The night I found her, she was so distraught it scared me," Thomas continued. "She felt like a failure. She blamed herself. I guess you could say the Naylor's were the first casualties of this war. I don't think Radek knew that Marlena was close to that family. I do believe he was pushing the boundaries though. Radek planned to assassinate Marlena and his first act of war was to release the hounds, so to speak. I wish we had known that at the time, but we were taken by surprise. We found out later that Radek openly condoned the killing of fae. He told his vampires they would never be punished for feeding on our people. He didn't agree with that clause in the treaty and decided not to honor it. Like I said that was just the first step. I think he already had plans to kill our mother. If the killing of innocent fae families didn't break the treaty, her assassination would."

The two of them sat in silence for a long time. Alex thought about the young family that was slaughtered by her half-brother or his followers. She thought about the war and about the losses. There were so many of them. Before tonight she'd only been counting the ones that had occurred under her watch. Thomas made her understand there were more. There were entire families that had been killed under her mother's watch as well.

"There were others," Thomas said as if he had read her mind. "The Naylor's were the first, but there were others that were killed before mom's death. She struggled with every one of them. She grieved for the losses and had compassion for the survivors. She visited each of the families and cried with them, comforted them and inwardly despised the son she had created. What I'm trying to help you understand is that Marlena struggled just as much as you are. She understood the pressure of being queen. She also felt responsible for what her own child was doing to her people. You think you're a failure because you couldn't heal everyone. She felt like a failure because her own child was killing people she cared about. You're both wrong. I don't know if Marlena had enough time to come to terms with it all. She recovered enough to plan for the future. We know that; for one thing, we have the fort to prove it. But I also know it because I heard her talk to her people. Marlena called for a gathering. She told us all to prepare for hard times. She encouraged parents to work with their children. She begged her people to start carrying

Progeny

weapons again. The people didn't believe her. Most of them left thinking she was paranoid.

Alex, the people loved Marlena and they still didn't take her seriously. As a result, people lost their lives. She struggled with many of the same problems you are struggling with. She lost friends and associates. She doubted her ability to lead during war time, she did all the same things you are doing right now. You have to make the same decision she had to make all those months ago. You are sitting here, staring into the vast expanse, teetering on the same cliff Marlena did. Only you can decide if you want to give in to the depression and the sorrow, or if you want to fight. Marlena was a fighter. So are you. I hope you make the same choice she did because your people need you. It's okay to be melancholy. It's okay to feel bad because Peter lost his father and Alveron lost his brother. Because Vivian is going to have to be strong for her mother and her brother. It's not okay to give up. For the past few weeks, I've been getting the feeling you have given up. We are at war and we need a strong queen. I know you have it in you. Dad knew you had it in you." Thomas stood and pulled Alex to her feet. "I love you, Alex and I believe in you. We lost a few. That just means we have to do better next time. And I think you're forgetting all the ones that you saved." He leaned down and kissed her cheek. "Keep this all in perspective. You're not alone. You have me and Dimitri and Victor and the rest of the vagabonds that adore you so much. Lean on us a little. We can take it."

Alex gave Thomas a slight smile then stood on her tiptoes and kissed his cheek. "I love you, too." She took a step back. "Thanks, big brother. I've missed our talks. I guess I took you for granted, too. You were saying you took the simple things for granted with mom and dad. I did too, but I also took us for granted. I never imagined finding someone as wonderful as Dimitri so I guess I always thought we'd be together, the way things were. Now that I've moved out, I understand how important you are in my life and this is one of the things I've missed."

"Me too, squirt. Me too," Thomas sighed. "I always knew dad was busy with the company and sometimes I noticed when he looked worn out or stressed, but I don't think I really understood just how much time it takes to run such a large corporation. Sometimes I wonder how dad ever had time for us."

"I know," Alex said with understanding. "It wears me out, too. Promise me we'll always make time for each other. I know we're adults and we're going to have our own families one day and our own priorities but promise me we'll always make time to keep in touch," she hesitated. "I need you."

"I promise," he said, then more lightly. "As long as you stop canceling my flights."

Alex smiled. "We agreed you wouldn't go to Vegas. That means Thomas Deveraux and Phillip Abercromby stay in New York. I'm worried about Dante, too. But neither one of us can get involved in this. You know what kind of power that would give Carlo Santora."

"I know," Thomas sighed. "And having Nick out there helps, a little."

"I still don't understand why you guys are sure Nick is going to do something violent," Alex said, frowning. "I've never seen Nick lose his temper. He's so respectful and mild mannered. I think you are all overreacting."

"That's because you haven't seen Nick lose his temper," Thomas mused. "Think of dad and how protective he was of us and Marlena. That's pretty close to Nick when someone messes with anyone important to him."

Alex frowned. "I've always worried about you because you seem to have inherited dad's temper. I have a hard time imagining Nick in the same light," she paused. "You are supposed to be putting my mind at ease, Thomas. If you're right, I'm going to be a basket case until the four of them get back home."

"We all are," Thomas said soberly. "Let's just hope Lillie and Cornelia have as much influence on Nick and Dante as Abby has over me."

Alex smiled. "I've got to get going."

"Where are you headed?" Thomas asked casually as they both stood and walked to the stairs.

"I'm going to pay Fira a visit," Alex frowned. "I'm going to try to talk her into paying Tighe a visit."

"Do you think she'll agree?" Thomas asked hopefully.

"I don't know," Alex said honestly. "But I have to try. Right now is not the time for the Queen and her Council to be at odds. If I don't do something I'm afraid they will vote to eliminate Fira as an alternate and vote Foster in. I won't approve that. I made my position clear on this and I can't back down now. You know that. It's one of the first principle's dad taught us when running a business, once you make a decision stick to it."

"I know," Thomas agreed. "And I agree. If you back down on this, it will give Avery and Warren a boost. Those two could get out of control if you let them. You have to stand firm. I hope Fira listens to reason, now really is not the time for conflict. The Queen and her council have to be united if we are going to stop Radek and end this war."

"I just hope Tighe will listen," Alex worried.

"He will," Thomas assured her. "And if you have Tighe's vote, I think this thing will be over. Foster and Fira will be alternates and we can focus on more important issues."

"What makes you so sure?" she asked, surprised.

"Drake is on the fence. He's following Tighe. Tighe doesn't believe Fira is Dahl's daughter. Drake agrees there should be women on the council, he's just not sure Fira can be trusted. If you get Tighe, you have Drake."

"That's good to know," she said, considering.

Progeny

"You already have Oberon and Orin's vote, if you can get Tighe and Drake that makes four," Thomas said confidently.

"But I need at least five. I would prefer six. If the vote is that close, Avery might challenge it because we are down one." Alex surmised.

"I believe if you get Drake, you will also get Elvin," Thomas continued. "Their wives are tight. Tianna has already told Breena she agrees with you. She thinks it's past time women were represented on the council. Wendy seems to agree with her. I suspect Elvin is getting pressure at home from Wendy to give Fira a chance. Again, it sounds like the only holdup is that nobody believes Fira is Dahl's daughter."

"I don't think she'll explain the situation to the whole council." In fact, Alex was sure Fira wouldn't do that.

"She doesn't have to," Thomas told her. "If she can just convince Tighe, the others will trust his word. Tighe and Dahl were tight. Warrior tight. I would compare their friendship to Nick and Dante's. The two council members were more like brothers than friends. That's why nobody believes Fira. I understand because you explained it to me. But it's impossible for those who knew Tighe and Dahl to believe Dahl had a secret life not even Tighe knew about."

"I know," Alex sighed. "That's why I need to get over and talk to Fira. Somehow I have to convince her talking to Tighe is the right thing to do."

They had reached the door. "Good luck," Thomas said with a smile. "I have work."

"Hey," Alex called after him. He was already out the door. "Why did you come by today?"

Thomas grinned. "I was having sister withdrawals. Now that I got my fix, I'm set for a while."

"Dimitri called, didn't he?" she scowled.

"Yeah," Thomas admitted. "But I had already decided to stop by. He's not the only one that worries about you. Don't give him a hard time about it. That man is worried, but it's only because he loves you so much. To tell you the truth, I'm worried about him."

"Worried about what?" Alex asked, frowning.

Thomas sighed. "He's distracted. When you hurt, he hurts. I know you've been preoccupied lately, but take a minute to look at him, I mean truly look. He's lost weight and his mind is constantly on you, not himself or even his safety. I can't stop him from fighting any more than I could dad, but he's not in a good place right now and it's dangerous. Dangerous for him and dangerous for anyone paired with him. He needs you to snap out of this funk more than anyone. Now, I've really got to take off. I'm late for a board meeting."

Alex stared at the car as Thomas pulled away. Had she really been so out of it that she hadn't seen the signs in Dimitri? She wasn't surprised he was stressing. He was so protective of her. Knowing she was struggling would upset him. She was surprised she'd been so caught up in her grief she hadn't seen his. Well, at least that was one thing she could fix and she intended to start immediately.

* * * *

Cornelia woke and realized Dante was still sleeping. She smiled, as her gaze moved along his tight body. He'd pushed down the blanket so it settled over his waist and legs. That left his broad chest and tight abs exposed. Her fingers itched to reach out and run a hand through his thick chest hair, then down over the tight muscles of his stomach, but she resisted. Momentarily anyway. A smile crossed her lips, why should she resist. They were married, weren't they? And technically this was their honeymoon. She pushed off the covers and lowered her body over his, straddling his hips. Then she began a slow, deliberate exploration of his body. First, she lifted his hands above his head and slowly smoothed her hands down, stopping at his biceps. She paused there, remembering how strong he was. How captivating he was to watch when he was fighting vampires. She continued her exploration, running her hands over his chest and down to his stomach. She couldn't stop herself, she wanted to taste him. Slowly, she lowered her lips to his chest and pressed a soft kiss to one of his nipples. Dante shifted slightly. When Cornelia lifted her head, she locked eyes with the sexy warrior. Yeah, he was awake. She laughed as he wrapped his arms around her waist and reversed their position so quick she didn't see it coming.

Dante lowered his mouth to Cornelia's for a long, sweet kiss. He pulled back and grinned at her. "Morning."

"Morning," she whispered, still breathless from his kiss. She smiled, "Sorry I woke you."

"I'm not," Dante said, trailing a finger over her collarbone.

"Well..," Cornelia said, still grinning. "I promised my man would get lucky last night. I was feeling a little guilty. We were both so tired when we got in, it was all either of us could do to get to the bed. I always keep my promises, so I thought maybe it was better late than never. If you're game that is."

Dante's kiss was his answer.

Some time later, the two of them snuggled in the bed. Dante was sitting, his back resting against the headboard. Cornelia was lying across his chest. Dante was playing with her hair; Cornelia was just enjoying the moment. "I have something for you," Dante finally said. He stood, shifting her body so her head now lay on a pillow.

Cornelia watched as Dante located his jacket and pulled something from the pocket. Then he returned to the bed sitting next to her in only his underwear. She forced herself to sit and pressed her back against the headboard. "The ring?" She asked, too many emotions swirling in her head.

Progeny

Dante opened the box and lifted the amazing ring with the gorgeous red diamond out with his fingers. Then he reached for her left hand.

Cornelia let him take her hand, all the time wishing this were real. Wishing this wasn't only a temporary arrangement. She loved Dante. She had for a while now. If only he loved her, too. Her eyes began to water as he gently slid the ring onto her finger.

"Now it's official," he said pressing his lips to hers. "You are my wife," he paused. "For as long as you'll have me." He added, not wanting to reveal too much, but wanting her to know she was in control. They'd be together as long as she would allow it.

Cornelia stared at the ring. She never knew how to take Dante in these moments. It would be so easy to believe he wanted her too. But that was impossible. She was part vampire. She knew she would never have forever. He was just being the gentle caring man he always was. He didn't know how to be anything else. "I still think it's too much," she told him gently touching the stone then holding her hand out to admire it.

Dante pressed his hand to Cornelia's face. "You are a special woman, Cornelia. There is nothing I could do that would be too much." He stood, then held out a hand to help her up. When she slid her hand into his, he pulled her against him. As they stood there, embracing Dante wished more than anything this would last forever. The thought of her leaving almost killed him. He sighed, then stepped back. "Let's go see if the others are awake. Nick and I have a lot to do today, we need to get an early start."

Chapter Twelve

"I love your ring," Lillie said as she and Cornelia approached the apple orchard. They had been wandering the grounds for over an hour. Nick and Dante were inside Waterson House meeting with Cam and Charlotte.

Cornelia hesitated. She loved it too, but she still felt so guilty about the purchase. It was way too extravagant. "Dante wants to spoil me," she finally said.

"He's a lot like Nick that way," Lillie agreed. "They are both so generous. I felt guilty at Christmas. Nick went overboard. I swear he bought me one of everything in the women's section. Expensive stuff, too. Silk blouses, designer jeans. He gave me a diamond and sapphire bracelet that had to cost a fortune."

Progeny

"It sounds like you got over the guilt," Cornelia observed.

"Maybe," Lillie hesitated. "I guess I just accepted it. Maybe it's easier for me because of the connection we share. Nick loves to give me things. I can feel it, his excitement and his love. How could I take that away by feeling guilty? It just ruins the gift. I know what's in his heart when he buys things for me. I guess now I just get caught up in his enthusiasm, which doesn't leave room for the guilt."

"I guess that makes sense," Cornelia considered. "But Dante and I don't have that connection." *We don't even have love,* Cornelia thought. *Well, not mutual love anyway.*

"No," Lillie agreed. "But you don't really need it. I mean it's great knowing, actually feeling Nick's love and devotion to me. If I could, I'd give that part to everyone I know. But sometimes it's hard, too. I know when he's upset. I know when he's worried about something. I came home from the hanger stoked. Ty's new plane was in and we spent an entire afternoon going through the amazing new features. I walked in the house soaring and found Nick in the study, brooding. He was so worried about Dante, out here dealing with Carlo all alone, it broke my heart."

"Dante wasn't alone," Cornelia said defensively.

"Oh, I know," Lillie said casually. "But he didn't have Nick. After everything that happened between them the last time Shannon and Carlo were in Dante's life, Nick was a wreck. He had to come out and help. I knew that, I felt it. That's why I pushed so hard to get Alex and Dimitri's blessing. We would have come anyway, there was no way around it," she paused. "Anyway, my point is that sometimes the connection is a curse, not a blessing. And other times it's the most wonderful gift I've ever been given."

"You've changed," Cornelia told Lillie. "It's more than just from human to warrior. You used to be so reserved. I remember that morning we were leaving Dante's cabin. You were so embarrassed when Nick showed you the slightest bit of affection."

"I know," Lillie admitted. "I used to be a loner. I hated socializing. I didn't have any friends and having Nick touch me, kiss me, hold me in public made me so self-conscious," she shrugged. "I guess it's that connection again. I love him so much and I can actually feel, deep in my soul, how much he loves me too. When Nick reached our table last night our emotions were raw, it was like his love, my love, our desire for each other was swirling in the air. It was so intense, I couldn't stop myself. I had missed him so much, and he felt the same. Then the whole scene with those two women, and the absolute euphoria I felt knowing he's all mine. Nick Moretti, the gorgeous, kind, loving man of my dreams is all mine. I just had to touch him, hold him, kiss him. I honestly didn't care where I was or how many people were watching us."

"I'm happy for you," Cornelia said honestly. "I don't understand it, but for some reason I've been drawn to you from the start. I knew almost instantly that you and I could be very good friends. I hope you feel the same."

Progeny

"I do," Lillie said linking her arm through Cornelia's. "I can't explain it either. Back then, when I was human, I was struggling with everything. My attraction to Nick, the trouble with Brad, the emotions I was feeling after my divorce. The others intimidated me. Mostly Thomas and Alex, but all of them a little. I liked Sam and I was getting comfortable around Ty but there was something different about you. Like you said, an instant connection. I'm glad you and Dante got together. He and Nick are so close. It's a relief that he found someone Nick and I already care about. The four of us are going to have so many wonderful times together. It's strange really, going from having no one to having so many friends. It's still a little surreal to know the four of us will be tight forever. Five hundred years from now, you, me, Nick and Dante will still be taking trips and making memories," Lillie froze at the look on Cornelia's face. It looked like the woman was about to cry.

"What's wrong?" Lillie asked immediately. "Did I say something wrong?"

Cornelia brushed a tear from her cheek and sat, leaning against a nearby apple tree. "I'm fine. But maybe we could relax for a minute."

Lillie moved in to sit next to Cornelia. "Talk to me," she soothed. "It doesn't matter what it is, you can tell me."

Cornelia shook her head. "I can't. If I tell you, then you will tell Nick."

"If this has to do with Dante, I guarantee Nick already knows," Lillie told her.

272

Cornelia shook her head. "Dante wouldn't tell Nick about this."

Lillie smiled. "Wanna bet? It's a good place for it, we're in Vegas after all."

"I'm serious, Lillie," Cornelia insisted. "Nick doesn't know."

"I'm serious too. Dante tells Nick everything. Nick is the same with Dante. I'm sure Nick does know because he was skeptical when they left together yesterday. Nick wasn't buying the whole 'we got married then decided it was the right thing to do' bit. When they got back, Nick was more relaxed about it. He's not worried anymore. Those two talked about you, your marriage, your future. I'm sure of it. Tell me what's upsetting you, I might be able to help."

Cornelia considered what Lillie was saying. Would Dante tell Nick about the arrangement? Most likely. But if he knew, why would Nick be okay with it now? That part didn't make any sense. He should be livid with her for trapping Dante that way. "Dante and I won't be together forever like you said. It just makes me a little sad that's all. And listening to you talk about the four of us, the close friendship was just more than I could take."

"Why do you say you and Dante won't be together forever?" Lillie asked.

"He only married me to protect me," she said ashamed. "And I let him. I let him talk me into dragging this thing out. I let him because I wanted as much time with Dante as I can have. I've been so selfish," the tears began to flow.

Lillie took Cornelia's hand and let her silently weep. "You think Dante doesn't love you," she finally concluded.

"He doesn't," Cornelia managed. "Our marriage was a drunken mistake. We'd both had too much alcohol and somehow found ourselves in one of those tiny chapels. We went to the bank and realized Carlo was responsible for your problems too. Dante took me back to the room and explained everything to me. I just wanted to take him out and show him a good time. I wanted to make him forget how he'd been used and discarded by that woman and his father. The man that is supposed to love and protect him, betrayed him. Then I woke up married. And now I'm using him, too."

"How?" Lillie asked. "How are you using Dante?"

"I already told you, for protection," Cornelia said, clearly annoyed.

"Then you don't love him?" Lillie asked, waiting.

"I do," Cornelia admitted. "That's the problem. I am so in love with Dante I can't think straight. That man can talk me into anything, even when I know it's wrong. I would do anything for him. He's so kind and gentle with me. Nobody has ever treated me the way he does. Oh, I know, he's macho and gruff when he's around the warriors but he's different with me."

"Like Nick is with me," Lillie said softly.

"No," Cornelia protested. "It's different. Dante is such an honorable and giving man that he would do anything to protect me. Anything to put my mind at ease, to make me feel safe and secure. Even marry me and deceive all his friends. This arrangement is no different than his marriage to Shannon. I didn't trap him for money, but I still trapped him for my own selfish reasons."

"You're wrong," Lillie said knowingly. "Dante doesn't feel trapped. No, just hear me out," Lillie rushed on, knowing Cornelia was about to argue. "I understand Dante better than most. We have so many things in common. We were both manipulated and used by our ex's. Both of them cheated on us, then discarded us. It's difficult to live with, for both of us. I shut out the world, Dante partied. He's had more time to deal with it than me, but he's still vulnerable. I can see it in his eyes. But when he looks at you, the only thing I see is love. Love and devotion and a little terror."

"It's the terror I see," Cornelia admitted. "Terror over the backlash he's going to take from everyone when he divorces for the second time. And resignation, because he's made his decision and he won't back down regardless of the consequences."

"Cornelia?" Lillie asked. "What would you do if Dante told you he loved you?"

Cornelia shrugged. "He doesn't, so I don't know."

"Maybe that's why he hasn't told you, yet," Lillie suggested. "You keep talking about leaving. Dante knows that the instant Nick told me he loved me, I bolted. I couldn't believe someone that wonderful could actually love plain old me. There had to be a catch. My husband never loved me, my foster parents never loved me, I didn't have any friends. How could Nick love me? Dante seems strong and secure on the outside, but he's still vulnerable. He's still unsure of himself. While all the other warriors were finding love and getting married, Dante sat back, sure he would never find that for himself. He might seem confident to you, but deep down he's a little insecure. You can trust me on this, I can see it. Sometimes when I look at Dante, I see myself. His father is so cruel. Shannon and her father schemed and manipulated Dante from the start. I suspect Dante doesn't trust what he feels for you. But more importantly, he can't imagine you could ever feel the same."

"But..." Cornelia started, then stopped. Could Lillie be right, or did she just want Lillie to be right because that meant she might have a chance with Dante?

"Don't argue with me," Lillie said standing. "Don't do anything. Just think about what I told you and enjoy spending time with Dante. You'll know. My wounds were fresh, but I decided to take a chance on Nick before we had this amazing connection. Now that I have it, it's impossible to doubt what we have. I can feel Nick's love like a blast of dynamite whenever he's near. You don't need that, Cornelia, neither does Dante. But he will need reassurance. If you truly want this to last, you're going to have to trust him. Not just with your life, but with your heart. And that my friend, is going to take a lot of courage."

They were headed back to the apartment building now. Cornelia's mind was reeling. She wanted to believe Lillie. She wanted Dante to love her more than she'd ever wanted anything. She felt so comfortable with him. He knew what she was and he'd accepted her completely in spite of her flaws. There's no way he could sit and casually drink a glass of blood with her if he had a problem with her defect. But accepting her for who she was didn't mean he had fallen in love with her. Sure the intimacy was wild and explosive, but was that love? How did you know? How would she ever know for sure that Dante was with her because he loved her, not because he wanted to protect her?

"This place is so amazing," Lillie said, studying the grounds. "I never knew you could have an orchard in the desert."

Cornelia smiled. "I know, and I love the concept." She glanced at the field where men, women and children dug rows and scattered fertilizer. Next fall they would be out there again, digging up potatoes. Off in the distance, she could hear the hum of a tractor. Some of the residents were preparing the fields to plant the alfalfa next month. Everyone chipped in, even the kids.

"They don't have much but they all seem so happy," Lillie observed. "I hope Trixie and little Bella Rose fit in. It would be a good place for the child to grow up."

"Can you believe how much that woman has gone through?" Cornelia asked. When they arrived, Lexie was waiting for them. She wanted to talk to Dante and Nick but didn't seem to mind Cornelia and Lillie being in the room. They had all gone into the large lounge, which was empty at the time. Most of the residence had already begun their work day. Lexie wanted to clear the air. She was also worried the new arrangement wasn't going to work out. When pressed, she proceeded to tell them her story. Her father was abusive, so she'd run off with the first man that offered. She grew up in Idaho. The boyfriend was headed for Vegas to strike it rich. He was a creep, verbally abusive and selfish. It didn't take long before he packed up and disappeared. A couple weeks later, Lexie discovered she was pregnant. Lexie got a job as a waitress and worked at the truck stop until the day before Bella Rose was born. A week later, she contacted her boss expecting to return to work right away. He informed her she was no longer needed.

Lexie was desperate, she had to pay the rent. For the next year, she moved from job to job, doing her best to care for her young child. She was fired several times because Bella was sick a lot and Lexie didn't have anyone to help her. She finally landed a job at a local club. She started out as a waitress, then realized she'd make a lot more money as a dancer. Things were going pretty well and she worked at the same job for a couple years. Then Bella Rose started to have problems. She passed out at pre-school and always seemed winded and tired. Lexie saved up and took Bella to a doctor. They discovered she had a heart defect. The doctors said it was common in children and could be corrected with minor surgery. Bella's valve was narrow, preventing her heart from pumping normally. She passed out and was tired because her body wasn't getting the oxygen it needed to function normally.

Lexie was devastated. She couldn't afford surgery, but Bella needed it to survive. She didn't have insurance, so the hospital required a large lump sum up front. Lexie had no idea how she was going to pay the rent and save enough to pay the deposit for Bella to have her surgery. Then she found her answer. One of the wealthy businessmen from the area, a regular at the club, approached Lexie with a proposition. Sex for money. He said he would pay her well, but didn't want the strings associated with a girlfriend. He had needs, but not the time to pamper a woman. Lexie hated it, but she would do anything for her child so she agreed. Pretty soon, the guy's friends were coming to her for the same arrangement. She had a few regulars and had decided not to take on any more clients.

That's when Dave Cunningham found her. He'd made her an offer she couldn't refuse. She'd only have to have sex with one guy and in return, she'd have a place for her and Bella to stay. They would be fed well and Lexie figured she could find a job at a local restaurant or café. Her entire check could go towards Bella Rose's surgery. Now, with Cunningham getting fired and Nick and Dante expecting her to work the fields she was once again in a bind. The men assured her Bella's surgery would be taken care of. Waterson House would pay the bill in its entirety. As long as Lexie contributed an honest day's work, she had nothing to worry about.

"I don't think anyone has ever done anything nice for Lexie or Bella Rose," Lillie smiled. "Our men came through on that one. The doctor is supposed to be here this afternoon. I bet little Bella Rose will have her surgery by the end of the week. Things worked out as they should. I hate the circumstances but I'm sure glad they ended up at The Waterson House. Lexie's life is going to get a lot better from here on out."

"I agree," Cornelia said stopping to open the large front door.

They wandered the halls until they heard Dante's voice. He and Cam were just exiting an office. Dante smiled at Cornelia when they met up in the hall. He took her hand and brushed a feather-light kiss on her lips in greeting. "I guess we won't have to call out the search team after all."

"Where's Nick?" Lillie asked, frowning.

"He should be back any minute," Dante said turning and leading the group toward the front doors. "He ran over to check in with Chen Lu again. He usually has good information and if Cam's cabin idea doesn't pan out, we're going to be back at square one."

"I would have gone with him," Lillie said starting to worry. "How long has he been gone?"

"Cool your jets young Jedi," Dante said pushing Lillie out the door. "Nick is fine. Chen's a little old Chinaman. I'm sure Nick can take him." He gave her a wink then turned back to Cam. "Ready to head over to the farmhouse?"

"Sure, but where's Charlotte? She wanted to go with us," Cam said glancing around for his new assistant.

"Already there," Dante said motioning to the house in the distance. "See, the lights are on. Charlotte said she was going to get the key and turn on the power so we didn't have to wander around in the dark."

"Um," Cam began. "Since there's no chance of her walking in on us, I wanted to talk to you about something."

"Go ahead," Dante said, watching Cam. Charlotte was staying, so he hoped these two could get along.

"Why didn't you promote her to Director? Charlotte I mean," Cam asked. "I don't feel right about taking that job away from her. She's been here a long time. She's efficient and could run this place in her sleep. It just seems to me she should get the director's job and I could be her assistant."

Dante smiled. "Charlotte is good, all that and more. But she's too kind-hearted and she doesn't have it in her to take charge when she needs to. I was very clear that I wanted that room left vacant. She knew that. She was willing to remind Cunningham of my directive but that's as far as she took it. I need someone like you to run this place. Someone who won't take any crap from anyone. I coerced you into giving the place a chance, but that's not the norm. Most of these people are here because they sought us out. They came here looking for a place to stay and have proven their worth. That's not always the case. We sometimes get people who come by looking for a free ride. Some of them are belligerent, some of them are good con men. Charlotte will have a hard time dealing with both types. She'll be intimidated by the ruffians and compassionate to the cons."

Progeny

Cam could see Dante's point, but he wasn't convinced. "But with me as assistant, I would still be here to back her up. I can get rid of the cons and the ruffians."

"Not going to happen," Dante said pausing to turn to Cam. "Look, Nick and I have talked about this. We were going to pull you aside and discuss it later, but since you're so adamant I'll talk to you now. We have a few places that have two directors, a partnership. Two people who work well together and play on each other's strengths. We're thinking about doing that here. Later, not now. Once you get settled and see how things mesh between you and Charlotte we'll talk again. It's going to be up to you. But if you think it could work, you can promote Charlotte to co-director any time you want."

Cam was silent for a long time. "It still surprises me, how much faith and trust the two of you are willing to put in me. I'm a stranger." He shook his head. "Rick was right. You come across as arrogant pricks, but the two of you are okay." He smiled then, "By the way, I called Rick last night. You have no idea how stoked he is that I accepted your offer. Mostly because he can find me now anytime he wants."

"Also because he can now set a date and make his woman happy," Dante said grinning.

"There is that," Cam said, as the group continued toward the old farmhouse. "He talked me into being his best man. So, I guess as soon as he sets that date I'll be asking for a vacation."

"Don't ask," Dante told him. "Just put Charlotte in charge and go. Go early, make sure you have plenty of time to spend with Rick and catch up before the big day."

"Good-2-go, thanks," Cam said, ascending the stairs onto the front porch and continuing on through the door Charlotte was holding for them.

The group toured the run-down house then headed back across the expanse to the main building. They had almost reached the property line when Nick pulled in and climbed from the car. Lillie quickened her pace and allowed Nick to pull her in for a hug when he intercepted the group.

"How's Chen Lu?" Dante asked.

"Wiley as ever," Nick said with a grin. "He really didn't have much to tell us. He was able to speak with one of the Pooch's associates. The guy said they had a meeting two nights ago and the Pooch was alone. No sign of Tiny. He thought that was strange, since those two hooked up they've been constant companions."

"That's true," Cam agreed. "It's the reason I haven't been able to talk to Tiny alone."

"Maybe Tiny had to stay back to guard Shannon," Cornelia suggested.

"Maybe," Dante said then shrugged. He turned back to Nick. "Everything else go okay?" He asked cryptically.

"Perfect," Nick told him with a grin.

Progeny

"Then it's time for us to leave," Dante said turning to Cam and Charlotte. "You both have our numbers if you need anything. You should have two doctors arriving later this evening."

"Two?" Cam asked. "Why two?"

"One for you and one for Bella Rose," Nick said, smiling. "Don't fight us on this. I've arranged for a specialist to come out and take a look at your injuries. He's going to do a thorough exam and see if anything can be done to give you more relief from the pain. It's a long shot, but give it a try."

Cam was touched, but he shook his head. "That's thoughtful, but there's no hope. I already got a second opinion. After the situation with Rick and the shrapnel they missed, I decided not to trust the VA. The second doc said the same as the first. This is it, I just have to learn to deal with it. Don't waste your money on a private exam, there's really nothing anyone can do."

"Do the exam," Dante ordered. "If the doc says the same, we'll drop it." Then he led Cornelia to the car and climbed in the back. "Nick, you get to drive. I drove last night."

* * * *

Nick and Lillie sat at a table next to the window of the Stratosphere. It was so romantic. Night had fallen and the bright lights of the city were breathtaking. The whole room rotated, slowly. By the time dinner was over she would have had a full 360-degree view of Las Vegas. There were no children here. This was an adult, romantic dinner for two type of place. Nick had insisted on leaving Dante and Cornelia back at the room. He wanted some time to dazzle the woman he loved. Lillie had reluctantly agreed, but she felt a little guilty about it. On the other hand, after her conversation with Cornelia earlier she thought it might be good for those two to have their own alone time.

The waiter brought the wine and Nick gave their order. He took Lillie's hand and pressed his lips to her palm. "You're beautiful tonight," he said softly. "Not just the dress, but you're glowing. I think Cornelia is good for you," he paused. "You two seem to be growing closer. I know you've never had a friend, not like Dante and Thomas are to me. Well, all the warriors actually. But you and Cornelia seem to click. It makes you happy to spend time with her."

"It does," Lillie admitted. "She has a rough background too. Maybe that's why we click so well. I don't know, but I really like her. She's someone I can talk to, open up to. I think she gets me and we have fun together. I hope her and Dante work out their problems so they can start being as happy as we are."

"Problems?" Nick asked.

"Yeah," Lillie hesitated. "She doesn't think he loves her. She thinks he married her out of obligation, just to protect her. She can't see past that to see just how much that man adores her."

Progeny

"You noticed that too, huh?" Nick asked.

"How could I miss it?" Lillie asked. "I know you see it and maybe because of our past I understand Dante better than most, but I just don't see how Cornelia can doubt how much she means to that man."

"They'll work it out," Nick assured her. "Now, there's something I wanted to ask you."

"Oh?" Lillie said, immediately engulfed by Nick's emotions. He was nervous, she could feel that but there was an overwhelming feeling of love and commitment.

Nick linked their fingers and smiled warmly. "I'd get down on one knee, but I think that would embarrass you. Unless you want me to," he hesitated.

"No," Lillie said immediately. "This is fine," she glanced around. The room was packed. She knew it was supposed to be more romantic for a guy to propose on his knee, but she never understood that. It just seemed uncomfortable to her.

"That's what I thought," Nick was concentrating. He wanted to feel every emotion Lillie was feeling. He wanted to know he'd done this right. She didn't want him on his knee. "I love you, Lillie Shepherd. I know we've already made a commitment. I know we already agreed to be together forever, but I want it all. I want you to be my wife. It took longer than I'd hoped to find the perfect ring, but I think I finally got it right." Nick opened a small box and set it on the table in front of her.

Lillie gasped. It was perfect. Tears formed in her eyes, she was so happy. "It's beautiful," she finally said.

"The sapphires match your eyes," he whispered. "They're not quite as bright and beautiful but I think it's a close second. I know it's not a traditional wedding arrangement but the moment I saw it I loved it. It felt right."

"It's perfect," she said smiling at the man she loved. "Do we have to size it?"

"Already done," he said lifting the ring from the box and taking her left hand in his. "Lillie Shepherd, will you make me the happiest man alive and agree to be my wife?"

"Yes," she said, captivated as he slipped the ring on her finger. "But only if we can wait and perform the ceremony in Italy. Only if we can give your mother the wedding she always dreamed of for her wonderful, special son."

"Deal," Nick said leaning forward to kiss her. "If that's what you really want. I know you're doing that for me and mom, but I want you to have the wedding you always dreamed of."

"I will," she said softly. "I'll be marrying you."

The waiter came and brought their meals. Lillie was happier than she'd ever been in her life. She knew they had already agreed to get married, but having the ring solidified their plans somehow. She loved the fact that it wasn't traditional. She knew this one was expensive, far more expensive than the one Brad had given her but that's not why she loved it. She loved it because Nick had taken the time to find something unique, something that fit her. It was just one more way he demonstrated his love for her.

* * * *

Alex, Dimitri and Fira sat in silence as they traveled to Tighe's house. Dimitri pulled the car off the highway and slowly made his way down the long drive that led to the modest home. Tighe had money. He was over 1200 years old, but he didn't believe in flaunting it. He and his wife, Leah, loved their little ranch and had no desire to upgrade. Dimitri knew their daughter, Carli, had loved growing up here too. Tighe had always raised horses and his property was large enough to keep a growing girl busy. Carli was older than Dimitri, almost twice his age if memory served correctly. But she was nice and tried to get down from Canada to see her parents as often as possible. Dimitri stopped the car in front of the farmhouse and silently walked to the passenger side, opening both doors to let the women out.

Alex heard noise in the stable and wondered if Tighe was still working on something. They hadn't called ahead. She was afraid he might try to put them off and she didn't want to wait. She'd talked Fira into confiding in Tighe and any delay might give Fira a chance to change her mind. "Let's check the barn first. I hear voices out there."

Dimitri took Alex by the hand and led the group to the large stable. When they stepped through the door he saw both Tighe and his wife, Leah. "Hey old man," he said with a friendly laugh. "You need a hand?" Tighe was standing on a footstool hanging a saddle on a wall hook.

"The day I need a hand from a sassy young man like you, is the day I gather up the horses and head to auction," Tighe said jovially. He stepped back, placing an arm around Leah's waist. "I thought you'd be busy tonight," he said, leading the group out of the barn and toward the house. "Shouldn't you be resting up, preparing for another busy night just in case?"

"We will be heading out once it gets dark but first, we needed to talk to you about something important," Dimitri said soberly. He hoped they wouldn't have another night like last night, but they were prepared if the vampires attacked again. Mason Cooper and Travis Monroe had their packs on alert as well. He was shorthanded but with the added manpower from the shifters, things should go a lot smoother this time.

"Would you like something to drink?" Leah asked. "Coffee? Tea? Soda?"

"No thank you," Alex said. "But a comfortable place to sit would be nice. This might take a while."

Tighe glanced at Fira, then back to Alex. He knew this was about Orin's nomination and the woman's claim she was Dahl's daughter. He had to admit there was a resemblance, but he just didn't see how it was possible. He and Dahl told each other everything.

Progeny

The group headed into the living room and settled in for a long discussion.

"I'd like to start this off if nobody objects," Fira began.

"I know you're here to try to convince me you are Dahl's daughter," Tighe objected. "I'm going to be honest, I think it's a waste of time. If Dahl had a daughter, I would know. He would have told me."

"Didn't he tell you there was someone he wanted you to meet when you and Leah got back from Dublin?" she asked.

Tighe paused, "Well, yes," he admitted.

"We were supposed to have dinner at Dahl's house," Fira told him. "I was coming out to visit for a couple weeks. He really wanted me to meet his best friends. Instead, my father was kidnapped and killed. He never got the chance to explain. That's what I'm here to do tonight, explain the situation to you. All I'm asking is for you to listen to my story. Then you can decide whether you believe me or not."

Tighe considered. How would Fira know Dahl had wanted him to meet someone when they got back from Dublin if Fira wasn't the person he was supposed to meet? It was an arrangement made between friends. He glanced at his wife.

"I'd like to hear what she has to say," Leah said placing a hand on her husband's thigh. "I don't see how it could hurt."

"Okay, go ahead with your story," Tighe decided.

"I really don't know how to begin so I guess I will just tell you my story," Fira took a deep breath. "I was born one thousand, one hundred and twenty-three years ago. At the time, my parents lived in New Zealand. I had a good childhood. I grew up with two loving parents and two sets of grandparents who I believed were too strict and old-fashioned but who loved me very much. I guess my point is that I was very happy, our family was happy and as time went on we prospered. One of the rumors I've heard lately is that I am claiming to be Dahl's daughter because I am after his wealth. I assure you, I don't need it. My family is very wealthy. I am very wealthy. I own and operate a very successful business and have done so for centuries."

"I think this would go better if you just told us your story. I am aware of the rumors, but frankly my wife and I don't put much stock in rumors." Tighe prompted.

"You're right," Fira said, taking a deep breath. "My father, Briant Williams, passed away twenty-three years ago."

"I'm sorry to hear that," Leah said. "That must have been difficult."

"It was," Fira admitted. "I thought losing dad was the worst thing that could happen. I loved my father very much, Briant that is," Fira paused. "Well, Dahl too.

Progeny

Anyway, a few months after Briant's death my mother paid me a visit. They were living in Australia at the time but I had moved to the states."

Tighe was listening very carefully. Was it possible this all had to do with Dahl's time in Australia? The time frame seemed to fit.

"Mom sat me down and told me she had a confession to make. She said Briant wasn't my biological father. She said she had met a wonderful man named Dahl and he was my father. I didn't believe her. Briant was the only father I had ever known. I didn't want to believe her. Then she told me her story," Fira paused.

"Which was?" Tighe prompted.

"Mom was 284 years old. Back then it was common for parents to arrange marriages for their children. My grandparents wouldn't even consider marriage until mom was at least two hundred and fifty years old. They believed she needed that time to grow and mature. They wanted her to have time to live before they chose her a mate. They didn't decide on Briant until she was 282 years old. Her parents and Briant's parents hashed out the details and decided their children would be married the following year. Mom objected. Not because she disliked Briant, but because she wanted time to get to know him. The four parents resisted at first but finally agreed to give the couple two years, then the wedding would happen without delay.

Mom and Briant spent some time together, but Briant was off exploring for months at a time. He was trying to make his own way in the world. Mom was disappointed.

She thought two years would be plenty of time to get to know her new husband, but as the prearranged wedding date grew closer mom began to panic. She cared for Briant, but she wasn't sure she loved him. A month before the wedding, mom ran away. She'd heard Briant talk about the amazing beaches in Australia. This was long before the European's had discovered either island so the place was remote and secluded.

Once mom got to Australia she didn't know what to do. She had never been on her own before. She'd never had to hunt for her own food. The one thing she could do was fish. So, she decided to stay close to the beach. That's where she met Dahl. He was handsome and charming and the two of them hit it off immediately. Dahl was so carefree and wild. Mom couldn't resist. She'd come from such a strict and structured life. This was her time to let go of her inhibitions and live a little. Dahl had built a small shack on the beach. The two of them spent the summer together in that shack. Dahl hunted, mom fished. They made love under the moonlight and never once talked about the future or responsibilities. At first, mom thought it was heaven. But as time went on, she began to miss her old life.

The idea of living forever with a man that didn't seem to have a plan, a nomad, someone with no future and no ambition frightened her. By the end of the summer mom longed for the life she had abandoned, and the man. Dahl left one morning to hunt. Mom got up, planning to fish again but she couldn't do it. The summer was coming to an end and she knew if she wanted to get back to New Zealand she had to go soon. Otherwise, she would be

Progeny

stranded on that Australian island all winter. Mom walked further from the shack than usual and came across a boat pushing out, headed for New Zealand. She was terrified, but she caught a ride with the strangers and never looked back.

When she arrived home, her parents were livid. They threatened to disown her and refused to let her stay with them for even one night. Mom was heartbroken. She knew she deserved their wrath, but she didn't know where to turn. She had no reason to believe Briant would forgive her, but she went to him anyway. He had settled at the foot of the mountains and spent the entire summer building a beautiful log cabin. The structure was finished but he hadn't furnished it yet. Mom told him how her parents had refused her and he insisted she stay with him. Before mom agreed, she told Briant the entire story. To her surprise, he forgave her immediately. That was the moment she knew Briant was the only man for her. They spent that night and every night afterward together.

Briant's parents wanted to plan a big wedding but the couple wanted something small and intimate. A week after mom returned home, she discovered she was pregnant. She was terrified, sure that Briant would change his mind about the wedding, but she told him anyway. Briant was elated. He knew he could give the child a good life, a better life than a drifter living in a shack. He told my mother he had been in a terrible accident years ago, when he was in his thirties, and it was impossible for him to father a child. For Briant, this was a miracle. They truly believed the nomad, Dahl, wouldn't be interested in being a parent anyway.

The couple got married immediately, raised me as their own and never told a soul that I wasn't Briant's. When she finished relaying the story, mom gave me an address. Dahl's address. She said that eventually she and Briant realized they'd been unfair to Dahl. Briant had tracked him down and discovered he wasn't a nomad. Mom was surprised to learn Dahl did have ambition. He did have a plan. She assumed he was doing the same thing she was on that island, escaping reality for a while. She considered contacting him, but by this time he was married to Chelsea and they had a son. She and my father decided it was better to leave things as they were."

"Dahl had a right to know," Leah said, appalled that something so important could have been hidden from her friend for so long.

"But you still didn't contact Dahl," Tighe said, sure he was right. Dahl didn't know about Fira twenty-three years ago. He would never have kept it a secret that long.

"No, I didn't," Fira agreed. "I wasn't a child in need of a father any longer. I was an independent business woman. I loved my parents and we spoke on the phone and emailed frequently but I rarely saw them anymore. I missed my father and still do but I didn't feel a need to fill the void he had left in my life. If I'm going to be truthful, I wouldn't let myself admit that there was a void. I continued on the way things had been for years. Mom and I still talked regularly on the phone. We sent emails at least once a week. Life went on."

"So when did you contact Dahl and why?" Tighe asked.

Progeny

"A little more than a year before he died," she admitted. "I was preparing for the grand opening of my shop in New Jersey. The day before I left, a client of mine stopped by the office. She was putting forth such an effort to go over the details, but I could tell her heart wasn't in it. I finally asked her what was wrong. This client was human and her story was much different than mine. She was adopted. She'd known that for years and had been desperately trying to track down her biological parents. After years of nothing, the private detective she'd hired called. He had a lead. The two of them traveled to Denver the following day. He was sure he'd located her mother. He had, but she was in the hospital dying. My client had a week to get to know her mother before the woman died of cancer.

This client of mine went on and on about how grateful she was to have that week. She was able to get to know the woman who had given her away. Her mother explained that she didn't want to give the child up, but she knew it was the best thing for the baby. She was poor and didn't feel like she had anything to offer. My client grew to love her mother in only a week's time. She wished she had found her sooner, but treasured the moments they had together. I started to wonder. Fae don't get cancer, but we do die. I asked myself if I would regret my choice if I never met my real father. I decided I would. So, once I opened the store in Jersey I headed to New York."

"It's hard for me to believe that Dahl knew he had a daughter for over a year and never told me," Tighe said, considering.

"He didn't believe me at first," Fira told him.

"How did you convince him?" Tighe asked. "No, wait. How long? How long did it take before he accepted you as his?"

"Four and a half months," Fira said. "And I didn't convince him, mom did."

"What is your mother's name?" Tighe asked. He was almost convinced, but this was important. If Fira said Rhianna, the pieces all fit.

"Rhianna Williams," Fira told him.

Leah gripped Tighe's hand. She was convinced. This really was Dahl's daughter. Everything fit too perfectly.

"And Rhianna contacted Dahl on your behalf?" Tighe asked.

"Yes," Fira nodded. "I told mom I finally went to visit Dahl. She wasn't surprised to learn he didn't believe me. She told me not to worry, she would take care of it. I tried to talk her out of it. I said it didn't matter. I had met my biological father and if he didn't want a daughter, he had that right. Mom called him anyway. I think Dahl believed her, but two weeks after my first visit, Dahl showed up at the shop in Jersey. He asked me if I was willing to have a DNA test. I asked him what was the point? He clearly didn't want me in his life, so why did he want to know if I was his," Fira smiled. "He said he would like a daughter more than anything. He told me I had no

Progeny

idea how much it would mean to him if he learned he really wasn't alone in this world. But he wasn't willing to accept me on face value. He had to know for sure. He couldn't have any doubt."

"That sounds like Dahl," Tighe said.

"So we did the test," Fira told them.

"You still have the results," Tighe realized.

"I do," Fira assured him. She pulled a file from her bag and handed it to him.

Tighe read the report generated by Bastian Carrigan himself. It was right there in black and white. The test proved by 99.9% accuracy that Fira was Dahl's daughter. "Why haven't you shown this to the council? The only holdup, the only thing standing in the way of you becoming an alternate council member is the council's uncertainty that you really are related to Dahl. This proves, without a doubt that you are."

"Because I don't want to answer all the questions," Fira admitted. "I don't want your people to judge my mother. I know her decision isn't going to be a popular one. I saw the look on your face, Leah, as I was relaying what happened. Most people will believe that Dahl had a right to know about me. I'm inclined to agree. However, I also understand my mother's position. She spent a wild, carefree summer with Dahl. They never discussed where they came from. Never shared the intimate details of their lives back at home. Dahl didn't know my mother was running from marriage. Mom didn't know Dahl was struggling with the pressures of the family business. They both escaped to an island paradise. He was a boy without a care, she was a girl looking for adventure. That's really all they knew about each other."

"I understand," Tighe told her and he did. "Dahl was struggling with the pressure his family was putting on him at the time. He needed an escape," Tighe figured he'd found one. It was much later, months after returning home that Dahl confided in him. He told him about the wild, sexy woman that had vanished as mysteriously as she had appeared. And how the loss of the woman was what pushed him into coming home and accepting his destiny. "I still don't understand why Dahl kept this a secret from me and Leah once you had the DNA results."

"That was probably my fault," Fira admitted. "I asked him to give me time. I talked to him about my dad, Briant Williams. He understood that we had a strong, loving relationship. I wanted to get to know Dahl but wasn't sure I would ever be able to accept him as my father. We decided to spend some time getting to know each other. If it worked out, if we enjoyed spending time together, if I was able to accept him as my father, then we'd share the details with others. I know it was hard for him to keep it from you," she smiled. "Every time he gave you a vague excuse for leaving, he asked me how it was going. He was anxious for us to meet. He wanted me to know you, but he also wanted you to get to know me. The secret was killing him. At first, I was worried we might not like each other but that concern was quickly eliminated. We clicked right away. But then I just wanted him to myself. I worried if he started telling people he had a daughter, I'd spend what

Progeny

little time we had together with his friends. I guess I was selfish, I wanted my father to myself. The more time that passed, the closer we became. Dahl was a natural businessman. I found myself calling him all the time, discussing problems with the business with him or just telling him about my day.

I was having some trouble at the New Jersey shop. Problems that needed to be dealt with in person. Dahl talked me into moving out here. He wanted me to stay at his place, but I resisted. I decided to rent a place in Jersey and drove over as often as I could. We agreed that as soon as you got back from Dublin, he'd set up a meeting. I flew out, found a place to stay and spent a weekend with dad. It was wonderful. I was so happy about the direction my life was headed. I think he was, too. I flew back to California to finalize the sale of my home and check in with my CEO. That's where I was when dad was kidnapped," Fira paused to wipe the tears from her face. "I will always regret that. If I'd been here, maybe I could have helped. Together we may have been able to fight them off. He may not have been kidnapped and tortured. I'll never know."

"If you had been there, you would be dead too," Dimitri told her.

"I guess my biggest regret is that it took me over twenty years to seek him out. If I had gone to him when I learned the truth we could have had so much more time. But I was stubborn. I convinced myself I didn't need him," she paused. "I was wrong. I did need him, I still do."

"You brought him joy," Leah said softly. "We didn't know what had happened, but we saw it. He was finally living again. Dahl had become such a recluse. He missed Chelsea and his son had died so long ago. He'd pretty much lost the desire to live until you came into his life. He needed you, too. Instead of regrets, focus on that. Focus on the joy the two of you gave each other."

"Thank you," Fira said sincerely. "I do, most of the time. I don't know how this information will impact your vote, Tighe. It may not matter one way or the other, but I'd like to follow in my father's footsteps. I would be honored to serve on the council. He talked about that, how important it was. About his philosophies, and the trouble you were having with the vampires. How the two of you would hash things out, sometimes for days, before you could agree on the best course of action. I think I was able to get to know dad pretty well in the short time we had together. If the council will have me, I plan to do my best to honor my father. Before I cast a vote on any issue, my first question will be what would dad do? If the council can't accept me, I understand but I truly would like this opportunity."

"You have my vote," Tighe assured her. "I can't speak for the others, but you have my vote. And before we vote the others will know I trust you and accept you as my best friend's daughter."

"Thank you for that," Fira said softly.

"I hate to cut this short, but we are out of time," Alex said hesitantly. "It's almost dark and Dimitri and I have to meet with the warriors before we all head out to patrol the streets."

Progeny

Tighe stood and moved to stand in front of Fira. He reached out his hand. Fira stood then took the hand he offered. Tighe pulled her forward and embraced her lovingly. "I'd like a chance to get to know you better," he finally said, releasing her. "Will you come to dinner sometime?"

"I'd like that," Fira told him. "I feel like I already know you, dad told me so many stories. I guess that gives me an advantage."

"I'm sure I'll catch up," Tighe said, smiling.

Leah stepped forward and embraced Fira. "We both loved your father so much. His death was very hard on both of us. We know it had to be equally hard on you. I hope you will visit us often. It would make us so happy to get to know the daughter of such an honorable man and a good friend."

"That would make me happy, too," Fira told her.

Chapter Thirteen

Nick, Dante, Cornelia and Lillie crouched in the shadows of the trees. After hours of searching, they had finally located the cabin. Well, a cabin that was obviously occupied anyway. They'd been watching for movement for the last fifteen minutes but hadn't seen a thing. It was time to approach the building.

"I think Lillie and Cornelia should remain here and keep an eye out while the two of us approach the cabin," Nick finally said.

"How about you two keep an eye out while Cornelia and I approach the building," Lillie asked, a little annoyed. He was just trying to keep her at a safe distance.

Progeny

"Because although you have many talents my dear, stealth isn't one of them," Nick brushed a soft kiss across her temple.

Lillie couldn't argue. She wasn't all that good at sneaking up on people.

"Then the three of you stay here and I'll go peek in the windows. It would be a lot easier for me to play the helpless and lost girl than either of you," Cornelia suggested.

"You might be okay at stealth, I don't know," Dante studied Cornelia. "But Nick's the best. The three of us will wait here. Nick go see what you can find out."

Nick nodded then headed through the trees before anyone could argue. Within minutes he was back by their side. "She's in there. I assume it must be Tiny with her. There's no sign of anyone else. I think it's just the two of them."

"Weapons?" Dante asked.

"None that I could see but according to Chen Lu, the Pooch is always armed. According to word on the street, Tiny is also carrying now," Nick paused. "If he really is on the level of a nine-year-old that could be dangerous."

"I agree," Dante said soberly.

"If Tiny is like a kid, a woman would be less threatening than either of you," Cornelia was thinking. "What if I go knock on the door and ask for directions?"

"No, too risky," Dante said immediately. "What if the Pooch actually is inside, just somewhere Nick couldn't see him? He might shoot you on sight."

"There's a pretty clear view of the living area from the other side of the cabin. It has a fairly large window. What if we station Lillie at the window? Cornelia can watch the back door in case they try to run. Dante, you stay on this side. That way you can watch out for the Pooch, but hang back in case you need to help Cornelia. I'll sneak up to the front door and see if it's locked. If it is, I can pick it."

"That leaves you hanging out too much," Dante argued. "And Lillie, if she sees someone coming and calls out to you. The attention is going to be drawn to her."

"She doesn't need to call out," Nick argued. "I'll feel her emotions. If something's wrong, I'll know immediately."

Dante considered, he'd forgotten about the connection. He turned to Cornelia. "What do you think about the plan?"

"It might work. If anyone comes running out the back it's going to leave Nick and Lillie to deal with whatever's happening inside, but I can't think of a better plan with just us four," Cornelia answered.

"I agree," Dante finally said. "There's only two, maybe three, of them. I know they have guns, but we're used to battling hundreds of vamps. If you removed the guns from the mix it would be a piece of cake, with the guns... it's more challenging, but I think we can handle it."

The group disbursed. Dante turned to Cornelia. "When Nick goes in, we go in through the back. I'm not taking any chances," Cornelia just nodded before heading to her post. The door was locked, but it was a cheap lock and easy to open. Nick turned the knob and pushed on the door, careful to stay in tune with Lillie's emotions. They were heightened a little, but not to the point he felt something was wrong.

Once Nick was inside, Lillie ran to the front and tiptoed through the door. Nick glared at her unhappily then pressed a finger to his lips and continued down the hall. Lillie followed directly behind him. So far, so good. There still wasn't any sign of the Pooch.

Nick reached for the door to the bedroom but was stopped by Cornelia. He looked up to see Dante right behind her. They must have come in through the back.

Cornelia shifted, positioning her body to the side of the door jamb. She pointed to the room across the hall and to the left. "Go in there," she mouthed. "I'm going to knock. If he shoots, the jam will help and the bullets should miss that room."

Nick and Lillie moved into the room, but Dante didn't budge. He knew the door jamb wasn't going to stop a bullet and he wouldn't allow Cornelia to take this risk on her own. He was going to be prepared if Tiny surfaced with a gun.

Cornelia rolled her eyes, "Then stay out of sight." Dante moved further into the shadows. Cornelia knocked softly and waited.

"Who's there?" Came a low, male voice.

"Cornelia," she said, forcing her voice to sound casual and light.

The door opened a few inches and Tiny peaked out. "I don't know any Cornelia's," Tiny told her, he was frowning.

Cornelia held out her hand and waited. Tiny only hesitated a second then he took it, giving it a quick shake then letting go. "Now you do," she told him.

In the shadows, Dante scowled. Was the woman always this reckless?

"I was wondering if I could come in there and talk to you," Cornelia asked. Before Tiny could respond they heard a noise in the room down the hall, the one Nick and Lillie were hiding in.

"What was that?" Tiny said nervously.

"Oh, that's just my friend Lillie," Cornelia told him. "She was worried you might not like us so she hid in the room over there. You're not mad at us are you Tiny?"

"I'm not mad," he said instantly. "But I need to see Lillie."

Progeny

Lillie stepped from the room with a smile plastered on her face. Cornelia knew it was fake, the girl was nervous but Tiny was satisfied.

"You probably shouldn't be here. The Pooch will be back soon and I'm not allowed to have friends over," Tiny admitted guiltily.

Just then a woman's voice came from the bedroom. "Help me. They kidnapped me and they're holding me against my will," then she screamed, "Help!"

Cornelia shook her head then glanced at Tiny.

"Shannon," Tiny said as if he were talking to a child. "The Pooch already explained this. We didn't kidnap you. We're having a sleepover. It's just for a few more nights then you can go home."

Cornelia and Lillie locked eyes, then they both nodded. Cornelia pushed open the door and stepped into the room, Lillie at her side. "Tiny?" Cornelia said softly, "Is Shannon a friend of yours?"

"I thought so, but she's mad at me. She's mad because the Pooch says she has to wait here. He says I have to keep her company until he can figure out a new plan. He said he couldn't find her husband so his first plan didn't work. He thinks her husband is home now, but he never leaves the house. Now we're having a sleep party until the Pooch decides she can go home," Tiny frowned. "The Pooch isn't nice anymore. I don't like him, he's bad."

Cornelia motioned for Dante and Nick to leave. She knew they wanted to, they would do more good outside watching and waiting for the Pooch to arrive. She could handle Tiny. She heard the slight click telling her the men had left the cabin. Her attention turned to the grimy window. Moments later she saw the slightest movement and her muscles relaxed. The men would take care of the Pooch and she could handle Tiny and Shannon.

"Do you mind if I sit down, Tiny?" Cornelia asked. "It looks like you have an extra chair."

"No, I don't mind," Tiny said returning to sit in front of a board game.

"Oh, are you playing Monopoly?" Cornelia said, feigning excitement. "Who's winning?" Cornelia was studying Shannon from the corner of her eye. The woman was a knockout. She had red hair, but it wasn't just red hair. It was about ten different shades of red, a silk flowing mass that somehow brought out her vibrant green eyes. And saying that Shannon was petite was a gross understatement. She was probably a size two and she looked fragile and delicate. Cornelia knew she could never compare to someone this feminine. That was the only word she could think of to describe Shannon Santora, feminine...and gorgeous.

"Shannon's winning," Tiny grumbled. "But I think she's cheating."

"Probably," Lillie said taking a step toward the woman. "That seems to be a habit of hers."

Progeny

Shannon glared at Lillie. Who were these women? "If you know what's good for you, you will get me out of these chains immediately," Shannon spat, irritated at the lack of respect or concern the women were showing her.

"Tiny," Cornelia continued as if Shannon hadn't spoken a word. "Shannon's husband is very worried about her. He asked us to come pick her up and take her home. He really misses her and even though you are supposed to have a sleep party for another night, we really have to take her home. He's pretty sad without her."

"Shannon's husband is sad?" Tiny said concerned.

"He's very sad," Cornelia said. "Do you know where the key is to unhook those chains?"

"In my pocket," Tiny said proudly.

"Really?" Cornelia asked. "Could I borrow it?"

"Okay," Tiny said, standing to pull out the key. He handed it to Cornelia who passed it to Lillie.

"Thank you," Cornelia told him. "Shannon's husband will be so happy."

"The Pooch is going to be mad at me," Tiny realized, frowning. "He said she had to stay until he decided she could go. Until he had another plan," he paused. "But he's already mad at me because I wouldn't let him hurt her. He got mad and wanted to hit her, but I wouldn't let him. I thought the Pooch was nice, but he's mean. He hurt me, too." Tiny pulled up his shirt sleeve and showed the two women a large bruise.

Cornelia trailed a finger over the bruise, gently. "That looks like a bad one," she commented. "Why did the Pooch hurt you?"

"He said his plan wasn't working and it was Shannon's fault. He said he was going to show her. He said she had to pay for his plan getting messed up and she refused to give him some drugs. I blocked the door and wouldn't let him in. That made him mad and he was mean to me," Tiny explained.

"This is ridiculous," Shannon yelled. "Stop mollycoddling that buffoon and get me out of here."

Lillie stared at Shannon. "Lady, I don't like your tone. You might want to dial it down a bit or I might just leave you here to rot."

"How dare you speak to me that way?" Shannon growled. "My husband will show you a thing or two once I tell him how I was treated. He must have hired you to find me. When I get finished, he's not going to pay you a dime."

"I'll stack my husband against yours any day and twice on Sunday," Cornelia said casually. "So shut up."

Lillie had removed one of the shackles and was starting on the other one when she saw him. Her eyes grew wide and she was about to warn Cornelia, but it was too late. The sound of gunfire echoed throughout the small room.

Cornelia saw Lillie's face and started to turn, but she didn't have time. The cold steel pressed firmly against her temple just before she heard a click, then a loud boom.

Nick and Dante had circled the cabin twice, then headed toward the woods. They located an overgrown trail that had obviously been used recently. Weeds were trampled, branches were broken. They silently followed the trail, worried about how far they were going from the cabin. Just as they were about to give up and turn back, Nick spotted the truck. It was an old Junker, backed off the trail and partially hidden in the forest. They snuck through the darkness careful to remain hidden behind the trees as much as possible. Finally, they darted past an opening and crouched in front of the truck. Nick went right, Dante left but they instantly realized the truck was vacant. Dante stood and placed a hand on the hood, it was still warm. "We need to get back to the cabin. It hasn't been here long. If I had to guess, the Pooch just got home."

"I agree," Nick said, turning and heading the same way they had arrived. The men had just reached the edge of the trees when a shot rang out. Panicked, both men ran for their life. Nick concentrated, he was sure he'd know if Lillie was injured. He was halfway across the yard when he felt her. Lillie wasn't hurt, but she was shocked and worried. That meant Cornelia. She had to be okay. Dante couldn't lose her now. Nick glanced at his friend, then picked up the pace.

Both men reached the front door at the same time. Nick yanked it open and followed Dante through the door.

Dante ran down the hall then stopped abruptly, relieved. A man was on the floor, clearly dead. Cornelia stood in the doorway, covered in blood. That made his breath catch, but she was standing. That was good, right? "What happened?" He demanded pulling Cornelia against his body and wrapping his arms around her. "Are you hurt?"

"I'm fine," Cornelia said a little shocked. "I'm fine," she said more forcefully. She glanced down at the man lying at their feet. "He's dead, isn't he?" The dead body didn't bother her but she was still shaken up at how close she'd just come to dying.

"Yes," Dante said releasing his hold and surveying the room. That's when he realized Tiny was holding a gun.

"Uh, Tiny my man. Maybe you could set that down on the table." He was trying to sound cordial but knew he failed.

"Tiny?" Cornelia said softly. "It's okay now. Let's put the gun down."

"He might get up," Tiny said shaking his head. "He might try to hurt you again. I won't let him hurt you. I won't let him shoot the nice lady," he said glancing at Dante.

Progeny

Nick was still standing behind Dante. The doorway was crowded and he couldn't get passed to reach Lillie. He was about to push his way through when Shannon spoke.

"Give me that," she ordered. "Give me the key you stupid girl. I've had it with your incompetence." And without warning, she slapped Lillie across the face.

Nick shoved at Dante, but it didn't help, his friend was still in the way. Dante had taken a step forward to defend Lillie himself but didn't get a chance.

"That's it," Lillie said, standing. Then she hauled off and punched Shannon in the face. Shannon's chair fell over as she slumped to the ground. Lillie had knocked her out cold. Lillie turned to face the room, chagrin showing in her eyes. "Sorry, I guess I don't know my own strength yet," then she frowned. "She's okay, right? I mean I didn't kill her or anything did I?"

Nick finally got passed Dante and pulled Lillie into his arms. "No, sweetheart," he glanced at Shannon. "Unfortunately, she'll be fine."

"Funny," Dante said taking the key from Lillie, then leaning down to undo the other shackle. "Nobody move anything. I need to call Dimitri and see how he wants us to handle this."

"Tiny's not going to jail," Cornelia said immediately. "He saved my life. He's not going to have trouble over this."

"I agree," Dante told her. "Take it down a notch. We'll take care of Tiny."

"Jail?" Tiny said, obviously distressed at the thought.

"I'm going to take care of you, Tiny," Dante promised. "Will you trust me on this?"

Tiny looked to Cornelia for guidance.

"You can trust him," Cornelia promised.

"Okay," Tiny said, relieved. "I'm hungry. Can we have McDonald's?"

Dante left the room and dialed Dimitri. He knew it was late in New York, but he also knew all the warriors there would be pulling an all-nighter.

"Yeah," Dimitri answered. "What's up?"

"You busy?" Dante asked, hoping Dimitri wasn't in the middle of a battle or something.

"No," Dimitri grumbled. "We haven't had any trouble tonight. I can't decide if Radek is taking a break or if he's holding the vampires off until later hoping we'll get complacent and go home."

"Sorry I'm not there to help," Dante paused, he really didn't want to lay another problem on Dimitri tonight. "And, uh...sorry for what I'm about to tell you."

"What happened?" Dimitri asked, alert now.

Progeny

"There's been a little incident," Dante confessed. "The Pooch is dead. Apparently, he was going to shoot Cornelia and Tiny, his partner, shot the Pooch."

"So what's the problem?" Dimitri asked. "Just turn Tiny over to the police and let them hash it out."

"Can't do that," Dante disagreed. "Tiny is like a nine-year-old in a thirty-five-year-old body. He won't be able to handle the interrogation. Is there anyone out here that can help?"

"Not that I know of. Let me call Travis Monroe," Dimitri said with a sigh. "I'll call you right back."

Dante heard the door and turned to see Cornelia standing on the front porch. His stomach clenched again at the sight of blood splattered across her shirt. He took two steps toward her when an eagle swooped in, shifted and landed. A tall, muscular man stood there taking in the scene.

"Monroe works quickly," Dante said, as his phone began to ring. "Hey, Dimitri," he said casually. "Chief Monroe's man has already arrived."

"Oh," Dimitri said, clearly surprised. "He must have been close. I just hung up about ten seconds ago."

"Monroe said this guy can handle it?" Dante asked, still sizing up the newcomer.

"Yeah," Dimitri assured him. "Travis says not to worry, tell this Capello guy what we need and he'll take care of it."

"Got it," Dante said. "See ya," then he clicked off the phone.

"I hear you've gotten yourself into a little trouble out here," Capello said, taking another step toward Dante. "Sergeant Mark Capello." He said holding out his hand.

"Dante Santora and this is my wife, Cornelia," Dante saw the recognition immediately.

"Santora, huh?" Capello sighed. "Chief Monroe left that little detail out of the conversation. I can't say that I blame him. If you're as much trouble as Carlo, I'm not sure I can help you."

"He left it out because I doubt he's ever heard of Carlo Santora." Dante motioned for Capello to proceed into the cabin. "And I guess I should warn you that the trouble here started with Carlo and his wife Shannon. Carlo is my father."

Capello shot him a glance then continued down the hall. He noticed the man lying dead on the floor, then the big man sitting in a chair just inside the room. The next thing he spotted was the woman lying on the floor out cold. "She dead, too?"

"Nope," Dante said, giving Lillie a wink. "Just a little bump."

Progeny

Capello moved across the room, stopping to crouch in front of Shannon. The shackles were still lying on the floor next to her. He lifted her head and saw the bruise forming on her chin. "Who cold cocked her?"

"I did," Lillie said sheepishly.

Capello just raised an eyebrow, stood and continued to take in the scene. "That the weapon?" He asked, pointing to the gun sitting on the table next to a Monopoly board.

"It is," Nick said, wrapping an arm around Lillie's waist. He was still trying to figure the guy out.

"So," Capello finally said turning back to Dante. "Shannon Santora was obviously shackled to that chair. The four of you arrived to rescue her and at some point there's a shootout. Who's the triggerman?"

"Technically right, but you left out quite a bit," Nick said politely. "Shannon was kidnapped by that man on the ground out there. Tiny says the dead guy is the Pooch?"

"Never heard of him," Capello said, studying the man more closely.

"Small-time dealer, he's new to the area," Dante provided.

"I guess that move didn't work out as planned," Capello mumbled under his breath.

"The Pooch kidnapped Shannon and brought her out here." Cornelia picked up the story. "Tiny says they've been here the entire time."

"Tiny seems to know a lot. You Tiny?" Capello asked.

"Yes," Tiny said, hands in his lap, head lowered.

"How are you involved in this?" Capello asked.

"The Pooch bought me a cheeseburger. He said we were just going to have a sleep party, then I could go to McDonald's." Tiny looked up at Capello. "Can we go to McDonald's? Cornelia says Shannon has to go home because her husband is sad."

Capello raised an eyebrow and looked at Dante.

"We figure he functions on the level of a nine-year-old, mostly. Sometimes he seems younger." This was taking too long. Dante just wanted it over, but they'd learned their lesson dealing with Rand McBride. Cops had their own way of doing things. Even shifters.

"Alright, you finish it then," Capello turned back to Cornelia.

"Apparently, Shannon isn't the most amenable hostage. She's been difficult since she got here. At some point, the Pooch went out for a while. When he came back, he was in a mood. Tiny had to block the doorway to save Shannon," Cornelia continued.

"Is that true?" Capello asked Tiny.

Tiny nodded. "The Pooch is a bad man," Tiny whispered. "He wanted to hurt Shannon, I had to stop him. He said the plan was ruined. He said Carlo was missing and then he wouldn't leave the house."

"If Shannon Santora was kidnapped, why are you handling this instead of the local cops?" Capello asked.

"That would be difficult to explain," Dante glanced at Tiny. "But there were concerns, this had to be handled privately. The four of us came out from New York to investigate the situation and locate Shannon. We found her here."

"Okay, tell me what happened once you got here," Capello prompted.

"We had a tip that the Pooch might be staying out here in the cabins. We searched for hours and finally came across this one. The only one we've found that's occupied. Nick was able to get up to the window and check it out. He spotted Shannon inside with Tiny. At that point, we made entry and searched the place for that man," Dante pointed at the Pooch. "When it was clear only Shannon and Tiny were here, the girls began to handle Shannon's release. Nick and I took off in search of the Pooch. Tiny warned us he would be back any minute."

"Okay," Capello nodded.

"Nick and I found a trail that led into the woods. The Pooch obviously parks his truck out there because it's easy to hide." Dante shifted closer to Cornelia when he saw Shannon moving. "We found the truck and spotted cash and drugs in the cab, but realized it was empty. The hood was still warm so we knew he'd just gotten back and would head to the cabin. We took off at a run, realizing the women were vulnerable. We just got back when we heard the gunshot."

"So you were outside when the man was shot?" Capello asked the men.

Both of them nodded. Capello turned to Cornelia and Lillie. "Were either of you present?"

"We both were," Lillie told him. "Cornelia was talking to Tiny, making sure he was comfortable with us and everything. Tiny gave us the key to unlock Shannon. I was crouched down taking off the shackles," Lillie paused. "Shannon was being belligerent and wouldn't sit still. She was making it difficult to undo the locks. Anyway, I had just released the first one and moved in to take off the second. I think Shannon may have said something and when I looked up I saw the man. The Pooch, that guy lying on the floor, had moved up behind Cornelia. I was about to warn her when he pressed a gun to her head. Before I could do anything, Tiny shot him."

Capello turned to Cornelia. "Do you have anything to add?"

"Only that Tiny saved my life," Cornelia said confidently. "The Pooch not only held the gun to my temple, but I heard him cock the hammer."

"I guess that explains the blood," Capello said without emotion. "Okay, so I'm going to have to call this in." He glanced around the room. "Is that a problem for anyone here?"

"No," Dante told him. "But Tiny doesn't spend time in jail."

"What?" Capello asked. "You said you didn't even know him. I can't promise that. He was part of the kidnapping."

"Then I'll make him disappear," Dante said casually. "He's just as much a victim as she is." He pointed to Shannon, who was starting to sit up. "He's just a kid, mentally, and he protected her and saved my wife's life. He doesn't do jail time. The guy needs a guardian, not a cell."

"I might agree with you on that but clearly, he doesn't have one. You got any candidates for the job? I'm certainly not taking on that responsibility," Capello argued. "He's a liability."

"He's a kid," Dante returned. "I want him to go to The Waterson House. Assign guardianship to the House. Cam and Charlotte will oversee his care from now on."

"The Waterson House?" Capello snorted. "I don't know who this Cam guy is, but Director Cunningham will crap himself if I show up with Tiny in tow and tell him the guy is his problem now."

"Dave Cunningham has been fired. Cameron Harris, former Lieutenant Colonel in the Marines, is now the Director of Waterson House. He won't crap himself. He can handle Tiny just fine," Dante paused. "I need you to make this happen. Do I need to call Travis Monroe to get you on board?"

Capello sighed. "No," he said resigned. "But I wish I had been a fly on the wall when you fired that slime ball Cunningham," Capello grinned, "Literally." He realized Dante must own the charity home. The guy just shot up a couple notches on the good guy scale for that.

"I might have invited you if I'd known," Dante said moving to stand over Shannon. "Get up."

"Wait," Capello corrected. "I need a picture."

"You are not taking a picture of me in this condition," Shannon objected. "I haven't done my hair in days. I can only imagine what my makeup looks like. If anyone saw me in such a state, I'd die."

"Sorry princess," Capello said as he snapped the picture.

Shannon jumped to her feet and began to yell. It was hard to keep up, she was going off on the police, Dante's incompetence, how much she despised Nick Moretti and the horrible way the women had treated her. It seemed to go on forever.

"Now you know why I punched her," Lillie said, looking at the cop. "You want me to do it again?"

Capello smiled. "More than you know," he admitted. "But that might get me in trouble. Everyone out." He yelled so he could be heard over Shannon's ranting. "I need the scene secured. Forensics is on the way. So are a couple detectives." Once they reached the front porch Capello shoved Shannon into a chair. "Shut up and don't move," he ordered. "If I hear one more peep out of you, I'm gonna cold cock you myself."

Shannon opened her mouth, but she must have seen the truth of the threat in Capello's eyes because she immediately pressed her lips shut, folded her arms tight against her chest and pouted.

Capello left the porch and pulled out his phone. Dante assumed he was making whatever calls needed to be made to arrange for Tiny. He took Cornelia's hand and led her to a small bench.

"I guess you think this means something now?" Shannon said, glaring at Dante then Cornelia.

Neither of them spoke.

"It doesn't," she said coldly. "We don't owe you anything. And don't think you can hold the money over Carlo's head the way you always do. The Waterson's won't take that away from us. They have to understand how much we need it. And now that you're married, I'm sure they're too busy protecting their fortune from her." She shot a pointy finger in Cornelia's direction. "Anyone can see she's just after your money." Shannon looked up and down Cornelia in disgust. "Those clothes are atrocious."

Dante was about to respond when he spotted three cars. He watched as they slowly pulled into the clearing. This could wait. The Vegas police had arrived.

It was over an hour later when Sgt. Capello exited the house and approached Dante. "We shouldn't need you here much longer." He glanced out, toward the forest. "I still don't know the whole story, why didn't you come to the police when Mrs. Santora was taken. It would have been a lot cleaner if you had." He rushed on when he saw the look on Dante's face. "I know you said you had your reasons," he handed Dante a business card. "I just wanted to let you know, if you're ever out this way again and encounter trouble, give me a call. I understand the sensitive nature of some of the uh...situations our kind find ourselves in. I just wanted you to know you can trust me and depend on me in the future, that's all," he shrugged. "I'll clean up this mess from tonight. I'll just tell my boss you guys are private dicks or something."

"Actually, my wife is a Private Investigator," Dante smiled when he saw Cornelia walking his way. "I introduced you when you arrived, but here she comes. I'll introduce you again." Dante reached out and wrapped his arm around Cornelia's waist. "My wife, Cornelia Santora, PI extraordinaire," he grinned at the confused look on Cornelia's face.

"Cornelia Santora?" Capello said. Something clicked in the back of his mind. Had he met this woman before?

Progeny

Cornelia stepped forward, "I used to be Cornelia Harris, if that helps. I'm used to working in the area, so Dante thought I'd be an asset on this case."

"Seriously?" Capello said happily. "You have no idea how much that is going to help me with my Captain. When I tell him the reason we weren't contacted was because the family wanted to keep things discrete and they hired Cornelia Harris, Captain Norton won't say another word," he grinned. "Good job on the Bateman case by the way. From what I understand, our people were stumped."

"Thanks," Cornelia said, dropping the subject. She was always embarrassed when the cops praised her on her cases. It was just a job. Sure, she did it well, but so did a lot of cops. They were just understaffed and didn't have the kind of time she did to track down all the leads. "And it was nice to meet you."

"Bateman case?" Dante asked as he watched Sgt. Capello walk away.

"It was a kidnapping case a few years back," Cornelia said, brushing aside her accomplishment. "The locals were at a dead end, so the family called me in to see what I could do. I stumbled onto a lead they'd missed and was able to get the girl back within a few days. She was a mess emotionally, but relatively unharmed."

"I didn't realize my wife was famous," Dante said, clearly impressed.

"Unfortunately around here I am," she confessed. "It's going to make it difficult to return in the future. My picture was splattered all over the papers. It might be safe in fifty years or so. There's a slight possibility I could return as Cornelia's granddaughter or something. Honestly, it wasn't helpful for my long-term plan."

"Long-term plans can change," Dante said softly. "Anyway, Sgt. Capello thought they were done with us, so let's grab Nick and head out." He made a mental note to search the internet for articles on the Bateman case and Cornelia Harris. He thought it would be interesting to read what the human world thought of his amazing wife.

It was late when Dante pulled the car into Carlo Santora's drive. After dealing with the police, he had to wait for Cam to bring the van out and retrieve Tiny. Shannon had thrown a holy fit over that one. She insisted they take Tiny to jail immediately. She said he was trying to kill her with boredom. Once Tiny was loaded in the van and on his way to a better life, Shannon turned on Dante again. She didn't even stop when Nick shoved her into the back seat of the car. Her tirade covered a vast array of flaws. Dante was an ungrateful child, he was a bully, he was a control freak, he was beneath her. The few years they had been married was the worst time of her life. Apparently, they had that in common. Nick had finally had enough. He silently slipped a bandana from his pocket and fastened it around Shannon's mouth. Then he wrapped a second one around her wrists so she couldn't use her hands to get free. Shannon kicked and screamed and tried to yell, but Nick just settled back against the seat and sighed in relief. Dante flashed a grateful smile, then accelerated. He couldn't wait to dump her back on Carlo and be finished with the whole mess.

Progeny

The instant the car came to a stop, the group of four climbed out. Shannon didn't budge. Before Dante could walk around and deal with it, Nick had crouched down so he was face-to-face with Shannon. "Get out of the car, or I'll pull you out." His tone was soft but full of promise and anticipation.

Shannon tried to look dignified as she climbed from the car and held out her hands. Nick reached out and pulled the bandana free. Shannon immediately yanked off the one tied around her mouth. She glared at Nick, eyes full of hatred and venom. Then she straightened her shirt in a huff and turned. She closed her eyes and when she opened them again, they were brimming with tears.

"Showtime," Dante said, rolling his eyes and following Shannon into the house.

Carson was in the foyer as they entered. "Draw me a bath," Shannon ordered. Then she continued into the study where she found Carlo waiting.

The instant he saw her, he rushed to her side and pulled her in for a hug. He scowled at Dante when he saw the tears flowing down Shannon's cheeks. "Are you hurt, darling?"

Shannon shot Dante a triumphant smile then pulled back, frowning. "Nick and Dante have been so cruel to me." She let out a sob. "It was terrible. And they talked the police into letting one of the men go. I insisted he needed to go to jail, but Dante wouldn't have it. Then the police were mean, they took Dante's side. I've never been treated so horribly." She sobbed again, this time a loud painful sound that would have made Dante laugh if he wasn't so annoyed.

"Is this true?" Carlo demanded. "Did you set the men free that kidnapped my wife?"

"No," Dante said, taking Cornelia's hand and leading her to the couch. "We're all tired so maybe we could do without the theatrics." His voice was nonchalant but annoyed.

"See!" Shannon demanded pointing at Dante. "I don't deserve this. I won't allow him to treat me that way."

Dante raised an eyebrow at her. "If you're after what you deserve this might get a whole lot uglier, be careful what you ask for princess."

"Enough," Carlo demanded. "I want to know about the kidnappers."

"The kidnapper is dead," Nick said, pulling Lillie with him as they too settled in for the discussion.

"I don't understand," Carlo looked from Nick to Shannon. "Why did she say you let him go?"

"He did," Shannon insisted, still whining. "There were two of them. Tiny shot the Pooch and then Dante talked the cops into letting Tiny go."

"Is that true?" Carlo demanded.

"Yes," Dante answered. "Now that we cleared that up, we need to talk about the fee and how things will proceed from here. Then I need to get back to our room so I can get a couple hours of sleep before we head back to New York."

"This is not cleared up," Carlo demanded. "Dimitri assured me you would resolve this completely. Allowing a man to go free, a man that kidnapped my wife, is not resolving anything."

Dante inhaled a long deep breath before locking eyes with Carlo. "It's finished," he said coldly. "Focus on pampering that spoiled brat and forget Tiny. He's out of your reach and he's not a threat. Drop it."

"I will not," Carlo said shaking his head. "If you think you can leave things like this you are mistaken. I'll call Dimitri. He'll make you take care of it."

"Go ahead," Dante motioned for the phone. "It is three hours later in New York than it is here, but if you want to wake Dimitri up at four o'clock in the morning be my guest."

Carlo glared at his son. He hated the man right now, more than he had ever hated anyone in his life.

Shannon stomped her foot. "Do something Carlo. The four of them have been cruel to me. That one actually punched me in the face. I think I'm going to have a bruise. And Nick tied and gagged me in the car."

Carlo rushed to Shannon and studied her face. He turned on Lillie. "You...Neanderthal," he exclaimed. "I'm calling the police. We'll press charges. I should have known something like this would happen with Nick Moretti in town."

"You actually put up with this for three years?" Lillie asked Dante. "No wonder you're screwed up."

Dante gave her the finger with a smile. Lillie smiled back as she returned his one finger salute.

"Do you think this is a joke?" Carlo spat. "You are all sadly mistaken. Maybe a night in jail will do all four of you some good."

He turned toward the phone but stopped when Shannon began to speak.

"They won't do anything," she sniffled. "The police won't do anything. I already tried. I was trying to explain things to them earlier. One particular vile cop shoved me into a chair and told me if I didn't shut up, he was going to knock me out again."

Carlo was across the room standing in front of Lillie. "You knocked out my wife?" His face was red, a vein pulsing with his heart beat. His anger was out of control. It had been simmering since Dante had walked into Thomas' study. Well, in all honesty, it was simmering since he went to New York and realized he couldn't manipulate Thomas Deveraux into doing what he wanted him to. Everything had gone downhill from there.

Lillie shrugged one shoulder but didn't answer.

Progeny

The woman's cavalier attitude pushed him over the edge. Before anyone knew what Carlo planned, he struck Lillie in the face. He aimed for her jaw, but she started to lower her head and his fist collided with her right cheek. Her head bounced against the back of the couch and her eyes watered as she lifted her hand in pain. Her cheek felt like it was on fire.

Nick jumped to his feet but was pushed aside by Dante who flew off the couch and across the room in almost a single motion. He was on Carlo instantly. Nick took another step toward Carlo then decided this was Dante's fight. He sat back down and cradled Lillie's head on his lap. "Relax, baby," he told her. "It will feel better in a minute. Once we get back to the room you'll have to drink a bag of blood. But you do need to stop letting the Santora's use your face as a punching bag."

"Can I hit him back for that?" She asked, only half joking. She hated drinking blood.

"We'll see," Nick soothed as he ran a gentle finger over her swollen cheek. "Right now Dante has it covered."

Dante had initially grabbed Carlo and threw him across the room. Carlo collided with the wall and sank to the floor. Dante loomed above him. When Carlo stood, he took a swing at Dante. Dante moved to the side and avoided Carlo's fist. Then he punched Carlo in the nose. Blood gushed instantly, trickling down his face and onto the tailored white shirt he was sporting. Carlo screamed and lunged for Dante. Dante simply sidestepped at the last second and Carlo lay sprawled on the floor again. As Carlo stood he tried to elbow Dante in the ribs. Dante grabbed his arm, spun him around and planted his fist in Carlo's side. The sound of Carlo's ribs cracking filled the room.

Shannon flew across the opening and leaped onto Dante's back. She was pulling his hair and scratching viciously. Cornelia moved silently across the room. She wrapped one arm around Shannon's waist and got a good grip on that gorgeous red hair with the other. It only took one quick tug to free her from Dante. Shannon was screaming at the top of her lungs while she frantically kicked and flailed her arms in an attempt to turn around and focus her attack on Cornelia.

"They make a good team," Nick observed. "Just like us." He brushed a finger lightly over Lillie's cheek, it was red and was going to bruise before they got back to the casino. "You okay now?" He was worried, Carlo was strong enough Lillie could have a cracked bone.

Lillie sat up and took a deep breath. "I really hate those two," she finally admitted. "I might even hate them more than Brad. If I never see them again, it will be too soon."

"I know," Nick said as he wrapped an arm around her shoulders and continued to watch the fight.

Cornelia finally knocked Shannon's feet out from under her. The instant Shannon hit the ground Cornelia was on her. She sat on Shannon's hips while she pinned her legs and arms. Shannon couldn't move. She bucked and twisted but couldn't get free. "Give it up, Princess," Cornelia said with disdain. "You'll never win. You're a lightweight." She glanced up to see how things were going with Dante and Carlo.

Carlo had to be in pain. Dante knew at least two of his ribs had been broken along with his nose. He didn't care. He could go on like this all night. Carlo was out of shape. Even in his prime, he wasn't that great at fighting, he was too lazy. Carlo kicked out and tried to connect with the side of Dante's knee. Dante twisted, pivoted then knocked Carlo's legs out from under him. Carlo went down hard. Dante scooped him up and plopped Carlo into a chair. He moved in, pinning Carlo in place. "How many bones do you want me to break before you give up? This is finished."

Dante stood and started to turn when he saw Carlo's fist headed for his temple. Dante grabbed his father's arm, twisted and heard the crack. Carlo went down in pain. This time, Dante left him on the floor. He moved to where Cornelia was pinning Shannon. "Your husband needs you. Do you think you can tamp down on the selfishness for a night and be there for him this time?"

"I hate you," Shannon growled. "I wish I never met you."

"Honey, the feeling's mutual," Dante said casually.

Shannon tried to spit but Cornelia saw it coming and leaned back out of the way. "You deserve each other. You're wife's just as uncivilized as you are," Shannon said angrily, annoyed Cornelia had robbed her of even that small pleasure.

"Thank you," Dante said, placing a hand on Cornelia's elbow to help her up. "Don't try anything. Cornelia was holding back, I've seen her fight. Go tend to your husband unless you want to find yourself knocked out cold again. On second thought, she might just throw you out the window."

Shannon stood, considered, but ultimately just walked to Carlo and knelt by his side.

"Now," Dante said turning to face his father again. "You have your wife back. Cornelia will be sending you a bill for our services. She'll also be providing me with a copy. I don't intend to wait for you to send the check in the mail. I'll be deducting it from your monthly allowance."

"I'll complain to your grandparents," Carlo bluffed.

Dante shrugged. "Go ahead. They don't control the trust anymore. I do, I already told you that. New York is off limits to you, both of you. If I ever see you within one hundred yards of the state border again, I'll cut off the money. No discussion, no negotiating, it's finished. Do you understand that?"

"I have a right to go to New York, a right to contact the council or the queen if I need to. This is a free country Dante, not even you can take those rights away," Carlo glared.

"True. If you have a legitimate problem, feel free to contact someone on the council or Dimitri. The queen, however, she won't be taking your calls," Dante assured him. "And do it from Vegas. There is no request, no need you might have, that can't be handled over the phone or by email. It is a free country and you can go anywhere you please. There will simply be consequences."

They both knew Carlo wouldn't risk losing the money. But that didn't mean he had to back down completely. "You are really that arrogant Dante? So arrogant you presume to decide whose calls the queen will and won't take?"

"Not at all," Dante said just as confidently. "Alex won't be taking your calls because Dimitri will object. And because Alex really doesn't have time for someone as insignificant as you."

Carlo wasn't going to take the bait. He continued to watch his son, content in the knowledge that Dante hadn't won this battle. Sure he may be stronger than Carlo, but not smarter. The instant Dante left, Carlo would be lodging a complaint. He didn't have to call Oberon. He didn't have to call anyone. He'd simply write out his formal complaint and email it to the entire council along with pictures of his injuries. When Dante returned to New York, a hearing would be waiting for him and all his arrogant friends. Let him try to talk his way out of this one. A grin spread across his face.

"We're leaving," Dante stood. "And that's the last time I do anything to help you or your pathetic excuse for a wife."

"Wait," Lillie said moving across the room. She crouched down next to the injured man. After taking such a beating he still had that same cocky grin on his face. She wanted to punch him, for the grin and the blood she was going to have to consume. Instead, she looked him in the eye and gave him her most menacing smile. "I have another message for you before we go."

Carlo glared at the woman. He just wanted these people out of his house. Who did they think they were? Nobody got away with striking Carlo Santora, not even his son, and the sooner they left, the sooner he could get started on his complaint.

"The message is from Abby Cooper," Lillie said casually. "I'm sure you don't know her so let me explain before I continue with the message. Abby is Thomas Deveraux's fiancé. She is also the daughter of Mason Cooper. They are shifters and Mason just happens to be the pack leader." There it was, the reaction she had hoped for.

Carlo sobered immediately. He'd run into shifters before. They had killed a friend of his years ago. Carlo knew how to work the fae system to his advantage, but shifters played by different rules. He didn't like this new twist.

"Since you've been estranged from Dante for several decades you may not know that your son and Thomas Deveraux are very close. More like brothers than friends, really." She shot a glance at Nick and her smile softened. "Very similar to the tight relationship Dante has with my Nick over there." She focused on Carlo again and her eyes hardened. "Because of that close relationship, Abby and I also share a very close, very protective bond with Dante.

Progeny

We all spend a lot of time together and us girls have decided Dante is a very special man. None of us will tolerate it if he's hurt, in any way, by anyone, not even his father," Lillie paused to look at Dante. "Your father doesn't deserve you, and never will," she grinned as Dante scowled, clearly uncomfortable with Lillie's support. "Anyway, back to Abby's message. She wants you to know that this little mistake as you call it, threatens her pack's safety. They were willing to let the fae handle it this time," she paused for effect. "But, if word gets back to any of us that you have done something that could expose our world to the humans again, well... all bets are off. The shifters are going to step in and handle the situation once and for all," Lillie shrugged. "I'm not sure what that means, but use your imagination."

"They can't..," Carlo began.

"Oh, they can," Lillie interrupted. "And they will," she assured him. "The shifters aren't nearly as um..." Lillie pretended to consider the correct word. "Civilized as the Fae. They are a bit animalistic when it comes to their rules and punishments."

"What does she mean, Carlo?" Shannon whined.

"If either of you does anything in the future that threatens our world, Abby's pack will take care of the problem...permanently," Lillie explained, grinning at Shannon. "Keep that in mind, princess. I'd say neither of you are cut out for the island anyway so a more aggressive approach is probably a blessing."

"They'll kill us?" Shannon shrieked. "They can't do that."

"Actually, they can and will," Nick said flatly. "Your greed and your recklessness threaten more than the Fae. The shifters have a right to protect their secret as much as we do. They stayed out of it this time as a favor to the queen. I know the shifters. Next time, they'll insist on handling the problem. And, I'm sure Alex will let them. Our alliance is very important to our people."

Carlo was furious. His son had attacked him. His nose was surely broken along with his ribs. And if that wasn't enough, Dante's friends were standing here in his home threatening him. "Get out of my house, now!" He demanded.

"I'm almost finished and then we'll gladly leave this tacky excuse for a home you live in," Lillie glanced around in disgust. "Like Dante told you earlier, feel free to send a memo to Dimitri if you have need of the warrior's assistance or to Oberon if you have business with the council. Otherwise, do not contact our people. Don't try to involve the queen or Thomas in any more personal problems. Never show up at the Deveraux home again. Do whatever you want here in Vegas as long as your greed and selfishness doesn't threaten exposure to our people. But never come to New York again," she paused. "Oh, and Abby had one more message for you." Lillie gave Carlo her most menacing look. "Don't ever mess with Dante in any way, shape or form again," she grinned. "Or the result will be the same. Abby will quietly send a small group of shifters out here to handle the problem...permanently.

Progeny

Abby wanted me to be very clear on this point. Remember, she's the daughter of the pack leader. As I understand it, men would line up to do her a personal favor. Dante is now married, the last thing you want is three pissed off women after you. If you think I'm a Neanderthal, just wait until you meet Abby Cooper. She makes me look like a debutante," Lillie shrugged. "People disappear all the time. It's tragic, but a fact of life. Being a pilot I know all kinds of remote areas. There are places in the desert very near here that I'm not sure man has ever explored and they aren't likely to anytime soon."

Carlo glared at her. He wanted to tell her he would mess with Dante if he wanted to, but the threat was effective. They all knew he couldn't handle a group of shifters. If he caused problems for Dante over this, he and his wife would die. The message was clear. It infuriated him, but he had to accept it if he wanted to live.

"Are we clear?" Lillie asked without emotion.

"You've delivered this Abby's message. Now get out. I get it, stay out of Dante's life or die."

"Good, sounds like you do understand," Lillie said standing. She turned to Nick and smiled. "Shall we?" She shuddered as she glanced around the room again. "I don't think I can handle another second in this awful, tasteless room."

Nick grinned at Lillie and shook his head in amazement. He was proud of her and Abby. He was also a little surprised that Lillie had kept this whole plan a secret. Carlo Santora would definitely be out of Dante's life for good now. Nick was sure of it. Dante had told Nick about the attack on Carlo's friend. Carlo was terrified of shifters and he was a coward. Nick hadn't gotten the chance to knock the man out himself, but this was better. It was satisfying to see Dante finally give the man what he deserved. Lillie had then topped it off with a healthy dose of fear. Nick had to admit the entire encounter had been a success.

Lillie giggled once they were back in the car. "That felt so good," she exclaimed as she wrapped her arms around Nick. "That man reminds me of my ex on steroids. He's so selfish and pompous. Instilling a little fear in the arrogant prick was so..."

"Orgasmic?" Nick and Dante asked together.

"Yes," Lillie agreed. Her smile widened as she glanced at Dante. "You're not mad at us are you?" She sobered a little, worried what his reaction might be. "Mad at me?"

Dante was sitting in the front passenger's seat. He turned to study her. Then he leaned into the back of the car, grabbed Lillie and pulled her to him planting a sloppy kiss on her mouth. "Thank you," he said sincerely. "That was one of the nicest things anyone has ever done for me. Of course, I'm not mad."

"Hey," Nick objected pulling Lillie back and wrapping an arm around her protectively. "Get your own woman. This one's mine."

Progeny

Dante laughed. "And you better treat her right, my brother," he paused, smiling at his friend. "Because she now has my love and devotion for life. Treat her right, or you'll have to answer to me," Dante winked at Lillie as he turned back and focused on Cornelia. "Now, let's get out of here. We only have a couple hours before we need to head to the airport. And I'm in the mood to celebrate," he gave Cornelia a seductive smile.

"You're always in the mood to celebrate," Nick joked. Dante's threat was delivered in a light, joking manner but Nick knew underneath the surface his friend was serious. Abby and Lillie had worked their way into Dante's heart. That was huge and permanent. He would love and protect them forever. As wives of his two best friends, Dante would have done his best to like them anyway. But the women's willingness to step in and stand between him and his father would create an unbreakable bond for life. Nick glanced at Cornelia, another woman willing to stand between Dante and his father. Nick was grateful Dante had her in his life. He just hoped she'd stick.

Dante turned his attention to Cornelia. She'd been quiet, too quiet. He casually reached down and took her hand. "You okay?" He asked a little worried.

Cornelia glanced at him momentarily and smiled. "Yeah, I'm alright," she paused. "Now, anyway. There were a few moments back there it was touch and go though. I seriously wanted to pick that man up and throw him through the window. A window at the top of a very tall building. And Shannon? Don't get me started on her. You are just lucky I have so much self-control." Cornelia was surprised at the anger that was still swarming through her. It was like she had an evil monster inside her itching to cause destruction. Well, didn't she? The evil monster had a name, it was called vampire. Dante could never know about her weakness. He'd never trust her in a touchy situation again if he did. It was just one more secret she had to keep from him. One more reason she could never have a life with him. The knowledge depressed her and dashed any hopes she may have had regarding a future with the man she loved.

Dante gave her hand a little squeeze. He was lucky to have her. He just wondered how long his luck was going to hold. He'd deal with that when the time came. For now, he was going to enjoy every second he had with his sexy vampire.

Chapter Fourteen

The following evening Nick and Dante sat, sipping a beer in the large study of the Deveraux mansion. Thomas, Abby, Alex and Dimitri were also there. Dante had just finished telling the group about their mission in Vegas. He glanced at Abby. "I hope I never get on your bad side," he was only half joking. "You can be a scary woman."

Abby smiled. "I planned to deliver that message myself. But when Alex canceled our flight and then Nick told Thomas he'd gotten the okay to head out west I called Lillie immediately. I suspect it was just as effective by proxy."

"And then some," Nick agreed. "Lillie was awesome. And I think it was scarier because he'd never met you. That whole fear of the unknown thing. It was great."

"How is Lillie?" Alex asked. "I can't believe they both struck her in the face. I wish I'd been there to knock them out myself."

Dimitri started to comment then stopped when the doorbell rang.

"I'll get it," Alex said jumping up and rushing to the door. A few seconds later she walked back in with Oberon. "I told him he missed all the fun and encouraged him to bug Dante until he relayed the story to him."

Dimitri was watching Oberon. One look at the man's face and Dimitri knew something was wrong. He'd known Oberon too long to be mistaken.

"Sorry to interrupt," Oberon said soberly. "But I have bad news."

Alex immediately moved in next to Dimitri. He wrapped an arm around her waist in comfort.

"I just got word that we did have an attack last night," Oberon began.

"Who? Where?" Dimitri asked. "We stayed out all night."

"I know," Oberon said, laying a hand on Dimitri's shoulder. "We know you did all you could. They hit just outside the city. We think they hit the Taylor's first then moved north and struck the Mitchell's."

Progeny

"I don't know them," Alex said turning to Dimitri in confusion. "I've never even heard of them. Are they all dead?" She asked shifting her attention back to Oberon.

"Yes, I'm afraid so," Oberon said soberly.

"How many?" Abby asked softly.

"Just the four of them," Oberon said taking a seat. "Jason and Diana Taylor. They were never able to have children. I think that might be why they liked being isolated. They've lived here a long time, but they don't attend social events and rarely shop where we do. They liked it that way."

"Four more dead," Alex said in defeat. No matter what she did, people were still going to die.

"The Mitchell's have a son, but they are estranged. He hasn't been around for years. Last I heard he was living in North Carolina and I think he has a daughter, but she would be grown now too. I'm not sure if they ever met their granddaughter," Oberon mused. "Anyway, the Mitchell's were difficult. There was an incident a decade or so ago with Warren. When the council and your mother didn't side with them, the Mitchell's basically cut off all ties with the community. They too lived on the outskirts."

"Are there any others?" Alex said, worried. "Any other families that we need to check on? Anyone else we didn't protect?"

"I'm certainly not agreeing with the way you put that because unlike you, I don't feel responsible for those deaths. I feel bad. It's unfortunate, but all four of them rejected our community. They didn't want anything to do with us and it left them vulnerable. They paid a high price for that decision, but you have to realize they were already vulnerable. Even if we weren't at war. They lived in a secluded area, the chance of an attack is a lot higher out there and they knew it," Oberon paused.

"But?" Dimitri asked.

"But another family was attacked," he admitted. "The Jenkins, who also live on the outskirts. But they're okay," he added quickly.

"Were the boy's home?" Dimitri asked.

"Yes," Oberon confirmed. "All three of them. I believe that's why they all survived. The boys heard about the trouble out here and came home a few months ago to keep an eye on their folks. The battle was pretty intense and all five of them have wounds."

Alex jumped up. "Why didn't you say so?"

"Because they're not life threatening. Some of the cuts are deep, but Stephanie knows how to treat them. She bandaged them up right nice. I just thought if you were available we could head over and take care of them just in case," Oberon didn't finish.

"In case there's another attack," Alex finished for him. "Just say it, we all know there's going to be one."

"Yes," Oberon agreed. "So they will be prepared for the next attack. We don't know if the Jenkins will be a target again, but we know there's going to be one. Which is another reason I'm here. The council met, via video conference and we all think the Fort should be shut down for now. We think the kids should be sent back home."

"But they're a lot safer out there," Alex disagreed.

"Yes, but their families are here. I suspect once word gets out, the kids are going to come home on their own anyway. Those kids, the ones willing and anxious to head to the Academy for training, won't stay out there when their families are in danger back here. Let's just shut the place down and send them home. That way, we also have more help here and we all know we're going to need it," Oberon suggested.

"I agree," Dante said hesitantly. He wasn't sure his opinion mattered. "At first, it might just be a few, but once word gets out most of the students will head home anyway. This way, they're not putting themselves in danger to get home and that gives us more homes that are prepared for the fight."

"Me too," Nick nodded. "It makes more sense to have them here."

Alex sunk back into her chair. "I know," she said in defeat. "I just liked the idea that at least they were safe."

Dimitri stood and held out a hand to Alex. "Come on, we need to go heal people," he turned to Oberon.

"Don't worry, I've got this. I know where the Jenkins live. When we get back Alex can call Atticus."

"I'll take care of it," Thomas suggested. "The Academy is mine too, and Alex might be busy for a while. I've got some time. I'll take care of this. After I talk to Atticus, I'll make arrangements for the plane. Oberon, can you call Orin and tell him the cabin's available and ready for them if they want to use it again? They might want to stay in one of Victor's apartments, but it's there if they want it."

"Yes, I will also call Victor," Oberon agreed. "He'll want to make sure the apartment is ready for Atticus and Tala, too."

"Thanks," Dimitri said. He turned back to the room. "It's going to be another long night."

"If you need me, call me at home," Oberon said before he left. "The council is going to have another meeting tonight. We need to come up with a plan to help our people prepare for these mini battles. The warriors can't be everywhere at the same time."

"Any news about Foster and Fira?" Alex asked.

"Yes," Oberon said. "They both received enough votes to join the council. Avery was going to notify Foster and ask him to join in the meeting tonight. Tighe said he'd talk to Fira and see if she can head over to his place. We can use any new ideas we can get so we all thought we'd invite them to attend."

"Wonderful," Alex said, truly happy about the decision. "At least something good happened today," then she turned to Dimitri. "Let's go."

Sam walked into Ty's office and leaned against the desk. "I have an idea," she said anxiously.

"You have about a million ideas every day. That's nothing new," Ty said, shutting down his computer.

"I have a serious idea," Sam said walking around the desk to stand next to Ty. "I'd like to bounce something off you before I take it to Alex."

"Okay," he said, shutting the lid on the laptop. "But you'll have to be quick. I need to head out soon. We're meeting at Dimitri's before we split up to head out and I can't be late."

"You mean we can't be late," Sam corrected. "I'm going, too."

"Not tonight," Ty said pulling her onto his lap.

"Yes, tonight," Sam countered. "Vampire problem, count me in. Warrior problem, count me in. Family problem, I'm in. Three out of three, I'm going. We agreed that you and I are a team. Don't fight me on this. I'm still not happy about the other night. You were out there alone. You, Victor, Bastian all of you could have been killed."

Ty sighed and leaned his head against hers. He knew she was right, but he hated it. "Okay, tell me your idea."

"Does that mean we're not going to argue about this?" Sam asked.

"That means we're not going to argue," he agreed.

"Good," she said smiling. "I hate it when we argue."

"Me too," Ty paused. "The idea?"

"Okay, so the biggest problem I see is that we are all out there wandering aimlessly trying to find the vamps. We have no idea where they're going to strike or who is in trouble," she began.

"I agree," Ty said with a nod.

"So I was thinking, they are closing down the Fort and sending all the kids back. Those kids are going to want to participate," she continued.

"No way," Ty said immediately.

"I'm not suggesting we send them out on patrol," she said annoyed. "Just hear me out."

"Fine, continue," Ty said, kissing her temple.

"What if we came up with an alert system?" she asked. "You know, kind of like that Life Alert thing the humans have for their elderly. We put a system in every home and have it connected to a dispatch center. Then we have a couple kids man the center."

"How will they get the information to the warriors? You know we can't carry walkies. It's hard enough to keep track of our phones." Ty liked the idea, but they had a few obstacles to overcome.

Sam pulled out a watch and handed it to Ty. "You'll wear this," she said pushing it to him. She watched as Ty studied it, then looked back at her. "This button is an emergency button. I doubt any of you would actually use it, but I thought it was important. Heaven forbid a mighty warrior admit he's in trouble. Basically, that's for life or death stuff. This one over here is for backup. You know, 'I'm by myself and headed into battle a couple hundred vamps, I could use a hand when you can get here,' sort of thing."

Ty laughed and took the watch from her. "Okay, I can see how it will help the warriors, but how is it going to help the community?"

"Because it has a GPS," Sam told him. "Built in. The watch will transmit your location to a map that will be at the dispatch center. When an alert comes in from someone's home a flashing house symbol will automatically show on the map. Then the kids can see who is closest to that house. Give me a minute. I'll be right back." Sam jumped up and ran out the door. Within minutes she was back in Ty's office.

"Okay, so here's my favorite part." She clicked a few buttons on the device in her hand and an address lit up on the watch. "You can adjust it so instead of lighting up, it vibrates. That way if you're trying to be stealthy, it won't interfere," Sam said, getting more excited by the minute.

"I like it," Ty said honestly. "And I don't think the warriors will balk at something this small. If it's on vibrate how do we get the address when we're clear?"

"Just press the face of the watch for 3 full seconds and the last transmission shows up," Sam answered. "Then if you can take the call, you just press this button on top and it sends a signal to dispatch that you're responding. It's a lot like the police systems that have been in place forever except more automated. Plus, I like this addition too, if you hold this button for 5 seconds you can talk directly into it like a walkie. We still have a long way to go and it's going to take time to install these systems in all the homes, but I really think it could help," Sam told him.

"I do too," Ty agreed. "Bring the stuff, we'll talk to Alex tonight. She's going to have to approve this because of the expense, but I wouldn't worry about that. We could always pass at least some of the cost on to the community."

"I'll go change, then we can head out," Sam said, even more excited now.

* * * *

Fira pulled into Tighe's driveway and stopped the car. She was nervous. What if they all hated her idea? She had just been voted in today. Could they fire her already? She had to time this right. She knew that. She'd been running a business for centuries and knew timing was everything.

Progeny

The council had been discussing the problem for over an hour. Fira wondered if this was unusual or if it was the norm. Did all men immediately jump to violence anytime they encountered a problem? Sure, they had to fight the vamps, but some of their ideas were just outrageous. It was now or never. She cleared her throat and spoke. "I realize I'm new here, so I'm not clear on procedure."

"We're just having a casual discussion tonight, Fira," Oberon told her. "Did you have something you wanted to add?"

Fira shifted her laptop then hit send. "I just emailed a map to everyone," she began. "I've spent the day identifying targets."

"What do you mean by targets?" Avery asked. He still didn't like having her on the council.

"Places we know the vampires have hit. Homes where people have been injured or killed. Other places, like my home, that was hit but saved by the warriors."

She had a large printout that Tighe was studying. It was good work.

"I don't see what this tells me," Avery continued.

"Well, it tells me my house is in the target area. So is Warrens," Tighe said, still studying the map. "It also tells me the likelihood the vampires are staying in that area to the north is pretty high. It's an easy access route from there to here where all the attacks have occurred."

"This looks like a lot of work, Fira," Oberon said, impressed. "And I agree with Tighe. It gives us a pretty clear idea of the danger area. I'm going to call Dimitri, it might help them patrol tonight," Oberon stood and pulled out his phone.

Foster was studying the map. It wasn't that long ago he was doing the same thing with a map of New York, trying to locate his mother. Well, not his mother, the woman who killed his mother then pretended to be his mother so he'd give her money. "When we were looking for Patricia and Lawson that cop had us create a grid, a small area of focus. On this map, it looks like a one mile circumference. All the attacks have occurred within this circle." Foster used the tool to draw a circle then turned his laptop to the screen. "The shifter bombings are outside the circle, but I think those were deliberate targets by Lilith. It wouldn't have mattered where they lived, she would have traveled to them."

"Where are they located?" Fira asked. "I think we need to add them in any way."

"And probably the Kahn attacks as well," Oberon said, rejoining the group. "If we're going to plot this out, we need to add in everything."

"I'm familiar with those," Foster told the group. "Maybe Fira and I could get together and finalize the map for the next meeting."

"Sure," Fira said enthusiastically. "We all know there will be more attacks tonight. I'll get with Alex and plot those as well."

Progeny

"I still don't see the point," Avery told them. "So we know where the attacks are. It's not like that's going to help us prevent them."

"No," Orin agreed. "But it will give us a clear picture of where the action is and it might help us see something we're missing. This is good work, Fira. I think it's nice to have a different viewpoint for a change. None of the rest of us would have thought to use visual effects this way."

"That's because we don't need them," Avery grumbled. The rest of the council ignored him.

* * * *

Martinez tensed at the knock on the door. Apparently, it was time for yet another test. With any luck, this one wouldn't be as painful as the last. He knew this was necessary, otherwise he would have left already. Last night he had only been questioned. Maybe they'd just go through the events again. Thank goodness he'd had a chance to speak with Sammael. The guy had filled him in on some details he would never have known otherwise. Details that may have gotten him killed if he hadn't known them. Martinez walked to the door and slowly swung it open.

"Hey," Sammael greeted. "You ready for this?"

"I guess that depends on what this is," he countered.

Sammael laughed. "It sounds like they are going to do another round of interrogation. Just stick to what you told them yesterday and you will be fine. I'm getting the sense this will be the last time. If you give the same story, you pass."

"Good," Martinez said, relieved. He could take whatever they dished out, but it was getting harder not to fight back when the woman, Lilith, decided to be sadistic just for the fun of it. And he couldn't fight back, not yet. But someday, her time would come and he was going to take great pleasure in watching her suffer.

Sammael entered the dimly lit cave and motioned for Martinez to follow. Martinez stepped into the room and surveyed his surroundings. As usual, Radek was sitting in the large lounge chair in front of the fireplace. Lilith was standing off to the side, watching his every move. He disliked the woman on so many levels. She was sadistic and conceited. It was obvious she believed the male race was her playground. He knew he was going to have to deal with that side of her eventually. The longer he lasted, the more tolerance he showed throughout this ordeal, the more excited she became. He was surprised the last guy, Hector, had gotten involved with her. She was trouble for sure. Martinez would not make that mistake and to be honest, he wasn't even tempted.

"We have some more questions for you, Martinez," Lilith finally said. "Why don't you take a seat and let's get started."

Martinez walked casually, confidently to the couch and took a seat. "Fire away," he said as he leaned back and crossed one leg over the other. He knew this game was dangerous, but took the calculated risk. His cavalier attitude might enrage the king, but he thought it was more likely to demonstrate to the dynamic duo that he wasn't worried about what they might ask.

Lilith grilled him. She wanted details. How had Felix been killed? How many vampires died with him? Where was the rest of the group? Why hadn't he been killed along with everyone else? Where had he been all this time?

Martinez walked them through the careful story he and Sammael had outlined. He told the truth about Felix and his friends Gomez and Zaphrey. He played up Tyrone's insistence that this Thomas guy was the first target, but his sister Alexandria was their prime target in the war. Then he explained how they were hustled to a plane and flown east. He really didn't know where they had landed, so it wasn't hard to convince them he was telling the truth. He had exaggerated the distance, though. If they hadn't landed in New York, they had been close. He made it sound as if they had traveled for weeks before reaching that fort. This is where things got a little trickier, the entire story was fiction. He told them about Jose, the large husky guy Felix paired him with to scout their route and locate safe hiding spots for the daytime. Then he explained that Tyrone had continued to use the two of them because they were such a good team. Jose was big and burly, Martinez was small and agile.

Martinez told Radek that he and Jose had been sent to scout for a cave big enough to accommodate the entire group. The rest of them hid out in the forest. Jose had located a large cave that was perfect for their needs. The two of them were headed back to tell Tyrone when they heard fighting in the forest. He took off at a dead run, but Jose wasn't as fast. Martinez didn't realize there was trouble until he heard the horrible screams of agony coming from behind him. He swung around and saw Jose being attacked by a fox. "It was like a rabid fox on steroids. I'd never seen anything like it before," he said, trying to feign shock. He hadn't really seen any vampiric animals. Sammael had described them to him and their effects. The guy had gone into so much detail, Martinez felt as if he'd witnessed an attack himself. He told them how he'd run back to help Jose, but it was too late. By the time he'd finally killed the fox Jose was gone. Then he noticed the forest was quiet.

It was obvious he had missed the battle, but he still needed to tell Tyrone and the rest of the survivor's where the cave was. Martinez claimed he had wandered around for over an hour trying to find someone, anyone, but they were all gone. He didn't understand what had happened and knew he couldn't leave the area without the others. Tyrone hadn't described where they were going in detail. He had only said they were headed to New York. Initially, Martinez had believed he meant the city but after the attack, he changed his mind. He decided they must be close to their headquarters because of the battle he had heard raging nearby.

Martinez then described the cave that Sammael had told him about. He said he had stayed out all night, searching for his group then slept in the cave. The following evening he went out searching again. The routine continued for over a month. He couldn't understand it. Even if his entire group had been wiped out, they had to be close to their destination. Finally, when he had searched everywhere possible, he decided to head to New York City. He thought there might be other vampires in the Big Apple that could direct him to their king. That's how he ended up here.

Lilith quizzed him. She drilled him on every detail. Where was the cave? How big was it? Describe the animal that attacked him and Jose. He answered every question, never faltering, never hesitating. Sammael had prepared him for this.

"Sammael," Radek spoke for the first time.

"Yes, sir," Sammael said, moving from the shadows.

"When you went to the fort to find Lilith, did you discover any caves that appeared to have been used recently?" Radek inquired.

"No sir," Sammael said meekly. This was the risky part. He and Martinez had decided they needed to relay events to make it sound like Tyrone and his group arrived after Sammael had rescued Lilith and brought her back to New York. If they had been in the area before, she would have seen the signs. The cave Martinez had described was actually the one Sammael had stayed in while he searched for Lilith. There was another small cave close to the forest he had occupied the day before he located Lilith's hiding place. He'd only stayed there because he'd followed clues all night and was sure he'd locate Lilith before dawn. By the time he'd finally given up there wasn't enough time to make it back to the safety of the upper cave. Both caves would show signs of occupancy. Months ago, when he returned with the injured Lilith, he thought claiming he'd stayed in the small cave while he searched would reinforce the image he had created of an ignorant, weak subject. Staying so close to the fort would have put him at risk. It's what Radek would have expected from him.

"Do you remember going to the area Martinez talked about?" Radek pressed.

"Actually, I think I do. I found a large cave in the area he described but it was so far from the fort, I didn't think Lilith would hide there. I decided to stay closer to the forest and search the surrounding caves down there," Sammael explained.

"Lilith," Radek turned to address her. "Send for Zorak. I think he's proven his loyalty. I want him to head out and find the cave Martinez claims to have stayed in. If there are signs of a recent fire or other indication's someone has been there, Martinez is cleared to join our ranks."

Lilith left the room and returned with a large, serious vampire. Martinez couldn't put a finger on it, but something about the man made Martinez wonder if Zorak really was loyal. After receiving his orders the vampire left.

"If he's cleared, I'd like to start working with him," Lilith told Radek. "He's new, he'll need instruction if we want him to be a valuable fighter."

"Very well," Radek said with a dismissive wave.

The three vampires exited. "Sammael, go away," Lilith said immediately. "I want to talk to Martinez alone."

Sammael looked at Martinez then turned and scurried away.

The instant they were alone, Lilith ran a hand down Martinez's arm. "I think we are going to become very close," she cooed. "I'm looking forward to sparring with you," she paused and gave him her most seductive smile. "In more ways than one."

It took effort for Martinez to remain perfectly still. "I look forward to honing my evasion techniques," he smiled. "In more ways than one," then he turned and headed for his room.

Chapter Fifteen

Dante strolled down the crowded street lost in thought. Cornelia just hadn't been the same since they returned from Vegas. It was driving him crazy. Had he done something to upset her that night he confronted his father? He knew she wasn't upset about the fight. Not Cornelia, she probably would have liked to be right in the middle of that debacle. So what was going on with her? He'd noticed the mood right away, on the plane ride home actually. Since they'd been here, he'd taken her to his favorite restaurants, cooked her dinner, and even bought her that diamond necklace and earring set.

Dante cringed. That hadn't gone over as planned. He thought women loved jewelry. Cornelia, on the other hand, had been furious. She was so uptight about him spending money on her. That's why he didn't mention the

Progeny

new wardrobe in the closet. He just loved buying her things, pampering her, taking care of her. He loved her. But nothing he did made her happy. He'd been so sure if she gave this marriage a chance he could win her over. Maybe that was the problem. Maybe she just didn't want to be stuck with him as a husband. The idea of losing her about killed him. But he would lose her, wouldn't he? Almost daily she reminded him that their marriage wasn't permanent. That as soon as everything settled, she would be leaving. He knew in his heart, if Cornelia left, she would never return. Just his luck, he finally found love and was destined to lose it. And worse, it seemed there was nothing he could do to change her mind.

He glanced up and a little flower boutique caught his eye. That was one thing he hadn't tried. Maybe flowers would cheer her up. Nothing else seemed to be doing the job. They hadn't even been intimate since leaving Vegas. He just didn't understand her. Their lovemaking had been explosive. It had been the one thing that had given him hope. Cornelia responded so passionately to his touch, now nothing. The whole thing frustrated and confused him.

Dante stepped through the door and was instantly engulfed by fragrant scents. As he glanced around the small room he knew immediately what arrangement he had to have. Half a dozen large, yellow Lilly's flowed from a simple crystal vase. They were surrounded by delicate white roses. It reminded Dante of Cornelia's bright, sunny personality. Well, the one she used to have anyway. The way she was before he bullied her into marrying him. Had he taken advantage of her the same way Shannon and his father had taken advantage of him? He didn't think so at the time, but now? Now he didn't know what to think.

Dante entered through the front door of his large home. It had been months since he'd gone through the front entrance instead of the door off the garage. Today he'd been on foot and it just seemed right somehow. Maybe because he'd felt less than welcome here since he and Cornelia had returned from their trip out west. He paused, wondering how Cornelia was going to react to his latest gift. He hoped she'd flash him that bright, cheerful smile he loved so much. Well, it was time to find out. He took a tentative step forward and that's when it hit him. There was a wonderful aroma coming from the kitchen. Was Cornelia cooking dinner? Dante continued down the hall and smiled as he stepped through the large kitchen door. Cornelia didn't notice. She was standing next to the sink chopping cucumbers, the bowl positioned next to her was full of bright red tomatoes and black olives. So, she was making a salad. Flowers and vegetables were a good combination Dante surmised.

Cornelia sensed Dante rather than heard him. She slowly turned her head, planning a friendly greeting when she saw the huge arrangement he was carrying. The contrast between the delicate white roses and vibrant yellow Tiger Lillies and the masculine man holding them was staggering. Once again it hit her just how much she loved him. How much she wanted a lifetime with Dante. And just like always, she knew she couldn't keep him. Dante deserved a life with a woman he could actually love. Not someone he felt responsible for. Not someone he stayed with to protect. Not someone with an angry demon

Progeny

inside. Not someone that couldn't give him children. She inhaled sharply, trying to hide the pain that knowledge always brought and turned back to her chopping. "Dinner's almost ready," she managed to choke out. She was frustrated at the tear that trickled down her cheek. The last thing she wanted was for Dante to know she was crying.

Dante frowned and set the flowers on the table then moved to Cornelia's side. "It smells wonderful," he whispered as he turned her to face him. He'd seen the tear and it broke his heart. He studied her as he gently wiped the liquid away with his thumb. "Will you please tell me what's going on?" he asked softly. "I can't stand to see you upset like this."

Cornelia sighed. She couldn't tell him she was desperately in love with him and every time he was kind, it broke her heart into a million pieces. She couldn't tell him she wanted a life with him forever when he only wanted to protect her. She couldn't tell him that as much as she didn't want to trap him, she needed him. She couldn't tell him that because she was part vampire, her mother was sure Cornelia could never have children. Cornelia shook her head. If she let her thoughts continue down that road she'd be a sobbing mess in seconds. "Happy tears," she said forcing a smile. "I saw you standing there with those beautiful flowers and it made me a little sappy, that's all. But you really shouldn't have gone to so much trouble. We both know I'm leaving soon. You don't need to waste money on me. Please don't make a big deal about this. I'm embarrassed enough as it is. "

Dante wasn't fooled. He knew she was trying to cover, trying to hide her real emotions from him. He just didn't know why. He pressed his lips to her forehead and gave her a gentle kiss. "Okay," he said pulling back. "Then I'll go wash up and be back to help. Just give me a minute," he turned and left the room.

Cornelia took a minute to stare out the window. She couldn't stand this. Dante was being so kind to her. They'd had an arrangement, an agreement, and she had reneged. Since they'd been back she always made sure she was in bed before Dante. Every night she closed her eyes and pretended to be asleep when he walked in. She wished she could just enjoy what she had, but knowing she would eventually have to leave made it impossible to live in the moment. Every second she spent in Dante's company she loved him even more and dreaded the day she would have to leave him.

Dante returned and silently began setting the table. The crack that had formed in their relationship since they'd left Vegas felt like a gaping chasm. He loved Cornelia too much to watch her suffer this way. Dante subconsciously rubbed at his chest. His heart was broken and the pain he felt knowing he had lost her was almost too much to bare, but he was going to set her free. Tonight, he was going to give her what she obviously wanted. He was going to give her a divorce.

The couple finished preparing and dishing the meal, then sat on opposite ends of the table in silence. Finally, Dante pushed his plate away. He couldn't eat. Just one more way he'd failed Cornelia. She'd clearly spent hours preparing him a nice meal and he was too upset to eat it.

Cornelia saw Dante push his plate away and cringed inside. She'd spent all day preparing her special lasagna then ruined it the instant Dante walked through the door. She was a horrible wife. She wanted Dante to love her, but she just didn't know how to be what he needed.

"Cornelia," Dante said softly. "We need to talk." Dante leaned back in his chair and waited.

Cornelia held her breath, knowing she wouldn't like what Dante was going to say. She pushed food around her plate, not wanting to face what was coming. When the silence continued she finally looked up.

Dante closed his eyes. This was the hardest thing he'd ever done in his life. The hardest thing he would do. "I know you're not happy here," he finally began. "I've known all along you didn't want to be my wife. I basically bullied you into giving me a chance. But I can't do this any longer. I can't stand to watch you suffer day after day. I thought maybe if I dated you, courted you I guess, bought you pretty things, took you to dinner, that you'd see I was an okay guy. That maybe you would develop feelings for me, a foundation so to speak. We didn't start out as a real couple but I thought..," he paused. "Never mind what I thought. The point is, you are unhappy. You don't want me as a husband. I know firsthand what it feels like to be forced into marriage. To live day after day with someone you really don't want to be with. I can't do that to you. I won't do it. I won't let you stay with me because you think you need my protection. I'm sorry I manipulated you into being my wife. I never meant to hurt you, but that's clearly what I've done. It's too late to do anything tonight but tomorrow I'll go see Jake. I'll get him to draw up the papers and we can be divorced within a few weeks," Dante stood. "Don't worry, I'll find somewhere else to stay until everything's final."

Cornelia sat in stunned silence. Dante hadn't manipulated her, she'd manipulated him. Now she'd run him out of his own house. What had she done? He'd looked so sad and miserable. So defeated and it was all her fault. She couldn't let him leave like this. She jumped up and collided with Dante. His big, strong hands clasped her shoulders in support. How long had she been sitting there? She really didn't know. Obviously too long. She opened her mouth to say something, but nothing came to mind. Dante immediately released her and took a step back.

"Nick and I are patrolling tonight," Dante said soberly. "Lock the doors behind me. I won't be back," he gave her a humorless smile. "I'll see if I can get Jake over in the morning to take care of things. I'm sorry for all of this. I'm sure it's a relief to know you're no longer stuck with me," he paused to look her in the eye. "And I'm sorry I made you so uncomfortable you thought you had to pretend to be asleep to avoid me. I thought you knew me better than that. I would never touch you if you didn't want me. All I can say is that I truly am sorry. Goodbye Cornelia," then he walked out the door.

Cornelia sank to the floor and cried. She was still there when the doorbell rang hours later.

Progeny

Lillie stood on Dante's large front porch. She knew Cornelia was home and she wasn't leaving until she found out what was going on. She reached up and rang the bell again. Then she pounded on the large wooden door and yelled. "Cornelia, let me in. I'm not leaving," still nothing. Lillie began pressing the doorbell over and over again. Eventually, she'd be a big enough annoyance Cornelia would have to open the door.

Cornelia couldn't ignore the door any longer. Clearly, it wasn't just a salesman. She pulled herself up and slowly, methodically made her way out of the kitchen. "For heaven's sake," she grumbled as the bell rang over and over again. She swung open the big door and growled, "What!"

Lillie pushed her way inside. No way would she risk Cornelia slamming the door in her face. She studied her friend. "Well, I'd say you look about as awful as Dante does."

"Gee, Lillie. Do come in," Cornelia said sarcastically.

Lillie ignored her and headed for the large living room. Once she sank into the comfortable lounge chair she studied Cornelia. Clearly she'd been crying, but the pain Lillie saw went much deeper. "I'm not leaving until you tell me what's going on," she declared.

Cornelia sank onto the couch. She pulled up her legs and laid her head against her knees.

"Cornelia," Lillie pressed.

Cornelia sighed deeply then raised her head. "I've made a mess of things. I think it's time for me to..."

"Yeah, yeah," Lillie cut her off. "It's time for you to leave. Time for you to run away. Time for you to abandon the one man that loves you more than anything in the world," Lillie stood. "So, go get your stuff. I'll call the airport and have Joe prepare the plane."

"What?" Cornelia asked, surprised and a little confused.

"I for one am tired of the threat. You sound like a broken record. It's no wonder Dante's gone crazy," Lillie raised an eyebrow. "You want to go? Pack your things. I'm a pilot, remember? Give me your destination and I'll file the flight plan. You can leave tonight, right now."

"But I don't..," Cornelia stumbled. "I can't..."

"Don't worry about the trial. We all know you'll come back. Rand or Monroe can appease the District Attorney. Rand has your cell number. He'll call when it's time for you to return to testify. Go on. Pack up, it's already going to be a long night."

Anger took over Cornelia's confusion. "I didn't realize you were so anxious to get me out of town," she said as she stood to pace the room.

"Not me," Lillie said shaking her head. "I'd like you to stay forever. It's you that insists you need to leave. Maybe you could enlighten me. What's so important? You already told me you don't own a home, you don't have a

Progeny

ranch or any other responsibilities pulling you away. You visit your mother in Utah regularly when weather permits but other than your mom, what's out there you don't have here?"

"You wouldn't understand," Cornelia said, sinking back onto the couch.

Lillie relaxed. She'd been terrified Cornelia would take her up on the offer. Dante would never forgive her if she just took off and flew Cornelia out of New York. Maybe they could finally talk this out. "I know what you have here that you don't have out there. You've made friends here, Cornelia. You have a husband that loves and adores you. You have a nice home and people who need your help. Yet, you still insist you can't stay. I'm beginning to think it's just a way for you to keep everyone at arm's length. If you make it clear you won't be around long, maybe nobody will push you into feeling too much."

The tears began to flow again. "I already feel too much," she sobbed. "You know I can't stay. My being here puts you and all your friends in danger."

"Your friends, Cornelia," Lillie countered. "They're your friends too. I'm your friend. And if you think I'm just going to mosey on back to my comfortable house and my comfortable life when two of the people I care most about are miserable, you really are nuts."

"I'm not nuts," Cornelia said defensively.

"What happened tonight?" Lillie asked again. "Why does Dante look like the walking dead and you're all alone in this huge house crying your eyes out?"

"I'm not alone," Cornelia countered. "Gladys Kravitz is sitting in my favorite lounge chair."

"Wow, you had television in that cabin of yours?" Lillie said, surprised.

"No," Cornelia confessed. "Re-runs."

Lillie smiled. "Anyway, back to my question. Seriously, Cornelia tell me what happened."

"We're getting divorced," Cornelia admitted. "Dante is going to talk to Jake tomorrow."

"What? Why?" Lillie asked, truly shocked.

"I was just as surprised as you are to tell you the truth," Cornelia admitted. "Dante has been so wonderful since we've returned. Well, actually he's always been wonderful but more so lately. Anyway, I wanted to do something nice for him tonight, something a wife should do. So, I made him my favorite dinner. I love lasagna and it's one of the few things I can cook well. I thought after everything he's done for me, it would be a way to give back a little."

"Okay, so you made him a special dinner and he said he wanted a divorce. That doesn't sound like the Dante I know and love," Lillie said even more confused.

Progeny

"I knew you wouldn't understand," Cornelia protested. "He shouldn't have bought all those things for me. He shouldn't have brought me flowers. He shouldn't have filled an entire closet with new clothes and shoes. He shouldn't..."

"Now that's the Dante I know and love," Lillie said, smugly.

"Lillie," Cornelia objected.

"Well, it is," Lillie insisted. "Wait until Christmas. But don't make the same mistake I did. I only got Nick two presents and he gave me a whole mountain of them. It was embarrassing and I felt so bad about that. Next year watch out, I'm going crazy with gifts," Lillie grinned.

"I think that's the problem," Cornelia said studying Lillie. "You look at me and Dante and see the same kind of relationship that you have with Nick. It's different with us."

"Oh, I know," Lillie agreed with the swipe of her hand. "You're leaving."

"Would you stop that?" Cornelia insisted.

"What?" Lillie asked, trying to sound innocent. "Does it get a little annoying? You know, having that thrown in your face all the time?"

Cornelia went white. "Is that what you think I'm doing?"

"How would I know? You won't talk to me," Lillie shrugged. "You won't tell me how you feel so I have to figure it out on my own. And when you are constantly reminding me that you're leaving soon, what am I supposed to think?"

Cornelia knew Lillie was making a point. Lillie thought that since she hadn't talked to Dante about her feelings, he was making assumptions. It was time to tell Lillie the whole truth. "My marriage to Dante is a sham," Cornelia confessed.

Well, that was a good start. Maybe Cornelia would finally open up and get it all out there.

"I already told you we were both drunk when we got married," Cornelia began. "It had been a terrible day. We'd just found out that Carlo was involved with the smuggling. Dante took me back to the room and told me everything. He told me about his marriage, his father, Shannon. It was horrible. I felt so bad for him and knew he was embarrassed to be telling such a dreadful story to someone he barely knew."

Lillie rolled her eyes at that. Dante was more than interested in Cornelia before they ever left for Vegas. And if he didn't trust and care for her, he never would have told her his worst secrets.

"I wanted to help. I thought maybe if we went out he could blow off some steam," Cornelia continued. "I've never been much of a drinker so after a few margaritas, I was toast. Dante was drinking far more than I was. To be honest I don't know how we made it back to the room.

Progeny

Somehow we stumbled our way into a little chapel, got married then crashed. The following morning we both realized we were married. I suggested we get an annulment. Dante refused. He said it was impossible anyway since we'd consummated the marriage several times the night before." Cornelia blushed and put a hand over her mouth.

Lillie moved to the couch and took Cornelia's hand in hers. "We're friends, Cornelia. Don't be embarrassed. I'm aware you and your husband have sex."

Cornelia's eyes began to water. "Not anymore. I'm such a horrible wife. I've been pretending I was asleep when Dante came to bed. I didn't know he knew."

"Are you sure he does?" Lillie asked, wondering why Cornelia would even want to pretend.

"Yes. He mentioned it when he left. It's just another way I've hurt him," Cornelia said quietly.

"Okay, but if you didn't want to be married, why didn't you just get a divorce right then?" Lillie pressed.

"Dante convinced me it was better for both of us if we remained married. I knew he didn't mean it. It was better for me, but he was only trying to protect me. He was being noble just like always," Cornelia lowered her eyes. She couldn't look at Lillie. "He stayed married to someone he doesn't want because he's honorable and selfless."

"Okay, there are several things we need to address," Lillie stood. "First, you are not in danger and don't need protection. I know," Lillie went on before Cornelia objected. "Radek knows you're here. He knows you defied him. Sure, that matters and we all have to be careful with you, but we all have to be careful anyway. You don't need any more protection than anyone else does. Alex is Radek's prime target. You don't see her running off to Siberia."

"That's not..." Cornelia said but was cut off again.

"As for Alex and the whole 'she's going to hog tie me and throw me in the vamp cave' thing. It's time to give that a rest," Lillie said, annoyance showing. "Alex wouldn't do that. Thomas wouldn't do that. Dimitri wouldn't do that and Oberon wouldn't do that. Exactly how long do you have to associate with these people before you stop villainizing them? I mean come on! It didn't even take me that long and I'm stubborn, hardheaded and opinionated."

"Well, that's definitely true," Cornelia agreed.

"I know your mom was afraid. I know she was sure if anyone knew about you, they'd never accept you. But since you've been here, has anyone ever done anything that made you feel like an outcast? Like they were just waiting for the perfect moment to throw you out?" Lillie pressed.

"Well, no," Cornelia said reluctantly. "But why would they accept me?"

"I don't think the problem is us accepting you. I think the problem is you accepting yourself," Lillie

Progeny

watched for a reaction. She wanted Cornelia to talk to her, but she also wanted her to listen.

Cornelia blinked. Then she blinked again. Was it really that simple? She knew she wasn't self-assured like Abby or Ariel. Put her in a battle and she was confident and secure. Put her in a group of people and she was shy and reserved. The only exception was when she was working.

"I know how you feel," Lillie told her. "Nobody ever loved me before I met Nick. Well, that's not true. My father loved me, so much he died trying to give me the things the state decided I needed. But I was very young when he died. Then I went into foster care. Those families never loved me. My first husband never loved me. I never developed friends or confidants. When Nick came along it was impossible for me to believe someone that wonderful could love someone like me."

Cornelia was surprised. She knew Lillie had been introverted. She didn't know she was insecure. Maybe they had more in common than Cornelia originally believed.

"You don't talk about your mother a lot, but I think she must have loved you, still loves you. That's why she went to such extremes to keep you safe. I don't necessarily agree with her methods, but it's the thought that counts. Am I right?" Lillie asked.

"Yes," Cornelia admitted. "Mom is great. She loves me more than I deserve sometimes. I know she seems

378

eccentric and strange to most people, but she has her reasons."

"I get it," Lillie said. "You don't have to defend your mom to me. My point is that, like me, you have one parent who loves you so much she would do anything to provide for you, to protect you. But like me, you've been isolated most of your life. The whole warrior change thing fixed my insecurities. Nick and I have such a strong, special connection. I don't have to believe he loves me; I don't have to have faith in him. In fact, my trust in him is never really tested because trust isn't necessary with the connection we share. Oh, I trust him. I trust him with my life. But more importantly, I trust him with my heart. I took that leap before he changed me into a warrior. You said your relationship with Dante is different than my relationship with Nick. Of course it is. How can it not be when you don't trust him?"

"I trust Dante more than I've ever trusted anyone in my life," Cornelia disagreed. "I trust him with my life, my secrets," she thought of all the things she was keeping from Dante and inwardly cringed.

"All of them?" Lillie pushed. "Have you trusted Dante with all your secrets? You said you made him dinner. Did you tell him you love him? When he suggested you get divorced, did you tell him you wanted to make this marriage work? Did you trust him enough to tell him how much you really care about him? Have you ever told him you don't want to leave him?"

"No," Cornelia said softly. "No, I've never told him any of that."

"Then you don't trust him," Lillie shook her head. "You know, I almost lost Nick forever because I was too scared to believe. He told me he loved me and I bolted. I told him I wanted space. He left angry and hurt and I went apartment hunting. I almost ruined everything. I came very close to losing the best thing that ever happened to me. I almost walked away from the perfect man because I was too scared to try. But I couldn't do it. I was more scared of losing Nick than of loving him, of believing he could love me. Because it was impossible not to see the love in his eyes."

"But Dante doesn't love me," Cornelia whispered. "I only wish he did."

"How can you say that?" Lillie said, exasperated. "That man is over the moon for you. I knew it that first night at the casino. Were you paying attention at all? I was worried before that. I love Dante and didn't want him to get hurt. I knew about his first marriage and was skeptical about your motives. But when Nick and Dante walked into that room together, I knew. The instant that man spotted you, it was like nobody else was even in the room. I recognized it because Nick looks at me the same way. They were both so focused on us they didn't even see those two trashy girls approaching," she paused. "If you have decided you need to leave for yourself, then, by all means, tie things up here and go. The longer you stay, the harder it is going to be for Dante when you go. But if you have somehow convinced yourself you are doing this for Dante, you couldn't be more wrong. You're leaving just might destroy that man. You need to think about that. While you're thinking, you might want to ask yourself if all those excuses you've concocted are real concerns or just a way to justify your fear. I know you don't want to leave, otherwise you would have taken me up on my offer earlier. So, what are you running from? Radek, or Dante? Because if you can't let yourself believe in Dante, his love is probably the bigger threat," Lillie stood. "I'm here for you if you want a friend. You made me feel welcome while I was still trying to find my way. I hope you'll let me help you through this, for your sake and Dante's," then she walked to the door and headed home.

Cornelia sat there, thinking for a very long time.

* * * *

Jake rang the bell and waited. He hated this part of his job. This divorce was going to be much harder on Dante than the first one. The man was so in love with his wife, he was sacrificing his own happiness for hers. The whole thing broke his heart. He wished Dante could find a love like he had in Marta. But then again, he and Marta had wasted so much time being stupid and foolish. He wondered why it was so difficult for warriors to open up and communicate with those they loved. Bastian had flown all the way to Ireland and came close to losing Kylee forever. And Thomas was so ensconced in his own troubles, he didn't recognize he was in love until it was almost too late. The front door opened and Cornelia stood aside to let him in with a sigh.

Jake pulled Cornelia into a big hug. She looked like she needed one. Moments later he stepped back and sighed. "I guess you know why I'm here," he said, pulling a stack of papers from his briefcase. "I've marked the pages that need to be signed. They'll have to be notarized of course, but most banks can do that or just bring them back to my office and my secretary will take care of it."

"Come into the living room, Jake. We need to talk," Cornelia said leading the way.

* * * *

Nick and Lillie stepped into the luscious executive suite. "Are you sure he's here?" Lillie asked.

"Yeah, I called already. Maggie said he'd be here all afternoon. Something about a kid that wanted to go to the fort but was denied. His parents filed a lawsuit and Jake's trying to sort it all out," Nick rolled his eyes.

"A human kid then?" Lillie asked, already knowing the answer.

"Yeah," Nick agreed. He paused at the large desk just outside Jake's office. "Hey, Maggie. Can we go in?"

Maggie, Jake's secretary, gave Nick a huge smile. "Go ahead, I told him you were on your way over. He's expecting you."

Nick and Lillie stepped into Jake's office and moved to the large chairs in front of the desk. "Hey old man," Nick joked. "We need a moment of your time."

Jake looked up, studying Nick. He knew the kid was here to talk about Dante, he just didn't know why. Or more to the point what position Nick was going to take on the matter. "So talk," Jake said reclining back to study the couple.

"I know Dante was here. I know he wants you to get Cornelia to sign those divorce papers. I'm here to ask you to stall." Nick thought being direct was the best approach to use with Jake. He hoped he was right.

"Stall?" Jake asked. "I'm not sure I understand. Do you want me to put off talking to Cornelia, or stall the divorce?"

"Well, both," Nick decided.

"I'm afraid that's not possible," Jake said, giving nothing away. "You see, I've already been to see Cornelia this morning."

"Did she sign?" Lillie asked, anxiously.

"Actually, no," Jake almost smiled. Cornelia had been a surprise. After talking to Dante, he'd assumed this was what the girl had wanted.

"So, what happened?" Nick asked.

"I'm not sure that would be ethical to discuss," Jake pondered.

"Oh, come on," Nick waved that away. "Cornelia's not your client. There's no attorney-client privilege here. Did she give you a reason she wouldn't sign the papers?"

"No," Jake said sitting forward. "She said if Dante wants to know the reason, he's going to have to ask her himself. But she vehemently refused to sign the papers. She said she doesn't want a divorce and to tell Dante she will fight this for as long as she can."

Lillie smiled. "Good for her."

Jake narrowed his eyes. "You know something about this?"

"Sure," Lillie said, relaxing a little. If Cornelia refused to sign the papers, Dante would have to go another route on this. A route that would take time. "But I'm not sharing either," she grinned. "Friendship privilege, it's even stronger than that attorney-client thing you're so fond of throwing in our face."

Jake grinned, but before he could respond, Nick reclaimed the conversation. "So what happens now? If Cornelia won't sign the papers, what's Dante's next move?"

"I've already contacted Dante. He wants me to file the papers and have Cornelia served," Jake sighed.

"Moron," Nick grumbled. "So can you stall it? Can you do some of that fancy lawyer stuff to make sure this doesn't go to court for months?"

"I could, but I'm not sure I will. Is there a reason you want me to screw over your best friend Nick?" Jake asked, still not understanding the situation completely.

"Yeah, because the idiot is in love with that woman. He doesn't want a divorce any more than she does. Those two belong together. They're just too pig-headed to figure it out on their own. If you work your magic, like I'm sure Dante expects and get this divorce finalized, it could ruin both of their lives forever. I'm just asking for time, Jake. Not for myself, but for Dante and Cornelia."

"I see," and Jake did. Dante looked terrible this morning when he rushed in and said he needed a divorce, yesterday. Then seeing Cornelia had broken his heart. She looked so sad, with those beautiful puffy eyes and red nose. Any fool could see she'd been crying. And he finally understood. He was dealing with two people who were desperately in love, but afraid to admit it. He knew a little bit about that. Actually, he knew a lot about that. "Well, since Cornelia is stonewalling I think I can give you the time you're asking for. She told me that if I tried to have her served, she wouldn't open the door."

Lillie smiled. "That's my girl," she pressed her lips together when both men glared at her. She shrugged. "Well, someone has to do something. At least Cornelia is finally taking a stand."

"You do realize Dante isn't going to accept that. He thinks she wants out. He's going to push," Nick warned Jake.

"I know how to deal with Dante. Leave that to me. But be careful, Nick. I was in love with Marta long before I found the nerve to act on those feelings. You know Dante's past. It's going to be even harder for him. Pushing too hard might have the same effect as the divorce," Jake warned.

"I also know how to handle Dante," Lillie assured him. "We're kindred spirits."

Jake's expression softened. He didn't know the details of Lillie's past, but he knew enough. "Then I'll wish you luck and get back to work."

"Anything to worry about?" Nick asked as an afterthought.

"No, no," Jake sighed. "Just an affluent couple that wants to spoil their son. He wouldn't belong at the fort even if it was what we pretend it is. He's a troublemaker with a history of expulsion. Just a nuisance really, but it has to be dealt with."

"Then we'll leave you to it. Thanks for your time," Nick paused. "How's Marta taking the news? I mean, about having to close down the bakery again?"

Jake smiled, "She'll be fine, but thanks for asking. Marta can adjust to anything. Better than I can, actually. See you two and take care of our boy. Nick?" Jake softened. "Dante could use a friend. He didn't look so good this morning and sounded worse when I talked to him this afternoon."

"I'll take care of it," Nick said over his shoulder as he escorted Lillie out the door. "It was a pleasure as always Maggie. Say hello to the grandkids for me."

Maggie smiled and waved as she answered the phone.

Lillie waited until Nick helped her into the car and pulled onto the highway. "So, what's the plan?" She asked.

"First, you're going to tell me the rest of the story," he glanced at her. "Clearly, you left out the good parts."

"Not on purpose," she said defensively. "I started to tell you about my visit last night, but as soon as I said divorce you were out the door, headed for Jake's."

"So spill it now," Nick pressed.

Lillie started at the beginning and told Nick everything. Once she finished she waited for a response. When Nick didn't speak she stared at him, waiting. "Well?" she finally said, annoyed.

"I'm speechless," he admitted. "I mean, what were you going to do if Cornelia packed her bags and said okay, let's go. I want to escape to the Bahama's?"

"I'm not sure," Lillie admitted. "I guess I probably would have called you so you could warn Dante, then I'd file the flight plan."

"Seriously?" Nick asked, stopping at a red light and glaring at Lillie. "That's hardly fair. You would really dump that on me without any notice like that. You know hearing the woman he loves took off without so much as a goodbye would kill Dante."

Progeny

"I know," Lillie said. "But I was sure she wouldn't go. I know it was a risk. I know I could have been putting you in a difficult position, but I had to push. I had to call her bluff. If Cornelia had said okay, I'll go pack, that would have meant I had made a mistake. That we had all made a mistake and in the long run, Dante would have been better off without her. The woman I believed her to be would never do that. Cornelia loves that man more than life itself. She just can't admit it. She keeps threatening to leave, but she's still here. We both know the D.A. can't make her stay. She's here because she wants to be. I was trusting that, combined with my instincts of course. I think it paid off. It sounds like she might finally stand up and fight for what she wants," she glanced at Nick and smiled. "You had to push me, you had to fight for me. Dante needs Cornelia to do the same. It's the only way he will ever believe in her love."

"I agree," Nick said, smiling. "You wanted to know what I have planned. Well, I plan to do a little pushing myself. I think it's time I had a similar talk with Dante."

Lillie considered. "I think I agree that's a good idea."

"You think?" Nick said amused.

"Yeah," Lillie said seriously. "I'm trying to decide how I would have reacted if someone pressured me when I was struggling with the concept of us. I knew I loved you, but I couldn't believe you loved me. I had to figure it out on my own, pressuring me wouldn't have helped. Only you pressuring me broke through. I was more afraid of losing you than I was of trusting you. I knew I couldn't live without you. I had to believe in your love. It wasn't easy for me to get there. But I knew I had to, otherwise, life wouldn't have been worth living."

"You and Dante are a lot alike, but you're going to have to trust me on this. I know him better than anyone. I can push him in the right way," Nick assured her.

"What does that mean?" she asked, worried.

"It means when we get home, I need you to head over and tell Abby and Thomas what is going on. We need reinforcements. I'm going to need help from Thomas," Nick said turning onto his street.

"And you're going to talk to Dante?" Lillie asked.

"Yes, but first I'm going to talk to Dimitri. I need him to give Dante the night off. He can use any excuse he wants, but I'd prefer it if Dimitri ordered Dante to stay home and work out his issues with Cornelia."

"Why?" Lillie asked.

"Because it will push him into going home," Nick said confidently. "If I know Dante he'll head straight over to Jake's house, demand the divorce papers and deliver them to Cornelia himself. I hope you're right and Cornelia is strong enough to handle the confrontation. She's going to need to stand up to him. I can't guarantee his moronic side won't rear its ugly head again. He's heartbroken and believes he has nothing to lose. He's already lost the woman he loves."

"She's strong enough," Lillie said confidently. Inside she hoped she was right. She hoped that pushing Cornelia last night had given her friend the strength she needed to do what had to be done in order to work this out with Dante. The man could be as stubborn as she was and that wasn't a good thing. Not in this instance anyway.

Nick pulled down his drive and stopped at the front of the house. "Wish me luck," he said leaning over to give her a quick kiss.

"You won't need it," she said kissing him back before she opened the door and climbed out. She turned back and smiled at Nick. "Like you said, you know Dante better than anyone. Go with your gut. It's always right," then she closed the door and watched as Nick pulled away. She stood there, watching his tail lights until they disappeared down the street. Only then did she turn and enter the house. Moments later she was in her car, headed for the Deveraux mansion.

Chapter Sixteen

Martinez rested his head against the flat pillow and stared at the ceiling. He had finally passed the final test. Zorak was back and he had found the cave Sammael had stayed in. Radek believed his story and Lilith was plotting her seduction. He laughed, the woman was persistent. Martinez was sure no one had ever turned her down before. She was starting to get impatient. Too bad. There was a first time for everything. No way would he give into that psychotic narcissist. The woman repulsed him.

Martinez heard a soft knock on his door. He hesitated, was it Sammael, Zorak or Lilith? He'd welcome the first two but dreaded another encounter with the last. He cracked the door and exhaled in relief. "Come in Sammael."

Progeny

"I only have a minute," Sammael said, slipping Martinez a sheet of paper. "Destroy it when you're finished. I'll meet up with you sometime tomorrow."

Martinez slid the door closed and sat back on the bed. He slowly opened the page and began to read. He grinned at the news and immediately knew it was from his new king, Typhon. He recognized the handwriting. The king had news about the mysterious woman. They were still unsure of who she was, but they'd been able to determine she was working with the fae queen and the warriors. In fact, she seemed to be closely associated with one particular warrior. Martinez pulled out his lighter and caught the corner of the sheet on fire. So he was to protect the woman as much as he could without giving his motives away. He could do that. He had no doubt that soon there would be some kind of confrontation. He still didn't know if it would be a direct, frontal attack or if Radek would try to use stealth to get close. He did know, the Fae Queen was his main target. Sammael had reported as much, but Martinez wasn't willing to take the other vamps word on what was happening here. He was determined to figure things out for himself. That, he had figured out pretty quickly. The problem Radek had was getting through all the warriors to gain access to the queen. Martinez personally thought he was destined for failure, but wasn't that the reason he was here? His main mission was to ensure Radek failed. His secondary mission was to find the key and retrieve it.

He was pretty sure Lilith had it. She wore a chain around her neck at all times with something heavy hanging on it. The other day, while she was sparring with Zorak,

392

Martinez thought he spotted a key on the end of the chain. When Lilith caught him watching her, she incorrectly assumed he was interested. He'd acted cool, pretending indifference. It didn't help. Lilith was even more aggressive now. He just hoped Radek really was done with her because she wasn't even trying to hide her interest. He'd just gained entrance to Radek's army, he didn't need trouble because Radek's ex-girlfriend couldn't keep her pants on. Once word came in from Zorak, Martinez had been paired with the large vamp and informed he would be expected to fight the following evening. He'd go out with the group, but he would not kill any fae or any warriors. He didn't think that would be a problem with Zorak but he was having a hard time reading the man. From all outward appearances, Zorak was loyal to the king. However, Martinez had seen something in the man's eyes. Something that made him doubt Zorak's loyalty. Maybe he could do a little fishing while they were out hunting. He was confident before the night was over he'd have a read on Zorak the barbarian.

* * * *

Nick climbed from his car and studied the sleazy motel, frowning. Dante seriously thought by staying in this dive Nick couldn't find him. His friend was losing his mind. Nick took the stairs two at a time and paused before he began pounding on the door. Dante opened it with a scowl.

"What?" Dante demanded when he spotted Nick. "Can't you take a hint? I mean after about the twenty-fifth call that went unanswered, I'd think even you would realize I don't want to talk."

"Good, then you can listen," Nick said pushing his way into the room. He surveyed the tiny space then lowered himself cautiously onto the closest bed.

Dante slammed the door, stomped across the room and plopped down on the other bed. Determined to demonstrate his annoyance as he glared at Nick. "Make it quick," he grumbled.

Nick shook his head. "Was I this bad?"

"You're worse," Dante countered.

"I mean, I know I was a royal pain when Lillie took off, but I don't remember taking it out on you," Nick said, leaning against the headboard trying to find a more comfortable position. The bed was awful. He was sure if he removed the blanket he'd see springs poking through the mattress.

"This isn't the same and you know it," Dante said, lowering his head into his hands. He so did not want to have this discussion right now.

"Right," Nick agreed. "Because you're the one that left. You are the one that asked the woman you love more than anything in the world for a divorce. I agree, this is totally different. If I didn't know it was impossible, I'd ask when you had the stroke."

Dante stood and walked to the window, it didn't help. The thing was so caked with grime you couldn't even see out. "I couldn't stand it anymore," he said softly. "She was so unhappy. I thought if I had time, if she would just come back to New York with me, I could dazzle her. I thought if I showed her how much I loved her, she'd eventually fall in love with me, too. It didn't work. She doesn't want me and no amount of time is going to change that," he turned around to face Nick. "It's killing me, but I love her too much to make her suffer that way."

Nick closed his eyes. He'd planned to confront Dante with his stupidity, but he couldn't do it. The guy was a mess. Lillie was right, yelling at him would only make things worse. Nick stood and walked over to Dante, pulling him into a hug. At first Dante resisted, but it only took a few seconds for him to give in. They stood there for a long moment as Nick searched for wisdom. It had been a long time since they had embraced like this. It was more like father to son, than friend to friend. Like they'd done centuries ago when Dante had come to him for direction.

Dante pulled away. "I don't know how to live without her," he finally choked out.

There was so much emotion in Dante's voice, Nick almost broke. "I don't think you have to," he said softly. "Don't get mad, but Lillie was upset after she saw you last night. Once we went out on patrol, she drove straight over to your house and demanded an explanation from Cornelia."

Progeny

"She what!" Dante said concerned. "I don't want you guys harassing Cornelia over this. I'm the one that got us into this. She shouldn't suffer because I was a bully."

"I disagree," Nick said shaking his head. "With the bully part," he added when he saw the anger building in Dante's eyes. "The two of you decided all of this together. You didn't bully her, she didn't bully you."

"She didn't bully me," Dante said vehemently. "Who said she bullied me?"

"She thinks she manipulated you," Nick supplied. "The thing is, Cornelia loves you. She's upset over this because she thinks she manipulated you the same way your father and Shannon did. She feels guilty and she can't stand it either."

Dante began shaking his head. "She doesn't love me. I only wish she did. She's upset because she thinks she's stuck with me. I can't blame her after the fiasco in Vegas. Seriously, who would want to deal with a family like mine? She has to wonder how much of Carlo I have in me."

"Dante, this isn't like you," Nick said, walking to the window. "I knew you should never have gone to Vegas in the first place," he turned and punched a hole in the wall. He was so angry. He couldn't stand seeing Dante like this. His friend was so broken, Nick wasn't sure he would ever pull it together, especially if he didn't work things out with Cornelia. "It wasn't even this bad after your first divorce. You were angry, frustrated and I know you felt ashamed and embarrassed over the whole situation but never defeated. I can see that something has died inside you and I can't figure out why. This is just a bump. I know it doesn't feel like it, but I promise you this is a bump. If you try, you and Cornelia can get back on track."

"She's leaving," Dante said flatly. "Even if I worked this out today, she would still leave me. Maybe not tomorrow, maybe not next week, but eventually. She reminds me of that every day. She can't wait to hop a plane and be rid of me. You can trust me on that, I know what I'm talking about. The only reason she's still here is because I keep talking her into staying."

"Not true," Nick said confidently. "She's here because she wants to be. I know there's something she's holding back. Something she hasn't told you. Lillie felt it last night, too. But when Cornelia started in on that 'I'm leaving' crap, Lillie called her bluff. She told Cornelia to go pack and Lillie would fire up the plane. Cornelia refused to leave. She's still here because she wants to be here. She loves you, Dante. I don't know how to be any more straightforward than that. Cornelia is madly in love with you, the same as you are with her. There's just something she's too afraid to tell you. Something she thinks is a deal breaker and you running off serving her with divorce papers really isn't helping the situation."

"You didn't see her face," Dante disagreed. "Since we've been back I've tried everything. I've taken her on dates, bought her jewelry, nothing helps. It only makes her more upset. The final straw was last night when I bought her flowers. It made her so sad, she cried. She tried to hide it from me, but she cried. I can't do this to her anymore. I can't be the reason she is so unhappy. We haven't made love since we left Vegas. She pretends to be asleep so I won't touch her. That's not the way a woman in love acts. Don't insult my intelligence by arguing otherwise."

"Not normally, no," Nick agreed. "But I think you should look at things from a different angle. What if she's sad because she loves you but thinks she has to leave you, for you? Does she know you love her? I know you bought her things and took her to expensive restaurants, but have you told her you are in love with her yet? I know it's not easy to open up like that. Hell, it scared me to death and I don't have your baggage. But don't you think she deserves to know the truth? You did not marry her to protect her. You did not stay married to her to protect her. Make sure she knows that. Especially after the fiasco in Vegas. Then if she leaves anyway, at least you know you did all you could. You were honest and she still wanted out."

"What if my telling her the truth somehow hurts her even more?" Dante wondered. "I'm only trying to do the right thing here, no matter how much it hurts me."

"I don't see how the truth can hurt her," Nick disagreed. "Telling the truth is always best. Go talk to her. Lay it all out on the table and see where things go. Have a little faith in yourself," Nick said closing his eyes for strength again. "Somehow that trip to Vegas has shattered your faith in yourself. I know you don't want to hear this, but I could kill Carlo and Shannon Santora right now. I want to kill them for making you doubt yourself this way. This is not who you are Dante. Put those two behind you for good this time. They are in your past. Don't let them take away your confidence or your future," he hesitated. "You are worth loving. I've been trying to help you see that for over thirty years now. I love you. Thomas loves you. Abby loves you and Lillie loves you. Abby loves you so much she's willing to kill the Santora's for you. Just say the word and Carlo and Shannon will disappear forever. Dante, you need to start believing in yourself again. If you can't believe in Dante Santora, how can you expect Cornelia to?" Nick stood and pulled Dante into another man hug. He'd said all he could say for now. The rest was up to Dante. "Call me if you need me," he smiled. "And get the hell out of this dump."

"Thomas found me about an hour ago and threatened to hog tie me and carry me to his hotel if I didn't move there on my own. I'm actually packed and just need to check out, then I'm moving to The Devierre."

"Good," Nick said moving to the door. "Then I won't keep you. I'm serious, call me Dante. Don't try to go through this alone. I made that mistake and you forced your way in. I'm grateful for that. Let me do the same for you."

"I'll call you tomorrow, unless we're paired together tonight that is," Dante promised. He glanced at the bed as Nick closed the door and spotted the crisp one hundred-dollar bill. He knew Nick had left it to pay for the damaged wall. Dante smiled, no one could ever accuse Nick Moretti of not paying his debts.

Nick sat on Thomas' couch. It was almost time for them to head out and patrol the city. Tonight he was working with Lillie. The women had banned together and insisted they were going to help, with or without the men's approval. All the warriors had given in and were paired with their mates. He was waiting for Dimitri's call. Any minute, his leader would phone to tell him how his meeting with Dante had gone. The warrior leader had been more than willing to give Dante the night off. Dimitri could feel Dante's pain. He knew his friend was distressed and not mentally sound enough to hunt tonight. Nick was so deep in thought, he actually jumped when his phone began to ring. "Hello," he said immediately.

"It's done," Dimitri said flatly. "He's not happy about it. He stormed out and took off like the hounds of hell were on his tail. I hope Cornelia's ready for this because I have a feeling he's headed her way."

Nick smiled, he'd called that one. He was sure Dante would make a stop at Jake's then he'd head for his house. "Thanks," Nick said soberly. "I hope this works."

"Me too," Dimitri grumbled. "I need you four to head out. Did Thomas give you the wrist units Sam and Alex developed? Tonight will be their test run, so I want you to use them as much as possible."

"We have them. Did those two have time to install the panic devices in the homes Fira and Foster identified?" Nick asked.

"Yes," Dimitri confirmed. "All the homes in the one mile circumference, as well as many of the farms and ranches outside the city limits, have panic devices installed in their homes. I sat down with Oberon this afternoon and identified the most likely weak spots. Alex and Sam should be able to get the units installed in those areas tomorrow but we're counting on the warriors to protect them tonight. Did you receive the list?"

"We did," Nick assured him. "We understand our mission, Dimitri," Nick said, hoping his people would be safe. "We'll call if we need anything."

"Be safe out there," Dimitri added before hanging up.

"Let's head out," Nick said, standing and holding out a hand for Lillie. "It will probably be a long night."

Lillie stood, hoping her head would be in the game if they encountered vampires. She was so worried about Dante and Cornelia. The rest of their lives would be impacted by what happened tonight. She paused and pulled out her phone. "I need to warn Cornelia Dante might show up tonight."

"I thought you said it would be better if she was surprised," Nick said, confused.

"I changed my mind," Lillie said then held up a finger to hold off further discussion. "Hey, Cornelia. Dante's been ordered to sit out tonight. He's not happy about it. I wanted to warn you he might pay you a visit. Be strong and don't chicken out. Tell him. He deserves to know exactly how you feel," Lillie paused then nodded, "Start a fire. If he brings them, burn them," Lillie laughed, "Of course I'm serious. Do it," then she shut off her phone and turned to Nick. "Okay, we're good to go. I'm your humble follower for the rest of the evening."

Progeny

Dante pulled his car to a stop in front of his house. The lights were on, so chances were good that Cornelia was still awake. He pushed open the door and climbed out, stomping to the front porch. It was one thing for Cornelia to want him out of her life. It was an entirely different matter if that decision was going to keep him from fighting. They were going to settle this once and for all so he could try to get his life back. He climbed the stairs and approached the door then paused. This was his house so he'd feel like an idiot if he rang the bell like a common visitor. On the other hand, he'd told Cornelia he wouldn't be back until after the divorce. She wouldn't be expecting him and he didn't want to frighten her. If he just opened the door and walked in, she might think he was an intruder or worse her father. He turned and ran his hand through his hair, what should he do? Dante spun back around when he heard the door open.

Cornelia stood in the doorway, studying Dante. He was clearly angry about something. "You gonna stand there all night?" she finally asked.

"I need to talk to you," Dante said moving to stand just outside the door. "Can I come in?"

"Sure, it is your house after all," Cornelia said, taking a step to the side.

Dante entered his home and silently shut the door. He followed Cornelia into the study. The room felt cozy and warm. Cornelia had started a fire, and he spotted one of his hardback books on the lounge chair. Apparently, Cornelia had been relaxing before he arrived. "Sorry to bother you," Dante began. "I know I said I wouldn't be back until the divorce was final but..."

"You're not bothering me," Cornelia said, "You are annoying me, though."

That stopped him. He swung around to study her face.

"Dante, this is your home," she began. "You don't think it's a little silly to stand out on the front porch waiting for an invitation like a stranger?"

"I was trying to be polite," he said defensively. "Sorry to annoy you. I'll make this quick." He thrust the divorce papers out, waiting for her to take them.

Cornelia hesitated, did she really have the nerve to toss the documents in the fire?

"I know Jake stopped by," he said, lowering his hand. "Is there something in here that you're not willing to agree to? I'm sure whatever it is, we can resolve it quickly and it will be finished. You can put all of this behind you." Nick's words ran unwanted through his mind. He considered them, then tried to push them away. "Tell me what you want and I'll give it to you."

Cornelia took a step forward and took the stack of papers. She inhaled sharply then tossed them into the fire. She braced herself as she turned back to face Dante. He looked shocked. Good, she shouldn't be the only one on unfamiliar ground here.

"What?" Dante said staring at Cornelia like she was nuts. "How? I mean...why did you do that?"

"I disagreed with all of it," Cornelia shrugged, trying to sound casual.

"Okay," Dante said slowly. "I guess we can start over, then. Tell me what you want," he ran his hand through his hair. "I'm at a loss here. Just tell me what you want and you can have it."

Cornelia walked to the window and forced herself to breathe. It was now or never. Did she have the guts to follow through with this insane plan? Well, she'd started down the path, she'd always regret it if she didn't follow through to the end. "I want you," she said softly.

Dante slowly lowered himself to the couch. "What did you say?" He asked, wondering if he'd really heard what he thought he'd heard.

Cornelia turned and faced Dante, bracing herself on the window seal. "I said I want you," she hoped she sounded more confident than she felt. Dante looked even more shocked now than he had when she'd tossed the divorce papers into the fire. She thought maybe that was a good sign. The tables had finally turned. Normally Dante was in control of their conversations, tonight she was in the driver's seat for a change.

"I'm not sure I understand what you mean," Dante finally said. Could Nick be right? Was it possible Cornelia really did love him? Was it possible she really wanted him? He hadn't believed Nick this afternoon, but maybe his friend was right about this. Nick was right about one thing, Dante's confidence had been shaken since the instant he walked into Thomas' study and spotted his father. The past had rushed forward and invaded his world with a vengeance. His confidence took another hit seeing Cornelia and Shannon in the same room. Cornelia was everything bright and good. Shannon was selfish and dark. Cornelia was real in every way; she was beautiful on the inside as well as the outside. Shannon might appear beautiful, but she was fake and self-serving. The contrast in his two wives made him doubt himself even more.

"I don't want a divorce," she said, watching Dante closely. He wasn't giving anything away. He was shocked, but shocked in a good way, or shocked because he wanted this over with already? Well, now was as good a time as ever to find out. "I feel like I manipulated you into marrying me. I'm so sorry for that. You shared something very personal that night and I repaid you by dragging you into the nearest chapel and tying the knot when you were too drunk to know what you were doing. Okay so I was also drunk, but I accepted your offer to remain married for my protection because I wanted you. I wanted to marry you. I wanted more time with you. I love you, even though I know I shouldn't. I can't help it. No matter how hard I've tried to keep my distance all I can think about is you."

Dante was across the room in an instant. He pulled Cornelia into his arms and held her close. "You love me?" He finally asked, emotion running through every molecule of his body. "No, don't answer that."

Progeny

"Yes, Dante. I love you," Cornelia said, hopeful for the first time in months. But reality crashed in. She had to tell him everything. He needed to know all her flaws.

Dante pressed his lips to hers to silence her before she could continue. "I am so madly in love with you, Cornelia," Dante whispered. "I don't deserve you, but I love you. I've been such an idiot. I should never have let you believe I wanted to stay married to protect you," he pressed his forehead to hers. "I want to stay married to you for you, period. There are so many things I need to apologize for," he straightened and lifted her into his arms. As he walked to the couch he pressed his mouth to hers again. Then he lowered himself onto the couch positioning Cornelia on his lap. "I wasn't sure I could live without you, but I knew I had to let you go. I thought that's what you wanted," Dante paused, not wanting to ask, but needing to know. "If you want me, if you love me, why have you been so miserable?"

A tear ran down Cornelia's cheek. This was the happiest and scariest moment of her life. Dante loved her. But would he still love her when she explained her worst fear? "I've been an idiot too," she cleared her throat as she wiped the tears from her face. "I want you to know how much it means to me that you said you love me."

"I do love you," Dante said, frowning.

"Okay, you love me," she gave him a faint smile. "But I won't hold you to anything until you know everything."

"There is nothing you could say that would change the way I feel, baby," he gave her a gentle kiss. "Tell me what you're worried about."

"Because I'm part vampire my mom is sure I can never have children. That's why I've been so unhappy. Since I was a teenager I've known I would never find love. I thought I'd accepted that, accepted that no fae would want me. I knew I couldn't allow myself to fall for a human only to lose him in such a short time. Then I met you. I think I loved you the moment I saw you, but I tried to stay away. I thought I was managing until that night I brought you home. I took advantage of you that night, too. I keep taking advantage of you while you're drunk."

"Before you go any further I need to make a confession," Dante interrupted. "I was slightly drunk that night when I left the building, but mostly I was in pain. Severe pain, actually. The alcohol was wearing off and I needed blood desperately. Once you provided that, I was fine just exhausted. Drinking does that to me. I wanted you, too. When you pressed that gorgeous body against me, I couldn't resist. I wasn't drunk and you didn't take advantage of me."

"Well, I kind of realized that the morning after when you remembered everything," Cornelia said shyly. "At the time, I thought you'd be too drunk to remember our encounter like you were on our wedding night."

"I wasn't drunk the night we got married either," he told her before he chickened out. He had to get everything out on the table like Nick suggested. She needed to know when he married her, he knew exactly what he was doing.

Progeny

"I remember everything. When you opened that door and walked into that quaint little chapel, I knew I should stop you. I knew you were too drunk to know what you were doing, but you looked so happy I just couldn't resist. I knew I cared for you more than I had ever cared about another woman. But, standing there in the front of that chapel I realized how much I loved you. I wanted to marry you more than I had ever wanted anything in my life. The next morning I was desperate. I needed an excuse to give me more time. I thought eventually you might fall for me, too. So I pretended you were doing me a favor if you stayed married. I pretended like it was a business deal because I didn't know how to tell you I loved you. I thought if you knew how strong my feelings were, you'd run screaming in the opposite direction."

"Silly man," Cornelia smiled and kissed his cheek. "I'm glad you remember. I only wish I remembered more about that night. I hate that I only have flashes of my wedding day. It was the most important day of my life and I was smashed."

At that moment, Dante knew what he wanted to do. If Cornelia agreed to stay with him, he was going to plan another wedding. A wedding with all their friends. A wedding Cornelia would never forget. "Just so I'm clear, you've been unhappy because you think you can't have children and you thought that would be a deal breaker for me?"

Cornelia sighed. "I've been unhappy because I don't feel like I'm enough for you. You deserve the world, Dante. You are so special. I know you've had a rough past and you think that reflects on you badly. It doesn't. Contrary to your belief that only makes you more desirable. I only wish you knew your own worth. Your horrific history doesn't have anything to do with who you are. Not in the way that matters. You overcame something so horrible and you came out the other side even more perfect. You're beautiful on the outside and the inside. You and Nick help so many people, you're rich as sin but still humble. I could go on for hours but I think you get the idea. You deserve a wife that can give you the world. I'm part vampire, I probably can't even give you children. The community would never accept me if they knew what I am. That alone is enough, but I sat in your father's house after we rescued Shannon and I wanted to kill that man and his wife. I was so furious. It was like an angry monster was alive inside of me. It was all I could do to hold back. When Shannon jumped on your back, I wanted to do more than pull her off you. I wanted to snap her head off. You're so kind and loving and I'm a monster," she was crying now. She'd shared all her dark secrets. There's no way he could want her now.

Dante was angry with Cornelia. "You are not a monster," he said forcefully. "Honey, look at me," he waited until she looked him in the eyes. "I love you. I'm not sure what I deserve in a wife, but I know you exceed it by leaps and bounds. You say I don't know my own worth, well clearly neither do you. I know you have some vampire in you. I don't care. I have vampire in me, too. So we both drink blood, it's just another thing we have in common."

Progeny

Cornelia was still crying and it was breaking Dante's heart. How could she think she was a monster? How could she think he could do anything but love her? How could he make her see how much all that stuff didn't matter? He only knew one way. If he couldn't get her to listen, he would show her. Dante stood, bracing Cornelia against his chest as he ascended the stairs.

"What are you doing?" Cornelia finally asked. The moment he stepped into the master bedroom she thought she knew.

"I'm better with action than I am with words," Dante said setting her on the edge of the bed. "So, I'm going to make love to you until you believe I don't care about any of those things. I don't care if it takes all night. In fact, I don't care if it takes all week. We're not leaving this room until you believe that I love you and I can't live without you."

"Dante," Cornelia protested. "We have to finish our talk."

"No, we don't," Dante said sitting on the edge of the bed to remove his shoes. "I love you and I'm going to convince you of that if it kills me. As for the baby thing, I kind of suspected that might be a possibility. I don't care."

"I know you want kids, Dante," Cornelia protested. "I don't think I can give you children. You would be such a good father. I can't live with that. I can't live my life knowing I'm responsible for you missing out on something so wonderful."

410

"First of all," Dante said as he pressed her back to the bed and lowered himself on top of her. "You don't know you can't have children. You just believe you can't. There's a difference. Second," Dante continued before Cornelia could object. "There's never a guarantee that anyone can have children. You know how difficult it is for the fae to get pregnant then to carry a child full term." He covered her mouth with his as she began to protest. When he was sure she'd remain silent, he pulled back. "Third, there are other options. If nothing else, we can adopt, then when the kid grows up, I'll use my change on our child. With the amazing improvements Bastian has made, the risk will be minimal."

"But..," Cornelia began.

"But nothing," Dante said as he ran kisses down her neck. "Take off your clothes," he demanded as he stood to do the same.

"This discussion is not over," Cornelia insisted.

"I agree," Dante grinned that wicked grin she loved so much. "I'm just getting started. And I'm serious, I don't plan to stop until you agree to stay my wife forever and you give up that ridiculous notion that you are in any way a monster."

"The first part's easy," Cornelia said seriously. "If you're sure you want me, you're absolutely sure, I'd love to be your wife forever."

"I've never been more sure of anything in my life," Dante said pulling her close.

Chapter Seventeen

Dusty and Nebi sat in the control room, exhausted. One more hour and the sun would come up. It had been a busy night. The only thing that had saved the community was the alert system. They were worried about the warriors. They had been in so many mini battles tonight, every one of them had to have injuries.

"I think we need more help," Nebi finally voiced her opinion out loud. She'd been thinking the same thing since the night began. "In here and out there."

"I agree," Dusty said. "We need to talk to Alex. There were plenty of kids at the fort. If she puts the word out I'm sure more of them will volunteer to help."

"Let's head over once we close down here. Alex will still be up." Nebi suggested.

"Sounds like a plan," Dusty agreed.

* * * *

Nick climbed out of the car and rushed to Lillie's aid. She'd held up tonight. He was actually surprised she only had the one wound. It was deep and needed attention but things could have been so much worse. Radek was pulling out all the stops. His tactic was working. The warriors were holding up, but barely. They didn't have enough manpower. Dante would be back tomorrow, but they would still be shorthanded. They needed the shifters to help. It would be the only way to survive this war. Nick's biggest worry was that Radek was leading up to something big. He was pretty sure it was only a matter of time before they were forced into another large battle like the one they'd had on New Years.

Lillie limped to Dimitri's front door and waited for Nick to ring the bell. Her leg felt like it was on fire. She was proud of herself. She was new to all this warrior stuff but she'd held her own in the battle tonight. Training every day with Sam's robot had saved her life. She knew if she hadn't been diligent in her training she wouldn't have fared so well. There were so many vampires for her and Nick to handle alone. When Dimitri opened the door Nick whisked her into his arms and carried her inside.

"What's wrong with her?" Alex said, worried.

"I'm fine," Lillie assured her. "Just a slice on my leg, nothing serious."

Progeny

"Put her on the couch," Alex sat next to Lillie and took her hand. She immediately began scanning and caring for her wounds. Lillie also had a minor cut on her shoulder and another one on her hand. "I've been so worried all night," Alex admitted. "Do you know if everyone else is okay?"

"No," Nick admitted. "I was hoping you had some news for us."

They all looked up when they heard the bell ring. Ty and Sam followed Dimitri into the room. They too had minor wounds, but nothing serious. Ty had a large cut on his forearm and Sam had a cut on her head. Alex was still healing Sam when Bastian and Kylee arrived. Bastian was carrying Kylee and his face was grim. Alex jumped up. "Put her on the couch," she ordered.

"She only has the one gash on her side, but it's deep and she's lost a lot of blood," Bastian said setting Kylee gently onto the couch.

Alex went into action, healing Kylee in seconds. "How are you feeling?" She asked, sitting back to study the doctor.

"A little weak, but fine," Kylee told her. "I'll be better if I can get a few hours' sleep. Please tell me we can go home and rest for a while. I am so glad this night is over."

Before Alex could answer the doorbell rang again. Victor and Ariel didn't wait for a response they entered the house and headed for the group. "Are either of you injured?"

"Nope," Ariel said, still pumped from all the fighting. "We're good."

Victor pulled Ariel close and leaned against the wall. "I'm good, too. I have a secret weapon," he said, grinning at his wife. "Tony and Megan called, they're okay too. Megan was beat so they headed straight to the apartments."

"Are you sure she wasn't injured?" Alex asked, worried again.

"I'm sure," Victor confirmed. "If she even had a scratch Tony would have brought her over so you could heal her. Trust me, Megan is fine she's just a little under the weather."

Thomas and Abby arrived next. They didn't even bother with the bell, they just walked in. "Looks like we're the last to join the party," Thomas said casually. "Hey, put those magic hands away. I don't have any wounds and neither does Abby. She's my superhero, remember. Nothing can get past my woman."

Abby laughed. "I'm going to talk to dad after I get a few hours' sleep. We were hopping out there tonight. We need help. I know Morrigan gets back this afternoon. He and Nadia will insist on joining us tomorrow night. Austin and Sherrie will probably join in as well. Dad can start working on a schedule to get us help from some of the others. This can't go on forever. I'm sure Monroe's pack will step up as well. Alex if you call Ryker the panthers will probably send us a few fighters, too."

"I've been hesitant to ask because I wanted to make sure the shifters are fresh if we have another big attack, but I guess calling them in would be best," Alex said.

"We'll be fresh," Abby assured her. "Dad will make sure of it. He'll work the men in shifts and insist on a break. In fact, we should probably do the same. Dante sat out tonight. Maybe two of us should sit out tomorrow night. Then two others the next night."

"Good idea," Dimitri agreed. "I sat out tonight, but Alex is insisting we help you guys tomorrow. I've agreed to give it a try. I'm just worried that if someone is hurt it's going to take longer for her to reach them."

"I don't think that will be a problem," Victor volunteered. "Even though we were split up, the fighting was condensed to a fairly small area. I actually think she's going to be closer out in the field than if we have to transport the wounded here."

"I agree," Bastian said. "I was worried about Kylee tonight. She was losing so much blood, I had to stop and bandage it before we could travel back to you. If you were in the area, she wouldn't be so weak."

"I'm not that weak," Kylee protested. "And it didn't take you long to stop the bleeding and get us here."

"That's because I have medical experience. Everyone doesn't have that. I'm just saying I agree with

Victor, having Alex close is going to be a big help. The downside is that she's going to be vulnerable. We all know she's Radek's main target. Maybe you two should pair up with one of us rather than heading out alone."

"That defeats the purpose of us helping," Alex protested. "I've already fought Dimitri on this, I'm not going to fight all of you. I'm not helpless. My people need me and I am going to help."

"Well then," Bastian said, grinning. "Consider me corrected. It won't happen again."

"Bull," Alex said, also grinning. "I know your job is to protect me, but Kylee and Lillie showed their worth out there tonight. As did Ariel, Sam and Abby. This won't be my first fight. Have a little faith in your queen, that's all I'm asking."

"We all have more than a little faith in our queen, Alex." Ty said. "But you can't blame us for being concerned. If Radek somehow discovers you're out there, he's going to send his entire army after you. It's not the same as Sam or Abby and you know it."

"Then he can't find out," Alex shrugged. "I'm certainly not going to tell him. The only way he could learn of my involvement is if Lilith is out fighting with the troops. Has anyone spotted her in the last couple nights?"

"No," Thomas sighed. He wanted to argue with her, but deep down he knew she needed this. She needed to participate if she was going to stop internalizing all the deaths. All they could do was watch out for her. She

417

wouldn't like it, but he knew all the warriors were going to do it anyway.

"Okay, so everyone is healed and we've settled the Alex dilemma. Who's going to sit out tomorrow night?" Dimitri asked.

The room went silent. Nobody was going to volunteer with their queen out and about.

"I don't think it's fair to ask any of us to sit out when we know our queen will be out there fighting," Victor finally said. "I say we start the rest period the next night. Ariel and I will sit out the following night. It will give me a chance to deal with some things at the club, but we want to be out there tomorrow. I'm sure everyone else in this room feels the same way."

The group nodded in agreement.

"Okay," Dimitri agreed. He felt better knowing all his men would be available with Alex in the open. "We'll start with Victor and Ariel, the next night Bastian and Kylee, then Thomas and Abby, then Ty and Sam. Nick, you and Lillie come next then we'll start over with Dante and Cornelia. I'll play it by ear. Alex and I will take a break when she needs one. Any questions?"

"Nope," Victor said pulling Ariel toward the door. He wanted to get home and celebrate their success with his wife. Then he wanted to crash for a few hours before he headed over to the shelter to check on things. He'd stop in at the club before nightfall and they'd be good to go for another night. The bigger issues could wait until his night off.

The rest of the men stood. "Me either," Bastian said, pulling Kylee toward the door. All the warriors followed.

Nick and Lillie were the only ones left. "Any word from Dante?" He asked hesitantly.

"Not a word," Dimitri said, watching Nick. "But I can tell you he's much happier than he was earlier. I can feel the shift in his emotions. I assume that means he and Cornelia have come to some kind of agreement."

"Then Lillie and I will be going home, too," he said taking Lillie's hand and heading for the door. "It's been a difficult night and tomorrow will probably be just as bad."

"Unfortunately, I agree," Dimitri said walking the couple to the door. "Sam and Alex will be installing more of those units tomorrow. Was any area more susceptible than another?"

"Not really," Nick said. "I think we were all equally busy between covering our assigned areas and responding to calls for help. I guess just focus on the area we guarded tonight and we'll move out from there."

"Get some rest," Dimitri said putting a hand on Nick's shoulder. "The last few weeks have been almost as emotionally draining on you as it has been on Dante. I know how close the two of you are. He's fine, now. Go enjoy a few hours rest with Lillie. I'm sure Dante will check in with you tomorrow."

Progeny

"Good night, Dimitri," Nick said as he headed for the car. He spotted Dusty and Nebi pulling in as he exited onto the highway. The kid's first night at the control center had been a busy one but they'd handled it. Those two were proving to be invaluable in this war. He knew Alex and Dimitri would make sure they knew it before they went home tonight.

* * * *

Cornelia woke confused and a little panicked. She couldn't move. Then she remembered why. Dante was wrapped around her like a vice. She smiled as she opened her eyes and studied her husband. That made her smile widen. She had a husband. Not just any husband, Dante was definitely one of a kind. And he was true to his word. He hadn't let up until she accepted his love. That hadn't taken long. Once she let herself believe, she could easily see how much he cared. His love not only sparkled in his eyes but she felt it in the gentle way he caressed her. The rest had taken a little longer. After their first round, he had held her down and insisted she admit there was nothing monstrous about her. When she didn't comply he proceeded to once again demonstrate his creativity.

Hours later, he had posed the demand again. He wasn't going to be happy until she gave in. By this time, it had become a game and she had playfully refused to admit anything. Dante had grown serious and proceeded to explain why she was basically just another kind of warrior. That intrigued her, but she had to admit his explanation made a weird sort of sense. He insisted that their body composition was basically the same. She was mostly fae with a little human and some vampire thrown in for durability just like the warriors. The only difference, according to her analytical husband, was how they each got there. She was a product of years of mixed breeding, he was a product of science. Then he smiled mischievously and disappeared into the bathroom.

A few minutes later he swept her off the bed and dumped her into the large Jacuzzi tub. He said they were going to determine which one of them was the better specimen. But, he would concede the competition if her claims were really true. When she asked him what claim he was referring to, he said the one about holding her breath under water. She agreed to a demonstration but knew he was up to something. She'd been right. The instant she emerged herself Dante began to demonstrate how good he was at water games. She'd only lasted seconds before she was gasping for air. Dante feigned disappointment but she wasn't fooled. He was enjoying himself as much as she was. And for the first time in her life, she didn't feel like a monster.

Dante woke to the feel of Cornelia snuggled against him. He loved the feeling and once again marveled that such a wonderful woman had fallen for him. Once she'd gone to sleep he had wrapped his body around hers, worried she might leave before he woke. He opened one eye and was relieved to see she was smiling. He studied her for a long moment before he reached out to run his thumb over her bottom lip. "It's nice to see you smile again," he said, surprised at the gravelly tone in his voice.

Cornelia turned, she'd been so deep in memories she hadn't realized Dante was awake. "How could I not smile after the night we had together? I'm the luckiest woman in the world." She leaned closer to give him a quick kiss. She'd only meant it to be a gentle peck, but Dante pulled her close and deepened the kiss. The man was insatiable.

"I think I'm the lucky one," he finally said, brushing the hair away from Cornelia's face. "Cornelia Santora..," he paused, "you know, that is a mouth full in the morning. Have you ever had a nickname?"

Cornelia pulled a face, scrunching up her nose in the process. "My mom calls me Corni, but I hate it."

"Yeah, that is a little...Corny," Dante laughed.

"Ha, ha," Cornelia said, not in the least bit amused.

"How about Corrie?" Dante asked, watching for the slightest reaction.

Cornelia considered. "I guess that's okay," she thought for another moment. "Corrie Santora, I think I like that."

"Then Corrie it is," Dante said rolling over and trapping her to the bed. He grasped her wrists and raised them above her head. "I like you this way," he mumbled as he brushed feather-light kisses down her neck and across her collarbone, then back up the other side of her neck. He began to run his hands down her arms and then across her rib cage. "Yes, I like you like this a lot."

* * * *

Hours later, Dante grumbled as he woke to the sound of his phone. He wasn't ready for reality to intrude on paradise. He fumbled around on the floor then pulled his cell from his pants pocket. "Hello," he barked, clearly annoyed at the interruption.

"Hello to you, too," Nick said just as annoyed. "You said you'd call me today."

"Well, the days not over yet," Dante said, glancing at the clock to make sure he was correct. He couldn't believe it was already one in the afternoon. He sat up and rested against the headboard. Where had Cornelia gone?

"If it's not too much trouble, I need your help," Nick grumbled.

"What's up?" Dante asked, concerned at the tone of Nick's voice.

"We have a problem at one of the Waterson Houses," Nick said soberly.

"What kind of problem?" Dante asked.

"One of the kids got into some kind of trouble. I got a call from the local police. They want a conference call with both of us ASAP. Do you want me to come there or do you want to come here?" Nick asked.

"I'll head over there. Give me ten, I need to jump in the shower first," Dante said climbing from the bed. He saw movement in the doorway and realized Cornelia had returned.

"See you in twenty," Nick said, ending the call. He had wanted to ask a million questions, but they could wait. If Dante wanted to talk, Nick would be there for him. Dimitri had been right, Dante sounded much better than the last time Nick saw him. He must have worked something out with Cornelia and that was enough.

"Sounds like you need to leave," Cornelia said moving into the room.

Dante turned and pulled her into his arms. He brushed a light kiss on top of her head. "Problems at one of the houses. I need to head over to Nick's for a conference call," he stepped back and rummaged around in his closet for clean clothes. Then he turned to face Cornelia. "What do you have planned for today?"

"Nothing much," she shrugged. "Alex called earlier. She and Dimitri are going out to fight tonight. It sounds like things were a little out of control last night. I think they need me...and you tonight. Most of the warriors have paired with their significant others. I plan to help, but if you'd rather pair with Nick..."

Dante was across the room in a second. He placed his hands on either side of her face and forced her to look at him. "We are partners now. Forever. If you're going out there, I want you by my side," he studied her. "Are you trying to keep us, our relationship, a secret?"

Cornelia shook her head vehemently. "No," she said swallowing the lump in her throat. She still didn't know how to act like a wife. "I just wasn't sure what you wanted. I mean Nick and Jake know about the divorce. And Lillie knows, which means Abby and Thomas probably know. I just don't want you to have to make explanations," she furrowed her brow. "I guess it's too late for that, huh? I mean no matter what, there are going to have to be explanations."

"We worked things out," Dante said kissing her softly. "It's as simple as that. No further explanation will be required. The divorce is off. You and I decided we are perfect for each other and we are staying married. Nick will have additional questions and I'll answer the ones I want to. Maybe Thomas, but the others won't pry. You may get a few questions from Lillie and Abby but handle it however you want to. I really don't care what you tell them as long as you're clear we're an eternal couple."

Cornelia smiled. "That, my handsome prince, is not a problem. Now, go shower and head over to Nick's. I'll be fine here. I have a little shopping I want to do anyway. Will you come back later or should I meet you somewhere?"

"I'll come back," Dante assured her. "I don't know how long this will take, but I will come back for you before I head out to fight," he stepped into the bathroom and closed the door.

Progeny

* * * *

Dusk was about to settle as the warriors split up and headed to their assigned areas. Sam and Alex had installed almost twice as many devices today as they had yesterday. The fae was on high alert and anxious to have a means to call for help. Word had spread quickly so very little explanation was needed before the install could begin. They were all hopeful that this new system would save lives. Between the new system and the addition of the shifters, everyone was optimistic. If they were lucky tonight would be less dangerous for the warriors.

* * * *

Martinez and Zorak headed into downtown New York. Martinez had insisted he was not going to fight until he fed. Zorak finally agreed after he gave a stern warning. If any trouble came their way over their disappearance, Zorak was not taking the heat. He'd rat Martinez out in an instant.

"Good to know you've got my back man," Martinez said under his breath as they approached a dark alley.

"Hey, Lilith is brutal," Zorak countered. "One session with that psycho and you'd be careful, too."

"One session?" Martinez asked, truly curious.

"Yeah," Zorak nodded. "That maniac tortured me for days. I didn't know a thing about that mystery woman

426

but did that matter? Not a lick. That woman is vicious. There is no way I'm taking the heat for your stomach."

"Seriously?" Martinez asked, considering. Lilith might be vicious, but she was also bats hit crazy, which was worse. "No wonder you get that look in your eyes every time she walks in the room. I was trying to figure out who the target was, Lilith or Radek. Sounds like I have my answer." But Martinez still wasn't sure. The look Zorak got around Lilith was contemptuous on the surface, but there was something underneath it. Martinez was beginning to wonder if it was admiration...or obsession. The guy was saying all the right things, but something was off.

Zorak froze in shock. Did his eyes really give him away? "I'm loyal to the king," he said defensively.

"Hey," Martinez said raising his hands in surrender, snapping his mind back to their conversation. "It's nothing to me. I just got here. I'm still trying to figure out why we're fighting the other locals and how that has become my problem. I mean, I'm from Mexico. Who cares if the woman, Alexandria is it, rules the fae kingdom? We're vampires aren't we? For now, I'm doing what I'm told but if I disappear one day, don't come looking. I think I'm more of a nomad than a team player." He was still playing things close to the belt. He wanted to trust Zorak, if things went horribly wrong they might need him, but he couldn't shake the feeling he was being set up.

"Sounds good to me," Zorak agreed. "I've about had it with all these battles myself. As long as we don't get caught, I'm all for ditching the action and doing a little feeding tonight."

"That's the spirit," Martinez said raising a fist so Zorak could knock knuckles. "Let's check out the alley then maybe we can get a little action of a different variety. We'll be sure to join the others in time. Lilith gave us our curfew. We'll meet it."

Zorak smiled. "I think I just might like you, Martinez. You're a man after my own heart."

Hours later Zorak and Martinez slid into the shadows of a nearby neighborhood. They had just come from a small alley where they had engaged in a friendly practice fight. They needed to look disheveled and war-weary before they tried to blend in with the group. The instant they arrived, Zorak became visibly angry. What was Radek thinking, putting Philip in charge of an entire group of vampires? He had no business leading himself, let alone others. He was about to step in and take charge when a warrior flew by and sliced his dagger through Phillip's heart. Dust erupted around them scattering Phillip's remains across the roadway. "That's enough," Zorak said stepping into the opening. "Retreat," he called, swinging his arm towards the north, directing the vampire's home.

As they approached the cave entrance Lilith blocked their path. "How did things go out there tonight?" She asked studying the pair. She hadn't seen them, but they looked as if they'd been fighting.

"The same as it's been going for days. We lost a lot of good men," Zorak said, clearly frustrated. "I thought

Radek wanted to build an army, not slowly get them slaughtered night after night."

"You have a good point, Zorak," Lilith grinned. "Why don't you head on over to the King's chambers and explain the error of his ways."

"As the kings' girlfriend, I'd say that's your job." He took a step forward. When Lilith didn't move, he brushed passed her anyway. "Get out of my way, Lilith," he warned. "I'm in no mood to deal with you tonight."

Martinez stepped in before this got ugly. "Actually, that's not a bad idea."

Lilith raised an eyebrow to the newcomer. "You've got more guts than brains if you're thinking about having a chat with Radek."

"Actually, I was thinking more along the lines of having a strategy session with Zorak," Martinez said casually. "He's right. This isn't working. The only thing Radek is accomplishing with these suicide missions is killing off men. Together I'm sure we can come up with something more effective. Something that can bring all this fighting and killing to an end."

"So, after what, two months as a vampire, you think you have what it takes to win a war?" Lilith said sarcastically. "Exactly how many wars have you won in your vast lifetime, Martinez?"

"I realize you're an old woman, Lilith, but even you must know who El Toro is. You know that little thing called the drug wars in Mexico. I've spent my life in a war zone. I'd say that qualifies me for an opinion."

Lilith studied Martinez then gave him her most seductive smile. "What do you say we ditch Zorak and you and I go back to your room and do a little strategizing of another kind?"

"I'd say no, the same as I said yesterday and the day before. The same as I'll say tomorrow and next week and next month. You might as well stop asking, it's never going to happen," Martinez said flatly.

"You seriously do not want to make an enemy of me," Lilith hissed. "It's bad for your health."

"I'll tell you what's not good for my health," Martinez answered. "Accepting a sexual offer from the king's girlfriend. Seriously, do you think I'm stupid? I'm new. You're trying to decide if I can be trusted. What better way to test me than to have the king's girlfriend hit on me and see if I'll take her up on the invitation. I can just see it now, we step into your room and it's off with my head. No, thank you. I think I'll pass."

"This has nothing to do with Radek," Lilith said, understanding. "This is between you and me. I can give you the time of your life and Radek doesn't need to know."

"Not in this lifetime," Martinez said pushing past her to enter the cave. "If anyone needs us, Zorak will be in my room."

Once they were behind closed doors, Zorak turned to Martinez. "You are walking a dangerous road here, man. Lilith is not a woman to scorn. She was right about one thing; she is not someone you want as an enemy."

Martinez shrugged. "I'll risk it. I'm not hooking up with Lilith. Now, let's see what we can come up with? These nightly mini battles can't continue."

With that, they both got comfortable and started to strategize.

Lilith stomped to her room and slammed the door. If that punk kid thought he could get away with rejecting her, he was seriously mistaken. She had a lot to think about tonight. First, she'd actually spotted the queen out fighting. She knew she couldn't act on it. The woman was paired with the warrior leader. If it had only been the two of them she might have gotten a shot, but she spotted the other two just in time. The fire thrower and the bad ass biker. They were lurking in the background, fighting a smaller group of vamps but they were close enough to jump in if she tried anything. The queen and her warrior had decimated Radek's best group of fighters. The woman would have to pay for that. And causing a little chaos would help calm Lilith's temper and take her mind off the public rejection she'd just endured. She was determined to find a way to get back at Martinez but for now, she'd settle for a strategically placed explosion. Too bad Lawson was no longer available. She'd run out of his bombs, but she'd found a replacement. He wasn't as good as Lawson, but the two bombs waiting under her bed would do nicely. She couldn't wait. Tomorrow was going to be a very good night.

* * * *

Nick and Dante sat in the large study with Thomas and Abby. Alex and Dimitri had just arrived. Alex insisted on making coffee and of course Dimitri followed her into the kitchen. "Thomas?" Dante began. "Have you heard from Dusty or Nebi? I'm just wondering how much time I have before we need to head out."

"I haven't heard a word," Thomas shrugged.

"Sorry, I was under the impression you lived here," Dante countered.

"I think I liked you better depressed," Thomas joked. "I have no idea where those two are. But we can't start until Alex has her coffee anyway so it really doesn't matter does it? They should be here any minute I would guess, those two are never late."

"It's getting dark," Dante worried. "I'm not sure how forgiving the community will be if we don't have anyone to man the controls when they press the alarm. Or any warriors out there fighting when the vamps storm the front door."

"Such an alarmist," Thomas said shaking his head. "What's this meeting all about anyway?"

"Are those the records for Dusty and Nebi?" Nick asked pointing to a large stack on the desk in the corner. He was trying to change the subject. Dante wasn't going to talk until Alex and Dimitri returned.

"They are," Abby smiled. "Those kids have their work cut out for them. If we're as busy tonight as we have been the last couple nights, I doubt they'll even have a chance to look. I might recruit some of the teens in our pack to go through them. We need to get the files categorized so we know where we have help and where we are the most vulnerable. Most of the kids that spent time at the fort have at least one skill they can use to help protect their families. But, we all know some of the kids are better fighters than others. Mapping everything out and knowing each households abilities will take time, but I think it's going to be worth it."

Alex and Dimitri walked in with the cart in tow. "Okay, let's get started. Dusty and Nebi should be here any minute," Dimitri told them. "I asked them to make a stop on the way over so we're going to be cutting this close. The rest of the warriors are heading out already. What did you want to talk to all of us about Dante?"

"I need to plan a wedding," Dante began, standing to address his friends.

Thomas laughed. "Isn't one wife enough for you?"

"Funny," Dante said, clearly not amused. "When Cornelia and I got married it was after a night on the town. We'd both been drinking; I was gathering information to try to find Shannon. Of course, I remember everything but she only has flashes. She mentioned how she wished she could remember her wedding. She never thought she'd have one because of the vampire thing. I'd like to give her the wedding of her dreams," he paused. "I'd also like to include her mother in the mix, but I'm not sure if that's possible. I'm hoping to keep this all a secret until the big day.

Nick and Lillie already know about this. I talked to them yesterday. I want it all, the white dress, the flowers, friends and family. I was hoping Oberon would perform the ceremony and I'd like it to be soon. I know that's a lot to ask, but I thought maybe between Abby, Alex and Lillie we could pull it off. If you're all willing to help, that is."

Abby ran across the room and pulled Dante into a big hug. "Dante Santora you are such a romantic. Of course I'll help," she grinned at Thomas. "Maybe if I keep assisting in other people's weddings someone will eventually propose to me."

Thomas winked at her and smiled. "Could happen, you never know." He was going to propose to Abby and she knew it. He even had the ring, he just wanted to pick the perfect moment and with everything going on, it just didn't seem right yet.

"Lillie has already agreed to help," Nick added. "In fact, that's why she's not here. She's with Cornelia, trying to get as much information as possible without giving anything away. I'll help in any way I can, Dante knows that too."

"We're all in," Alex said, grinning. "I can't wait. This is going to be so much fun. We could use a little fun to counterbalance everything else. Just so you know, Sam, Kylee and Ariel are going to want in, too. Together I'm sure we will exceed all Cornelia's expectations."

Talk continued about colors, guests and cake. Dimitri glanced out the window, it was completely dark now. They would need to join the others, soon. But, he could give them a few more minutes. As soon as Dusty and Nebi arrived he'd have to break this up.

* * * *

Martinez ignored the knock on his door. How was he supposed to develop a plan when he couldn't get one lousy minute to himself? When he didn't respond, the door creaked open and Sammael slipped in. Martinez didn't offer a greeting. These two were supposed to be partners in this, but so far all he was getting from the man were orders and lectures. He continued to stare at the ceiling, trying to formulate a plan.

Sammael watched the newest member of their group as he continued to ignore him. He was running out of patience with the man. "Are you going to stare at the ceiling all night or will you be joining Zorak for another wasted evening of parties and women?"

Martinez forced himself to hold back the sigh. "Was there something you needed, Sammael? I'm busy."

Progeny

Sammael narrowed his eyes. If it wouldn't blow his cover, the man would have been ground to dust by now. "I need to know how much of our plans you have shared with Zorak," he finally said, doing his best to hold back his anger. "I have a mission to fulfill and I need to know how badly you have messed things up for us."

Martinez sat up, swinging his legs over the edge of the bed. "None of it," he said, never taking his eyes off Sammael.

"Nothing at all?" Sammael asked eyebrows raised in disbelief. "The two of you have become inseparable. You seriously want me to believe you haven't confided in the man?"

"Believe what you want," Martinez said, settling back down to stare at the ceiling again. "If that's all, I'm busy. It's impossible to think while you prattle on about nonissues."

Sammael was across the room in a second. He yanked Martinez to his feet and glared. "Nonissues?" he spat. "I suppose you're busy planning new, creative escapades for tonight with your new best friend? Have you ever stopped to wonder why Zorak has taken such an interest in you? I mean, until you came along he was a loner. Now all of a sudden he's the great companion."

Martinez let one side of his mouth tip up in response. So, the little hellion wasn't as patient as he wanted everyone to believe. Martinez allowed his gaze to move from Sammael's eyes, down to the hand that was still grasping his shirt then back to Sammael's eyes. He lifted a brow and waited. Finally, Sammael relinquished his hold and took a step back. "Jealous?" Martinez finally asked.

"Of course I'm not jealous of that big, stupid oaf," Sammael said with contempt. "We are simply running out of time and so far I don't see you making any progress. In fact, from where I'm standing you are jeopardizing the mission more than anyone has thus far."

"Then maybe you should move," Martinez said, lowering himself to the edge of the bed. "Are we partners or not?" he finally asked. "Because since I've been here, the only time I see you is when you stop by to give me orders. I'm trying to work this out on my own, but it would be nice if I got a little cooperation from you. Maybe a little input on the current problem at hand before I end up either dead or explaining why Zorak is dead."

"So you don't really trust the man?" Sammael asked in surprise.

"Of course I don't trust the man," Martinez said with exasperation. "I'm not an idiot. The only reason the guy hasn't tried to slip behind me and stab me in the back, literally, is because he knows it would displease Lilith. But eventually, Zorak is going to have to disappear. I need a plan. A way to get him out of the way without raising suspicion."

"Not that I don't agree with you but tell me why," Sammael asked. He had to admit he was surprised. He'd thought Martinez had been taken in by Zorak, he'd been worrying for weeks that the kid was going to ruin all their hard work. Which is why the only time they spoke was when Sammael was passing on messages. Until now, he hadn't trusted the new guy. Now? He wasn't sure. But he wanted to hear what the kid had to say.

"We have two missions," Martinez said with a shrug. "I think we can achieve the main goal with Zorak around, but I don't see how we can get the key from Lilith unless Zorak is out of the picture."

"You found the key?" Sammael asked, impressed. It seemed like he'd been looking for that thing forever and it was nowhere to be found. "Where is it?"

Martinez looked at Sammael, alert. "You don't know?"

"No," Sammael admitted. "I spend some time every night looking while the vampires are hunting and fighting, but so far I've come up empty."

"That's because it's not here when we're all out hunting. Not unless Lilith is here. The woman never goes anywhere without it. At least she never goes anywhere without the key hanging from the chain she wears under those seductive clothes of hers. I can only assume it's the key we are looking for."

"I'm not even going to ask how you know what that woman wears under her clothes," Sammael said, not hiding the worry from his tone.

"Not on your life," Martinez said rolling his eyes. "She's not even a temptation. I know because I've seen it, every time I train with the two of them. The same way I see that Zorak is obsessed with the woman. He hates my guts. You're supposed to be the master spy; you can't honestly tell me you haven't seen the way he looks at me. Especially when Lilith is making advances right in front of him. I haven't been able to get a line on her feelings for him, but Zorak wants that woman for himself. If I ever accepted one of her offers, I'd be dead within twenty-four hours, tops. Which is why we can't go after Lilith without having to deal with Zorak as well. And we can't blow your cover or we risk the main mission."

"I can't say for certain, but I believe Zorak and Lilith are lovers," Sammael supplied. "I know they were previously, but who Lilith sleeps with currently is anyone's guess. Zorak hated knowing Lilith was sleeping with Hector, but Zorak was afraid of Hector so he tolerated it. He would not tolerate you, we can agree on that. He would find a way to take you out and try to talk his way out of it."

"Hum," Martinez considered. "So, did Lilith really torture Zorak over the mystery woman or is he exaggerating?"

"No, she tortured him," Sammael admitted. "She was ordered to do so by Radek. It pissed her off when Radek ordered me to stay in the room with her while she did it. Otherwise, I think they would have used the time in a more...intimate manner. With me there, she had no choice. Both Radek and Lilith consider me beyond loyal to the king. Also, Lilith and I have not hidden our dislike for one another. She knew she had to perform some torture on Zorak, but I knew she was holding back. As far as I know, they are not aware of my knowledge where the two of them are concerned."

"So how do we make Zorak disappear without casting suspicion on me?" Martinez asked. He'd been going around and around in circles and still had not found a solution to the problem.

"I think I can provide the answer you are looking for on that one," Sammael said moving to sit next to Martinez on the bed. "The only question is how to get word to Ammit."

"Can't you just text him?" Martinez inquired.

"I do not have cell service inside the cave. I will have to try to sneak out tonight and make plans for tomorrow," Sammael said regretfully.

"I have text service, just not phone service," Martinez said pulling out his phone. "What message do we need to send?"

"I think it would be best if Ammit sent Gallo to meet with me. I could explain the situation in person then the kings could come up with a plan and get word back to us on when to strike," Sammael told him. "I just worry if the message comes from you, Ammit might suspect a trap. I mean, why would you ask for a meeting with Gallo?"

"Tell me what you have in mind first," Martinez pressed.

"A small number of vampires just arrived from Canada," Sammael told him. "Radek sent Clay up to hunt and bring back another contingent because we've lost so many over the past week. Anyway, he told Clay to take them to a cave nearby and start their training. Radek hasn't decided who to send to train them yet. I believe I can manipulate him into sending Zorak."

"That might work," Martinez said nodding. "Then, Gallo or Trumak could intercept him and question him. But if Zorak doesn't arrive, won't Radek find out his new vampires are running around without supervision?"

"Those vampires are from Canada. King DeMarco is probably already here. If not, he will be here within a couple days. We can just turn the vamps back over to the Canadians and they can decide what to do with them," Sammael supplied.

"I like it," Martinez said standing to pace. "I think it just might work, as long as Lilith doesn't try to head out to the cave for a little side action between training sessions."

"She's not that attached to him," Sammael said confidently. "Oh, she keeps him around as a backup because he's so easy to control. Which is why she went after Hector and now you. The fact that you have refused her only makes her more determined. You have now become a challenge to her, and I'm sure you've noticed Lilith doesn't get many challenges around here. Zorak isn't strong enough to keep her for long. Once she gets what she wants from him, I have no doubt she'll kill him herself."

Progeny

"Gives a whole new meaning to psycho ex-girlfriend, doesn't it?" Martinez joked as he sent a text to Typhon requesting a meeting with a runner. Seconds later he had a response. "How do you want to work this meeting?"

"Tell them to go to the east side of the cave. There is an opening, but it's very difficult to find. As far as I know, Hector and I were the only ones aware of it. I will meet them an hour after the group leaves to go hunt and fight. It's going to take me that long to get Radek situated and sneak away. I'll only have enough time to give them the basics. The runner will need to take the information back to the kings and return tomorrow night with a plan. Same arrangement. I'll be there an hour after everyone leaves to receive further instructions. We'll have to act fast though, before Radek selects a new trainer," Sammael said, thinking.

"I think it's safe to go ahead with that part of the plan," Martinez provided. "Start dropping hints tonight if possible. It's not going to hurt if the kings don't like the plan. It still gets Zorak away from me for a while and I can start working on getting that key. With Zorak gone, I'll have to train with Lilith and I'll be able to get a better look at the thing anyway," he glanced down at his phone then gave Sammael a satisfied smile. "Gallo will be meeting you as requested."

"I'm not even going to ask how you managed that one," Sammael said, for the first time thinking he might have misjudged his new partner.

"It was easy, I left it up to them to select the runner. I just told them they would be meeting you. Gallo was the obvious choice," Martinez supplied as he moved to change his shirt. "Now I need to be ready to head out. The last thing we need is to cause suspicion tonight."

"Agreed," Sammael said as he moved toward the door then slipped into darkness.

* * * *

Cam stepped from the cab and paid the fare. He barely noticed the car drive off. The house was magnificent. He knew it would be, of course, the Deveraux's were beyond rich. He just stood there, taking in air then letting it out slowly. He wouldn't say he was nervous. He was a Marine. Marines could handle anything. He was just surprised. Not at the fact that the two behemoths who were now his bosses knew the Deveraux's, that didn't surprise him at all. The surprising part was the casual way they had invited him to join them here. As if he were an old friend stopping in to chat. Stopping in at the Deveraux's, the most powerful family in the world, was mind boggling. He'd never met anyone quite like these guys before. The top notch products Deveraux Industries produced had saved his butt more than once in Iraq. He'd heard the old man had died not too long ago and the kids had taken over. He hoped they were as on the ball as their father had been. There were a lot of lives depending on their products.

Progeny

Cam took one more soothing breath and headed up the drive. The solar lights bordering the pathway made it easy to find his way in the dark. He glanced again at the large house, illuminated in the darkness. He'd like to see it in the daylight. He was sure it was old and just as sure it would be even more majestic and intimidating during the day. That's when he spotted the kids. They were young, teenagers, early twenties tops. Obviously, they were in love. The two of them were joking around, engaging in horseplay like so many of his men did when they first came to him, innocent and full of life. Untouched by the ugliness of war. Just a few months in Iraq and the playfulness, the joviality, disappeared completely. Sure the men sometimes wrestled around, but it was never the same. They were never the same.

Nebi laughed and jumped backward when Dusty tried to grab her arm. "You're never going to catch me, babe. You might be bigger, but I'm quicker."

Dusty pretended to ignore her. He continued up the driveway, forcing his body to relax. If he tensed in anticipation, she'd sense it. He took another step, feeling her more than seeing her. She was right behind him. Another second and he'd have her. Dusty shifted and lunged for Nebi. She was too quick; the girl was like a gazelle. Nebi was laughing, bouncing from one foot to the other, waiting for him to attack. Dusty couldn't help himself, he started to laugh and lunged just as the world exploded.

Cam continued up the drive, lost in thoughts of war and destruction. Senseless fighting that altered young

444

men's lives forever. He heard the explosion but at first it didn't register. For the slightest instant, he was back in Fallujah, bodies everywhere, bullets flying, the blood of his friends seeping into the powdery sand. But, no. He was at the Deveraux's, not Iraq. He shook his head, forcing his mind back to the present and realized he hadn't imagined the bomb.

The two kids were lying on the ground. The boy was bleeding profusely from his leg and the girl was either dead or unconscious. He didn't think, he just sprinted toward the kids. He went to the girl first, she was still alive, her pulse was a little weak but steady. The guy was a different story. A story he'd seen way too many times to count. The explosion had blown off the kids' foot and part of his shin. Cam had just finished tying the tourniquet when he saw a dozen men approaching. Their faces were hard and their eyes...what was going on here? Nobody had such vibrant green eyes. If it had only been one of them he'd think they were contacts, but every one of the men had the same spooky green cat eyes. He rushed to the girl and slid her as close to the guy as possible. She was still out cold. Unfortunately, the guy wasn't and the kid was in pain.

"You need help," the kid croaked. Cam saw him pull a large dagger from a sheath secured to his belt. He appreciated the gesture, but the kid was not going to be any help. Cam slowly stood, prepared to defend the wounded. He grimaced at the pain that shot through his knee. His damn injury was going to be a problem. He felt that old pang of annoyance, he hadn't even run that far.

Progeny

The closer the group got, the more certain Cam was that those things were not normal men. What in the world had he got himself into? Well, it didn't matter. He'd defend the kids or go down trying. Wouldn't that be a kicker, to survive Iraq just to come back to the Big Apple and be killed by freaky cat eye things, whatever they were? Fate had to be a woman, no man would be this cruel.

One of the attackers was ahead of the others. He had zoomed in on Cam and was headed straight for him. Cam focused and prepared for the attack. He'd never been shy about fighting and rarely lost one, but now that he was in the Twilight zone that might change, especially since he had a handicap. He braced himself trying to anticipate the impact.

Nick, Dante, Thomas, Abby, Dimitri and Alex were deep into wedding plans when they heard the explosion. They immediately jumped to their feet and headed for the door. Dante reached it first. The instant he stepped out on the porch his heart nearly stopped. Halfway up the drive Cam was trying to fist fight with a vamp. Several others were gathering in the distance. Dusty and Nebi were lying on the ground. A vampire was circling the kids, every few seconds it would lunge, then back off when Dusty flailed his arm, dagger in hand. There was so much blood surrounding the kids and Nebi wasn't moving. He immediately pulled his dagger and flew off the porch in a dead run toward the trouble. He heard the pounding of boots and knew the rest of the group was directly behind him.

Cam had never fought anything like this thing before. His knee was swollen, almost inoperable and his back was killing him. That last impact was brutal. He'd flown across the driveway and collided with a tree. One of the branches had split open his shin, but that was nothing compared to the excruciating pain radiating in his lower back and buttocks. Cam took a deep breath then forced himself upright. He stood there, hands on his thighs, hunched like an old man and spotted Dante and Nick running toward him. There were others, people he didn't know and all of them had large daggers drawn. Cam swallowed the lump in his throat, determined to force himself upright and finish the fight when he saw Dante plunge his knife into one of those things. Cam was no stranger to blood, so he didn't flinch, he just stood there, waiting for the thick red liquid to start seeping through the guy's shirt. But that wasn't what happened. The thing disappeared. Poof, he was gone. Cam watched in shock as dust disbursed over the barely lit driveway. A slight breeze caught part of the remains and scattered them over the lawn and onto the tiny lights outlining the flower bed. "What in the hell?" He blinked, blinked again and then realized his attacker was coming at him again. Cam quickly reached into his pocket and pulled out his Benchmade. He'd gotten it years ago and never went anywhere without it. That tactical knife had saved him too many times to count. He was grateful he had it now.

Cam hadn't wanted to deliver a fatal blow before. He was on Deveraux property and a family like that didn't need the kind of publicity a dead body in their driveway would bring. Things had changed now. No body, no problem. His training kicked in. He continued to watch as the man that threw him into the tree lumbered toward him. He'd only have one shot at this, so he'd better make it good. The guy, or whatever it was, came at him. Cam stood his ground, perfectly still until the thing was close enough to reach for his neck. Then he plunged his knife into its chest. Just like before, the guy poofed. Dust settled around Cam's feet. Well, that was weird. After three tours in Iraq and one in Afghanistan, he thought he'd seen it all. But he'd never seen anything like this battle before and hoped he never did again. He took a couple tentative steps, aiming for the last spot he'd seen Nick and Dante. As Cam looked up, he realized Nick was in trouble. He was fighting off four of the things and another one was headed straight for Nick's back. Cam stumbled forward, his back was killing him and every other step put pressure on his knee. He could tell the thing wasn't injured, just aggravated and swollen.

He barely reached Nick in time. Just as the freaky monster raised his arm to slice through Nick's shoulder, Cam lunged forward and struck it through the ribs. The thing fell to the ground taking him with it, but it didn't disappear. Cam knew he was still in danger. Until he killed the thing, it would just keep coming. He rolled, forcing himself onto his good knee and plunged his knife through its heart. If it had one that is. Cam didn't know, he just knew the thing faded into the dirt and gravel of the driveway. The pain was too much, Cam knew his fight was over. He sank back to the ground and hoped the rest of these guys would protect him. He rolled to his side and pulled his knees to his chest, sometimes that relieved enough pressure to stop the spasms.

Cam glanced up just in time to see the girl, the one that was unconscious, spring up and then turn into a wolf. No way, there is just no way that was possible. Maybe he'd hit his head on the way down. He closed his eyes, counted to ten then looked again. He watched in amazement as the girl, or wolf, killed one after another. Nick and Dante were still battling, two or three of the things at a time. There were others, the group that had followed Nick and Dante out of the house. He was trying to force himself into a sitting position. He had to watch. The whole thing was too surreal to miss. Once he got upright, he looked around. He spotted a woman he didn't know fighting off two attackers. Once she obliterated the last enemy everything went quiet. The attackers were gone. Within seconds, Nick was crouched in front of him.

"You okay?" he asked, clearly concerned.

"I'll live, if that's what you're asking," Cam said as he tried to stand.

Nick moved behind Cam and effortlessly pulled him to his feet.

"Thanks," Cam said, taking a deep breath as he looked around again. "Uh, you mind telling me what those things were?"

"Later," Dante said, moving in beside the two of them. "We need to get you into the house."

Dante glanced at Nick and knew they were both thinking the same thing. The cut on Cam's leg would draw any remaining vamps in the area directly to them.

Progeny

Nick helped Cam hobble up the stairs. The three of them paused at the door. Cam looked back and saw a couple men carrying the injured kid toward the house. "I have to say, I'm having second thoughts about leaving the simple life of that tent."

"No, you're not," Dante said, laughing. "A couple of weeks in a nice comfy bed has ruined you. We may never get you back to New York, but I'm willing to bet that Las Vegas suite we set you up in still looks mighty good."

"Maybe," Cam agreed. "But the Big Apple is definitely overrated," he paused, remembering the blast. "I think that bomb is still hot."

Before either of the men could respond a black SUV flew up the drive and came to a screeching stop. Cam watched as another large man and a beautiful red head jumped from the vehicle.

"Ty's here," Dante said casually. "Problem solved."

Cam watched as one of the women moved from the injured kid's side and approached the new arrivals. She spoke quietly, motioning toward the explosive device then walked back to accompany the kid inside. The man turned toward the bomb, then stopped. He and the woman got into what looked like a heated argument. The woman stopped and waited, but she didn't look happy about it. The guy moved in and crouched next to the bomb. He began fiddling with it before Cam could respond. "Uh, you might want to call the bomb squad. That thing might be unstable and poking at it if you don't know what you're doing could blow us all to la-la land."

"Ty knows what he's doing," Nick assured him. "Now, let's get inside."

Cam hesitated but realized the group carrying the injured kid was almost to the front porch. If they didn't move, they'd be in the way. "The kid's going to need a good support system to deal with that leg," Cam thought aloud.

"He's got one," Nick said confidently as he ushered Cam into the study.

Once Dusty was settled in the back room, Dimitri, Alex, Thomas and Abby joined the trio.

Alex studied the man sprawled on the couch, wondering what to do about him. He was clearly human and a risk. He'd seen way too much tonight. But he'd also saved Nick's life and protected Dusty and Nebi when they couldn't protect themselves. She was just sick over what happened to Dusty. For the first time in a long time, she was aggravated and annoyed with her gift. She healed Dusty the best she could, but she couldn't regenerate the foot. Dusty's condition was permanent and he wasn't taking it well. In fact, he'd been downright nasty to Nebi before he ordered her out of the room.

Cam felt the scrutiny of the petite woman and the Goliath man and took that as a hint. "I'm kind of short on time," he said to Nick and Dante. "If I could just have a minute, I'll get out of your hair." He pulled a large sheet of paper from his inside coat pocket then looked around for a place to lay out the plans.

"Why don't you take that into the kitchen? We'll be in shortly. It's out the door to the left. Just follow the hallway through the door," Nick suggested.

"Got it," Cam said, slowly rising to his feet. He knew he looked ninety but there was nothing he could do about it.

Once Cam was out of earshot, Alex turned to Nick and Dante. "I could heal him. He's seen enough that one more shock won't matter."

"Victor and Ariel are on their way over," Thomas supplied. "They're bringing Tony and Megan."

"Good," Alex said, relieved. If there was a problem, Megan could handle it. "Then why don't I heal him? If it's a problem, Megan can take care of that, too."

Nick and Dante studied each other for several seconds. Dante was the one to speak, knowing Nick was thinking the same thing. "If you do, we'd like you to heal all his wounds."

"Of course I'll heal them all," Alex said defensively. "When have I ever left a job unfinished?"

"Don't get your panties in a bunch, your highness," Dante joked. "I was talking about old wounds. Wounds he got in the war, in Iraq."

"We'd like you to take care of those as well as the ones he got here today," Nick added. "Let me fill you in on his story."

Cam studied the diagram. He was pleased with it. Sure, it needed a little tweaking, but it was good enough. He pulled a pencil out of his pocket and made a slight alteration. He flinched at the sound of a chair sliding across the floor and crashing into the wall. Cam took a deep breath. It wasn't his problem, he told himself again. The girl was a wolf. He glanced over his shoulder and sighed. She looked so miserable and he knew he might be able to help. She wasn't a wolf, she was just a kid. She wasn't crying, but he could tell she was angry. Just then she covered her face with her hands and growled.

Cam moved silently, albeit slowly, across the room and sank into the chair next to the girl. He didn't say a word, just waited.

"What?" Nebi finally asked in challenge.

Cam shrugged. "Nothing," he said casually as he straightened his legs and crossed one ankle over the other.

"Then stop staring," she grumbled. "What are you a pervert?"

Cam grinned, "Nope. Well, there was that woman in Reno, but...never mind. That's way off topic and not appropriate for a young squirt like yourself."

"Humph," Nebi said, trying not to smile. She was almost successful, but her bottom lip did twitch just a little. "So what do you want old man?" she finally asked.

"Nothing," Cam told her. "I was just trying to figure something out, that's all."

Progeny

"And what might that be?" Nebi asked, curious but wishing she wasn't.

"Well, I was wondering why you let him kick you out," Cam said casually. "I can see you're pissed about it, frustrated and maybe a little scared of the situation. Of course, he's feeling all those same things, too. But if you really love him, I just can't figure out why you let him banish you to the kitchen."

"You don't know anything about this, so mind your own business," Nebi grumbled.

"I know more than you might think," he said soberly, thinking about all the kids that had gone home without a limb. "So? Do you love him?" he asked.

Nebi didn't answer.

"I don't just mean a casual fling kind of love or childish puppy love. I'm talking soul deep, down to the bone love? Because that's the only thing that's going to get him through this," Cam glanced at Nebi and smiled. The girl was listening; she just didn't want him to know she was listening.

Nebi turned to him, glanced pointedly at one arm then the other, then she moved her attention to both of his legs. "Since you seem to have all your body parts intact, I don't see why you think you know anything about this."

Cam ignored her. He didn't have all his body parts intact, but this wasn't about him. "Your man in there is broken. I'm not talking about the leg. It will heal and eventually he'll learn to get around, to function, to go on. I'm talking inside. In his soul. He's broken, he's scared and he's worried about his future. Based on what I saw out in the driveway, he knows you're a strong, capable woman. You can take care of yourself, so why would you need a broken guy like him around?"

For the first time, Nebi realized this human had seen her shift. When she regained consciousness, she wasn't thinking about secrets, she was thinking about survival. And she was pissed that the vampires had set off another bomb, a bomb that had the man she loved lying on the ground missing a leg. She'd snapped. She looked at the stranger in shock and wasn't sure what to say or do.

"Don't look at me that way," Cam muttered. "I'm not talking about the freaky Teen Wolf thing. I'm just saying you are strong willed and, for whatever reason, you can protect yourself. Let's just leave it at that. I don't want to talk about the rest."

"Freaky teen wolf thing?" Nebi asked, amused.

"Yeah, you know Michael J. Fox, Teen Wolf? Basketball?"

Nebi furrowed her brows, she had no idea what he was talking about. The guy in Teen Wolf played Lacrosse.

"Never mind, you probably weren't even born in the 80's," Cam grumbled, feeling older by the minute. "My point is that your man in there is a strong, honorable man. I don't know if he's involved in all that woo woo stuff, but clearly he knows about it."

Progeny

"How do you know he's honorable? You don't even know him," Nebi took a deep breath, she was beginning to like this guy, but wasn't ready to trust him. He might just be blowing smoke to try to make her feel better.

"No, I don't know him. Not really," Cam agreed. "But I know his type. He's a good soldier. A solid, honorable, strong fighter. Those traits show character. When I reached you, the guy's foot had been blown off, you were lying there unconscious and he was basically bleeding to death. Once I got the tourniquet on, do you know what he did?"

"No," Nebi said, but she had a good idea.

"He pulled out a dagger and told me I needed help. The guy was barely conscious himself but he wanted to fight and he did. I was trying to keep those things away from the two of you, but your man in there continued to fight them off. Anytime one of them got close, he swung out and tried to kill it," Cam paused, thinking about all the kids lost in the war. "I've seen a few men, I say men but they were really just kids, a few of them have that kind of courage. That kind of honor, that kind of grit to fight 'til the end... but not many. Your man in there is special," he glanced at Nebi. "I think you have the same grit. And that's what's eating at him."

"If you think Dusty cares that I'm strong and capable you're wrong," Nebi said defensively. "He loves that we're equally matched. He loves that we can work together."

"Exactly my point, sweetheart," Cam said soberly. "He doesn't feel equally matched anymore. He's broken and he thinks you deserve better. Which is why you're out here pissed and he's in there miserable. And that brings me back to my original question. Are you in love with the guy? Do you love him enough to push back? The natural tendency is to pamper. That's not what a guy like that needs."

"Which brings me back to my original question. You haven't lost a leg, so what makes you think you're an expert on it?" Nebi asked, curious not defensive this time.

"I have injuries, ones that will be with me for the rest of my life," Cam sighed. "But, I'm a Marine. I've been to Iraq. I've seen more than my share of kids get limbs blown off. In battle, from car bombs, from IED's. It's a freaking mess over there and too many kids have come home just as broken as your Dusty in there. Good men, good soldiers who never made a mistake, never screwed up, they were just in the wrong place at the wrong time," he studied her. "And nine out of ten of them try to push those who love them away, especially girlfriends or wives. Sometimes their kids. I've seen it enough to know what I'm talking about."

Nebi thought about that. Maybe he did, he certainly had more experience in this area than she did. "So, what should I do?" she finally asked.

"I can't tell you that," Cam said softly. "You have to figure out what works with him for yourself. What I can tell you is that by leaving, by letting him throw you out of that room, you have already given him the upper hand. Fix that, right now. Go back in there and don't let him bully you. He's injured, there is no way he could physically throw you out of the room. Take advantage of that."

Nebi wasn't about to tell him that Dusty wasn't injured any longer. Alex had healed him. His leg was as good as it was ever going to be. "How does pissing him off from the get go help my cause?"

"It's Nebi right?" Cam asked. "We haven't exactly been introduced but I thought I heard one of them call you Nebi."

"Yeah, it's Nebi," she agreed.

"I'm Cam by the way. Anyway, like I said, I'm also injured. Sure I have all my limbs, but not the strength I used to have. Not the flexibility or the mobility. That doesn't make me an expert, but I can tell you I hate it when people pity me. I don't want to be given a break because I got hurt. I don't want to be pampered or get special treatment. So I got injured, who cares. That's life. Life's hard. I could have gotten cancer, or a brain tumor, or died from a heart attack. I don't have it any worse than anyone else does. I want to pay my way, take care of myself, be independent," Cam said, staring out the window.

"So I shouldn't give in to Dusty's demands and I shouldn't pamper him?" Nebi asked, considering.

"I know that's going to be tough. Especially while he's healing. You love the guy; you're going to want to help him. But he needs to know that nothing has changed," Cam supplied.

"But things have changed," Nebi disagreed.

"They don't have to," Cam told her. "I don't know how serious you two are. But if you were talking about marriage, college, kids. You need to keep talking about those things and make sure he knows you expect him to continue with your plans. There's no reason Dusty can't go to college. There's no reason he can't get a job and provide for a family. In fact, he has an obligation to do just that. The leg hasn't changed anything. Even the fighting and we are not going to get into that. But, once he's healed if he's a freaky Teen Wolf too, he can still be a freak," Cam shrugged. "He just has to be a three-legged freak."

Nebi did smile now. "We're not freaks. We're unique. You're just jealous," she challenged.

"Yeah kid, sure I am," Cam shook his head. Was he really having this conversation? "My point is that, even with my disabilities, I found a way to matter. Dusty needs to know he still matters. He needs to know he's not as broken as he thinks he is," he paused. "But don't get me wrong, this won't be easy. He's going to push you away. He might even be cruel about it. In his mind, you are better off without him. That means anything he does, he's doing out of love. Remember that, because it's going to get harder before it gets better."

Nebi wondered if she could take it if Dusty got any worse. He'd been so cruel when he kicked her out of the room. But Cam made sense. Dusty would be stupid enough to try to push her away. She wanted to help him get through this, so she had to be strong enough to take whatever he dished out. Even if it shattered her heart into a million pieces. Nebi gave a quick nod then stood. "Then I guess I better get back in there and set my guy straight on a few things."

"That's the spirit," Cam said, pleased with her tenacity. He hoped they made it. He had a feeling they were good for each other.

"Consorting with the enemy?" Dante asked Nebi as he and Nick walked into the room. "I'm surprised at you."

"Cam's not the enemy," Nebi said, looking him in the eye. "In fact, for a human he's okay. He's ancient and moves like he's about a hundred, but I think he's alright." She turned, strode through the bedroom door and closed it silently behind her.

"She's young," Nick joked. "Her judgment can't be trusted." He turned to the diagram on the table. "So, tell us what you've got here old man."

Cam chuckled as he slowly rose from the chair. He did move like he was a hundred, but he had meant every word he'd said to Nebi. As long as he could pull his weight, as long as he felt independent and worthwhile, it didn't matter. Once he reached the table, he sat back down. He wished he could do this standing, but his knee and his back were killing him.

Dante studied the diagram then turned his attention to Cam. "I don't think this needs much explanation. It's a great idea, might be a little pricey, but I like it."

"Yeah, me too," Nick said, calculating the cost in his head. "Give us the details," he prompted. "Who will you have do the work?"

"Well," Cam began. "I figured we already have the manpower to clear that field over here," he pointed to an area that was mostly weeds. He knew it was rocky, but the tenants already living at Waterson could handle the clearing.

"True," Dante agreed.

"Once that's done, I figured I could start taking tenants. We could set up an area over here," he pointed to one edge of the field. "For tents. It takes a lot of time to travel to the alley from the House. If I moved those people that depend on me out here in the tents they could work for their keep. I'd oversee the construction of the cabins, but most of them are healthy and able. They can do the hard labor."

Nick sat back. It was a good plan. "Is Charlotte on board with this?" He finally asked. If they approved this, it would be adding a lot of extra people, extra responsibility for Charlotte and Cam.

"Yeah," Cam assured them. "She's already scoured the books and squeezed out enough to get the project going. She wants to make additional cuts, but I'm not on board with all of them."

"If you guys can come up with thirty percent of the cost out of your own budget, Nick and I will cover the other seventy," Dante offered. "You okay with that?" he asked Nick.

"Absolutely," Nick agreed. "I like this idea enough to throw in one hundred percent, but I think it would be good for the House to pitch in. The thirty includes labor, so if the tenants help that's less cash you need to provide."

This was more than Cam had hoped for. The three men went over the plans in more detail. Cam was excited about the project. The first step was moving himself and Charlotte into the old farmhouse. He'd take the upstairs and Charlotte wanted the basement. Then he'd clear the fields and set up the tents. He'd been serious, driving out to the alley every other day was time-consuming. He'd move the people he cared about into tents and get them started on building the small cabins. Each one of them would be given one of the cabins to live in for their work. Then he'd get started on remodeling the big house. Dante had been right, they needed at least one apartment for a large family. Moving himself and Charlotte out would give them two more apartments for guests. He also wanted to convert the two large offices into one more apartment. The more people they could house, the better.

It was almost an hour later when Alex stepped into the kitchen. "Dimitri and I need to head out. I was hoping I could take care of Cam before I left. And Dimitri said you two have somewhere to be as well."

Cam stood, slowly. His back spasms had subsided, but his knee was stiff and hard to manipulate. "Ma'am," he said as he took her hand. "I'm sorry I kept you all here so late. I'll head out now, too. I'll just need to call a cab.

I have an early flight in the morning and I'll need to get some ice on this leg or I'll never survive the trip to Colorado. Anyway, I think we've talked this thing to death already."

"Cam, I wasn't implying you'd overstayed your welcome. I'm just a bit tired and I too have a long day ahead of me tomorrow." She glanced at Nick and then Dante. "Megan says there's no risk in this, so we don't have to worry about that."

"Good," they both said in unison.

"Anyway," Cam said dropping Alex's hand. "It's been an honor to meet you and your brother. I have to tell you I can't count how many times one of your devices has saved my butt. Thank you for that. The men and women out there fighting for our freedom count on you and respect you. I hope you know that. What you do, it matters. And it saves lives."

"Thank you, Cam," she said humbled. "That means a lot coming from a war hero like yourself. I know there's a lot of speculation now that my father died. We've been able to maintain most of our contracts, but there's also grumblings. Guys wondering if we can maintain the high standard Luke had when it comes to technology. I can assure you, Sam's on top of that. D-Tech couldn't have a better director. She worked for my father and has already done a lot to improve quality and efficiency. We really do care about our soldiers. I hope if you have a chance, you will relay that to your friends."

"Will do, ma'am," Cam said as he took a careful step toward the door.

"Cam?" Alex said softly.

Cam turned. "Yes."

"I was wondering, after all you have given for this country, if you would give me the opportunity to do something for you," Alex said, taking a step toward him.

"That's really not necessary," Cam said, smiling at Alex. She was a very classy lady. He could tell Deveraux Industries was in good hands.

"No, I don't suppose it is," she agreed. "But I'd be honored anyway." She stepped in beside him and took his hand. "I spoke with Nebi and she's informed me you have very strong feelings about freaky things," she grinned.

"Oh, I uh..." what could he say to that. There was no way he was going to insult Alex Deveraux.

"That's okay. I have some very strong feelings on the topic as well." She didn't let go of his hand. "Do you think you can handle a little more...what did you call it?" She paused, thinking. "Oh yes, woo, woo?"

"Uh..," he looked to Dante and Nick for help.

"The surgeon I sent to examine you told me there was nothing he could do to help you," Nick supplied.

"Oh, yeah," Cam said confused. "Well, it's okay. I told you it was a waste of money, but you have so much I guess you don't mind throwing it away on a lost cause." His hand felt warm and he didn't know why the woman wouldn't let it go.

"I didn't see it that way," Nick assured him. "But Alex is Plan B."

"Huh?" Cam said, truly confused.

"Alex is a healer," Dante said impatiently. "We'd like her to heal you. Are you opposed to that? Would you miss hobbling around like an old man? Have you become attached to those back spasms you're pretending you aren't having?"

"Well no," Cam said carefully. "A healer?" He looked at her, still confused.

"I'd like to take care of your wounds. The slice you got on your shin, the one you've tried to hide all night. The one that should have had stitches but didn't because I plan to take care of it."

Cam glanced down at his shin. So maybe he hadn't been as clever as he originally thought.

"And since I'm going to fix the wound you received protecting us tonight, assisting us with our war, I thought I'd take care of the rest while I was in there," Alex said happily.

"In there?" Cam asked, terrified of what that meant.

"Don't worry, it won't hurt," Alex said, focusing on Cam's shin.

Progeny

Cam stood, amazed. A warm, tingling sensation hit his lower leg. Then, almost instantly the pain was gone. Before he had time to wrap his head around that, his knee felt better than it had in years. A few seconds later he straightened, knowing he would never have problems with his back again. Gratitude swamped him and his legs buckled, then gave out. He'd heard about people going into shock, but actually experiencing it was indescribable for him. His mind was no longer controlling his body's reaction. All he could think was that he could never, in a million years, repay this act of kindness.

Alex continued to hold Cam's hand as Nick quickly slid a chair forward to catch Cam's ungraceful decent. "We are trusting you with a very precious secret," she finally told him. "I'm sure you can imagine what would happen if anyone knew I had the ability to heal."

Cam couldn't speak. All he could think about was the enormous debt he owed this woman. Then her words registered. He did know what would happen and the prospect wasn't pretty. "Yes." He choked out as he looked to Nick, then to Dante. "I hope you won't take this the wrong way, but Ms. Deveraux you should never, ever do that again."

"Call me Alex," she said, smiling. "And I'm not offended."

"I couldn't possibly begin to vocalize my gratitude for what you just did. I am forever in your debt. I'm serious about that. If there is ever anything, anything at all, that I can do for you I really hope you will give me that honor. But I'm familiar with the military, with politicians, with Washington. If anyone, and I mean anyone, knew what you could do, no amount of money would save you," Cam explained. "I am grateful, don't get me wrong. You have given me a miracle and I swear I will never tell a soul. But using your gift is dangerous. If anyone knew, they would capture you and dissect you. I know you are strong and powerful, but you also have a lot of military contracts. One day you would be contacted to come to a secure location where you could renew a contract and you would never leave that facility. Do you understand how serious this is?"

Alex patted Cam's arm. "I understand Cam and believe me I would never let that happen. I'm careful with my gift. There are other things you don't know. Ways we have of knowing who to trust and who not to trust. I trust you, and I believe you. If the government knew what I could do, my life would change forever. I like my freedom; I won't take chances with it."

Cam relaxed. He didn't know exactly what she meant, but she could heal and the girl was a wolf, so surely they would have other ways to protect themselves. "Good," he finally said. Then he turned to Dante. "I was wondering if you could answer just one question before I leave."

"Maybe," Dante said, a little amused at his new employee. The guy was one of a kind.

"Can you tell me what those things were? The things we fought out there. Initially, I assumed they were some kind of human experiment gone wrong. That's why I was just fighting. I didn't want a scandal in the Deveraux's front yard. But then I saw you kill one and it vanished into thin air," he shrugged, "Gives new meaning to the phrase dust to dust."

Dante smiled. "They are vampires and that too must be kept secret."

"So you guys, all of you, are some kind of superheroes that protect us humans from...what? Evil?" Cam finally asked.

"No," Dante said. "Nick and I are just a couple of guys that fight vampires. That's the only threat there is. Well, besides other human's that is."

"I saw you fight, you have superhuman strength," Cam argued.

"It's hereditary," Nick provided. "My father fought vampires, Thomas' father fought vampires. So did our grandfathers. Back as far as I know," he shrugged. "I guess it's a form of evolution. We adapted, we're big and strong to fulfill our destiny."

Cam paused, considering. "Okay, I'll buy that," he finally decided. He knew they weren't telling him everything, but he also didn't think he wanted to know everything. "I only have one other question," he finally said.

"Okay," Dante was curious what else the man might want to know.

"I was thinking it might be good for the kid, Dusty I mean, to spend some time with me and Rick in Denver. I realize Rick is getting married and I'm sure there's a honeymoon planned and all, but the kid will need time to heal..." Cam stopped.

"Yes," Alex confirmed. "He's already healed."

"So why couldn't you fix his leg?" Cam inquired.

"Apparently, I can only heal what's still there, I can't regenerate what was lost." Alex knew her voice shook a little with that confession, but she was so distressed over Dusty's loss.

Cam put a hand on her shoulder. "I'm not sure you know what a great blessing that was for him. I know, I've watched people I love suffer through the pain until their wounds healed. It will also get him mobile a lot faster, which will help him psychologically. Be grateful for what you can do, not upset over what you can't."

Dimitri moved in behind Alex and wrapped his arms around her waist. "I've been telling her that for a long time now. Maybe she'll listen to you since she pays little attention to me."

Alex leaned against Dimitri's chest. He was so strong and somehow he always knew when she needed him. "I listen to you," she disagreed. "I just don't like my restrictions and I wish my gift didn't have such limitations. Anyway, enough of that. I thank you for the offer, but I think that Dusty is better off here."

"I'm not sure about that," Dante disagreed. "Cam forgot to mention that Rick was in Iraq with him."

"Yeah, and he was injured as well. At the same time Cam was. The two of them were sent home together," Nick supplied.

Alex furrowed her brows. "I don't see why that is important. Dusty needs to be around people who love him. People to care for him and help him accept his disabilities."

"That's exactly why I think it would be better for him in Denver. Rick can help him more than anyone and..." Cam paused. "I think, at first at least, it would be better for Dusty to be away from the hovering. Nebi should join him of course, I think Darla could help her as well."

"Well, again, thanks for the offer but for now I think we'll decline," Alex said, still unclear why Dante would suggest such a thing.

"Alex," Dante continued. "Rick lost a leg, too."

"Oh," Alex said in understanding. "I'm sorry to hear that."

"Rick's amputation was above the knee. He's dealt with all the emotions, all the obstacles already. I agree with Cam, Dusty and Nebi should go to Denver with him. If it doesn't work out, they can always come back," Dante decided.

Nebi took a step forward, showing herself. Initially, she'd planned to head to the room and try to get a little rest.

Dusty was finally sleeping, rather than pretending to sleep so he didn't have to deal with her. "If I have any say in this, I think we should go. Cam's right. At least about me. It would help me to talk to this Darla woman that Rick is marrying. She's already had to deal with this. If Rick is a friend of Cam's, I'm sure he's just as macho and pig headed as my guy. Maybe she can help me deal with the pain." A single tear ran down her face and she impatiently brushed it away.

Alex studied Nebi for a long time. "If you're sure," she finally said. "If this is what you want, I won't stand in your way. We're going to have to talk to his parents about it. I've already told them about the injury. They'll be here first thing in the morning."

"Okay then," Cam said turning to head out the door. "Let me know when your flight comes in and I'll make sure I'm there to pick you up."

"I know you're anxious to see Rick and Darla, but we'd prefer it if you flew out with Dusty and Nebi," Dante interrupted. "I'll let my pilot know you'll be flying out tomorrow afternoon. That should give Dusty enough time with his parents and Nebi enough time to talk to her folks and get packed."

"Oh, I..." Cam stopped then as a huge smile spread across his face. "Do you have reclining seats?"

Nick smiled too. "That's just one of the perks of flying Air Santora."

"Well, if you insist," Cam continued to grin. "I guess I can accommodate you," he stopped, then decided to get it out of the way. "There is one other thing."

"Oh?" Dante said, raising an eyebrow.

"Uh..." Cam hesitated. "Well, it's just the other stuff. The freaky Teen Wolf stuff."

Nobody responded, the room was completely silent.

"I mean, Rick's solid. If he saw the girl turn into a wolf... or some other happy shit he'd be fine. I'm just not sure about Darla. She seems more...grounded. It might freak her out, that's all," he paused again, not sure how to continue. "Unless you can't control it. If it's spontaneous I'll find a way to explain it. Like I said, Rick's solid. He'll take it all in stride, same as me. It's just his wife, or wife to be..."

"It's not spontaneous," Nick assured him. "It's deliberate. And, under the circumstances, I'm sure the two of them can control all the 'happy shit' as you so delicately put it."

"Okay, well," he looked to Dante then to Nick. "Good to know. I guess I'll hear from you sometime tomorrow."

Chapter Eighteen

Foster shifted again. He still couldn't believe he'd let Fira talk him into this. He was never what you would call the outdoors type. His brief time trying to track and catch Victor when he was a child was a testament to that. Even an eight-year-old could out maneuver him in the woods. So how he now found himself perched high in a tree, a sharp branch poking his behind, was still a mystery.

"Stop moving," Fira scolded. "It's starting to get dark. They should be exiting within ten, maybe fifteen minutes. I do not want them to sense we are here."

Foster was about to respond when his phone vibrated. He quickly pulled it from his pocket and whispered a greeting.

Progeny

"Foster?" Dimitri said, confused. "Where are you? I can barely hear you."

"Uh...well, that's a little hard to explain at the moment," Foster whispered.

"Get off the phone," Fira hissed. "Unless you have a death wish. In a matter of minutes, hundreds of vamps are going to exit that cave, hungry and looking for a fight."

Dimitri caught part of Fira's warning. "Foster," he said more sternly. "What are you two up to?"

"About twenty, maybe thirty feet I'd say," he paused. "Fira has narrowed Radek's location to one of two caves. She got this wild idea to stake them out. I couldn't let her go alone, so we're currently up a tree outside that large cave where Marlena was rescued all those years ago."

"You're what!" Dimitri bellowed. "Of all the hair brained, irresponsible..," he stopped himself. "We have people watching that cave already. There is no reason for the two of you to risk your lives playing secret agent. Get out of there, now!" He was not giving either of them a chance to claim they hadn't understood his directive. "That's an order, Foster. I want you far away from that cave before night falls and the vampires swarm the woods."

"Hold on," Foster handed Fira the phone. "He's ordered us out of here. You explain to Dimitri why you're planning to disobey his command. And let him know I can't leave you here alone. Unless you go, I can't go."

Fira took a deep breath and pressed the phone to her ear. "Dimitri, this is important."

"Fira," Dimitri said, trying to rein in his fear and anger at her recklessness. "We have people in those woods. I already have the place under surveillance. You are not only risking your life, but you are risking Foster and our entire operation. If you get yourself into trouble my spies will have no choice but to step in and help. That gives them away, their hiding place away and it gives Radek a heads up that we are watching. Now get out of there now. Once you are a safe distance away, I need Foster to call me. Tell him I need him to head to Patricia's old farmhouse and evacuate Kathy and Bobby. They are human and we think they may be in danger from Lilith. They need to be moved before nightfall," he hung up, so Fira couldn't argue.

Fira shoved the phone at Foster, frustrated. This was important, she knew it. But she also knew she couldn't disobey an order from the Warrior leader. She was new to this community, but that much was clear. If she ever wanted to fit in, she had to do what Dimitri said. "Come on," she finally said. "We're leaving."

"What did Dimitri tell you?" Foster demanded.

"That we need to head to Patricia's old place. Apparently, there are some humans there that are in danger from Lilith. That's all I know, Dimitri wants you to call him once we reach the car," Fira let out a sigh as she slowly climbed from the tree.

Sammael stayed frozen in the shadows as the man and woman climbed from the tree and headed out of the forest. *What was Lilith up to now?* There was no reason she would need to go out to that old cabin property. That's where she used to meet up with Lawson to pick up her bombs. Nobody knew he had knowledge of that. He hadn't even told Ammit. He was worried the king might blame him for the havoc Lilith had wreaked with the humans. Her need for vengeance had threatened exposure. Now she was headed back to the cabin. *For what?* He'd have to inform Gallo. Maybe someone could tail Lilith and see what she was up to now. He knew she had more bombs because she'd set one off last night. Was she having more of them made? And what were the fae up to? Clearly they had located Radek's hiding place. *Why didn't they do something about it?* Were they planning a raid on the caves? If so, he and Martinez were in danger. He breathed a sigh of relief when he saw Gallo silently moving through the trees, headed in his direction.

"The plan is in place," Gallo said, not one to waste time. "DeMarco has his men ready to take over the newborns once Clay is sent back to Radek. The kings want to wait for Zorak to arrive and relieve Clay himself. That way Clay can report all is well and Radek will forget his new soldiers until it is too late. Once Clay is out of the area, DeMarco's men will move in to secure the vampires. Trumak and I will take custody of Zorak. We believe the questioning may take a while, possibly several days. That should give you and Martinez plenty of time to take care of Lilith and retrieve that key."

"We have a new development," Sammael said soberly. "Our timeline may be compromised," he proceeded to tell Gallo what he had overheard and his suspicions that the fae might be planning some kind of offensive on the caves. "If I'm right, things are going to get dicey for myself and Martinez. We will be directly in the line of fire. I have found a couple places inside the cave walls that will provide temporary shelter, but the warriors are thorough. I don't believe we can simply wait things out. It might be possible to sneak out one of the hidden exits, but only if they come at night. If they launch an attack during the middle of the day we're trapped."

Gallo considered. "It would be easy to pull Martinez out without causing alarm. He hunts every night. If he disappeared, everyone would think he was killed in battle. You, on the other hand, will be a problem," he paused. "If you just up and left, Radek would grow suspicious. Most likely he would send out a search party. We can't allow that. Anyone searching the area for you would stumble onto our camp. Don't worry, my friend, we will not abandon you. Somehow we will come up with a plan to protect you. Keep your phone close. With fae in the area, our meetings are becoming too dangerous."

"I agree," Sammael said soberly. "However, the two that just left did not seem to be aware that an ancient can go out during sunrise and sunset. They were clearly under the mistaken assumption it had to be fully dark before they would encounter a threat. That works in our favor. Martinez would not be able to withstand the sun during those hours, but I could. It's something to think about."

"I agree," Gallo said with a nod, then disappeared into the shadows of the forest.

Dimitri ended his call and placed his phone back into his pocket. "Thank you, Megan. Once again, you have saved lives with your gift." She did not look well. "Foster and Fira are headed to the farm. They will get Kathy and Bobby to safety. Foster plans to tell her one of his brother's criminal friends is in the area and he fears for her safety. She won't risk the boys' life, especially since Foster plans to offer her a room at the hotel where she works. It will be convenient and safe. I can't figure out why Lilith would go there in the first place. It made sense when Lawson was around, but why now? There's nothing there for her."

"I agree," Victor said, still perplexed. "Nothing that we know about anyway. Maybe Lawson buried some bombs or something. She has to be running short. Ty said the devices left at Thomas' last night were not made by Lawson. So if she has a new supplier why bother with the farm? None of this makes any sense."

Alex returned with some tea for Megan and coffee for the rest of them. "When are you due Megan?"

"What?" Victor said, looking at Tony for confirmation.

"Yes," Megan agreed. "We're pregnant. Which is the second reason we came to see you tonight," she said to Alex. "It was just lucky that Victor was here planning strategy with Dimitri. That was our next stop. We have decided to return to Ireland."

"That would be best," Alex said, sad that her friend was leaving, but relieved that she would be safe. "Megan,

478

come into the kitchen with me, I have something I want you to take back to Ireland."

"Oh?" Megan said surprised. "What is it?"

"Breena has made a tea that helps our people deal with the difficulties of pregnancy. It's safe, don't worry about that. Breena used it herself and we've had three other members of our community use it as well. So far there have not been any side effects. Once you reach the third trimester, she has a different formula that helps with the growth of the baby and seems to calm them as well. Breena is a genius with herbs and I can see this is already taking a toll on you."

Once the women disappeared down the hall Tony spoke. "I'm sorry, Victor." He was sorrier than words could explain. "I hate leaving you here when I know you need me. I hate knowing I'm abandoning my brother in such a dangerous time, but Megan has to come first. I hope you can understand that and forgive me."

Victor moved to embrace Tony. "There is nothing to forgive my brother." He gave his friend a clap on the back. "Congratulations!" He paused. "Elizabeth must be ecstatic."

"Mother is over the moon with the idea of having a grandchild, but she too understands your community could use my fighting skills. We are both torn over this decision. You are as much a son to her as you are a brother to me. We will worry about you every day until this conflict has been resolved. Be safe and don't take any chances. My child needs to meet his Uncle Vic," Tony swallowed hard. "And I need my brother. We nearly lost you once already."

"I'll be careful," Victor promised. "We all will. And stop worrying about leaving. You are doing the right thing. I can fight better, less encumbered knowing that Megan and the baby are safe in Ireland. Sure we could use your help, but it's not like you could send Megan away alone. Her worrying over you might be enough to lose the baby. She is vulnerable right now. Go home, be safe and take our gratitude with you. The two of you have already been invaluable in this war. Take comfort in knowing you have done enough."

"As long as you are in danger, it could never be enough," Tony disagreed. "Especially with this new puzzle concerning Lilith. I still can't believe that moron kept the information to himself. What did he think you would do to him if he brought it to you?"

"Earl Jackson is a nervous wreck these days," Dimitri supplied. "He still holds a grudge against Victor and Atticus but can't voice his opinion for fear of repercussions from the queen. Add in the sanction they received from your mother at the ball, and he is jumping at shadows. I'm not surprised he didn't share the information. Frankly, I don't think he would have known who to share it with. I find the fact that he was struggling with the problem promising. He wanted to warn our government, he just hadn't figured out how to do it. I think eventually he would have done the right thing. Unfortunately, his procrastination may have caused Kathy and Bobby their lives. I'm just grateful you and Megan stumbled onto this so quickly."

"It was hard not to," Tony grinned. "We walked into the store and his mind was practically yelling. With Megan being so ill, she couldn't block or filter it. His frantic rambling shot right through Megan's mind and into mine. I've heard her apologize before, telling people she didn't mean to intrude but they were yelling their thoughts at her. Until I experienced it myself I did not truly understand how disturbing it could be. Anyway, he never did say how he knew Lilith was at Patricia's old farm and we didn't stick around to ask questions."

Alex and Megan returned to the men, Megan had a large sack in tow. She smiled at her husband. "Alex has loaded me up. She is very confident I will be feeling much better within a few days," she held up her stash. "She has also promised to mail replacement supplies to the castle so I won't run out," Megan placed a hand on her stomach. "She can't have our first born, but if she's right, we owe her anything else she could ever ask for."

Alex laughed. "Not me, Breena. She's the one that came up with the formula. We all owe Breena for one thing or another."

"We are so sorry to dump this on you and leave, but we still have to contact the airlines and book a flight. We're hoping to get out of here tomorrow, but it's such late notice I'm worried it might take us a few days." Megan moved to Dimitri and gave him a hug. "Take good care of that one. We all adore her." She kissed his cheek softly and turned back to Alex.

"Don't worry about travel plans," Alex said pulling Megan into another big hug. "I'll call the hanger and schedule the jet."

"Oh, we couldn't," Megan began.

"Don't be silly," Alex shrugging off her protests. "I want to do this for you. It will be so much more comfortable for you. It's a long trip and the jet has a bed. Why be miserable all the way to Ireland when you can be comfortable. It's really no trouble. The jet isn't scheduled to go anywhere until next week."

"Thank you," Tony said, moving forward to pull Alex into a hug. "It will make a much better flight for Megan, and myself of course. As usual, your hospitality is overwhelming."

Alex kissed Tony on the cheek then brushed a tear off her own face. "I am going to miss both of you so much. Tell Elizabeth hello and hopefully we'll get out to see her soon."

Tony moved to Victor and the two embraced again. "Keep me up to date," Tony whispered. "I'm going to go out of my mind with worry for you and Ariel until this thing is over. You have no idea how much I hate leaving you like this."

"I know," Victor said, choked up himself. He knew Tony needed to take Megan out of the danger zone, but having his best friend nearby these past months had reminded him how alone he always felt when they were apart. He had Ariel now and that would make things easier, but he was still going to miss Tony. "It's been nice having you so close. Let's not wait for another decade or two before we see each other again. Time passes so quickly, but we've both been lax in keeping in touch. Promise me we won't let that happen again."

"I promise," Tony said, blinking back the moisture forming in his own eyes. He really was going to miss his friend. "Anyway, Tala and Atticus are here now. We have to come back to visit. Tala won't tolerate being away from her daughter and grandchild for long."

Alex grinned. "I hope you will stop in to visit us when you get into town. I know Tala and Atticus, as well as Victor and Ariel, will be your priority but Dimitri and I would love to see you too."

Dimitri stepped forward and placed an arm around Alex's waist. "We would," he agreed.

"I promise we will keep in touch," Megan said as a final farewell, then they disappeared out the door and into the night.

"It's hard to see them go, but I really do think it's the right thing to do," Alex finally said. "Tony couldn't leave Megan alone. She'd be too vulnerable at the apartment in her condition. And you were right, Victor. If Tony sent Megan to Ireland alone, she would just worry herself to death. I'm not sure the baby could take that kind of strain. Not right now, anyway. Megan is pretty sick. I did a scan. It's nothing serious, but she's extremely dehydrated and she's losing weight because she can't keep anything down. The tea is going to help with that, but she's already in danger of losing that baby. Unfortunately, only time can fix it. There was nothing I could do."

"I could see she was sick but didn't realize it was that bad," Victor said soberly. "Do you think Tony knows?"

"I don't think Megan has been completely honest with him. As we all do with those we love, she tends to shield Tony from things. He knows she's sick, but I'm not sure he knows just how sick."

"Megan probably hasn't told Tony, but he knows it's serious," Victor decided. "Otherwise, he wouldn't be leaving. Megan is the only thing that could pull him away from what he sees as his responsibility. Not just because of me and Ariel either. His family feels they owe a huge debt to your family, Alex. Megan's health is the only thing that would have pulled him away from this fight. And he still feels guilty about his decision."

"I sensed that," Alex agreed. "Do you think he'll stop by and tell Ariel goodbye?"

Just then Victor's phone rang. "Let's find out," he said as he answered the phone.

"I just got off the phone with Tony," Ariel said. "I'm both excited and depressed over the news."

"Me too," Victor agreed. "Where are you?"

"On my way over there," she replied. "We had a new family arrive at the shelter tonight. A mother with two small children. Mom is pretty beaten up but this time, her boyfriend took out his frustrations on her seven-year-old boy. She says it was the last straw, I really hope so. Anyway, they arrived just as I was leaving and it took longer than I planned to get them settled. Did you take care of things at the club or do we still need to spend some time there tonight?"

"I think I've taken care of most of the problems," he replied. "I will need to stop by later, though. Jessie will think I'm gone for the night. I want to see how he reacts when I show up unannounced. Do you mind?"

"Not at all," Ariel said pulling to a stop and exiting her car. "Now open the door, babe. I want my hello kiss."

Victor laughed and swung open Dimitri's large door. The instant he did, Ariel jumped into his arms. "We should ask for a night off more often," he teased. They had been scheduled for the previous night but with the bombings, it was decided they should postpone the schedule for a night. "I think I might get lucky."

Ariel grinned and lowered her legs back to the floor. "You are already so lucky you don't know what to do with yourself," she grinned at Alex and Dimitri. "Hey, you two," she laughed as Dimitri pulled her into a hug. "I wish I had gotten here just a few minutes earlier. I could have seen Tony and Megan before they split," she paused. "On the other hand, I probably would have cried, so the phone was the better bet. Tony said you're loaning them your jet. Thanks for that. You're awesome, Alex. It's going to be so much more comfortable for Megan than a commercial flight. Tony is a wreck. He feels so guilty about leaving us but he's doing the right thing." They had all walked into the study and Ariel lowered herself onto the couch.

"We told them that, but it won't help," Victor said, taking a seat next to his wife. "He's loyal that way. This has torn him apart. He needs to take care of his wife, but he wants to be here for you and me and the rest. I just hope nothing happens to any of us, he will never forgive himself if anyone gets seriously injured and he wasn't here."

"I know it's always a possibility, but I refuse to consider it," Ariel said trying to shake off the fear that idea brought. "We have Alex and all of us are stronger now. The seven warriors have all found their mates. That makes each of you stronger. Having a partner doesn't only improve our home lives, it makes us all better fighters. I know that is true for me and Victor and Abby has mentioned the same thing when she fights with Thomas. I just won't accept any more losses in this war."

The room was silent for a long while. Each of them contemplating the future and what this war could do to their lives if anyone close to them was lost. Finally, Victor stood. "Enough doom and gloom for one night. Ariel and I are going to head out and find something to eat, would you two like to join us?"

"I think that's a great idea," Alex said, standing. "After we eat, Dimitri and I are going to head into the field for a while. I want to check on things and make sure nobody needs me."

The four of them left the house, locking up before they went.

486

**** One Week Later ****

"I don't know what she's doing inside that old barn, but I don't like it," Trumak told the three kings. DeMarco had accompanied his people back to Canada to get the new vampires settled and into a training program. Now, all that remained was Ammit, Typhon, Maedoc and their contingencies. "Maybe it's time to pull Martinez out," he didn't like that plan, it left Sammael vulnerable, but something was brewing, he could feel it.

"We've discussed that, and rejected it," Ammit said impatiently. He was not abandoning his friend that way. "We all agreed the fae would not launch an attack during the day. If they strike at night, Martinez and Sammael can escape through one of the tunnels. Sammael knows that cave better than anyone. He's had plenty of time to develop an escape plan. I trust him, you should too."

"We do trust him, friend," Maedoc said soothingly. "We're just all on edge. Something is in the air. We did agree the fae are unlikely to attack during the day. Tactically that just doesn't make sense. If there is one thing they have demonstrated throughout this war, it is common sense and good reasoning. Sending their people into an unknown environment where the enemy has no means of escape is not good tactics. We have to trust ourselves on this one. Martinez and Sammael can handle themselves. So let us stop debating the same issues again and again. We need a plan. Lilith's absence has made it impossible for Martinez to retrieve the key."

"You could order him to give into Lilith and have sex with her. That might make her vulnerable enough for

Progeny

Martinez to snatch the key away. While he's at it, he could just kill the bitch and be done with it," Alastar, Maedoc's First Lieutenant suggested.

"No," Typhon said forcefully. "We tried that once with Hector and we all know how that turned out. Martinez will not be sacrificed any more than Sammael will be. There has to be another way."

The group continued to debate the dilemma well into the afternoon.

* * * *

"Something is up," Thomas said, as he paced the large room full of people. "Lilith is up to something. She's been spending more and more time out at the farm house. In fact, she's not even leaving during the day anymore. Why is that? What is she doing out there? So far no one has been able to get close enough to see what she's doing."

"I could, but some big oaf won't let me near the place," Abby grumbled.

"That's because that big oaf loves you," Alex said diplomatically. "I don't want the shifters anywhere near that place. She could be using chemicals or any number of things that could be harmful, if not fatal. I won't risk lives because of curiosity."

Abby understood their caution, but she didn't agree. It would be so easy for a shifter to go in, do a little spying then get out. Lilith would never know they were there. The only thing stopping her was her father and Morrigan. She'd made the mistake of confiding in her brother, who in turn took the matter to her father. Mason Cooper had been very clear on the topic. Abby was not to go near the old place for any reason. Her mind shifted to all the things Lilith had been responsible for in this war. The most recent tragedy was Dusty. "Has anyone heard from Dusty or Nebi lately?" She said, changing the subject.

"Nebi called last night. Dusty is being as uncooperative as usual," Alex sighed. "I know he's upset about losing his leg, but does the boy have to take out his frustrations on that poor girl? She's dealing with just as much as he is."

"Ego," Ariel said, between bites of pizza. Dimitri had called a planning meeting so she and Victor had stopped off and grabbed a dozen of them. They'd both suffered through Dimitri's planning sessions before. "Our men have egos," she continued. "So of all people the seven of us should understand. Dusty is an alpha. He's too young to be the pack leader, but he's got that kind of drive in him. His ego is getting in the way of logic." She smiled at Victor while she rubbed her most recent diamond through her fingers. This time, Victor had purchased a necklace. Most of the time when he showered her with gifts they were both responsible for the disagreement. But, there was no way she'd turn down diamonds of any kind, so she just accepted the peace offering and then promptly gave him her own.

Victor grinned at the subtle reminder Ariel was sending him. "In Dusty's case, I guess you could call it ego but I think the kid honestly believes he's doing the right thing. His heart is in the right place, even though he's breaking Nebi's in the process. Give the kid a break, it's been less than two weeks since his life was changed in a drastic way. They'll work it out. I just hope he doesn't damage the relationship too much in the meantime."

"Nebi's strong enough to take it," Alex sighed. "I just wish she didn't have to."

"Okay," Dimitri cut in. "Back to that pesky war. We need a plan. It's obvious Lilith is planning something. Lately, her plans have been far more destructive than anything Radek is doing. He seems to be sticking with the mini battles. We haven't lost anyone since the alert system went into use, but we still have major injuries every night. He's wearing us down and I'm afraid it's going to get worse. With Lilith on the loose, we always have the possibility of explosives. That means I can't lose Ty. Until I say otherwise, the practice of having the night off is suspended. That means each of you will need to arrange your schedule to get plenty of sleep during the day. I know I'm asking a lot, but I don't see any other option."

"We don't need the night off," Bastian supplied. "Kylee and I talked about this a while ago. Sure, it was nice to have a break, but our schedule allows for plenty of down time."

"That goes for us, too," Ariel said, snagging another slice of pizza. "We had a few hectic days, but it's been ironed out and Victor and I are good to go."

490

"Dante and I have that one project that is taking up a lot of our free time, but we can adjust," Nick turned to face his friend. "Right?"

"Right," Dante agreed. He was hoping the wedding could take place next weekend, but if he had to postpone it, he would. The safety of his people was their priority. Plus, Tala and Atticus had not returned from Utah yet. He was determined to have Shaylee here for her daughter's big day.

"Dad still has some of our guys out hunting every night. He's also developed a schedule to monitor the caves. We're convinced Radek is still in the large one. I can't believe he didn't relocate after Luke and the boys rescued Marlena and Alex, but I guess it goes back to ego. That vampire has a whopper," Abby slid a large slice of pepperoni pizza onto her plate and grinned at Ariel. "Thanks for this, I was starving."

Ariel laughed and gave a nod, "You're always starving."

"So, do we focus on Lilith?" Ty asked. He was afraid he knew what Lilith was working on. And if he was right, he just hoped she was never successful.

Sam decided to voice the concerns her husband had left out. "We think she might be working on a bomb," she paused. "I mean a big, massive bomb. If we're right, it means she is no longer loyal to Radek. She's working on her own. Radek never leaves that cave. If Lilith creates a bomb of the magnitude we suspect based on the supplies arriving at that farm, the cave will collapse and kill Radek along with anyone else unlucky enough to be near him."

Progeny

"How do you know what supplies are being delivered to the farm?" Abby asked. "I thought we were all supposed to be staying clear of the place."

Ty cringed. "We are," he shot Sam an annoyed glance. "I have contacts. I put the word out months ago. Any large order is reported to me along with the delivery address. Lilith has been making large orders."

"I see," Dimitri said, considering. "So what is her most likely target? My house? That would take out the new warrior leader and the queen with one shot."

"Maybe," Ty shrugged. "I think the big question is where her loyalty lies. Is she working on this for Radek or herself? If she's no longer loyal to Radek, would she care about killing you or Alex? Or is Radek her target? With Radek gone, it would be a natural step for her to take over. Maybe she plans to blow up the cave on purpose."

"That's an interesting theory," Dimitri mused. "But I don't think we can count on it. There are just too many unknowns," he paused. "Foster and Fira brought over a new map this morning. They have identified possible strongholds in the forest. The two of them still believe an offensive just after dusk is our best course of action."

Alex put the new map on the large screen. "Their argument has merit," she said reluctantly. "They are very persuasive. In fact, they have almost convinced me they are right."

Lillie smiled. "Do you think there is something going on with those two?"

"Other than the obvious?" Abby asked. "Yeah. I think they have the hots for each other, but neither one wants to admit it. They both have family baggage and both of them are alternates on the council. They're walking a fine line, but I think given enough time, one of them is going to act on the attraction."

"How will the council react?" Cornelia asked Alex. She was still wondering how the council was going to react when they found out a warrior had married someone that was part vampire.

"Stop worrying," Alex shrugged. "The council has no say in the matter of love and that includes you, Cornelia. They don't know you're related to Radek. Not because it's a secret, but because it hasn't come up. Once they learn of it, some like Avery might balk but it won't matter. I have accepted you. Oberon has accepted you and the people will accept you eventually. They simply do not have a choice in the matter. I made it clear that the warriors are my family; as Dante's wife you are now my family. The community knows how I feel about family. That alone would be enough but as Radek's daughter, you are my blood. You are my niece. As far as I'm concerned the issue is closed for discussion."

"Thank you," Cornelia said, humbled by the vehemence in Alex's voice. She really was accepted as a member of this family. Her mother had been so wrong. Her mother had suffered all this time unnecessarily. Cornelia couldn't wait to tell Shaylee Harris it was no longer necessary for her to hide out in the mountains. She could visit the city any time she pleased. Once Radek was

Progeny

eliminated that is. Would her mother be pleased, or would she stick to her old ways out of habit? Cornelia didn't know, but at least they had options. She smiled when Dante pressed a gentle kiss on her lips. Then pulled her close, wrapping his arm around her shoulders.

"Back to the real topic," Dimitri said, clearly frustrated with the constant subject changes. "This is a map of the area where Radek is located. Here is the cave opening. Our scouts have identified three more entrances. Unfortunately, we have no idea if those additional three give full access to the cave or if they dead end. We do know for sure that the main entrance branches off and all areas are accessible from that location," Dimitri pulled out a large file. "This is the operation plan from 1987 when the warriors went in after Marlena and Alex. Radek has had plenty of time to make changes and improvements, but the basic layout should still be the same." He handed the file to Bastian then turned back to the map. "Pass that around while I continue. Foster and Fira have plotted out the best areas for an ambush," he nodded at Alex who put another map on the screen.

"This would take a massive joint effort," Alex supplied. "I'd have to call in Mason, Monroe and Numair's packs as well as all our able-bodied members to assist," she glanced at Dimitri. "As you can see, we would have to break up into groups large enough to handle massive amounts of vampires. Our scouts have determined that every night there is a mass exodus just after dusk. As the vampires head into the forest, they split into groups. Those groups proceed to their targets and begin the attacks. At some point each group breaks for a few hours to feed, then they move to their next target."

"So, the plan is to wait until they split off, then take each group out one by one," Victor asked, intrigued. "That might work as long as our groups are large enough. Especially if we have the element of surprise in our favor. The vampires won't be expecting a battle in the forest. They will be counting on anonymity until they reach the city," he glanced at Ariel.

"We could set something up like we did when we rescued Lakisha and Abby." Ariel was studying the map. "We rigged booby traps that gave us the edge along the way."

Thomas stood and moved closer to the map. "We could set up something similar here." He pointed to an area away from the cave. "It's far enough away that we could work on it all day and the noise won't reach back to the cave. Even if some of it did, the vampires wouldn't know it was us. There are hikers and backpackers in that forest daily."

They continued to study the map, generating a plan. It would take at least a week to set everything up, but the more they discussed, the more optimistic they became. The large open meadow nearby was going to be an asset to the fae, not the vampires. It would be a good place for the battle to occur and the vampires would be inside the opening before they realized there was danger.

Progeny

Dusty sat against the headboard, dreading what he was going to do. He hated hurting Nebi, but it couldn't be helped. She deserved better. There was no way he would sit back and let her ruin her life over him. He closed his eyes, wishing for strength when the door silently slid open. He knew it would be Nebi, bringing him dinner. And once again he was going to break her heart...and his.

Nebi pushed the door with her foot, but it didn't close completely. Well, she'd just take care of it once Dusty had his dinner. At least Dusty never raised his voice. She didn't think she'd be able to stand it if he did. The pitying looks were bad enough, if they actually heard what Dusty said she'd be mortified. He didn't just order her out now, he was cruel. If it wasn't for Cam, Rick and Darla's encouragement she probably would have left days ago. She wouldn't admit it to anyone, but she was starting to doubt herself. Maybe he didn't love her the way she loved him. The way she used to believe he did. Maybe he wasn't pushing her away out of love like Cam insisted. Maybe he truly didn't want her in his life. How was she supposed to know for sure?

"Nebi, it's time for you to go back to New York," Dusty said, pulling Nebi out of her thoughts.

"We wouldn't be able to get a flight for a couple of days, I'm sure. But if that's what you want, I'll call Dante and see when he can send a plane for us," she said, deliberately misunderstanding his intent.

"I didn't say I was going back to New York, you are," he pushed, annoyed. She knew what he meant, she just chose to ignore his suggestion. "I'll be going to Jersey."

Jersey? Was he going to live with his parents? Nebi knew that wouldn't last. The solitude would drive Dusty crazy. He needed the chaos of the city as much as she did.

"Well if you want to visit your parents before we head back to New York, that's okay with me."

Dusty growled in frustration. She just had to be difficult about this. Couldn't she just move on already and leave him to deal with the loss on his own? "*We* are not going to visit my parents." He was trying to sound calm but knew his frustration echoed in every word. "*I* am going to move to my grandparents' old cabin," he paused. "The place will need a lot of work, but I think even I can manage the repairs. I'm going to live in the cabin and ask my father if he still needs someone to handle the books. He'll hire me, if not to do the books then he'll make something up I can handle. That should give me enough money to buy food and incidentals for one. We both know you couldn't live like that so do us both a favor and go back to New York."

"We both also know you can't live like that. It's the reason you turned your father down the last time he offered you a job and the time before that and the time before that." She took the lid off the dinner plate and turned to set it aside.

Progeny

"Nebi, this has to stop," he said, raising his voice. "I've made my decision. You are just going to have to accept my wishes and move on. I know my injury cut our fling a little shorter than we planned, but it couldn't be helped."

"I agree," Nebi said coolly. If he called this relationship a fling one more time she just might punch him. "Your injury couldn't be helped. This nonsense about hiding out in the woods and living in your grandparent's cabin, now that's another story."

"Nebi, look at me," Dusty ordered. It was going to kill him, but he had to do this and he had to do it while he looked her in the eye and made sure she believed him. Believed the lies he was about to tell. "We both know things were moving along fine before I got hurt. It worked for both of us at the time. We were at the top of the class, it only made sense for us to hook up. We used each other to get what we wanted. We were both willing to do anything to help with the war. You and I hooking up made that possible. We were able to do our part and have a little fun at the same time. This thing between us wasn't permanent. It was never going to be permanent. Sure we had some kicks and a lot of action, but that's it."

Nebi didn't move. She forced her features to remain perfectly still. She would not show him how much he was hurting her. She would not give him the satisfaction of seeing her heart break into a million pieces. Was he telling the truth or was it just the anger and fear over the loss of his leg that was driving him? She just didn't know how to tell anymore.

Dusty watched Nebi. He knew he was hurting her, but she was just so damn valiant. She wouldn't show weakness and she wouldn't back down. He loved her even more for that, how was he going to live without her? But he had to. She deserved better. He loved her enough to push her away. "I didn't want to tell you this, but I had already decided the fling was over. It was time for me to move on. Now that everyone's been called back to New York, our partnership is no longer necessary," he paused, not wanting to continue but knowing he had to. "I've wanted to date other women for a while now, but I didn't know how to tell you. In the beginning, I was attracted to your spirit, to your guts, but your body...well, not so much and we're both too competitive to stay together for the long haul. I have needs, Nebi. Intimacy with you was okay, but I'm ready for a change. A woman with bigger boobs and more curves to start."

The vice grip strangling her heart relaxed. He was lying. He was trying to be cruel to force her away, but he'd just made a huge mistake. Dusty loved her body. She never understood why, but from the very beginning he hadn't been able to keep his hands off her. She initially believed a guy like him would be attracted to a beautiful curvy blond, like Tiffany Richards. She'd been so jealous of Tiffany at first, but it hadn't taken her long to realize Dusty never gave Tiffany a second glance. He only had eyes for her. The realization was baffling but invigorating. And the intimacy, that was explosive. So far removed from okay, it was comical. "So, you don't like my body then?" She glanced down, slowly letting her eyes trace down her body and back up, then locking with Dusty's again.

Progeny

"Funny, you never seemed to mind it when we were in bed."

"What? You thought I'd outline the areas that were lacking? I'm pretty sure that would have ruined the mood and since my only goal was to get into your pants..," he trailed off, hoping that would do the trick. He couldn't go on like this. He couldn't keep lying, insulting her when none of it was true. He loved Nebi's body and had from the instant he'd seen her. Watching her eyes trail down those amazing curves then back up made him want her right now. Man, did he want her? He clenched his fists and waited for her to leave. He just hoped she didn't start crying. He'd cave for sure if she cried.

Nebi watched Dusty. His eyes were giving him away. He wanted her, right now. She could use that against him. She slowly moved forward, running a finger down his biceps. "So Dusty," she whispered seductively moving her hand to his chest. "If this was all about fun, you surely wouldn't mind one for the road, would you?" She licked her lips and watched him through slitted eyelids.

Dusty swallowed the lump that had formed in his throat. "Sorry, sweetheart. I just don't think that's a good idea." He couldn't touch her or he'd cave. Every molecule in his body wanted him to cave, but Nebi deserved better.

Nebi reached the hem of his shirt then slowly rubbed her hands up his abs, all the way to his wide chest, then back down to his stomach. She glanced up and gave him a crooked smile, "Oh, come on. Be a sport. If this was all for fun, why can't we have one more for the road?" She leaned in and pressed her lips to his. The kiss was soft, feather light and sent chills up Nebi's spine.

Dusty tried to hold back, he really did. But the electric shock that speared through his body at Nebi's soft kiss sent him over the edge. He couldn't stop himself no matter how hard he tried. He crushed his lips to hers and pulled her on top of him. He needed her. He needed to hear her beautiful laugh, see her cocky grin, watch her strength as she fought off the enemy. He needed to run his fingers through her silky hair and he needed to feel her soft luscious lips against his. But it wasn't fair, not to her. "Nebi." He tried to pull back, to push her away.

Nebi felt Dusty's frustration and knew he was raging a silent battle with himself but she was determined to win this one. She straddled his hips and sat up. "Don't tell me we're going to go over all that crap about you not wanting me again. Really Dusty, I've had about all I can stand for one day. If you keep this up, I'm going to have to invest in hip boots. It's the only way I'll be able to wade through all this bull," she wiggled against him.

How did she know he was lying? Did his eyes give him away, the same as hers did for him? He pulled her to him, kissing her, loving her. He never wanted to stop. "I can't fight you anymore. I know it's wrong. I know it's selfish, but I just can't fight this. I need you, just one more time. I need you, Nebi."

That stopped her. One more time? Forget that. Nebi pushed back from him. "Sorry champ, but no way. You can have me. Just as soon as you promise to stop trying to push me away. I'm not leaving, get used to it. If I have to

Progeny

follow you to Jersey, so be it. Living there for even a month will probably drive me insane, but if you insist we'll make it work. Where you go, I go," she looked at him. "Seriously, whatever possessed you to dis my body?"

"Desperation," Dusty mumbled, unsure what to do now.

"I mean seriously, you honestly thought I'd buy that bigger boobs crap?" She was getting mad now. How stupid did he think she was?

Dusty watched a bird fly past the window then take perch on the roof, after a couple seconds it got spooked and took off again. "I can't make you happy anymore Nebi. I can't provide for you, for a family. I can't protect you. I'm not a man anymore."

Nebi's first instinct was to argue, but she'd been doing that for weeks now. She leaned forward and pressed a soft kiss to Dusty's temple. "It kills me that you think that," she finally whispered. "From where I'm sitting, nothing has changed."

"How can you say that? Everything has changed," he scowled.

Nebi sighed. "Dusty, before the explosion you were going to talk to Ty. You love that Tech Geek stuff and we both know that Ty would steer you in the right direction even if he couldn't hire you at Tyson Electronics. You have experience helping your dad run his company and combined with the tech stuff it's a perfect fit. I saw how excited you got over those goggles Sam and Ty developed

502

for the obstacle course. And you had so many cool ideas I would never have thought of. How does losing a foot change that? Last time I checked you don't type with your toes," she paused. "But if you want to, I bet Sam could develop a combo system, fake foot wired to a keyboard or something just to give you a challenge."

"Very funny," he scowled.

"Nothing has changed," she insisted. "You knew you would have to go to school, get some training then hopefully go to work for Ty. I was planning to find a job somewhere to pay the bills until you brought in the big bucks. Nothing has changed," she said again with more emphasis. "You can still go to school and I can work just like we planned. We both knew at first we'd have to stay in a small, cramped apartment but it didn't matter before. Why do you think it matters now?"

Dusty didn't answer. It mattered because he wasn't whole anymore. Because if they were attacked, he couldn't protect her.

"I know that look," she said narrowing her eyes. "And I don't need your protection any more now than I did a month ago, or four months ago while we were on the road tracking vamps. I need a partner, not a protector. I thought you had finally realized I can hold my own."

Dusty pulled Nebi onto the bed next to him and rested his forehead against hers. They sat there for several minutes in silence before he spoke. "I think I had, for the most part anyway. It's in my nature to want to protect you.

Progeny

I couldn't stand it if we were attacked and you got hurt or worse killed because I couldn't fight."

Nebi placed a hand on Dusty's cheek. "You can still fight, baby," she said softly. "Sure, you'll have to get used to romping around as a freaky teen wolf with only three legs." She grinned at the private joke. "But so what. You are so much stronger than me, most of the time you don't change to fight, anyway. When you do, just pick something like a wolf or a bear that has four legs. You can be just as effective running on three of them. You can do anything Dusty," she paused. "If you want it bad enough. That's part of the reason I love you so much," she considered their past. "You didn't dump me when I would only shift into a panther. That limited my effectiveness but you understood I did it to honor my aunt. What you may not know, is that I also refused to shift into anything else because it scared me. I knew every time I did it I would think of mom and dad. I was afraid I couldn't handle the pain. I know you're scared," she grinned at the look Dusty gave her. "But you don't have to be. Just like you helped me overcome my obstacle, I'm going to help you overcome yours. We can do this together. Sure, there might be a few adjustments to make but so what?" She smiled and ran her hand down his chest, then down to his stomach. "The important parts still work."

Dusty caught her hand and brought it to his mouth to kiss her palm. "How can you still love me after the way I've treated you?" Dusty asked.

"Because I understand what you were doing. I know you only said those things and treated me that way because

504

you love me." She tried not to think about how much Dusty had hurt her.

Dusty could hear the pain in Nebi's words. She was trying to hide it, but he had hurt her deeply. He wanted to grasp onto her hope. He wanted to believe they could still make this work, but did he dare? Or would he just end up hurting her worse down the road?

"Don't think you're off the hook," she finally said. "I'm giving you a pass on this one, but it's not free. You hurt me," she said, choking back the pain. "Don't do that again. We've always worked together before this. I need you to promise me we will work together from now on. And I need you to promise me you will work at getting your confidence back. I expect you to get the training you need and to convince Ty he'd be lost without you. I also expect you to start shifting again when we get back to New York," she glanced at the door, "it's not safe to work on that here. But when we get back, your physical training is going to start immediately. You want to deserve me, you're going to have to work and not give up," she scolded.

"I thought you were supposed to pamper me and cater to my every need," he said, finally grinning.

"Sorry, you fell for the wrong girl if that's what you wanted." She sat up, serious again. "You didn't fall for the wrong girl, Dusty. And I didn't fall for the wrong man. I won't give up on you, so stop giving up on yourself."

"I don't deserve you," Dusty sighed.

"Of course you don't," she agreed. "But I deserve you."

"How soon do you think we can get back to New York?" Dusty asked. "I'd like to try to change. I need to see how much it's going to impact my ability to fight."

"I'll call Dante and see how soon he can send a plane," Nebi said moving to stand.

"That can wait," Dusty said holding onto her. "I have a lot of making up to do."

Nebi smiled. Finally, they were getting back on track. She knew the struggle wasn't over, but it was a start.

Chapter Nineteen

Dante stepped into the large room and immediately sank into a chair. "There's still no word from Tala, Atticus or Shaylee," he ran his hand through his hair. "I need Shaylee. Do you think she ran them off?"

"No," Nick said, handing Dante a beer. "If she had, I think they would have called us immediately," he paused to move back to the chair, then smiled when Lillie walked in with Abby and Thomas. "I think they are in the mountains, out of cell phone range. I think that Shaylee is terrified of Radek and it's taking more time than we thought to convince her she will be safe here in New York."

"Maybe Abby and I should have gone instead of sending Tala and Atticus," Thomas provided. "I mean, if she got it straight from the source, maybe she'd trust us. Maybe she would finally believe that her story is a tragedy, she's a victim and in a way so is Cornelia. The Deveraux's, the council, none of us have a grudge against her. In fact, I consider it my job to protect her."

"I don't think that would have helped," Dante shook his head. "In fact, I think the instant she realized who you were she would have panicked. Maybe even bolted. No, this way was best. I guess I'll just have to wait until after the battle to have the ceremony. I don't see any other way."

"It would make for a nice celebration," Abby supplied. "A great way to celebrate our victory. We have all the decorations stashed here at Nicks. And we've thrown together more than one wedding in the past with less time to prepare. Stop worrying. This will work out, Dante. And in the end, you will be giving Cornelia the wedding of her dreams."

"I hope so," Dante sighed. "I just wish I could find my grandparents. I know they are going to be disappointed when they hear they missed it, especially Grams. I wanted to fly them in for the big day," he shrugged. "But that can't be helped. I won't do this without Shaylee though. She has to agree to come, it won't be the same without her."

"She'll come," Lillie assured them all. "If I have to, I'll borrow Ty's plane and fly out there myself. Tala and Atticus are diplomatic. I'll just kidnap the woman. I might need some help when I land, but with all you big strong warriors around I'm not worried."

Nick laughed. "You would, wouldn't you?"

"Of course," Lillie laughed, too. "Shaylee is scared, but she's going to regret it if she misses her only daughter's wedding. Cornelia will regret not having her mother there. I have no problem kidnapping Shaylee because it's a good cause. It's the right thing to do."

"There will be no kidnapping," Dante said, trying not to grin. He did love Nick's mate. "Where are we at on the forest project?" It was time to get back to work.

"It's coming along," Thomas said, allowing Dante to change the subject. The problems with his wedding couldn't be solved tonight anyway. And Thomas knew Atticus would not leave until Shaylee came with them. The wedding might have to be postponed, but it would still happen and Cornelia would love Dante even more for the gesture. Thomas might not know much about women, but living with Abby had taught him what was really important. Making his woman happy was at the top of the list. This wedding would definitely make Cornelia happy. "It sounds like Alex and Oberon have finally got the council on board. At first they were hesitant, just like we were, but once the two of them went through the battle plan they all jumped on board pretty quickly. The biggest selling point is the fact that if we pull this off, the war will be over for good. We're not talking about a capture and trial mission here. The goal is to eliminate Radek once and for all. If possible, we want to take out Lilith, too. With the two of them out of the picture, I think we can return to some semblance of peace around here."

Progeny

"I agree," Nick said, taking Lillie's hand. "And maybe then your girl will get that ring she's been wanting so badly."

Thomas scowled at Nick. The man knew that was a touchy subject. Thomas wanted to propose to Abby, he just wanted to do it his way. His way took time, something they didn't have at the moment. He was determined to give Abby a romantic getaway where he would propose in style. But, Abby was growing impatient. Especially now that Dante was married and planning to renew his vows. Alex had also set a date, her wedding was going to be on April 25th, Marlena's birthday. The only other couple in their group unmarried was Nick and Lillie. The only reason they hadn't tied the knot already was because they wanted to make Zarah happy. Nick's mom had dreamt of his wedding since the instant he was born. And that wedding had always occurred in their garden, in Italy. Lillie knew the importance of delaying, he just wished Abby could be that understanding. But, she wasn't. She was growing impatient and Thomas was going to have to act soon. "Thanks a lot, Nick," Thomas grumbled, then glanced at Abby. She, of course, was scowling.

"Happy to help," Nick said, laughing at both of them. It was a standing tradition between the three friends to exploit weakness. He was thoroughly enjoying his turn. Thomas had certainly earned it.

Dante stood and headed for the door. "Sorry, but I have to run. I need to check on some things before we head out to fight tonight. You guys still scheduled to work in the forest tomorrow?"

"Yep," Thomas and Nick said at once.

"Then if I don't run into you tonight, I'll see you tomorrow afternoon," then Dante headed for the door.

Once they were sure he was long gone, the four remaining members looked at each other. "Do you have an update on his grandparents?" Thomas finally asked.

"Last I heard they were stuck in Germany," Nick grumbled. "I think the delay with Shaylee is fate. The authorities are taking issue with the Waterson's passports. I guess they've been out to sea too long this time. They don't have enough stamps or some nonsense and with all the terrorist activity, they are being held for questioning. I'm sure they'll work it out. We just need to be patient. Are you sure you don't mind them staying here once they arrive?" He asked both Thomas and Abby.

"Not at all," Abby smiled. "I've heard so much about them, I can't wait to finally meet them. And they can't stay with you. Dante spends too much time at your house. It's too risky. We don't want to ruin the surprise."

"I agree," Nick said, relieved. He'd let the Waterson's stay with him, but Abby was right Dante would discover them before it was time. This way was much better. Plus, his parents were on alert. Once they received word, they planned to fly out immediately and stay with Nick. He had plenty of space, but with Lillie living with him and his parents joining them, his house would be a little cramped. "We have some time before we need to head out, you two want to grab a bite to eat."

Progeny

"Absolutely," Abby said, enthusiastically. Abby was always enthusiastic about food.

* * * *

Lilith set the metal container in the middle of the floor. This workshop was antiquated at best, but it was serving its purpose. The best part was the cellar. It was dark enough that she could sleep underground and not have to return to the cave every night. If she could just get this to work, her troubles would be over for good. Now came the difficult part. If she was wrong, the entire building was going to blow up around her. If she was right, she had the ingredients she needed to blow up that stupid cave and take out Radek, Sammael and maybe Martinez once and for all. Kaboom and her life would be perfect. Martinez, she would regret. In time she was sure he would have been fun, but the kid wouldn't budge. He was too afraid of Radek to act on his desires. She was sure he desired her. Every man did. That meant he was weak and as queen, she would not tolerate weakness. This way she could savor the memories. Well, the fantasies anyway. Martinez would be memorialized as the one that got away. This way, she would never have to be disappointed... like she had been once she hooked up with Zorak. From the beginning, she realized she would have to take Zorak out herself. That fact was becoming more and more obvious with each passing day. But, she'd have to accomplish that task in some other way. Once he returned from training the new group of vampires, she'd find a way to eliminate him. That vamp was becoming a serious nuisance. He seriously believed that once she was queen she'd have the same rules that Radek had. That she would limit herself to one vampire lover, him. Man, was he delusional. Lilith and only one lover? *As if?*

She slowly made her way to the pot of magic liquid. She was going to have to be quick. Just drop it in and run. Then if it didn't explode around her, she'd come back, light a fuse and stand a safe distance away to see what happened. She'd never made a bomb before, but really how hard could it be? After all, if a human could do it she certainly could. After taking a deep, calming breath she dropped the flask and ran. She had barely made it out the door when her world erupted, then went black.

Lilith crawled under the protective branches of a large tree. It was completely dark now, the blast from the explosion had knocked her out cold. Her skin was on fire. Ancient vampires, those more than five hundred years old, could survive during dusk and dawn. Those few minutes before or after daylight were shaded enough from the sun that ancient vamps could withstand it. The protection was limited but sufficient for such a short amount of time. Unfortunately, it took concentration, a vampire had to focus and cool their bodies from within. Something she couldn't do when she was lying unconscious on the hard ground. As a result, her skin was a mass of burns. She supposed that was her punishment for being impatient. Just an extra ten to fifteen minutes and the injuries would have been avoided. Even ancient vampires rarely used this gift, which is why it wasn't known in most circles. The risk typically wasn't worth it, as she had just learned firsthand. Some of her burns were more severe than others and she

Progeny

assumed that was from the blast. The burn on her side was especially deep, the pain felt like it went all the way to the bone. The workshop was destroyed. The house was barely standing. The windows were all blown out and the backside was leaning to the side. She had to get out of here. The human police would be arriving any minute. The last thing she needed right now was to be taken to a human hospital.

Lilith forced herself to stand. That mixture she'd created was lethal. In fact, she was lucky to be alive. The mistake was big enough for her to realize she was out of her league. She could not make a bomb and if she continued to try, she'd just kill herself. She was not going to kill herself. If anyone was going to die, it would be Radek. She slowly made her way through the forest, headed for the caves. Radek would be beyond angry but she'd smooth things over. She always did. He'd rant and rave, but then he'd forgive her. She wondered if Sammael had a secret cure for burns. Probably, he'd known what to do about everything else. Once again, she wondered where that knowledge had come from. She was sure Sammael was older than he had let on. Still, he wasn't an ancient so how did he know so much about healing vamps? She would probably never know. Maybe the explosives had been a bad idea, but somehow she was determined to take Radek out and his mousy sidekick with him. She'd just have to come up with another plan and soon, she was running out of time.

As Lilith approached the cave, she hesitated. Radek's moods were more erratic lately than they'd ever been in the past. He might kill her instantly and ask

514

questions later but she couldn't come up with any other options. She couldn't hunt like this, she couldn't fight and she was done experimenting with explosives. She needed Radek and the safety of the cave. She'd just have to risk it.

Radek looked up when Sammael stepped into the room. "She's back," he said softly.

The kid was still a weakling. Radek was growing impatient with Sammael. He'd done everything he could think of to toughen the kid up. Nothing seemed to help. Sammael was still queasy and intimidated by everything, including his own shadow. No matter how loyal, Radek would not surround himself with weak subjects. Eventually, he was afraid Sammael would have to be dealt with. The kid's death would be as painless as Radek could make it. He'd at least earned that much. Once the war was over, he'd give Sammael one last chance but he couldn't allow more than that. He'd already been too lenient with the kid. "Tell her I want to see her immediately. Here, in my chambers."

"I can try," Sammael said, looking at his shoes. Radek thought it was because he was the bearer of bad news. Actually, Sammael was having a hard time keeping the smile from showing on his face. Lilith was barely alive. Somehow she'd been burned by the sun, but that wasn't her only wound. She was bleeding. He didn't know where the wound was, but it was pretty serious. He could tell from the smell of blood loss. She'd walked in whining so profusely over the burns he wondered if she even knew she had another wound. If he was ordered to, he could deal with the burns. He wondered if he could fix the other wound. Maybe she'd finally gotten herself into a big enough bind she wouldn't recover. He could always hope.

"What does that mean?" Radek demanded, breaking into Sammael's happy thoughts. "Try?"

"She is injured," Sammael said softly. "It looked like she was barely able to make it to her own chambers. I'm not sure she has enough strength to make it to yours."

"That woman is going to drive me insane," Radek said, pushing himself to his feet and stomping to the door. "What has she gotten herself into this time? For the life of me, I have no idea how she's survived this long. If she's not getting herself doused with holy water, its vampiric animals and now this," Radek continued to mumble all the way down the hall and into Lilith's room.

Sammael followed the king, keeping a safe distance between them. The last thing he wanted was for Radek to catch him eavesdropping. He stopped just outside Lilith's door. Radek was inside, but he hadn't bothered to close the door. Sammael had been counting on that. Radek had a habit of leaving doors open, then he was completely taken by surprise when everyone knew his business.

"Explain yourself," Radek said, horrified by the sight of her. She was badly burned and clearly miserable.

"I've been working on a secret weapon," Lilith croaked. "I wanted to surprise you with it. I was hoping I could design a bomb big enough to wipe out half their force, if not more."

Radek rolled his eyes. He didn't understand Lilith's fascination with explosives.

"I figured you could set off the bomb, then sit back and watch. Once the dust settled you could send in the troops and fight off the remaining warriors, the queen if she was still alive and maybe the council. After that, the community would give up. Without their leaders they would be lost," Lilith continued. She'd thought about her cover story all the way home. The only way out of this predicament was to make Radek think she was doing this for him, that she was sacrificing her own safety to help him achieve his goal. He'd fall for it, she knew he would.

"I assume the experiment failed," Radek said coldly. He was disappointed. If Lilith had succeeded, this war would be over. But, once again, she had failed him. How many times could he allow her failures before he was forced to make an example out of her? He was afraid she'd just reached her limit. One more mistake and she would have to go.

"Yes," she admitted. "And, as you can see, I was injured in the process. I wrongly assumed I could get to safety even if the experiment failed. I was mistaken. I was thrown from the building and knocked out. I'm not sure how long I cooked in the sun before night fell, but these burns are severe. Do you think Sammael has a cure? Or at the very least something to relieve the pain? I am in so much pain, Radek." Lilith let a single tear trickle from her eye. She was in pain, but she never allowed herself the weakness of crying. Not unless something was gained by it, anyway. Much could be gained if Radek bought her distress.

"I'm not happy with you, Lilith," Radek said, turning to pace the small room. "You disappeared without a trace. I feared the warriors had finally killed you. Or worse, that they had captured you and were torturing you for information."

Lilith wondered if that was worse because of the pain she would be forced to endure, or worse because it would leave Radek vulnerable. She decided on the latter.

"Then Sammael notifies me you have returned," Radek stopped and glared at Lilith. "And I discover you have been off hiding on your own, working on some secret project. Correct me if I am wrong woman, but I thought I was King around here."

"I meant no disrespect," Lilith whined. She was so tired of dealing with this man. "It was supposed to be a surprise. I only wanted to please you. I thought if I could succeed, you would finally win the war. If I could not, then you need not get your hopes up only for them to be dashed again. I only wanted to save you from disappointment my love." Lilith closed her eyes. If she had to keep this up much longer she was going to gag.

Sammael moved away from the door. So, Lilith was trying to create a bomb. That explained her need to hide out. It also explained why she hadn't been around for days. Too bad the explosion didn't throw her hard enough to dislodge the key from around her neck. She still had it, but if Radek asked him to care for her, he might get a chance to remove it. He quickly slid into the shadows and made his way to the other side of the cave. Radek would summon him soon and he wanted to be safe inside his room when word came down that the king needed his help. If he hurried, he might also have enough time to send Ammit a quick text.

* * * *

Dante lounged on the bed watching Corrie slide into a delicate silk nightgown. He didn't know why she bothered, but he was grateful she did. Within seconds the thing would be lying on the floor, but in the meantime he had to admit the way it hugged her body was a major turn on. His gaze continued up her body until his eyes collided with hers. He smiled, knowing she'd caught him mid-fantasy. His eyes never left hers as she walked gracefully across the room and sat next to him on the bed.

Cornelia ran a finger across Dante's chest. "You sure this is okay?" She asked, frowning. Dante had a massive cut that trailed from his left shoulder diagonally across his chest and ended just above his navel. He'd received it in battle that very night. The fighting had been worse than usual. There were more vampires to contend with and they seemed more aggressive for some reason. Maybe they were as tired of the fighting as the warriors were.

Dante caught her hand and pulled it to his mouth. "Positive," he said as he kissed each finger, then turned her hand over and pressed a gentle kiss to her palm. "But I know what would make it better." He smiled that wicked, mischievous grin of his then raised his eyebrows in question.

Cornelia couldn't help herself, she laughed. "You have a one-track mind."

"Of course, I do," Dante said, pulling her on top of him then faster than lightening flipping her over so he could straddle her hips. "What else is there to think about?"

"Oh, I don't know," she said rolling her eyes. "Maybe survival, battle strategy, how we are going to spend our time once this stupid war is over."

"Which my dear," Dante said leaning down to kiss the tip of her nose, "Brings me right back to that single track of mine. We might never leave this bed. Creatures that live millennia have nothing but time. I plan to spend mine wisely."

Cornelia laughed, then gasped as she settled in to enjoy this wise man of hers. If life could be this good with all the turmoil and uncertainty surrounding them, it was sure to be spectacular when they finally found peace and normality.

* * * *

Two nights later, the large group was gathered in a conference hall a few doors down from Mason Cooper's home. Council members from the fae and each shifter pack were present as well as Alex, Dimitri and all the warriors and their mates. Orin was the only one absent. Oberon had to order him to stay home with his family. The council knew this fight was going to be dangerous and had decided one of them needed to sit out, just in case things didn't go as planned. Someone on the council needed to survive. The vote was unanimous in favor of Orin, mostly because he was the youngest and he was just starting his family. Orin and Breena were living in the Deveraux cabin again but this time, Breena's parents had joined them. It would be their job to take out any vamps that got past the outer perimeter. They both knew that was unlikely, but they were also grateful to have a job they could do and still protect their infant son. Orin was present by video conference.

Mason stood and whistled, a high pitched ear-splitting noise that silenced the crowd instantly. "We need to begin." He surveyed the group, he didn't know many of them and hoped they had each rounded up enough volunteers to finally finish this thing. "I'm going to turn the time over to Alex and Dimitri to explain the plan. Then we will hand out field assignments. We are going to mix warriors and fae with shifters. I think that will give us the biggest advantage in this battle. Does anyone have any questions before we get started?"

One hand went up. It was from a shifter Mason had never met before. She must be part of Monroe's pack or maybe Numair's. "My family lives on the outskirts of town. We have been the target of several attacks already. With myself, my husband and my son here to fight, it

Progeny

leaves my daughter and my two youngest children vulnerable. The fae were kind enough to install one of those alert systems into our home, but if there is trouble will anyone be monitoring tonight?"

"That's a great question," Mason replied. "And the answer is yes. We know that many of you have left your homes vulnerable. It's not perfect, but the kids who have been training at the Fort are on duty tonight. We've only pulled those kids away that were not needed at home. We also have a couple of the kids manning the dispatch center as usual. You can believe me when I say your homes and your families are not going to be left vulnerable while you go into battle."

"But they are just children," Donald Hovey protested. "You want us to feel secure in the fact that children are being sent out to protect children?" Donald was a panther, he also lived on the outskirts and didn't socialize regularly.

"If you are not familiar with the fort that Luke and Marlena started and Thomas, Alex and Dimitri have completed I can understand your question. However, anyone in this room who has children, relatives or neighbors that have attended the fort know those kids are more prepared to battle vampires than most of us are. In fact, many of them have already participated in more than one large battle. I for one have faith in their abilities."

"So do I," someone yelled. Soon there were shouts of "Me too," and "So do I."

Mason whistled again. "I'll now turn it over to Alex to explain the plan."

Alex and Dimitri walked them through every detail of the mission. They outlined known entrances, obstacles and described the preparations they had made in the field. If the vampires got through the first line, the second line would be prepared to handle them. They answered questions, then covered the basics again. Finally, it was time to leave.

"Shifters," Monroe called. "Pick a form and use it. We don't want you traveling in cars for this one. The fae don't have a choice but if we park hundreds of cars on the side of the road it won't only tip our hand to the vampires, but the local police will be called in. The last thing we need is for some overzealous human cop to stumble onto our battlefield."

And with that, the group started to file out the door.

"Is this going to work?" Oberon asked Mason and Monroe when the majority of the people had left the room. He realized Dimitri was herding the warriors out a side entrance. Dimitri was thorough. No doubt he was taking the opportunity to give his men final orders before the battle began.

"It has to," Chief Monroe answered. "The alternative is unacceptable."

"I agree," Mason nodded, then smiled when his wife slipped her hand in his.

Progeny

"I didn't hear my name on the list, will I be fighting or tending to the wounded?" Jackie Cooper asked soberly.

"At first, you will be fighting with my group," Mason told her. "However, don't be surprised if you are called off early to help deal with the wounded. We know Alex is a miracle worker, but she also wears herself out. You and Kylee will need to deal with as many members as you can. We'll leave the most serious wounds to Alex. We will be in the upper field, Kylee will be stationed with Bastian in the middle area and Alex is going to work the lower field. We think the really serious injuries are most likely to occur down there, on the front lines."

"I agree," Jackie said, worried. Alex did always wear herself out. "Do we have tea available for Alex? If this goes on for long, she's going to need something to keep her on her feet."

Abby stepped forward and gave her mom a hug, then her dad. "The tea is ready and stored in one of the cars the warriors will be using. I'm going to leave it up to you where you want to hide it once on scene. Mom, Dimitri will watch over Alex, but they could get separated. Please check in with her occasionally. You know how she is. She'll push and push until she drops. Keep her hydrated. Breena also added a little something special in there for an energy boost. I guess it's something she's been working on since the last battle."

"I promise," Jackie said, pulling Abby close. "Be careful out there honey. I can't be everywhere at once but I'm going to worry. My whole family is in danger. I know you and Morrigan can take care of yourselves and you both have wonderful mates but that doesn't mean I can't worry. It's a mother's right."

"We'll be careful, but follow your own advice and keep that one out of trouble." She pointed a thumb at her father. "And keep your fingers crossed. If this works, the war will be over for good this time."

"I hope that makes the losses worth it," Jackie said softly under her breath. She wanted to be optimistic, but she also knew any major battle was bound to result in losses, they had lost so many good people already.

Abby pulled a wrist unit from her pocket. "Put this on now, mom. It's similar to the ones the warriors are wearing. You, Alex and Kylee all have them. You are working on your own frequency so you will only be able to communicate with each other. The warriors can't hear you and you can't hear them. This is strictly to coordinate medical needs. We are working in pairs, so if you need to relay something to the warriors, go ahead and relay through Kylee or Alex. They can pass the message to their partner."

Jackie held out her left arm and Abby slipped the unit in place. "Gotta go, I'm already late." She gave her mother one last kiss then ran across the large room, skidding to a stop just before she disappeared out the same side door the warriors had used.

The instant Victor stepped outside he spotted the helicopter. He glanced at Bastian then focused on Dimitri. "I thought we were trying for stealth."

Progeny

"We are," Dimitri agreed. "Bastian is going to fly us to that little church just off the main highway. We have a couple cars waiting to get us further into the forest to our staging area. I wanted to make sure we arrive before the rest of our people. This will give us a head start. We probably won't beat the shifters, but we won't be far behind," he smiled when Alex slipped her hand in his.

"Kylee," Alex interjected. "Do you have your wrist unit?"

"All secure and ready," Kylee said holding up her arm.

"Jackie is going to hang back with Mason. The upper field will be the medical evac area. Any wounds that are not life-threatening will go there. Dimitri and I will be at the north end of the field. Most likely that's where the worst injuries will be. I'd like you and Bastian to stay in that middle area, somewhere between me and Jackie. It's a large area for only three of us to handle, but we're going to have to make due."

"Got it," Kylee nodded.

"Okay listen up," Dimitri commanded, he was clearly in warrior mode and everyone knew it. "Thomas, Abby, Dante, Cornelia, Nick and Lillie I want you to head out first. Then Bastian will return for the rest of us and we'll meet up in the forest."

"Maybe I should go with the first group, too," Kylee offered. "That will leave more room for you guys heading out in the second group."

"But that will leave you alone until I get back," Bastian argued.

"I can wait in the second car if I need to. You're stopping at the church. There won't be trouble there. We're too far from the caves and it's still light outside."

Nick considered. "I think it will be okay. It's not going to take long to drop us off, return for the others and get back to the church. Like she said, she can wait in the vehicle. Just give her the keys so she's not stranded. If she runs into trouble, she can just drive down the road a ways, then come back when she spots the chopper."

"I'll be okay," Kylee said, trying to sooth Bastian. "I can also shift and fly away if I can't get to the car."

Dimitri handed Kylee a set of keys. "I think it's a good plan and the risk is minimal," he turned and placed a second set of keys in Dante's hands. "Let's get loaded up. We're wasting time."

* * * *

Alex stood on the edge of the large clearing watching the sunset. It was beautiful here. They were in the upper field, the last line of defense. Mason Cooper would be in charge of operations for this section. She knew she needed to get moving. They needed to be in place before darkness surrounded them and the vampires headed out for the night. But she couldn't move. The instant she stepped from the vehicle a memory had hit her, so powerful it was almost like being five years old again. It was a memory of her father, she was having those more often lately. She wasn't sure why that was but for the most part, she was grateful. It was nice knowing her biological father was such a good man. Not because someone told her he was, but because she could remember him for herself. She sighed deeply when Dimitri moved in behind her and wrapped his strong arms around her body.

"You okay?" he whispered in her ear.

"I will be," she said, leaning back to enjoy the strength of him just for a second.

Dimitri pressed a kiss to her temple as he wiped a tear from her face. "Tell me," he said softly.

"It's stupid and entirely inappropriate for the moment," she admitted. "I had another memory of my father. It's a happy memory, but it makes me a little sad and angry. Radek has taken so much from me. I'm always torn in two when I remember the good times. I loved Luke so much and if Radek hadn't killed my father and kidnapped us, we wouldn't have met him or Thomas. I wouldn't have had such a wonderful life as a Deveraux. I may never have met you. It's just hard sometimes to remember, to realize what I missed out on. Then I think about what I might have missed if things had been different. I have a hard time reconciling all my feelings sometimes. Don't get me wrong, I love that I finally have my own memories of James and I hate knowing someone so wonderful was killed by someone so horrible.

Anyway, I guess this one was triggered by the forest. I think I was five, so it must have been shortly before he was killed. Dad took me, Sam and Michael camping. We didn't go far from the house, just far enough to set up the tent and build a fire to roast hot dogs for dinner. Afterward, dad taught us silly campfire songs while we roasted marshmallows," she shrugged, "Like I said, not appropriate just before we head into battle."

"It's good that you are remembering him," Dimitri said, turning her to face him. "And I don't think it's inappropriate at all. In fact, I was just thinking about my own father. I was wondering if he would be proud of me, or disappointed. I mean, I'm leading our people into a battle I don't know if we can even win. The risk is outrageous."

"He would be proud," Alex said, brushing a soft kiss on Dimitri's lips. "I know because I'm proud of you. And as risky as this plan is, at least we're doing something. I'm tired of sitting around waiting to see what he comes up with next. I'm tired of trying to not only anticipate Radek's moves, but also Lilith's. I'm tired of always second guessing myself. We all agreed, this is the right thing for our people. Some strategist centuries down the road might claim there was a better way, but I don't see one and neither did anyone else. No matter what happens tonight, you are not responsible."

"Neither are you," Dimitri said pulling her against his chest. "Remember that, sweetheart. We're all in this together. You can't take the blame on yourself and I won't take the blame, either. We're going in with our eyes wide open. People might die fighting for our freedom, but we will make sure they don't die in vain. Agreed?"

"Agreed," Alex said wrapping her arms around his waist. Dimitri pulled her closer against his muscular body. In that instant, Alex could feel his love, his fear and his strength. She loved this man more than anything. She was surprised to realize she felt safe. How silly was that, they were standing here on a battlefield waiting for the fight of their lives to begin and she felt safe. "I'm sorry," she whispered as she laid her head against his chest. "I am so sorry for what I've put you through these past few months. I'm sorry I didn't see how my grief and depression were impacting you. I put you in danger, I won't do that again. I couldn't stand it if you got injured because of me."

"We've already discussed this, Alex," Dimitri sighed. "When you hurt, I hurt. It's that simple." He placed his hand under her chin to lift her head so he could look her in the eyes. "You are my life now. I love you beyond words. Remember that while we're out there fighting tonight. I need you, baby. Your safety and your happiness are the only two things that are important in this world."

"I disagree," Alex interjected. "You forgot us. Our happiness and our safety are important, but the most important thing in the world is us. Our partnership, our love, our future."

Dimitri lowered his head and gave Alex a soft kiss. "I agree," he smiled.

"So, let's get out there and conquer the world already," she linked her hand with his. "We need to get into position. It's almost time," she turned and gave his arm a tug.

Dimitri smiled and let himself be led to the battlefield. They walked in silence, each of them deep in thought, dreading what was to come. Hoping it would finally be the end of the war and the beginning of a new, wonderful, peaceful life.

Chapter Twenty

Vampires were coming from all directions. Alex had assumed there would be a lot of them, but there were even more than she had imagined. Alex and Dimitri were still on the front lines but they were now cut off from most of the warriors. She wasn't sure how isolated they actually were because she couldn't see anything through the massive volume of vampires surrounding them. The traps they had been setting all week were working and thank goodness for that. Each time one exploded it took at least a dozen vampires out. The downside was all the smoke. It was making visibility even worse. The battlefield was huge. As hard as they tried, they couldn't prevent the vampires from getting through the front line. She had no doubt Mason Cooper and his group were far busier than they originally planned. It was going to be a very long, trying night. She was currently healing a shifter. The man's wounds would have been fatal without her. She'd lost track of how many people she'd healed already. So far, she was holding up fine, though. Whatever Breena had put in that tea was giving her a slight buzz, but it was keeping her energy up so she wasn't about to complain.

"Do you think you can stand up?" Alex asked the man she'd just healed. "We need to move as soon as possible. If you can't get up, I'll help hold them off until you catch your breath."

"No, I'm fine now. Thank you," the man said as he sucked in a long breath and slowly let it out. Then he stood and got back into the fight. Alex took a second using her gift to scan the area. She started in the backfield, checking on Jackie and Mason Cooper. Things were fine with them and not as busy as she'd feared. Jake was with Elvin. Foster and Fira were also helping keep the vampires away from the wounded. Next, she spotted Tianna and Drake. Thank goodness Tianna had joined the effort. Jackie could use all the help she could get. The two of them were tending to the wounded with a calm expertise that only came with years of experience. She paused when she saw Dusty and Nebi. They were further into the meadow, working their way towards the middle battlefield. The fighting was just as fierce in that area as it was up here in front. She was so proud of those two. Dusty had turned into such a wonderful man. Even with the missing leg, he was an awesome fighter. Those two were amazing both on and off the field. She would never have guessed Dusty had such a hidden talent in electronics. He never said a word to anyone the entire time they were at the fort. Nebi was the one who had set up the meeting with her and Ty the

Progeny

moment they returned from Denver. Initially, Nebi had led the conversation but Dusty quickly took over. The ideas Dusty, Cam and Rick had come up with to modify the droids so they could be used in a combat situation were mind blowing. D-Tech and Tyson Electronics were going to begin another joint operation immediately. Ty had insisted Dusty and Nebi move into his apartment complex. Dusty would be starting college full-time next semester and Nebi was planning on looking for work. It was nice to know those two were going to be okay. Once Dusty graduated, Ty had promised him a job in his company.

Alex moved on, searching the field for the rest of her loved ones. Rand and Caleb were doing fine, Bastian and Kylee were okay, too. She started to search for Thomas and Abby when she was knocked to the ground. Something heavy was lying on her back. She began to struggle, pushing her arms against the hard ground trying to dislodge whoever was on top of her. After a few seconds, she was able to roll over. That's when she realized it was a man, an injured man and he was unconscious and wounded. Which was probably why he fell on top of her. She knelt before him, placing her hands on his chest and surveyed his wounds. He had a large slice across his lungs, it was bleeding internally and she was sure he was no longer breathing. She went to work, trying to repair what she could. Once the wounds were healed he still wasn't breathing. Just when she was about to give up, thinking she'd been too late, he coughed, sucked in air and tried to stand up.

"You need to sit down, catch your breath and maybe have some tea. Then you can think about returning to the battle." Alex studied her surroundings and spotted the shifter she'd just healed. She called to him, then called again. She watched as he plunged his knife into a vampire then jogged to her side. "I need you to help this man to the upper field. He's been healed, but he's still too weak to fight. Take him to Jackie Cooper, can you do that for me?"

"Sure, no problem," the man said as he braced an arm around the fae man she had just healed and fought his way through the battle. Once again, Alex wondered if they had made the right decision. The mini battles had been tough, but this was insane. She took a deep breath and got to her feet, ready to help the next casualty.

The instant she stood, Dimitri was pulling her toward another wounded soldier. She took a deep breath and tried to keep up. A vampire came from nowhere, barreling toward her, knife outstretched. She stopped, planted her feet and waited. Seconds later she swung out and plunged her dagger into its chest. She only had a second to refocus when three more headed her way. She kicked out knocking one vampire into a tree, then swung her dagger and struck a second vamp in the chest. The third one got in a good slice. Alex gritted her teeth against the pain searing through her upper arm and waited. Then, she pivoted, kicked out and struck the vampire in the stomach. He went down hard. Alex was on him instantly. After one quick jab, the vampire dissipated. She stood and glanced around, searching for Dimitri. That's when she spotted the small lump lying on the ground. Before she could register what was happening, Dimitri was pulling her toward the injured body. He only said one word, Cornelia. Panic ran through Alex and she began to run.

Progeny

Cornelia was on the ground, but that didn't mean she was done for. Dante had his hands full trying to protect her but she was determined to help in any way she could. Eventually, Alex would find her. She had to believe that. She knew she was losing a lot of blood, but she didn't have any way to put pressure on the wound. Cornelia gritted her teeth and inhaled the cool night air. She had to breath, she had to focus, she would not give into the blackness that was trying to take her over. She was not going to pass out.

Alex slid to a stop and fell to the ground. Terrified she was too late, not knowing what she would find as she reached a hand out and pressed it against Cornelia's neck. She barely noticed when Dimitri knelt down beside her. "She's okay," Alex breathed in relief. "Go help Dante. He needs you."

Dimitri hesitated then focused on Cornelia. "Promise me you won't leave her alone."

"I promise," Cornelia croaked out. "Please, Dante's in trouble." She pushed at the ground, trying to force her body into a sitting position but she just couldn't do it. She needed to help Dante. She had to protect her husband.

"Cornelia," Alex said sternly. "Dimitri will help Dante. I need you to relax. Lay back and let me do my job."

Cornelia settled back onto the ground, wincing in pain. She was dying and she knew it. But Alex was here now and Dante had backup. She had to believe everything was going to be okay.

Alex pressed her palm to Cornelia's stomach and focused. She had to get the bleeding stopped or Cornelia would be in trouble. Actually, she'd lost so much blood she was already in trouble. Moments later her job was done but Cornelia was still too weak to move. "You've lost a lot of blood. I think you need a minute to recover."

"I know," Cornelia said forcing herself to a sitting position. "I'll be okay, just help me stand up."

Alex slid her hands under Cornelia's arms and lifted. She was glad to see Cornelia stand but was still worried about her condition. "What do you need?"

"I'll be fine," Cornelia said again. She took a deep breath in an attempt to ignore the nausea and dizziness trying to overtake her. "Really, the only thing that would help is blood and I'm not going to get that until we're finished here. Don't worry about me. I'm sure there are others that need your help. Let's go. Lead the way, I'll follow you."

Alex glanced around and spotted Dimitri. He and Dante were fighting for their lives. Vampires had them completely surrounded. She took a step toward him then stopped. The two men were holding their own. She paused for a minute to watch her man fight. He was amazing, so was Dante. Alex always loved to watch the warriors fight. It was what they were born to do. She glanced back at Cornelia then took a deep breath and utilized her other gift, the one that allowed her to see an overview of the battle. She was looking for injured, but instead she spotted Sam. What was that girl doing? It looked like she was running toward the forest. Before she could react, Alex had a flash of something. It was nothing like she'd ever experienced before. Sam falling to the ground, a large dagger protruding from her chest. "No!" Alex yelled as she broke into a run.

"Where are you going?" Cornelia yelled, running after Alex. She was winded and lagging behind.

"Go help Dimitri and Dante," Alex called back. "Sam's in trouble and needs my help."

"No way," Cornelia said when she caught up to Alex. "I promised Dimitri I wouldn't leave you alone."

Alex just nodded and continued toward the cave.

"Alex," Cornelia said in surprise when she realized where they were going. "This is dangerous and nobody will know where we are."

"Right," Alex nodded. She pressed a button on her wrist unit. "I'm entering the caves," she yelled. "I don't think my wrist unit will work once I'm deep inside," she turned to Cornelia. "That's going to have to do."

"Yeah, if anyone heard you," Cornelia grumbled. They were in trouble and she knew it. She had a very bad feeling about this.

The caves were massive, much larger than any of them had anticipated and they were still close to the entrance. Alex was focusing on the map inside her head as she rounded another corner. That's when she spotted Sam. She was lying on the ground, and there was a large knife protruding from her chest just like she'd seen in the vision. "Sam!" She yelled as she dropped to the ground and wrapped her hand around the large handle.

"Wait," Cornelia said lowering herself next to Alex. "Let me do it. Don't argue. Once we pull this from her chest the bleeding is going to be out of control. I need you to get in there and start working before I pull it out."

"Okay," Alex said, trying to hold back tears. She had to save Sam. She just had to. Alex closed her eyes and pressed her palm to Sam's stomach. It was below the wound, but it was close enough to stop the bleeding instantly as Cornelia pulled out the knife. That's when she realized Sam was not breathing.

* * * *

Sam was getting angry at Ty. The guy was doing his best to make sure she didn't have anything to do. He was forcing the vampires away from her every chance he got. Right now she was fighting off two of them and he was surrounded as he tried to herd another large group in the opposite direction. "Stop it, Ty," she screamed as she took out the two vamps he'd left her. She swung around to go after her husband and froze. Lilith was hiding in the forest about fifty yards away. She was staring at Sam in shock. Sam didn't think, she just ran.

Ty chuckled at his wife. He knew he was frustrating her, but there was no way he was backing off. He was stronger than she was. He knew she could handle herself, she'd been training every day, but he wasn't willing to take any chances with her safety. That's when he felt it, Sam's excitement. He glanced back and saw her running for the forest. Ty panicked. She was chasing Lilith away from the fight. He pushed his fighting into high gear, slashing and kicking like a mad man. He had to get to his wife.

Dimitri inhaled sharply when he felt Ty's panic. "Something's wrong," he said to Dante, immediately turning to find Alex. She was gone. Disappeared without a trace, Cornelia was gone too. Dimitri killed another vampire and frantically searched the field. "Dante!" He called, not even trying to hide his distress.

Dante kicked out, knocking a vampire into a tree. A protruding branch easily slid through the vampires back, killing him instantly. At the same time he lunged forward slicing his dagger through one vampire, then another. "What's wrong?" He called back to his friend. He could hear the panic in Dimitri's voice, but he was too busy to survey the area for what had caused it.

"The women are gone," Dimitri called back.

"What do you mean gone?" Dante asked, worried now.

"I don't know," Dimitri said, clearly frustrated. "One minute they were there with Alex healing Cornelia and now they're gone." Dimitri took his frustration out on the surrounding vampires. He had no idea what to do. How was he supposed to protect that woman if she couldn't follow directions?

* * * *

Jackie stared at the device on her wrist in surprise. She immediately ran to Mason. "Alex just said she's going into the caves. The transmission was broken up, so the rest was unclear but I know I heard her say she was heading into the caves. I tried to call Kylee but she's not answering."

"Go find Abby," Mason said immediately. "She'll be with Thomas and he can advise the rest of the warriors."

"Do you think she's been kidnapped?" Jackie worried aloud.

"Let's not borrow trouble," Mason grunted as he took out another vampire. "We both know what that would mean for Dimitri and I don't want to go there. Shift and go find Abby. She'll take care of it. Then hurry back, I need you here."

Abby was surprised when she saw her mother land beside her. Jackie immediately pulled out a knife and began to fight. "What's up mom?" Abby asked the instant she had a break.

"Alex came across this wrist thing and said she was going inside the caves," Jackie said not wanting to waste time.

"What?" Abby asked, shocked. "We all agreed it was too dangerous in there. Why did she change the plan? Was she going after Radek or did someone drag her against her will?"

Progeny

Jackie shrugged. "I only caught that she was going into the cave. Nothing more. I'm pretty sure this thing won't transmit in there. I tried to call her, but she's not answering. Your father said to get the information to Thomas so he can let the other warriors know. Kylee hasn't responded either so I don't know where she is or if she heard Alex any better than I did."

"Thanks, mom," Abby said, twirling around and slicing through a vampire's chest. She had shifted only her arm so she had large talons for fingers.

"I need to head back. Your father needs my help," Jackie said hesitantly.

"Go," Abby said as she kicked out and knocked over a vampire then sliced through another one.

Jackie took a second to kill two more vampires before she shifted into a hawk and flew back to her husband. He needed her help, but it was so hard to leave her daughter fighting for her life. She knew the wounded needed her now more than ever. She just hoped she didn't encounter a serious wound, with Alex missing the chance of survival wasn't good.

The instant Abby notified Thomas he was spreading the news through his wrist unit. Within seconds, all the warriors were aware of Alex's location.

Victor tossed out two of his stars then turned to Ariel. "Babe, we need to head toward the caves."

"What?" she asked, throwing fire from both hands and taking out five vampires at once. "No, we agreed that would be too dangerous. We don't know how many vampires are still in there."

"Alex announced over her device that she was entering the caves. Jackie tried to call her back but got no response. Dimitri wants the warriors with him when he goes after her."

"Okay, let me tell Monroe," Ariel said as she threw fireball after fireball. "He'll have to handle things out here."

"I agree," Victor said. "I'm fine here. Go tell Monroe and make sure he gets word to Oberon in case he hasn't already heard."

Within minutes Ariel was back. "He's got this. Let's go," the two of them took off, jogging across the field. "Mason will handle the upper field with Foster and Fira. Dad's now with Travis Monroe and Jake, Dusty and Nebi have moved forward to help handle the center. Monroe said Numair and some of his pack were also moving forward. Can you see if anyone is near Morrigan? He's going to have to handle things to the north. I think Rand and Caleb can help there, and Austin and Sherrie are also making their way to the front lines. I hope it's enough. We're leaving them awfully shorthanded."

"I know, but it can't be helped," Victor relayed something over his unit then waited.

Progeny

"Abby's taking care of it," Victor finally said. "She'll make sure Morrigan is clear on the plan and the location of his men," he laughed when Ariel glared at him. "And women," he added to appease her.

Morrigan checked on Nadia and was surprised to see Abby battling beside her. Austin was to their left, Sherrie to his left. He rushed to his sister, knowing there must be trouble.

"Morrigan," Abby called as she sliced through a vampire, then swung her leg back and kicked another vampire several feet away. "Alex announced she's inside the caves. We don't know why. Dimitri has ordered all the warriors to go in after her, which means you are losing the women too. That leaves you in charge here. I know the worst fighting is in this area, but I'm sure you can handle it. Just know, with Alex missing and Kylee heading in with Bastian, mom and Tianna are the only ones with medical abilities left and they're both in the upper field."

"That sucks," Morrigan said, slicing through a vampire then swinging around, kicking his leg out to shove back another one. "Do what you have to do, Austin and I can handle this."

"Thanks," Abby said leaning in to give him a quick kiss on the cheek. "I'll be back as soon as I can."

"Be careful," Morrigan called as Abby shifted into a raven and disappeared.

* * * *

Sam was running as fast as she could but she still couldn't catch Lilith. She knew the woman was heading for the caves. She also knew they had agreed not to go in there. She had an internal battle raging inside her head but ultimately decided to continue following Lilith. Ty couldn't be too far behind her. She'd not only sent him the message but also as many clues as she could so he could easily find her. Sam watched the vampire disappear through the dark opening and hesitated. It was now or never, what should she do? What if Lilith was retrieving bombs? She took a deep breath then slowly made her way into the dark cavern. Once her eyes adjusted, she realized there was a dim light showing the way. She wasn't sure if the light was coming from the moon or if her warrior vision just made it seem like there was light. Either way, she was grateful. She could smell Lilith and knew the woman had come this way. Judging by the strength of the smell, she couldn't have much of a lead. It still amazed her, the way a warrior could actually track a vampire through smell. She pressed her back against the cave wall and slowly slid around the next corner. Before she knew what was happening, Lilith jumped down from above and drove her dagger through Sam's chest. Sam thought of Ty and only had a second to regret her decision to go after Lilith alone.

Ty was frantic. It had taken him too long to dispense with the vampires and go after Sam. He thought he saw Alex and Cornelia enter the woods, but he couldn't be sure. He was now running through the forest, darting around trees, trying to follow the path he'd seen in Sam's head. He knew she must have been sending images to him, otherwise

Progeny

it would have been harder for him to pull her route from her mind. Ty paused, looking for the broken branch Sam had sent him when the pain hit. It was so severe it caused his knees to buckle. He went down, bracing his weight with his hands as he sank to the ground. Ty sat up, fear immobilizing him for what seemed like hours. Sam was dying and he was too far away to help. He leaned back, clutching his chest as he tried to breathe. He barely noticed when Dimitri placed a hand on his shoulder.

"Alex went after her," Dimitri said softly. "You have to get up. We need to find them. Ty?" Dimitri said more forcefully, "You have to keep it together. You have to lead us to our women." Dimitri closed his eyes and prayed for strength. He just hoped Alex made it to Sam in time. "Any idea what prompted those girls to deviate from the plan? We all agreed going inside the cave was too dangerous."

"Lilith," Ty choked out as he forced himself to stand. He could very well lose Sam forever. How could he live without her?

"Well, that explains it," Dante mumbled. "We should have known. Where that woman is concerned, our girls are too emotional and reckless."

"I agree," Dimitri said, taking Ty's arm and pulling him to his feet. "Ty, we have to have faith. I believe in Alex, if she can make this right, she will."

* * * *

Alex focused on Sam. Her energy was surrounding the knife on all sides. She knew it hadn't struck Sam's heart, but it did slice through an artery. "Count to three then pull. I'm going to help push from the inside and try to heal the hole as the knife is expelled."

"Can you do that?" Cornelia asked, amazed.

"I hope so, it's the only thing that is going to save her life." Alex knew tears were running down her face, but she couldn't stop them. Sam was dying. She wasn't breathing and Alex didn't know if she could save her or not. The instant Cornelia pulled out the knife, Alex healed the wound. Very little blood was lost due to the unbelievable coordination she and Cornelia had managed. But still, Sam was not breathing. Alex blocked out everything else and focused on Sam. She had to find out why Sam was still dying.

Cornelia heard a noise the instant the knife was pulled from Sam's chest. She swung around to see about twenty vampires descending upon them. She was still feeling weak, but the adrenaline rush she'd experienced the last few minutes had helped. She hoped it would be enough. Alex was too focused on Sam, she wasn't going to be any help and Sam still might die. It was up to Cornelia to protect the two until Alex could do her magic and get Sam back on her feet. She took a step forward and braced herself for the attack.

Sammael slid from the shadows and moved several steps forward. Lilith was gone now, the coward. Sammael always knew her tactics were underhanded, but she'd ambushed that poor woman. In no way was that a fair fight. He turned back to Martinez. "She's sent a group of vampires back to finish off the job. We're going to have to fight our own. The Kings were very clear that we need to protect the vampire woman at all cost. Can you handle it?"

"Of course," Martinez said, annoyed. As if he had some emotional connection to Radek's vampires. None of them had accepted him. He assumed that was Zorak's doing, but Lilith could have had something to do with it too. Martinez knew the two of them were trying to keep him isolated so he would have to depend on them. It wasn't working. He'd rather be a complete loner than depend on either one of those vampires.

Sammael moved into the opening and surveyed the scene before him. He was instantly impressed with the woman vampire. She was one of the best fighters he'd seen in his lifetime and he had lived a very long time. Radek, Lilith and the rest of these guys assumed he was fairly young, not even an ancient. They would be surprised to learn he was over one thousand years old. And he knew for a fact, the female before him was a better fighter than most ancients he knew.

Martinez slipped in beside Sammael and stared. "She's amazing," he whispered. "I mean, truly amazing, look at how she moves. It's like she anticipates what they are going to do before they do it. I've never seen anything like it. Is that normal? I mean for an old vampire."

"No," Sammael said, taking a deep breath and forcing his gaze from this amazing woman. "Let's go. If we split up and attack from the back, we'll take them by surprise. I'll handle Murray. He's the oldest one here and he can be tricky. You focus on the others."

"Got it," Martinez said, taking a few steps to the side. He glanced back at Sammael and on his nod, they moved in and began to fight.

Alex didn't know what to do, there didn't seem to be anything wrong with Sam, but she still wasn't breathing. She was out of time. *Think Alex*, she told herself. *Think!* An idea hit her and she decided to try it. She closed her eyes and focused on Sam's lungs, forcing air in and out, funneling it through Sam's system. Basically providing life support until Sam started breathing on her own. A few minutes later, which seemed like forever, Sam finally coughed out a strangled gust of air then began breathing on her own. A few seconds after that, she opened her eyes. Alex immediately pulled Sam into a big bear hug. Then she stood and turned, thinking she'd see Cornelia directly behind her.

What she saw surprised her beyond anything she ever could have imagined. Cornelia was battling vamp after vamp. But the thing that was truly amazing was that two of the vampires had joined her. The three of them were working through the growing army together. They were protecting her and Sam until Sam recovered. Alex took a step forward then hesitated. Was Sam well enough to handle it if one slipped through? Probably not yet. Alex watched as Sam slowly pushed to her feet. She was holding onto the wall of the cave for support, but at least she was breathing on her own and she was standing.

Progeny

"What's going on?" Sam asked, clearly confused.

"I have no idea," Alex whispered back. "Do you think you can handle it if I go out and help them?" She glanced down the long hall and hoped for reinforcements.

"Yes," Sam nodded. "I'm not ready to fight yet, but I'm getting better by the second." She closed her eyes and tried to send a signal to Ty. She needed him to know she was okay. She knew how frantic he was going to be.

Alex stepped forward and began to fight. She took a deep breath, shook out her hands and tried to focus. It took some effort; she was still shaken up over Sam's injury. She so easily could have lost her forever. But she couldn't think of that right now, she needed to concentrate on surviving. Alex turned just in time to witness one of the vampires save her from another vamp. She'd been so deep in thought she hadn't sensed him behind her. One more second and the vampire would have plunged his dagger right through her side. Her attacker must be old because he knew to aim for her lungs. She didn't have a chance to thank the vampire who had saved her. He had moved away, still deep in battle with the vamp that almost killed her. Alex studied the vampires face. She was determined to remember him. If she had the chance, she was going to return the favor someday. Then she swung around and entered the battle.

Ty, Dimitri and Dante thundered around a corner and stopped in shock. Sam was leaning against the wall, dagger in hand. She was obviously too weak to fight, but she was keeping a defensive stand in case she needed it. Alex, Cornelia and two vampires were battling hundreds of vamps. The things just kept funneling from the hallway into the large space.

"What in the hell?" Dante asked awestruck.

"I have no idea, but let's figure it out later," Dimitri said, moving in next to Alex and joining the fight. He watched as Dante moved to the other side of Cornelia and did the same.

Ty rushed to Sam's side, pulling her close against his chest. He pivoted so his back was to the wall. He knew it put Sam at a disadvantage, but he was certain he could protect her back. He also knew the others would protect both of them. "Baby, are you okay?" He moved his hands to cradle her face. "I thought I lost you."

"I know but I'm okay," Sam said, taking another deep breath, finally getting back her strength. "I want that bitch," she pushed away from Ty. "I'm going after her. Are you coming?"

"Sam," Ty began to argue.

"We don't have time for this," Sam countered taking a step away from him. "She went that way. We can slip past the few vampires blocking the way and go after her. Lilith has to die tonight."

Ty wanted to argue, but he knew she was right. Lilith did have to die, tonight. As soon as possible. He wasn't sure if Sam had thought of it, but it was likely Lilith had additional bombs. If she set one off inside the cave, they would all be dead.

Progeny

"I have thought of that," Sam said as she slipped behind a vampire and shoved her dagger through its back. Ty moved in beside her and did the same. They slowly made their way through the room and into the long hallway. "I can track her," she said to Ty. "I would recognize her smell anywhere." And with that, the two of them proceeded to track their worst enemy.

* * * *

Gallo led the way through the hidden entrance and down a narrow hallway. The small group of vampires hoped they were in time. Trumak had seen the women enter the cave, they were chasing Lilith. Everyone understood the importance of getting to the traitorous woman before the warriors did. If she was killed with the key, it would be lost to them forever. If a vampire was holding something in their hand at death, they would instinctively drop it and it would be spared. Any jewelry, or in Lilith's case the key, attached to their body would disintegrate with the vampire. They weren't really sure why, it was assumed that at the instant the blade hit a vampire's heart, their body became so hot, their essence was turned to dust. In the process, any clothing or jewelry on their body was also heated to the point of destruction. In other words, if Lilith was killed, the key would turn to dust along with her body.

Gallo paused, trying to remember Sammael's instructions. He wasn't sure which way to go.

"This way," Ammit said confidently. The group followed his lead. Moments later they were standing on a large ledge bordering the top of an enormous room. There was no way to get down. They were stuck. And Radek was pacing below.

Radek picked up a chair and threw it across the room. "How did this happen?" he bellowed. "I'm losing the battle. How am I losing the battle? And where is that no good woman of mine?" He didn't notice the slip but the other vampires in the room had. None of them considered Lilith Radek's woman any longer. They knew the two of them had stopped being lovers months ago. They also didn't believe Lilith was acting in the best interest of their king. Lilith's number one priority was Lilith and everyone knew it. Nobody noticed as the woman in question slipped into the room and hid in the shadows.

Alex, Dimitri, Cornelia and Dante continued to fight until the vampires stopped coming. The instant they were sure it was over Dimitri spoke. "Sam is on a mission to take out Lilith. If I'm reading Ty's emotions correctly, he agrees. Ty wouldn't disobey an order so I have to believe he's worried about bombs."

"She could have them," Dante agreed. "If anyone can find and disarm them, Ty can."

"I agree, but that puts us all in danger," Dimitri said, looking at Alex. "I think you should get out of this cave."

"Nice try," Alex said, pushing past Dimitri and heading down the hallway.

"Alex!" Dimitri said, exasperated. "Will you listen for just a minute?"

"Look," she stopped and swung around to face the group. "We're wasting time. Sam isn't a hundred percent better. If she's going after Lilith, they need us. Ty can't deactivate a bomb and protect Sam at the same time. I almost lost her once, I'm not dealing with that again. So follow me or leave, but I'm going after Sam."

Dimitri looked at Dante and Cornelia. "You don't have to follow. We all know if a bomb goes off in here none of us will survive. You two head out and warn the others."

Cornelia shrugged. "I haven't come this far to turn around now. There's no way to know where Lilith went. What if she ran to Radek? He's going to have vampires guarding him. They can't handle this on their own and neither can you. I'm in."

"Me too," Dante agreed. Where Cornelia went, he went. But he would have gone in without her. She was right. If Radek was here, it was the perfect chance to kill him.

Dimitri hesitated a mere second then turned and headed down the hallway.

* * * *

Victor was frustrated. The vampires were funneling out of that cave like rats abandoning a sinking ship. He was afraid that's what the cave was, a death trap. He was almost out of stars so he pulled out his dagger and did his best to push forward. Nick and Lillie stood to Ariel's right, Bastian and Kylee were directly behind them. Abby and Thomas were up ahead, but they were having just as much trouble fighting through the masses.

"Abby?" Thomas finally yelled. "Can you fly us out of here?"

"Sure, but what about the rest of them?" Abby asked, concerned for her friends.

"Get me ahead of the group then come back for Vic and Ariel. Once you show the way, Kylee will follow," Thomas decided.

"Are you sure about this?" Abby asked.

"Yes," Thomas said as he killed another vampire. Before he said another word, Abby had shifted into a pterodactyl and locked her talons gently over his shoulders. Thomas reached up and gripped her legs then held on as she flew to the opening of the cave.

"Wait for me," Abby ordered, knowing Thomas would be tempted to go in alone. She rushed back and landed next to Ariel and Victor.

Progeny

Victor didn't hesitate, he grabbed Ariel around the waist and tossed her onto Abby's back then he scrambled on behind her. Within seconds, they were lowered to the ground as Abby shifted back into human form. Victor glanced up just in time to see Kylee lower Nick and Lillie to the ground and shift to stand beside Bastian who was already beside Thomas.

"Well, that was fun," Kylee said, grinning. "Are we going in?"

The group cautiously entered the cave in search of their friends. When they came to a large opening, they stopped abruptly. "A serious battle occurred here," Victor said, crouching to study the remains on the ground. "The good news is I don't see any casualties from our side. The bad news, there's a lot of blood over here next to the wall."

"Let's keep going," Ariel said, guiding the group down the hallway. "I can smell Lilith from here."

"Dimitri and the others have been here as well," Victor added.

* * * *

Sam slid into the large room and spotted Radek. For a minute she froze, her mission forgotten. She would recognize those violet eyes anywhere. This was the vampire that had killed her family. The vampire she had watched so callously snap her brother's neck like he meant nothing.

556

Ty slipped his arms around Samantha's shoulder. "Breath, honey," he whispered softly in her right ear. He could feel her distress and understood why. They had accidentally stumbled onto Radek, the King himself. Samantha had lived with the memories of seeing this man kill her entire family far too long. Ty understood why she wasn't prepared for the encounter.

Samantha still hadn't recovered from the shock of seeing Radek in person when she spotted Lilith. The woman was hiding in the shadows. Seeing her like this shifted something inside of Sam. Ever since their encounter in the woods, Sam had feared Lilith. Not only feared her, but her mind had built the vampire into something that was impossible to defeat. Now Lilith was afraid, Sam could smell it. She was so afraid she was hiding in a corner hoping the king would protect her. That knowledge gave Sam's confidence a boost. She could finish this. She knew she could.

"That's my girl," Ty said, glancing toward Lilith. He leaned in close. "Go get her. I'll keep the others away. We'll take care of Radek once you're done."

Sam's head shot around to study Ty. He wanted her to fight Lilith? Of course he did. He was the only one who could really understand how much it meant to her to be the one that killed that vicious vamp. She gave Ty a subtle nod then slid into the shadows.

Chapter Twenty One

Alex, Dimitri, Dante and Cornelia approached a large door but paused. Dimitri turned to face the group. "There are a lot of vampires in there," he said soberly. "Ty and Samantha are in there, too. I'm not sure what we're going to encounter once we step through that door. What I do know is that Ty is on edge and Sam is excited, nervous and very focused. I can't read the situation accurately from here. That means we're going in blind. This is your last chance to turn back. The others could use your help out in the field."

Dante glanced at Cornelia then back to Dimitri. "I'm not leaving Ty. You do what you want, but I'm going in." He took a step forward and felt Cornelia slip her hand into his. The two of them walked into the room followed by Alex and Dimitri.

Cornelia's blood had turned to ice. At first she thought it was from her injury, then the adrenaline, that the ice in her veins was due to lack of blood. Now, she knew it was something entirely different. The second she and Dante stepped into the room, she froze. She told her feet to move, but they wouldn't budge. Her eyes locked on her father and she couldn't breathe. Radek turned and his eyes met hers. Cold, violet eyes studied her intently. She felt light headed and seriously thought she was going to pass out. Was her body doing this, or was he? She felt it the instant he realized the connection. His eyes actually darkened and something wild danced with the hatred, was that lust? *No. It couldn't be,* Cornelia assured herself. He was her father. Cornelia's breath slowed as those violet eyes continued to glare at her. Then, she stopped breathing altogether, terrified of what would happen next.

* * * *

Radek sensed the group as they mingled out of sight. He stopped pacing to watch them enter the room. He wanted a glimpse of the reckless fools before he sentenced them to die. At least there were no shifters in the group. He was no longer surprised that the shifters had joined ranks with the fae. At first, that had made him angry. They were supposed to form an alliance with him, hadn't he made that perfectly clear? Why else would he have abducted the pack leader's daughters? But after he thought about it, he didn't mind. It would actually make things easier in the end. Once he conquered Alexandria's kingdom, he would have her allies as well. Then he could finally get started making that heir.

The small group finally stepped through the door. Radek barely noticed the warrior, his eyes were drawn to the woman. The vampire woman that was fighting against him. The woman who had disobeyed his order, more than once. She had finally come to him. He couldn't stop staring at her. There was something about her. Something familiar, but not. Something unusual. Radek took a deep breath and continued to study her intently. He was vaguely aware that two additional people had entered the room. He didn't care who they were, he couldn't stop looking at the woman. He hated her, she was trying to take his kingdom.

Then it hit him, a smell so strong it couldn't be denied. He had a daughter. That woman, the one he kidnapped so long ago, had tricked him. She had conceived his child, then she had run off and deprived him of what was rightfully his. This vampire's mother was going to die for her betrayal. That Fae woman was going to pay for stealing his child. Sure, she was a girl and he'd never wanted a daughter. But as an adult, she was intriguing. The more he considered, the more he grew to relish the idea of the two of them ruling together. She was certainly strong and beautiful and she was all his. He could do whatever he wanted to her. She was his property. Then it struck him, he could create an heir with his daughter. Her offspring would have his strength and hers. Their son would be even mightier because he carried Radek's bloodline from both of his parents, not just one. He would be unstoppable.

Dante stepped in front of Cornelia, blocking her path. "Breath baby," he whispered. "You have to breathe." He knew he had blocked her view of Radek, he'd done it on purpose. "Corrie, you have to look at me." She was white as a ghost and she still wasn't breathing. He had to do something. They were surrounded by vampires but for some reason, none of them were advancing. Radek must have recognized her, just like she said he would. Maybe he had given the order to stand back so the king could deal with them himself. Even more reason to snap out of this. Dante leaned forward and pressed his lips to hers. She was so cold. He deepened the kiss, forcing her out of her shock.

Cornelia couldn't see Radek anymore. Had someone stepped in front of her? She kept telling her lungs to suck in air, but they wouldn't listen. She couldn't breathe, she couldn't move, she was too afraid to do anything. As she stood there, she had this vague feeling that someone was talking to her. He sounded familiar. Who was that? She was so cold and she felt like she was going to pass out. Then warm soft lips were pressed against hers. Who was kissing her? Then he deepened the kiss and she knew, Dante. Her eyes flew open and she gasped, pulling air into her lungs.

"That's my girl," Dante said, relieved. He started rubbing his hands up and down her arms. "Now, we need to move. We're out in the open and if things go to shit, we have no cover. Can you walk with me?" He asked as he gently moved behind her and slipped an arm around her waist. He maneuvered her slowly across the room, stopping when they reached the far wall. He could shield her between himself and the wall if he needed to. It was a risk, they were now deep within the room but at least Corrie was as far away from her father as she could get.

Cornelia continued to force air in and out of her lungs. It took effort and concentration, but she was slowly getting her wits back. She was standing in the same room as her father. The evil, sadistic man who had kidnapped and tortured her mother. She could feel his eyes on her. In fact, she was pretty sure he hadn't taken them off her since she'd entered the room. He knew who she was. That meant she had to kill him or die trying. He could never capture her. He would never forgive her mother for keeping such a secret from him. She read it in his eyes. The anger, the hatred, the vengeance. She frowned when she felt the hard rock press against her back. Dante had led her all the way across the room. He was trying to protect her. She loved him for the effort but he couldn't protect her from this. It was her destiny, she felt it in her soul. Just then she remembered Alex and Dimitri. Where were they? And Sam and Ty? They had gone after Lilith, who was also somewhere in this very room. Cornelia could smell her.

"Better?" Dante asked as he moved in beside her. He wanted to get his bearings, he had to know where Alex, Dimitri, Sam and Ty were. They might have to fight their way out of here before the others arrived. He was relieved to see Ty and Sam in the back of the room. Ty was guarding Sam as she slowly circled Lilith. There were a few vampires in the area, but none of them appeared to notice the fight that was brewing. Well, that wasn't quite true. There were two vamps that were slowly making their way toward Ty. He was watching them closely, intent on keeping Sam safe.

Dante turned his attention to Alex and Dimitri. They had made their way to the center of the room. Alex was now standing directly in front of Radek. The King hadn't noticed. The area where he was standing was slightly raised, three to four feet higher than the rest of the cave. The platform made it easy for him to see over Alex and Dimitri. His attention was still focused on Corrie. Dante frowned. He didn't like the look Radek was giving his wife. Where in the world were the others? This could get ugly, especially when Alex confronted Radek like he knew she was going to. It was just the way she rolled.

"Radek," Alex said, taking a step towards the large king. He didn't respond. He continued to stare at Cornelia. Alex took another step forward and called his name again, louder this time. That should get his attention, but it didn't.

* * * *

The three kings stood on the balcony watching the scene unfold. They weren't quite sure what to make of it. It was clear the group had two targets in mind, Lilith and Radek. They were prepared to let the woman take Radek out, but Sammael or Martinez needed to get that key before the fighting got too serious with Lilith.

"We have to do something," Ammit said softly. "We are going to have to intervene somehow."

Progeny

"There is only one option and we all know how risky that is. If we try to exit the ledge and make our way to the floor it will be too late," Maedoc mused. "We don't know our way through the maze down there."

"Then we must intervene," Typhon said with a shrug. "It's only risky because the man is crazy. With three of us, we should be able to control his mind. The insanity isn't bad enough to cause permanent damage. I'm sure of it. We are all too old and strong. Now if we had tried it on his father that's a different story. Balthazar was loonier than a stomped ant."

"Let us use that as a last resort," Ammit told them. "Look, that woman is taking on Radek alone."

The three men and their bodyguards looked on in fascination as the scene before them became even more interesting.

* * * *

Alex took another step forward trying to find an easy way onto the platform. The rocks were old and worn and looked slick. The last thing she needed was to trip and fall. She smiled at the thought. Wouldn't she look fierce as a klutz? She was still studying the obstacle when she felt the air shift somehow. Something had changed. She looked back at Dimitri. He had noticed it too. A quick glance at Ty told her he had also felt it. He shifted slightly and continued to glare at the vampires in his immediate area. Alex recognized one of them as the vampire that had saved her life. She didn't know what to think of that but couldn't deal with it now. Was Radek giving his men an order, telling them to fight? She glanced around and saw Dante and Cornelia against the far wall. Dante was in front of her, it looked like he was holding her back.

"Corrie," Dante whispered urgently. "You have to stop." Even his pet name for her wasn't breaking through the trance she was in.

Cornelia took a step forward, the voice in her head was getting so loud. "Come to me," it beckoned. She was aware of Dante. He had moved in front of her and was whispering in her ear. The voice called again, stronger this time, but not so strong she couldn't resist. She wasn't out of control, mindlessly forced to obey the command. It was a command, she knew that, she could see it in Radek's eyes. He was commanding her to join him. She wouldn't, of course. She could make the choice, not Radek. But his demand was driving her insane, repeating over and over in her head like a broken record. Somehow she had to make it stop.

"Honey, I really need you to look at me," Dante said as he gently put his hands to each side of Cornelia's face and turned her away from Radek. "I need you to look into my eyes. Can you do that for me?" Nothing. She was still focused on Radek. "Corrie, baby," he pled. "Ignore your father. Your husband needs you." Dante gently lifted Cornelia into his arms and moved further into the corner of the cave. It was the best protection he could find. He realized Radek was playing mind games with his wife and he was desperate to find a way to stop it. Once again he pressed his lips to hers, hoping the connection would be enough.

* * * *

Typhon was curious about the woman. There was something about her that intrigued him. He had moved to the far end of the balcony to get a better look when he heard the warrior mumbling softly. The guy was trying to break the connection Radek had on her. Typhon knew what Radek was doing. He'd heard the commands as had the rest of the Kings. This only made Typhon more curious. How was the woman resisting? The command was getting stronger and stronger with each passing second. Then he heard the man tell the female to ignore her father and focus on her husband. Had he heard that correctly? Was this vampire Radek's daughter? He rushed back to the others to relay his findings. An answer to their final question had just presented itself. They needed to act fast if they were going to control the situation.

* * * *

Morrigan sent a panicked look at Austin, they were in trouble. It had all changed so quickly. One minute they were battling like they had been all night, the next every vampire on the field was headed their way. "We have to stop them," Morrigan yelled over his shoulder. He hoped Austin could hear him. "Radek must have given the order to retreat back to the caves. The warriors must be winning. We have to stop them."

"I agree," Mason Cooper said, landing softly beside his son. "Something has changed and I think you're right, Radek is calling them back," Mason kicked out and stopped one vampire at the same time he plunged his knife into another one. "I've left orders for Jackie and Tianna to stay in the backfield. They need to continue to work on the wounded. Drake is staying with his wife and Avery and Tighe are remaining behind to protect them. I have Foster and Fira working to secure the area between us and Jackie. They will make sure we don't get cut off from each other. I've ordered everyone else forward. We need to make a line across the front and ensure none of the vampires return to the cave. Help me spread the word. I want our best fighters up front, the rest will fall in behind us."

"Sir?" Vivian said softly to Oberon who had just joined Mason and Morrigan. "I have a suggestion if I may."

"Yes, dear what is it?" Oberon asked gently. This girl had been through so much, lost so much in this war, he didn't want to scare her.

"Gerty and I have been stationed over there," she pointed to the forest. "Taking out the vampires with our bow and arrows. We've been each other's backup. Now I think we need to split up. We could move even further into the woods and take out any vampires that manage to get through the line. But we need spotters. Two people that can have our backs and retrieve arrows as we need them."

Progeny

Oberon considered. This was a good idea, but the job was going to be dangerous. He turned to Morrigan. "You've been fighting beside these men all night, what two men can handle this? They need to be good, strong fighters. Its possible vampires might come at them from both directions, from the field and from the caves," Oberon plunged his knife into a vampire's chest impatiently. It was difficult to communicate, to develop a plan when they were also fighting for their lives.

Morrigan studied the men as he continued to fight, killing vampire after vampire. Finally, he made a decision. "Johnson, Stewart I need you back here." The two men rushed to Morrigan's side, got their orders then proceeded into the forest, Vivian and Gerty close behind. Morrigan considered their line. It was as good as it was going to get. Travis Monroe, Numair and Ryker were at the far left end followed by Caleb and Rand. Austin and Sherrie were next to him then Nadia and his father. To their right was Dusty, Nebi, Jake and Oberon. The rest of the men had fallen in behind them. As he refocused on the vampires he wondered if any of them were going to survive.

* * * *

Victor and Ariel rounded a corner and finally saw the corridor they were looking for. They had somehow taken a wrong turn and had to backtrack. "This has to be the way," he said confidently.

"I agree," Ariel said, inhaling sharply to see if she could catch a scent she recognized.

568

Abby moved in behind them. "This is definitely the right hallway. I don't know how we missed it before," she scowled as Thomas took her hand and began running forward. Abby slowed their pace and smiled at Thomas' angry look. "We aren't going to do them any good if we are completely worn out and winded when we arrive." Thomas pulled in a deep breath then slowed his pace to match Abby's.

As the group rounded yet another corner they came to an opening that led to a large door. Abby pulled away from Thomas and moved in next to Kylee. "We're here," she whispered. "Kylee, follow my lead. We're going to be the only two shifters there. If I shift, you shift and do whatever I do. It might be the only thing that saves us. There are so many vampires in there."

Kylee nodded. She only paused for a second then she called out to the group. "Radek is in there, I can smell him," she scrunched up her face at the smell. Sometimes having an extra sensitive nose was a hindrance, not a blessing. Standing here, outside a room full of vampires she could barely breathe. The smell was atrocious. It wasn't something she could explain to anyone, it was strong and unique. Kind of like stepping into an enclosed barn where an animal had died then roasted in the heat for a couple days. It was pungent and overwhelming. She braced herself, knowing the instant they stepped into the room it was only going to get worse.

Thomas jerked his head around so he could see Abby. "Is Alex...?" He couldn't finish. His sister had to be okay.

Progeny

Abby moved back beside him and nodded. "This is the hot spot. Lilith is in there, too. Ty, Sam, Alex and all the others. We need to be prepared for anything."

As the group moved in, they weren't exactly sure what to expect. Each of them studied the large room and moved flawlessly into action. Kylee and Bastian moved in next to Ty, determined to protect Sam while she continued to fight with Lilith. A few vampires backed away the instant they took a stance. Nick spotted Dante and Cornelia and immediately pulled Lillie with him across the room. Something was wrong with Cornelia and Dante needed them to have his back. Victor, Ariel, Thomas and Abby headed for Dimitri and Alex. Victor and Ariel took the right side, Thomas and Abby the left.

The air was explosive inside the large cave. There were so many vampires, but none of them were attacking. As the new arrivals took everything in, they were still confused. It looked like Radek was trying to somehow control Cornelia. Dante was doing his best to comfort her. Alex was standing almost directly in front of the King but he didn't seem to realize it. Sam was trying to fight Lilith, but the vampire was skittish and kept jumping away. That was new. Normally Lilith was the aggressor; not this time. Sam was trying to fight and Lilith was trying to flee. There were two vampires close to Ty. They looked like they wanted to jump in the middle of Sam and Lilith, but Ty was holding them off.

Abby glanced up and saw the contingency of vampires on the upper balcony. She briefly wondered who they were. Three of them looked like royalty. They had the same air about them as Radek, only more intense. There were three other men standing in the background, bodyguards maybe? She was definitely going to keep an eye on them. She glanced back at Alex and wondered what the girl was planning. It was obvious she had something planned by the look on her face.

Alex finally spotted a section she knew she could climb without losing her footing. She glanced around the room before moving in. She hoped her people, the warriors, would take her lead. She was worried about Cornelia. Radek was so focused on her, she knew he was trying to control her mind. So far, Cornelia was winning but it was impossible to know if Radek had reached his limit or if he still had more tricks up his sleeve. She was grateful the others had found them. It had taken so long, she thought they must have run into trouble. She glanced back at Sam and Ty just in time to see Bastian grab her vampire protector around the neck and smash him against a wall. "Bastian," she called out. The entire room turned their attention to her. Well, everyone except Radek. He was still focused on Cornelia.

Bastian was itching to kill the scrawny little vampire. He thought he was sneaky. While Ty was focused on the guy's partner, this one tried to slip around the group and move in to help Lilith. No way, this was a personal matter between the women. No men allowed. He'd reacted immediately, grabbing the scrawny vamp around his neck and slamming him against the wall. He was just reaching for his dagger when Alex called his name. He kept his hold tight on the vampire as he turned to look at his queen.

Progeny

"Don't kill him," she ordered. "He saved my life. I want him to live."

Bastian turned back around and studied the vampire. "Why?" He finally asked. "Why did you save our queen? I thought you had orders to kill her." That little revelation didn't make sense.

The vampire lifted his arms to pull at Bastian's grip around his neck. Okay, so he probably couldn't talk with the vice around his windpipe. Bastian set him down but didn't move away. This one was wily and he wasn't taking any chances with him.

"My orders were to protect your queen if possible and the other woman, the vampire woman, at all cost," Sammael began rubbing his neck. He'd heard about warriors all his life, but up close and personal like this he couldn't help but be impressed. For so long he'd questioned the validity of rumors. Fear of the unknown had a way of generating tall tales. But now that he'd seen one in action, and several others disbursed around the room, he believed every tale he'd ever heard.

Bastian was still confused. That didn't make any sense. "Whose orders?" he demanded. Radek would never have given those orders.

"My King's," Sammael said, glancing at the balcony. "And the other King's as well."

Bastian glanced up and realized they had more company. Three large men, or vampires, were standing close together on a balcony. They were watching Sam and

Lilith closely. Bastian didn't like their stance. He didn't like anything about the situation they were in. He wouldn't kill the wily vamp, but he wasn't going to let him hurt Sam either. And that's what the three kings on the balcony seemed to be ordering him to do.

Sam was annoyed. She'd expected a challenge. Lilith wasn't even trying to participate. What had happened to this vampire? She certainly hadn't acted this way at the fort, out in the forest when she attacked and almost killed Sam. She hadn't acted this way on the rooftop either. In fact, she hadn't acted this way ever before. "What's wrong, Lilith?" Sam taunted. "You should be the confident one. Here we are in your home, surrounded by your friends and you're afraid to fight me. Why?"

"You should be dead," Lilith finally spat out. "Why are you not dead?" *And how did I not know you were a warrior when I had you in those woods*, she silently wondered? If she'd known, she would have finished the job. Lilith had seriously believed this woman was a human. The wounds she'd inflicted would have been fatal to a human. But this female was a warrior, they healed. She had been so intent on torturing the girl, on making her pay for all she'd done, Lilith hadn't even picked up on the warrior scent. She'd run out of time when the two men rushed in, but she hadn't been at all worried about that. A human would have died, anyway. This woman was more clever than Lilith had realized. And that scared her. Lilith wasn't even sure she could win a fight with the warrior on a good day. In the past, she'd only bested the girl because she'd caught her by surprise. This was a headon battle and it wasn't a good day. Sammael had cured her burns, but the large cut in her side was still tender. The woman standing before her was to blame for that as well. The holy water she'd splashed on Lilith all those months ago was still making her weak. Before Lilith knew what was happening, the warrior grabbed her by both arms and slammed her into the cave wall. Lilith saw stars, bright specks erupted in her eyes the instant her head hit the wall. Instinct took over and the fight was on.

"Sammael and Martinez are trapped. They won't be able to get to the key in time," Typhon said urgently. "We must step in and take control."

"I agree," Maedoc said with a sigh. "Let's do this now, before what we came for is lost forever."

Ammit moved forward and clasped hands with his friends. The three kings focused on Radek, blocking everything else from their minds.

* * * *

Alex leaped onto a rock and pulled herself up until she was standing face to face with Radek. Only, he wasn't looking at her face. He was still focused on Cornelia. Alex glanced at Dante then shoved Radek, hard. He looked at her in shock then lost his balance and fell to the ground. Alex was on him instantly.

Radek was enraged. How had he not noticed the queen enter his domain? He had the upper hand here and he could finish this war once and for all. The nerve of that woman, coming after him and attacking him while close to a hundred vampires watched in fascination. Radek jumped to his feet and began to fight. He was surprised at his sister's ability. He'd assumed she was weak and would be easily bested. That was not the case. He had to release his grip on the vampire, his daughter, to concentrate on his sister.

* * * *

Morrigan was tired, injured and his spirit was wavering. He'd finally accepted that they were all going to die. He didn't want to die out here in a lonely field in the middle of nowhere, but he knew he was going to. He was just thankful that he had found Nadia when he did. They were a good team and they were going to die together. The knowledge made his heart ache. He had wanted to grow old, have children, enjoy Nadia for centuries if not millennia, but apparently that wasn't what fate had in mind for them. They were all fighting valiantly, but the vampires were crazed. They were in a desperate frenzy to get back to the cave. He'd never seen anything like it. He wished he wasn't seeing it now. They couldn't let them get by, but his men were just as tired as he was. Many of them had serious injuries. They couldn't hold out much longer.

That's when it happened. Instantly, the vampires froze. Right where they were standing, every vampire on the field was as still as a statue. Morrigan looked around, trying to find his father to see if he knew what was going on. He spotted Mason, bloody and tired walking his way.

Progeny

Out of the corner of his eye, he saw Austin. His friend took one step toward Morrigan, then fell to the ground. Morrigan didn't think, he just ran. He reached Austin in seconds and frantically started to run his hands down Austin's body. "Where are you hurt?" He demanded. They needed Alex.

"I'm okay," Austin said, pushing himself up into a sitting position. "I'm just a little weak, loss of blood I think."

Morrigan pulled a chocolate bar from his pocket and shoved it at Austin. "Eat this."

Jackie Cooper looked up when the field went silent. It was an eerie sound. She wasn't sure what to make of it, but she had a desperate need to find her husband. She took flight and landed next to Morrigan seconds later. Austin was injured. Morrigan was frantic and Mason was headed their way. She pushed Morrigan aside and knelt in front of her son's oldest and dearest friend. "You look a little out of it kid. Where are you injured?."

Austin pulled at the side of his shirt and revealed an ugly, deep cut. It was bleeding pretty heavily and Jackie could see the kid was about to pass out. "I don't think that chocolate is going to do this justice. You need stitches. You okay if I take care of this, or do you need a pain killer?"

"Just do it. I'm fine," he said lying back down as his wife, Sherrie dropped down beside him. "Hey, babe," he whispered as he took her hand.

Mason joined the group, decided Austin was going to live and demanded Morrigan's attention. "I know you're worried about him son, but your mother will take care of this. I need you to focus."

Morrigan looked around the field in amazement once again. "Have you ever seen anything like this before?" He asked his father as Travis Monroe and Oberon joined them.

"No," Mason answered, considering.

"Me either," Oberon supplied.

Numair joined the group. "My people want to finish them off. I think I agree with them. If we destroy them while they're...frozen for lack of a better term, it will cut down on casualties to our men."

"No," Mason said immediately. He didn't like it. It seemed dishonorable somehow.

"I agree," Oberon added. "But I do have an idea."

"Tell us," Monroe ordered. He was torn between honor and expediency. Taking out the vampires while they were in this condition would solve their problem. Prior to this development, they were all about to die. He knew that as sure as he was standing here. The others had to know it too. Plus, they were dealing with vampires. Those monsters didn't care about honor when they sent dozens of men to attack a single family. Why should honor apply to them?

Progeny

"We send the women out to collect their weapons," Oberon declared with authority.

"And the men?" Mason asked.

"The men will use whatever they can find to tie the vampires up. We need to make sure if they awaken they are no longer able to fight. Tie them to a tree, to another vampire by their feet, whatever. Just make sure they are no longer a threat to us when this spell wears off."

Nadia stepped forward. "I'll get Sherrie and we'll start to spread the word."

Morrigan grabbed her and pressed his lips to hers. At first it was gentle, then it became deep and urgent. "Be careful. We don't know how long this is going to last."

"That goes for you, too," she said before she turned and motioned for Sherrie to join her.

The women got busy collecting the weapons and storing them in a pile away from the battlefield. They were close enough someone could guard them if the fighting started up again. The men secured the vampires as quickly and efficiently as possible. They got lucky, most of the vampires were men and as such, they were wearing pants with belts. It was fairly quick and easy to pull the belts from the straps and secure the vampires. They worked together, battle weary and apprehensive. The vampires could come back to life at any minute

* * * *

The instant Radek released his daughter, his body became frozen. He couldn't move, he couldn't fight, he couldn't do anything but swivel his head. Had his daughter done this to him? Was she that strong? No, he didn't want to believe that. If she could control him, their partnership would never be possible. He could not work with a woman that was stronger than he was. The air was knocked out of him and he gasped for breath when Alex kicked him in the chest. The impact knocked him to the ground. He still couldn't move his body but Alex had stopped her attack, weak thing that she was. You better believe if the tables were turned, Alex would be dead already. He would have taken advantage of the situation and eliminated her once and for all. He tried to concentrate. Tried to force his limbs to obey him, but no matter how hard he tried he couldn't move. That's when he felt them, the three kings. Had they come back to finish him off like they had warned? But if that's what they planned why was he still alive? He slowly raised his head, searching. They were on the balcony. The three of them, flanked by their three toughest soldiers.

For the first time, Radek glanced around the room. All the warriors were here, as well as what Radek assumed were their women. He wondered why his men hadn't reacted. He'd given them specific orders that if anything happened to him they were to attack. It took him a minute, but he realized they were all frozen too. "What have you done?" he demanded, looking toward the balcony.

Progeny

"We had no choice," Maedoc said casually. "Something very precious to us was about to be destroyed. We had to stop them."

"Stop who?" Radek raged. "Look around you, the warriors and the fae queen now have the upper hand. You are going to get us all killed. Release me at once."

Ammit was surprised at how easy it was to manipulate Radek's mind. All this time they believed he was a strong ancient that should be watched closely. In reality, he was a weak coward. It was hard to believe this man was even an ancient. He was a little crazy, but not as far gone as his father had been. There might have been hope for Radek if he hadn't believed in fantasies. His obsession with having an heir that could shift was making him mad. This war with the fae was putting all of them at risk. It couldn't continue.

Typhon was growing bored with all of this. Radek wasn't a mighty force to be carefully watched and controlled. He was weak and delusional. Why not experiment while he was in here? Typhon began to search Radek's mind. With this mind control technique, three against one, it was so very easy. He found the memory of the fae woman, kidnapped, locked in a cell, only to be taken out when Radek chose to have her, by force. This angered Typhon. He believed women were objects to be worshiped. They brought a man such pleasure after all. Then he saw how the woman had escaped. She was a clever little one, that one. He glanced at the vampire woman in the corner. She was in control now as she studied her father. Yes, it was true. Radek was her father.

Typhon wondered if he could get into that mind of hers. If he could see what made her tick. He had to try.

The headache erupted in Cornelia's brain instantly. Someone was trying to get into her thoughts. She fought the intrusion with everything she had. The pain intensified. Her hands immediately flew to the side of her head, trying to somehow block out the pressure. No luck, but she didn't stop resisting, nobody was getting inside her head and that included her father. She assumed he was the one attempting the intrusion and she pushed back. Two could play at this game.

Dante panicked. What was Radek doing now? "Corrie?" He said pulling her into his arms. He could see she was in pain and he had no idea how to stop it. He tried rubbing her temples but that didn't seem to help. He pressed Cornelia against the cold rock doing his best to shield her with his body. That didn't seem to help either. He began running soft kisses over her face, her neck, her lips. All the while massaging his fingers through her hair. It was killing him to stand here and watch her in pain. "Alex, can you do something?"

Alex wasn't sure what was happening at first, but then she figured it out. It wasn't Radek, it was the three men standing above them. "Stop it," she demanded. The men ignored her. Alex glanced at Abby then back to the men.

Abby didn't hesitate, Cornelia was in trouble. She shifted into a pterodactyl again, lifting Thomas off the ground with her as she flew to the balcony. She was relieved to see Kylee had done the same. She and Bastian landed on the opposite side of the balcony less than a second after Abby and Thomas. Bastian grabbed one large guard around the neck, Thomas did the same with another one. Kylee and Abby moved to the center to deal with the last one together. The three kings stood, a little surprised by the quick response. Gallo, Trumack and Alastar were completely useless. One wrong move and they would be lost forever.

"We mean no harm," Maedoc said. "Tell them not to hurt our men," he was speaking to Alex and nobody else.

Alex glared at them, then slowly glanced at Cornelia then back to the man who was speaking. Her message was clear.

"Typhon," Maedoc said impatiently. "Unless you want to get us all killed, I suggest you cease and desist immediately."

Typhon shrugged and released the woman. He wasn't getting anywhere with her anyway, which fascinated him. When was the last time anything had fascinated him? So long ago, he couldn't even remember.

Cornelia was released so quickly she almost stumbled to the ground. The only thing that stopped her from falling was Dante's big arms wrapped around her protectively. How she loved this man. She rested her head on his muscular chest and considered what she had learned. The man was trying to enter her mind, but she had been pressing back so hard that when he released her, she had gotten a glimpse into his. They wanted Radek dead and they needed a key. That was why these men were here. She might be able to use that knowledge to their advantage.

"Now it's your turn," Maedoc demanded of Alex. "Typhon released the woman, now you order these fighters to spare my men."

"I'm not sure you are in a position to make demands," Alex said evenly. But she gave Thomas then Bastian a slight nod. She felt Dimitri move in next to her and took his hand. "Who are you?" She demanded. "And why are you here?" She looked at the one called Typhon. "I know you are not from New York. Not dressed like that. I'd say the jungle somewhere." She turned to face the dark skinned man standing next to him. "And you are most likely from the Middle East somewhere. You are dressed like an Egyptian I would guess." She turned back to the man who had been addressing her. "I'm not sure about you, I think you could be from anywhere."

"Ireland," Victor supplied. "He is from Ireland."

Maedoc shifted his gaze to the large warrior and frowned. Did he know this man? He couldn't recall ever having an encounter with him. So how did the warrior know who he was? "Do I know you?"

"Obviously not, or you wouldn't have to ask," Victor said as he and Ariel moved in next to Alex. "But I know you," Victor told him casually. "I witnessed an encounter with you and Queen Elizabeth some time ago."

"Ahhh," Maedoc said in amazement. "You must be the notorious warrior, Victor. The youngest son's sidekick

Progeny

I presume," Maedoc wouldn't let it show, but he was honored to meet the man. He had such a reputation among his people. A man nobody would dare mess with. And here he was, standing before Maedoc valiantly protecting his queen. Wait, wasn't Elizabeth his queen? "But what of Elizabeth, did you two have a falling out?"

"I guess you have heard of me," Victor said amused. He and Tony had made sure the vampires in Ireland feared the royal family and the repercussion they would face for misbehaving. They were especially persuasive after a small group of vamps were found tormenting a young girl from a nearby village. Tony was going to be so bummed that he'd missed this encounter.

"It is an honor to finally meet you in person," Maedoc said. He wouldn't show weakness, but it wouldn't hurt to show a little respect.

"Can't say I feel the same under the circumstances," Victor grumbled.

Ammit and Typhon had also heard the rumors of the mighty warrior, Victor. They were just as star struck as Maedoc to see the man standing before them. If even half the stories were true, they could all be in trouble. They would need to tread lightly if they wanted to get out of this alive.

"So," Alex continued. "We have a vampire from Ireland, one from Egypt and one from the jungle with us here today. To what do we owe this honor? Did you travel all the way to New York to ensure Radek won this pathetic war?"

"No." All three men said at once. Then they glanced at each other and paused.

"I am from the Amazon," Typhon corrected. "And we are here for two reasons. Neither one is to help Radek win this war."

"So, what are they?" Alex demanded, growing impatient with these three. They only answered a direct question and never elaborated. She was afraid this might be a long negotiation and only hoped the group outside was doing okay.

"Our first objective is to retrieve something that was stolen from me. Something very valuable to my people. Lilith is in possession of this item right now, which is why our two men are trying to get to her. I'm afraid you are misreading the situation. Sammael and Martinez are not trying to aid Lilith in her fight with the female. They are trying to get to my property before it is destroyed," Typhon assured Alex.

Lilith glanced at the key hanging from her neck. Had Felix stolen it from King Typhon then put her in danger by giving it to her? And what did the key open? She'd been wondering that ever since Felix entrusted her with it and told her never to let it out of her sight. If the man wasn't already dead, she'd kill him herself. Not for giving her the key, but for failing to warn her of the dangers. And did that man just say Sammael, the loyal weakling Radek trusted so implicitly, was his man? She knew that weasel couldn't be trusted.

Progeny

"I would ask, in the interest of justice of course, that you let my men reclaim my property. Once we have it, I assure you, we will not interfere with your plan to kill Radek or the traitor Lilith," Typhon continued.

Sam saw Lilith cringe and smiled. She was terrified of one of the men up there, maybe all of them. If Sam had to guess, they were all kings too. Did they really just want whatever Lilith had hanging around her neck, or did they want Lilith? Sam would never let that happen. Lilith was hers, and the vampire was going to die tonight.

Lilith spoke up, clearly trying to manipulate the situation to her advantage. "Your majesty. I can only assume you are searching for this key. A token that a man I once thought I knew gave me. I thought he was giving it to me out of love. Apparently, he betrayed my trust. Had I known it belonged to you, I would have returned it immediately," she lied, giving the Amazon a very seductive smile. "I'm more than happy to give it to you now," she glanced pointedly at Sam. "In return, I hope you will demand my safe release. If this key is truly valuable to you and your people, the least you could do is assure my safe passage from this precarious situation as a reward for its safe return."

Maedoc, not Typhon answered Lilith's request. "Typhon might be willing to grant you safe passage for the return of his property, but I am not. There is the little matter of my nephew that needs to be addressed. He is still devastated by your betrayal. His family has forgiven him of course, but I will never forgive you. I think you are exactly where you need to be at the moment. Fight your way out of this or die trying," he continued to glare for several seconds before he returned his focus to Alex.

Ty saw the defeat in Lilith's face. While the kings were preoccupied with Alex he knew he could move in, remove the key, then let Sam finish her off. His timing had to be perfect, but he was confident he could pull it off. Only the two vampires guarding Lilith were still mobile. He took one small tentative step to the left then moved in, snatched the chain and tugged. The thing easily tumbled into his hand and he took a meaningful step backward. The two men were now staring at him. Clearly they wanted to rush in and grab the key, but they were hesitant to do so.

Typhon laughed. "Well now, it looks like one of your men just solved our first dilemma," he turned to face the other kings. "Let us release the hold we have on Lilith and let the fighting resume. My money is on the young warrior. I can see the passion in her eyes. Whatever is driving that fire will be motivation enough to end this quickly."

Maedoc looked at Alex. "Do you have any objection to Typhon's request? The key is secure and the woman's mate is standing guard. He could provide reinforcements if necessary. Can the fight between the condemned Lilith and your girl resume?"

Alex glanced at Sam, who gave a slight nod, then turned back to the kings. "How do I know this is not a trap? If Lilith dies, you will be losing one of your own. It would be easy to convince the vampires in this room that Lilith's death must be avenged."

Progeny

"That would be true if she was one of us," Ammit spoke. "She is not. She is a traitor who took Maedoc's nephew's innocence and left him heartbroken when she discovered she could not access his riches or the family's power. She also possessed stolen property that is valuable beyond measure to its owner. Lilith is not one of us and therefore will not be avenged."

"She is mine," Radek bellowed, frustrated with the way things were progressing. "I will avenge her."

Ammit laughed. "You will be dead. I'd like to see you avenge anyone from the grave."

"You underestimate me, brothers," Radek sounded more confident than he was. "I plan to win this battle with my sister."

"Well, that's a nice plan," Ammit continued. "However, there is that little warning we gave you. If somehow you are able to kill the queen, which I highly doubt, you will still have to face our wrath. You will not survive that, I am quite confident."

Alex hesitated, wondering if this was a delay tactic. One designed to give the vampires outside an advantage. She turned to ask Dimitri his thoughts when she saw Oberon, Mason Cooper and Travis Monroe enter the room. They glanced around quickly then moved to her side.

"I see whatever has the vampires outside in its grips also has taken hold of the vampires in here," Oberon said to Alex. "Any idea what it is?"

"You mean who," she corrected and pointed to the three kings.

Mason saw his daughter and reacted. He shifted into a dragonfly and landed on the balcony. Within seconds, he had the third man in the same choke hold Thomas and Bastian had on the other two. His left arm was around the man's neck, his dagger pressed against his side. One wrong move and the vampire would be dust.

Maedoc scowled, then turned back to Alex. "You are not playing fair dear queen."

Alex shrugged then turned to Oberon, "The battle has stopped then?" She had to be sure.

"Yes," he assured her. "And even if the vampires are released, they have been taken care of. The battle will not resume, I assure you," Oberon looked around the cave. "I can't say the same for in here." Suddenly, his attention was focused on his daughter, then her immediate surroundings looking for answers. For some reason, a ball of fire had just flown from Ariel's fingertips, barely missing the wild looking vampire on the balcony.

Ariel smiled. "Watch your back, Kylee. Typhon is getting bold."

Typhon grinned at the fae woman. "Amazing," he whispered. "Simply amazing. No wonder Radek could not defeat this group. There are so many anomalies, it's hard to keep track."

Progeny

"Typhon, I swear if you get me killed I'll come back and slaughter you from the grave," Maedoc grumbled.

"Stop this recklessness," Ammit chimed in. "We are trying to negotiate our safety, not enrage this group of fighters."

"Sorry. I was just curious," Typhon said with a shrug. "It's been a long time since something has intrigued me. Life gets boring after so many years."

Maedoc glared at his friend. "Well, stifle your curiosity before I do it for you."

Typhon laughed. "Lighten up, dear friend. They are not going to kill us. If they were, the fire thrower would have aimed for my chest, not my hand," he turned toward Ariel. "Isn't that right, beautiful myrmidon?"

Ariel laughed. "I'm not Greek and I had nothing to do with the Trojan War. So, I can only assume you believe I am a loyal follower," Ariel shrugged. "I guess I would carry out any order Alex gave, but most of the time I act as I see fit. The name's more wrong than right, I think...but it will do."

Typhon laughed. "Beautiful, lethal and smart. My kind of woman," he sobered when he heard the growl coming from the mighty warrior named Victor. "I meant no offense," he quickly added, hoping to appease the warrior.

Ariel grinned and slid her hand into Victor's. "He's my hero and protector. He's also my husband. I'd caution you not to make him mad. You wouldn't like him when he's angry," she mimicked the movie the Hulk, but didn't expect any of the kings to understand.

Typhon surprised her. "He may look a little green, but I highly doubt he could grow any bigger my dear. However, I will apologize once again. I meant no offense. You are a lucky man."

Victor looked at Ariel and smiled. "You have no idea," he said brushing a tender kiss across her lips.

Ammit was intrigued. It seemed this group of mighty fighters, were willing to act at a moment's notice, but when it came to their mates they were soft-hearted, tender and extremely protective. He'd never seen anything quite like it. Maybe they could play on that somehow. If they found the right angle, they just might be able to escape with their lives.

"So," Alex reclaimed the conversation. "What is the second reason you are here?"

"To ensure Radek's death," Ammit said with authority.

Radek lost it then. Ranting and raving about the injustice and how these three kings should have stayed in their own countries. He went on and on until the kings couldn't take it any longer. They shut his mouth by force, freezing his head the same way they had frozen his body.

"Thank you," Thomas said behind them. "I'd had about all of that I could take."

591

Progeny

"Just so I'm clear," Alex began. "You want us to believe you traveled all the way here to retrieve a key and ensure that Radek was killed in this battle? Why? Why would you want a fellow king killed by his enemies?"

The whole room went quiet when Ty slammed a vampire to the ground.

Maedoc sighed. "Martinez, what in the world were you thinking?"

"I thought I could get the key while he wasn't paying attention," Martinez shrugged, but it took effort since Ty still had him pinned to the ground. "I guess I was wrong."

Cornelia took Dante's hand and stepped forward. "If it helps, I can confirm that is what they came for. While that man was trying to enter my mind, I was able to push back. When he finally released me, I got a glimpse of his mission. They desperately need that key. It provides access to some kind of vault. And they want Radek to die. Only..." she paused and looked at Alex and then Dante. "They want me to do it." She turned her attention to the balcony. "Why is that important? I sensed it was very important that it was me, not Alex that killed my father."

Lilith's eyes grew wide. Was this vampire Radek's own child? How had he not known? She knew why the kings wanted the offspring to destroy Radek. With that one revelation, all her hopes and dreams flew out the window. She was wasting her time here. She had to find a way to escape this female warrior and flee. Maybe she could go to Canada. DeMarco didn't have anything against her. He'd never met her. Maybe she could hook up with him and be his queen. Clearly her time with Radek had been wasted. But she'd heard rumors that DeMarco was a passionate man. Surely he would welcome another woman into his bed. And in time, she could convince him she was worthy of marriage. It might still be possible to rule her own kingdom, she just had to think. She was clever enough to escape and smart enough to get what she wanted.

"Since you are not vampires, I can understand how you would miss the importance of this moment," Maedoc began. "The girl is correct. We do want her to be the one to eliminate Radek. It is cleaner that way. Before tonight we did not know Radek had a daughter. Our initial plan was to set the stage for you to do it and then do our best to keep the vampires in line. But now?" He turned to face Cornelia. "Now there is another way."

"I still don't understand," Alex admitted. "Explain yourself."

Ammit was the one who responded. "For our people there are only two ways for a king to lose the throne, both require death. The first is for a member of his coven to challenge him to a fight. The one who survives takes the throne. The second is for a member of the king's family to challenge him. This is the best way, but the least common. In most instances, the king has turned many of his subjects. This tie is very strong, the bond between the master, or Dom, and his sub. It can only be broken in death. This is why it is better for a member of the king's family to issue the challenge. Any vampires that were turned by the king could be controlled by his heir as they have blood in common. The transition is immediate. A nonblood

Progeny

member of the coven who issues the challenge would not have this benefit. He would have power over his subjects, but it wouldn't be as strong."

Cornelia was reeling. She could see where the kings were going with this. They wanted her to fight Radek, kill him and then take over as queen of the vamps. She didn't think she could do it. She hated vampires. How could she rule them? She immediately started shaking her head.

"But we are family." Alex countered seeing Cornelia's reaction. "Radek is my half-brother. We share a blood line; wouldn't the tie transfer to me?"

"We do not know," Maedoc admitted. "Which is why we initially planned on setting him up so you could take him out, then remaining in the area to see if you could control the vampires or if we needed to step in. Once we knew the female vampire was working with you, we had hoped she could remain to help."

"I see," Alex said, turning her focus to Cornelia. "How do you feel about all this?" She finally asked.

"No, I can't do it," Cornelia said immediately. "I won't," she turned to face Dante. "You said they wouldn't make me live with the vampires. You promised," she knew she was near hysterics but she didn't care. "I trusted and believed you. You can't let this happen."

"Corrie, sweetheart," he soothed. "Nobody is going to make you do anything you don't want to do. But I think we should consider this."

Cornelia began shaking her head and whispered, "No, no, no."

"Can you give us a minute?" Dante asked Alex. "I'd like to step out in the hallway so we can talk in private."

"Take all the time you need. But before you go, I have something I need to say to Cornelia," she paused waiting for Cornelia to look at her.

Cornelia couldn't speak, she just nodded once in acknowledgment hoping Alex would say whatever she had to say.

"We all love you," Alex said softly. "There is nothing anyone could say or do that would convince me to back on my word. This is your choice, not mine. I would never force you to live with the vampires. Even as queen it would be your choice," Alex glanced at Dante. "In fact, I would insist on finding another way. Dante is too valuable to me as are you. We need you in the city. If you do this, we will figure out a way to make it work. But we will figure it out together. Maybe we could find a liaison. It will be hard to find a vampire we trust, but not impossible. You decide what you think is best, what you can live with. I don't want to influence you too much. However, I do think it would rock if my niece were a queen, too," she smiled, then motioned for Dante to continue out the door.

Cornelia turned to Dante as soon as they stepped from the cave. "Was she serious?" It all seemed so outrageous. "She really wants me to accept this challenge and kill my father?"

Progeny

"I believe she is," Dante said cautiously. "But what really matters is what you want. Think about what she said, though. If you were the Vampire Queen and Alex was the Fae Queen, it would be easier to enact laws to protect our people. The two of you could make history, in a good way."

Cornelia began to pace. Could she do it? Killing her father, sure no problem. But taking over his kingdom and ruling the vampires? Dante had a point. She and Alex could enact laws and rules to protect the fae. They could force the vampires to adhere to those laws or suffer the consequences. If she didn't do this, someone else was going to. Would they be missing out on a unique opportunity? "But that would mean we would have to interact with the vampires," she told Dante. "And yes, I did say we. If I do this, I'm not doing it alone. You are going to have to be by my side the entire time. They will have to learn to respect you as well. Do you think vampires could do that? I can't have you in danger."

"Of course we would do this together," Dante said rolling his eyes. "You think I'd ever let you walk into these caves alone? Silly woman. And as far as respecting me?" He shrugged. "Warriors are part vampire, a small part yes, but still part. And after I slaughter a few that get out of hand, the rest will have to respect me."

Cornelia nodded, still thinking about the possibilities. "I have some questions for the kings." She took a deep breath and smiled at her husband. "Let's go back in, I have a few questions before I agree to this."

"Good girl," Dante said, pulling her close and kissing her quickly. "We can do this. I know we can."

"I'm glad you're so confident because I'm scared shitless," Cornelia stepped back into the room and moved in beside Alex. "Do you have to kill when you feed?" She blurted. Why beat around the bush?

"No," Maedoc answered. "In fact, in Ireland my vampires rarely kill when they feed." He glanced at Victor, the warrior and Prince Anthony were responsible for that particular law. "The same is true for Typhon's followers. There are fewer humans in the Amazon. Most have moved away, migrated to civilization. Typhon has strict laws against killing during feeding."

"So, what is the punishment if they disobey?" She asked Typhon.

"It depends on the situation," he admitted. "Just carelessness or callously disregarding the law is punishable by death. If a vampire comes across a fae and is overcome by the blood lust, we have less permanent punishments. I would be happy to share my laws with you if death is your concern." Typhon glanced at his two friends to make sure they didn't object. When neither said anything he continued. "We would understand the need for strict changes to your laws after the mess Radek has made here. If you are worried about our interference, don't."

"Okay," Cornelia hesitated then continued. "I don't know anything about vampires. I probably shouldn't admit that, but I don't. I was wondering if you could tell me how it all works. I mean Radek was king here, but the three of you stepped in to punish him when he got out of hand. Is that normal? Is there some kind of ruling council that decides when a king should be sanctioned?"

"That is a good question," Ammit answered. "And unfortunately, we cannot give you a direct answer. The quick answer would be no. There is no official ruling body that controls the actions of other kings. However, the three of us as well as your neighbor, DeMarco of Canada, have banned together to try to keep our fellow vampire communities in line. I guess you could say we are a self-appointed ruling body. We have been around for a long time. A threat from one of us would cause alarm. A threat from all of us tends to keep our brothers in line. If you do this thing, if you take care of this problem, we would ask you to join our alliance," he glanced at Typhon and motioned to Martinez.

"Martinez back there is from Mexico," Typhon began. "He has proven himself worthy over the past few months. We will be asking him to return to his home country and rule that region. If he accepts, he will also be invited to join the alliance. I believe the six of us are capable of making sure something like the fiasco here in New York never happens again."

Cornelia's mind was racing. Not only would she rule the vampires here in New York, but this was an opportunity to make a difference worldwide. She turned to face Dante, she couldn't do this without his support. He smiled and gave her a solemn nod of approval. If she chose to do this, he was all in. "Won't the other kings resist? I mean, they're kings. Won't they be angry if they are managed by others?"

"Sure," Typhon said grinning. "That just makes it more fun."

Ammit and Maedoc shook their heads, sure their friend wasn't helping.

"I agree," Cornelia said to Typhon. "Everyone loves a challenge." She turned back to the other two kings. "Release my father. I am challenging him to a duo. Wait," she turned to Sam. "Alex agreed to give up her right to kill Radek herself Sam, but I haven't asked you. He killed your entire family. You have as much right to him as anyone. Are you okay with this, or would you rather take him out yourself?"

Sam slowly walked to the front of the cave. She stopped in front of Radek and just stared at him. *Could she let someone else deal with Radek?* Sam wondered. Revenge had been her only goal for so long. Something inside her shifted. When had her focus changed? When she met Ty, that's when. And suddenly she knew it didn't matter. As long as Radek was dead, it really didn't matter how or who inflicted that final blow. She could give this to Cornelia for the greater good and deep in her heart she knew...she would never have a second thought about this decision. After a moment, she turned back to Cornelia. "He's all yours," she smiled. "As long as I get to take care of Lilith, you can have him," she motioned to Radek with a jerk of her head. "I only have one request."

"Anything," Cornelia agreed.

Progeny

"Make him suffer," Sam said soberly. "Make him suffer for what he did to my family, your mother, Luke and Marlena and all the other casualties of his selfish war. That's all I ask." She started to turn, then looked back at her friend. "And I want to watch."

"It's a deal," Cornelia promised. Then she turned to Alex. "How should we do this? I mean, should we release all the vampires or just Radek?"

"If I may," Maedoc cut in. "We are controlling the rest of the vampires through Radek. If we release him, we release them all. If you want the female warrior to have her shot at Lilith and give her the opportunity to watch the fight between you and your father, we must release her first. Once that fight has concluded, we can release the rest."

"That okay with you, Sam?" Cornelia asked.

"Peachy," Sam agreed. She wasn't thrilled with the idea that the whole world would be watching the battle, but the pressure would keep her focused.

Sammael and Martinez stepped around Ty and moved to Lilith's side. Each one placed a hand under her arm and moved her to the center of the cave. Lilith was ranting the entire time. "I knew you were a traitor Sammael," she spat. "I told Radek not to trust you. The idiot thought you were loyal just because you were weak. I knew better. I told him there was something about you."

The instant Sammael set Lilith down, he turned and punched her in the mouth. "You are the weak one," he said coldly. "I've never had to patch anyone up as frequently as I've healed you. From the holy water to the vampiric animals to the burns. You are a walking catastrophe. You have no idea how many times I wanted to show you my real nature, but I held back. I let you believe I was weak for my king. Now I will watch you slaughtered by the warrior. The only way this day could get any better is if I was able to fight you myself," then he turned and walked away.

The instant Lilith was released, she tried to escape. She turned and bolted for the door, only to be captured by Martinez and hauled back to the center of the cave. He glanced up at the kings then turned to Alex. "This would be easier if the three bodyguards were allowed to block the door."

Mason, Abby and Kylee latched onto the large men, shifted, and landed at the back of the cave. "Try anything and I'll kill you myself," Mason warned. The three nodded to their kings, then took up position.

It was in that instant that Lilith realized she was going to die here tonight. There was no escaping and even if she did, she couldn't go to Canada. DeMarco was clearly in bed with Maedoc, Ammit and Typhon. None of them would let her live after the things she had done. She gave herself a little shake and prepared for battle. Nobody had said what would happen if she won. If she killed this female warrior, Sam, would she be allowed to live? She could always hope. If she fought a fair fight, they had to let her go, right? That was the law of the land.

Progeny

Sam waited, sure Lilith was going to attack. Well, she was going to let her. Lilith would view that as an offensive move, but Sam had a plan. Each time she had battled Lilith, the woman had favored her side. Sam wondered if that was a result of the holy water she'd dumped on the woman or something else. Hadn't the little vampire just said something about vampiric animals? The reason didn't matter, Sam was sure Lilith's side was a weak spot and she was going to exploit it. Lilith came at her with a vengeance, but Sam was ready. She ducked, pivoted and kicked Lilith in the side.

Lilith screamed in pain. One for me, Sam thought as she crouched and prepared for another attack. Lilith didn't come at her head on this time, she stopped a few feet away and darted to the left then swung around and kicked Sam in the back. Sam went down, but it was intentional. The instant her hands hit the ground, she kicked out with both legs connecting with Lilith's right knee. It was a direct hit; the loud crack could even be heard over Lilith's angry scream. Lilith jumped up, but she was limping. She could barely put any weight on her knee. Sam didn't give her a chance to recover. She planted her feet and punched Lilith in the chest. First with her right hand and a second later with her left.

Lilith couldn't get away; she couldn't find a safe place to retreat to catch her breath. Her knee was on fire and she couldn't breathe. Sam was now hitting her in the face. One hard punch after another. Lilith went down, hard. She tried to push her body up but she couldn't put pressure on her knee. Her hands were in front of her, bracing her body up off the floor, she was on one knee, the other leg was spread out straight, her weight pressing on her foot. Sam came from behind and knocked her good leg out from under her. Her weight slammed down, forcing her knee against the hard surface of the cave. She screamed out in agony. This fight wasn't about killing her, it was about payback. Sam was exacting revenge for that night in the forest. The night the warrior should have died.

Sam leaned down and whispered in Lilith's ear. "That was for Dusty."

Dusty? Who was Dusty? Lilith had no idea.

Sam kicked Lilith in the side, she immediately fell to the ground in pain. "That was for Nebi," Sam said, circling the vampire. She kicked Lilith in the other side. "That was for all the shifters injured in that stupid bombing incident last year," she kicked her again. "That was for Victor and Ariel and all the pain you caused them by bombing our celebration," she kicked Lilith in the face. "And that is for my husband, who almost died because of what you did to me in that forest," Sam leaned down and rolled Lilith over. "And this, bitch, this is for me," she plunged her dagger into Lilith's chest and watched silently as her worst enemy dissipated into dust.

Ty was there immediately. Pulling Sam to her feet then crushing her against his chest. "I am so proud of you baby," he said softly in her ear.

Sam smiled up at him. He was proud of her? She was amazed by that. She knew she had been cruel to Lilith, but the woman was responsible for so many tragedies. She was personally responsible for so much pain, so many injuries, so many deaths. She couldn't just kill her, she had to make her pay. At that moment, Sam understood why Thomas had killed Hector in the way that he had. She understood that sometimes death just wasn't enough. Sometimes you had to exact a little pain, it was the only way for justice to prevail.

Ty tore off a piece of his shirt and pressed it to Sam's temple. He didn't think she even knew she was bleeding. Standing there, watching her battle with Lilith was the hardest thing he had ever done. He wanted to step in and kill the evil vampire himself. Lilith had tortured Sam almost to death, almost killed Victor, injured so many shifters. She was the one who had planted all those bombs he'd had to deactivate. She was the one that had taken Dusty's leg. Sam had exacted revenge for all of it. He was so proud of his wife and just wanted to take her home and pamper her. But, this wasn't over. Not until Radek had been dealt with. Once Cornelia battled that evil monster, they still had to hammer things out with the three stooges on the balcony. Ty didn't think he would be needed for that. Hopefully, he could just take Samantha home and deal with the rest in the morning.

Dante was nervous. Cornelia was good, she was better than good, but she was also dealing with some pretty big baggage. He wondered how she was going to feel about killing her father. He thought about his own sorry excuse for a dad and knew he couldn't do it. No matter how bad his father was, he couldn't be responsible for his death. That was a second reason he hadn't let Nick kill the guy all those years ago. It was 99% to save Nick from the consequences and 1% because he didn't really want his father dead.

But Cornelia was going to do this. He didn't know all her reasons, but she would do it for the community, she would do it for her mother, she would do it for him and an Aunt that she was just barely getting to know. Dante was pretty sure once it was done, she wouldn't look back. They might have a few bad moments, times when Cornelia questioned her actions, but he didn't think they would last. That was just the type of girl his Corrie was. He knew she'd been serious when she'd offered to head over to Carlos Santora's and take him out. To exact revenge for the wrongs committed against Dante years ago. She would do the same with her father, exact revenge for the horrific wrong committed against her mother centuries ago. Then it would be finished.

Cornelia turned to Alex. "This isn't right," she finally said. "We are a democratic society, so are the shifters. I can't just exact Radek's punishment because those three kings say so. Shouldn't we imprison him? Have a trial, then if he is sentenced to death I can do it?"

Alex looked to Oberon, then Mason and Travis. "It's your call," she finally told them. "Cornelia has a point. There are many communities that should have a say in this. Numair should have a vote. We are a democratic society. Let's not forget that just because we are at war."

Mason Cooper and Travis Monroe had a brief conversation. "We do not want to wait," Travis finally answered. "But we are willing to move this to the battlefield. We will secure Radek and move him outside.

Progeny

Once there, Mason, Numair, Oberon you, Alex, and I will all have one vote. We will determine his fate tonight. This has to end, and I for one am not willing to risk that man's escape."

"I agree," Oberon said, nodding to Alex.

"That sounds like a good compromise," Alex agreed. She turned to the three kings, "Release him. We will be moving this discussion to the fields and Radek needs to be more than physically present when we decide his fate. He needs to be aware of his surroundings."

The kings released Radek and the rest of the vampires began to move around. Dimitri ordered his men to get into position. They needed to be ready if this was a trap. That's when the world erupted. The vampires flew forward in a massive attack. Radek must have given them a silent command to fight.

* * * *

Morrigan straightened and watched as the vampires came alive at once. They were fighting against the bands that held them in place. "Be prepared," he called out to the group. "If any of them get free we will be forced to fight."

Most of the bands held, a few vampires were able to get loose. The group was tired and worn out but still alert enough to take out the few vampires that were intent on fighting to the death.

Thomas was trapped on the balcony with the three kings. He wondered if they knew what was going to happen the instant they released Radek. Probably, they had been occupying his mind all this time. He searched the crowd below until he spotted Abby. Once their eyes met, he climbed onto the railing and fell backward into the crowd. Abby was there to catch him. She had shifted into a large gorilla and held out her hands. He landed with ease, cradled like a child. Then, Abby lowered him to the ground and shifted back to a woman.

Typhon couldn't take his eyes off the battle. His head was moving around so quickly he was starting to feel dizzy. "Amazing," he said in awe, "they are all so amazing," he glanced to his left as an enormous mountain lion landed with ease onto the balcony. The remaining warrior climbed onto its back and the two gracefully retreated the way the large cat had come, bouncing with ease from rock surface-to-surface until it reached the safety of the ground. Then the woman shifted again and the two joined the fight.

Bastian climbed from Kylee's back and instantly joined the battle. His woman wasn't as theatrical as Abby Cooper, but she was just as effective. Kylee returned to her normal form and joined the chaos. These vampires had to be Radek's best. They were larger than the vampires out on the field and clearly older as well. All of them were seasoned fighters.

"I think you are drooling," Maedoc said to Typhon as the three kings continued to watch the battle.

Progeny

"Probably," Typhon said, studying Cornelia as she circled Radek. "I can see why Radek was losing this war. The fire thrower can take out five or six of our kind with the flick of her wrist. And look at the warrior, Victor. The stories about him were not figments of the imagination. He is a mighty warrior and nobody I would care to tangle with."

Ammit spoke softly so only his friends could hear. "You do realize an alliance with these people is essential for our very existence?" He watched as the warrior who had killed Lilith took out three more vampires, her mate by her side taking out five. "We would never win a battle against them. There is not a big enough army to defeat them."

"I agree," Maedoc said to his friends. "It is even more essential that Cornelia kills Radek. It is the only way. Once she is one of us, she will be less likely to obliterate us. We are not like Radek. We certainly are nothing like his father, Balthazar. Cornelia must join us so she can see, we are not all that different from them. We are simply another species. True, if our kind is allowed to run amok, function without rules and laws, we are more likely to get out of control than others, but that is the exception, not the rule. We must show her our good side. We must show her our kind can live among the humans and the fae without bloodshed and violence."

"That is an ironic statement, my friend," Ammit said soberly. "Considering the battle that is raging below us," he watched as Gallo, Trumack and Alastar joined in the fight, taking out any vampire that attempted to leave the room. The three kings watched as Cornelia continued to circle her father.

Cornelia hadn't wanted things to turn out this way. "What have I done?" She asked no one in particular.

Dante moved in closer and answered anyway. "Not you, him," he said motioning to Radek. "He did this, but you can stop it," he pivoted, twisted and sliced through another vampire. "Go take care of him and all of this will stop. He's the one controlling them," Dante moved to the side to block two more vampires from getting to Cornelia.

Cornelia continued to watch Radek. Dante was right, of course. Radek was giving the orders. If she took him out, maybe the battle would end. She took one step forward, waiting, anticipating, calculating her response. She knew Radek was going to attack. He believed himself a better fighter, and maybe he was. *But, I'm smarter*, she assured herself. She was prepared when Radek attacked. He rushed forward, his black robe billowing behind him. Cornelia waited, calculated, then at the last minute ducked and rolled. She used her dagger to slice across the back of Radek's shin as she went down.

Radek winced at the pain but refused to acknowledge it. He practiced fighting every day with a different vampire. He could win this, sure his men never actually hurt him, but so what. The principles were the same. The moves were the same. He was going to win.

Cornelia watched Radek as he calculated his next move. She was surprised at how cocky and self-assured he was under the circumstances. He was now injured, she was

Progeny

not. Training and practice were far different than an actual battle. He had to know that. Or, maybe he didn't. Maybe he believed that training was enough. Cornelia knew better, though. In battle, there were injuries. Agonizing pain that you had to work through if you were going to survive. She was more than happy to teach Radek that lesson. He came at her from the side this time. She hadn't been ready for that and was late getting out of the way. Radek's elbow collided with her cheekbone and the pain brought tears to her eyes. She worked through it. Stretching out and snatching Radek's knife right out of his hand. Radek kicked her legs out from under her. As she went down, she pivoted, reached out and drove the knife straight through Radek's left foot. Then she rolled in the opposite direction. Once she reached the wall, she jumped to her feet in one fluid motion ready to resume the fight.

Radek roared in surprise, he was in so much pain. His daughter was quick, a very worthy opponent. He hadn't seen that one coming. He bent down and yanked the knife from his foot, forcing his mind to ignore the ache and throbbing that followed. If he kept telling himself he wasn't in pain, maybe he could forget his injuries and move on. He was amazed at how much he was craving a drunk. Just one hit of the alcohol saturated blood would relax him enough to get through this fight.

Cornelia studied Radek, he was in more pain than she was, but not enough. She needed to give him a more significant wound, one that would incapacitate him. It was the only way she'd be able to get close enough to reach his cold, black heart. Radek chose a head on attack this time. He came barreling forward, counting on his large stature to

610

give him an advantage. Cornelia had dealt with men like this before. More often than she cared to admit. It was the price of choosing a career as a private investigator. He didn't know it, but that was the worst thing he could have done. She stood her ground, waiting, waiting, then at the last minute, she ducked and pivoted, reaching back and slicing a large gash across his shoulder blades. The wound was deep and had to be painful.

Radek fell backward and collided with the stone wall. His head hit a rock with such force he nearly blacked out. But he had to hold on. The minute he let himself go unconscious, was the minute he died. He held onto the wall for support as he considered his next move. His robe was a mess, he impatiently shoved it off and stumbled toward his daughter again. He had to admit she was a worthy adversary. He smiled. Tonight he was wearing black Levi's and a long sleeved, dark turtleneck underneath his robe. Normally, he would have been naked. He wondered what kind of reaction that would have gotten from his daughter. Would she have been able to continue the fight, or would it have stirred her sensual desires to the point she was unable to continue? Changing her passion for the fight to a passion of another kind. Too bad he wouldn't find out. His dream of having her as a mate had been short-lived. Tonight, one of them was going to die. He was determined to make sure it was her.

Radek straightened and went after Cornelia again. This time he paused, shifted and came at her from the left. She anticipated that move and pivoted, ducked and swung back around, her knife slicing deeply across his stomach. Cornelia didn't hesitate, she gripped a protruding rock and

Progeny

swung her legs around, colliding with Radek's knee. She heard the bone crushing sound of his kneecap shattering as her hand slipped and she fell on her butt.

She stood, pretending the impact hadn't rattled her hip bone. She was definitely going to have a bruise from that one. "Had enough yet, old man?" Cornelia asked. She was breathing hard and hoped to infuriate him enough to make a mistake. He was a good fighter and she had to stay on her toes but she was still confident she could win. At what cost was the only question. She had an idea. Most likely one that was going to hurt. One that would certainly piss Dante off, but one she had to try. Her friends were out there fighting for their lives. She had to end this. She had to get in close enough to finish the job.

The arrogance of the little imp, Radek thought angrier than he'd been in years. The woman was flaunting her abilities. Radek smiled, surprised by the pride he felt in his daughter. Then it hit him. He was the one that would die in this fight. His offspring had more practice than he did. His child would win. She would take over his kingdom. All was not lost. His heir would take his place. His dynasty would continue on. His progeny would rule the world just as he'd hoped. Sure, he'd believed it would be a son, but a daughter would do. His blood, his father's blood would continue to rule his people. This legacy... his legacy, would continue on through his descendants. First through his daughter, then her children and so on. If his life had to end to make this happen, then he was okay with that. He would live on forever, through Cornelia the Queen of his vampires. He smiled, that didn't mean he was going to make it easy for her. He stood, bent at the waist and charged.

Cornelia saw Radek coming and knew this was her chance. She might get injured, who was she kidding, she was going to get injured. But if she aimed just right the fight, the war, would be over. As she stood there, waiting, watching, anticipating she thought of Dante. They had come so far, she hoped she wasn't making a deadly mistake. Dante needed her. That was the most amazing part of all of this, having a warrior of such strength in body, mind and character need her. She couldn't die, she had to be smarter than Radek, that was all there was to it. As the blade sliced through her left shoulder, Cornelia gritted her teeth. She had to ignore the pain. Then she grabbed Radek by the shoulder and plunged her knife through his chest cavity. She saw the shock on his face an instant before he disappeared. Dust settled onto the cold rock beneath them and an eerie silence filled the room.

Chapter Twenty Two

Cornelia felt it the instant Radek turned to ashes. A shifting, or expanding rather in her brain. She turned to face her friends and the other vampires still left in the room. Her eyes widened and she let out a horrified scream. "Noooo!"

Alex saw the instant Cornelia killed Radek. She was relieved. Maybe now this war would be over. She shifted and ducked as a vampire came at her from the side. She didn't see the one coming at her from behind. She looked at Cornelia in confusion as her niece let out a blood-curdling yell.

Dimitri was fighting off three vampires; as he turned, he saw Alex take on a vampire approaching from the side. He knew she didn't see the one racing toward her from the rear. He was too far away to do anything but watch in horror as the vampire got closer and closer to the only woman he'd ever loved.

Sammael slowly moved through the shadows, stalking Dingo's every move. It was going to be so satisfying to take that sadistic prick out. The guy had criticized, tormented and humiliated Sammael at every opportunity. He slid closer to the rock and pounced, taking Dingo by surprise. He only had a second to revel in the feeling of besting one of his many adversaries when he spotted Titus. He had that gleam in his eye, the one that always meant trouble. Sammael slowly, stealthily moved in behind him and waited. Who was his target? Titus gave it away almost instantly. Alex, the Fae Queen. Sammael would not let that happen. She had saved his life; sure, it was because he had saved hers but that didn't matter, not to him. As Titus moved forward, Sammael moved with him. Finally he was in reach, but so was the queen. Just as he was about to take out Titus, the vampire raised his arm and lunged forward. Everything seemed to happen in slow motion for Sammael. Titus lunged, the queen pivoted to take out another vampire, moving her body closer to Titus and his knife. Cornelia, the new queen screamed and he only had an instant to tackle Titus and plunge his knife upwards into the wide, muscular chest of another nemesis, Titus the fool. Before Titus dissipated, his knife connected with the queen's leg. Blood trickled across her shoe and landed on the slick ground. Nobody moved.

"Stop," Cornelia yelled. "These are my friends. Stop this fighting at once," she glared at the vampires, daring just one of them to disobey her order. Not one of them did, they all froze in place unwilling to make a move for fear of the consequences. "Look around you," Cornelia ordered. The vampires ignored this command and continued to stare at the floor. "Look," she screamed when none of them obeyed. "These warriors, the fae, the shifters, everyone in this room is off limits to you. You will not hurt one hair on their heads or you will answer to me, do you understand?" Nothing. "Nod your heads if you understand."

The vampires glared at Cornelia but in unison, they all nodded once then looked at the ground. Clearly they were not happy with their new Queen. "Well, that's just too bad," Cornelia mumbled under her breath. She rushed to Alex and grabbed her hands. "Are you okay?"

"Thanks to this little guy, again," Alex said, smiling down at the tiny, but vigilant vampire. "Sammael I presume?"

"Yes, ma'am," he said with a smile.

"Thank you," Alex said sincerely. "That's twice you have saved my life tonight. I will never forget it," she looked back at the three kings. "We are finished for tonight. We will meet back here tomorrow at sunset to discuss the future of our people, the vampires and that key you so desperately need." Alex leaned back as Dimitri moved in behind her and placed his hands on her hips. "Until tomorrow gentlemen," then she turned and led her people out of the cave.

"But..." Alex heard Ammit's voice trail off as she hastily walked out into the darkness toward the battlefield.

Once they were a safe distance away from the cave she turned. "Does anyone need medical attention?"

"Bastian's bleeding, but he's trying to be all manly about it," Kylee told her. Alex was by his side in an instant, healing the deep cut to Bastian's stomach.

"Anyone else?" She asked. "If I find out any one of you had a wound that you didn't let me heal, I promise there will be consequences."

Sam moved forward and let Alex heal her head wound. Victor had a large gash on his back and Dimitri had a fairly deep wound on his right bicep. Alex shifted her attention to Travis Monroe. Then raised her eyebrows as he looked away. She slowly walked towards him, stopping directly in front of his large body. "Where is it?" She demanded. Monroe gave her his most intimidating glare, but she wasn't fazed a bit. "Where?" She asked again.

"It's just a surface wound, nothing that won't heal on its own in time," he shrugged and started to move around her.

Alex wasn't having any of it. She grabbed Monroe's arm and pulled him into the trees. "Where?" She asked as she closed her eyes and surveyed every facet of his body. When she found it, she grinned.

"It's not funny," he grumbled but was relieved when the stinging pain just beneath his right buttock disappeared completely.

Progeny

"Sure it is, but your secret is safe with me. You can be a pain in the butt sometimes, but you shouldn't have to suffer from one," Alex said, still grinning. Men were so difficult sometimes.

As the group entered the field, Alex went to work. There were so many injured. Jackie and Tianna were still in the upper field, stitching and bandaging as quickly but efficiently as possible. Jackie looked up and saw Alex approach. "Thank goodness," she said, letting out a long breath. "Some of these are bad," she admitted. "The worst are over there. We've tried to keep them in groups hoping you would return in time to take care of them."

Alex rushed to the large row of men and women lying motionless on the ground. She knelt down and began to heal them one by one.

* * * *

The following evening Cornelia, Dante, Alex, Dimitri, Oberon, Mason Cooper, Travis Monroe and Numair entered the cave in search of the kings. They were a little surprised when they rounded a corner and spotted Sammael. He was apparently their escort this evening. The group was taken to a large room. Inside were the three kings, Martinez and a fifth man sitting at a long table. Maedoc motioned for the group to sit.

"Are we holding council?" Cornelia asked. "I'm surprised I wasn't invited."

"You were," Maedoc said without emotion. "Did you think we didn't know the queen would bring you tonight?"

Cornelia shrugged and took a seat, Dante settled in next to her. "Are we negotiating terms then?"

"We hope that is not necessary," Ammit cut in. "Our requests are simple. First, Typhon's key must be returned. That is not negotiable. Everything else is up for discussion."

Alex began to turn the key in her hand. "Cornelia told us that this key opens some sort of vault, but I still don't get why it is so valuable to you."

"We are not at liberty to discuss that," Ammit said, clearly annoyed.

"Then I am not at liberty to return it," Alex said just as coldly.

"Alex," Typhon paused. "May I call you Alex?"

"Sure," she said casually. She actually could grow to like this king. Ammit, not so much. The verdict was still out on Maedoc.

"Alex," Typhon continued. "The key opens an ancient vault. One located in a secret area of my kingdom. It was stolen from a trusted friend of mine, who was killed by a man who betrayed me. This man was working with Lilith. I cannot go into detail with regard to what is in the vault. It would be fatal to my current guard if word got out about its contents. What I can tell you, what is common knowledge among our people, is that the vault contains our history. Ancient vampires many, many millennia ago came together. They realized there was a need to pass down information, history, ancient discoveries to their descendants. They also realized that this information, in the wrong hands could be devastating to our people and others. Therefore, it was divided into three sections. Each king would take a third of the knowledge and secure it in a specially made vault. That key opens one of the vaults. It is so complex, it cannot be duplicated."

"Is that where Radek got his knowledge to murder my mother?" Alex asked, not sure she wanted them to have access to that kind of knowledge.

"No," Maedoc assured her. "It is true that we do have some information regarding your kind in the vaults, but that information is limited and speculative at best. The information Typhon described pertains to our people. Knowledge about healing certain types of wounds, certain plants that are harmful to our species, things like that."

"Why wouldn't you want that kind of information readily available to all your people?" Alex asked, truly not understanding. Was it just about control and power?

"The healing remedies would be fine. It is the harmful substances that we need to guard and protect," Maedoc explained. "Can you imagine what Radek or his crazy father, Balthazar might have done if they knew a certain kind of plant, placed in a certain liquid would kill another king instantly? It is because of men like those two we must keep this information guarded. We have researched the remedies. In fact, Sammael has a unique fascination with the books and knows more cures for our ailments than any other vampire I know."

Ammit cast a proud look Sammael's way. "Sammael is a very dear friend of mine. He spent years studying the books in my vault, then requested permission to visit Maedoc here. He again spent years studying the materials in his vault. He has not yet had the opportunity to visit the vault in Typhon's region. Radek's war took him away. I know he would like that opportunity someday. An opportunity that can only be achieved if you are willing to return Typhon's rightful property."

"Sammael?" Alex called out. "In addition to cures, can I assume you have read about the toxins? You have the knowledge to kill a vampire if you wish?"

"Uh," Sammael did not know how to answer that. He did have that knowledge, but he would never use it. He hadn't even been tempted to use it on Radek. The death was usually horrendous and very painful.

"Yes," Ammit answered for him. "Sammael does have that knowledge."

"And will you be returning to Egypt with your king now that Radek is out of the picture?" Alex continued.

"I do not know," Sammael answered honestly. "That depends on the queen."

Alex smiled. "Me or Cornelia?"

Progeny

"I guess both," Sammael answered honestly. "I believe Cornelia will take your lead and if you want me out of your country she will order it so."

"Why did you save my life?" Alex asked pointedly.

"The first time because I felt Lilith was being underhanded. Also, because my king, Ammit, gave specific instructions that you should be spared if at all possible. The second, because you saved my life," Sammael responded.

"Well, at least you are honest," Alex said, considering. "Do you want to return to Egypt?"

Sammael glanced at Ammit, then back to Alex. "I do not," he said softly. "I love Ammit, he will always be a dear friend, but I have grown to enjoy life here in America. I am more suited for a life here in New York than in the deserts of Egypt." He ducked his head, then looked at Ammit. "I am sorry, friend."

"Do not be sorry," Ammit said, tears in his eyes. "I admit I was looking forward to having you return. But I can see why you would like to stay. I hope you are happy here and that your new queen treats you well."

Sammael nodded once then took a step back. He was not part of this discussion and knew his place was not at the table.

"I can see you are loyal to Ammit," Cornelia finally said. "Do you think you could also be loyal to me?" She knew she was taking a chance, but this guy had saved both her and Alex. She was going to have to use someone as a liaison, she might as well start with him.

"I already am," Sammael said softly. "I will protect you with my life if necessary."

"I don't believe that will be required," Cornelia said. "I just hope I don't regret this. I know you will always be loyal to Ammit. I also know you were good enough to fool Radek and spy for your king. I hope our working relationship will be a better one."

"Yes, ma'am," Sammael said with a nod.

"Then it's settled," Cornelia said to the large group. "Sammael will be my first lieutenant. If any of you need to contact me, I expect you to go through him. He and he alone will know where to find me. I insist on this arrangement for two reasons. I intend to have a life with my husband. I will not be threatened by vampires every minute of every day. I will not be interrupted by them either. I require my privacy. The second reason is just as important. Sammael must demonstrate his loyalty to me. If he reveals my location, I will know he cannot be trusted and I will be forced to find a new lieutenant."

"We all know how to get in touch with Sammael, that is not a problem," Typhon agreed. "Just know, our spies have reported problems in the northern region. Dealing with the king up there may require some travel. Travel by all six of us, if we are to be successful."

Progeny

"I understand. I get that I will have responsibilities to the entire world if I agree to join this alliance. I am willing to accept those responsibilities," Cornelia said.

"Then you will join us?" DeMarco asked, enthusiastically glancing at Dante. The man had a confidence he had never seen before. He was looking forward to getting to know the vampire queen's partner. He had heard this queen was loyal to only this man. That alone intrigued DeMarco. The man must be amazing to demand such loyalty from a vampire.

"I will," Cornelia said, looking each vampire in the eye then turning to Alex.

"Cornelia and I will be working together as well," Alex added. "Can you live with that?"

"We can," Ammit spoke for everyone. "In fact, we anticipated that."

Maedoc pulled a large stack of papers from a briefcase and handed them to Cornelia. "This is a copy of the laws I have enacted among my people. There is also a copy of Typhon's laws. Ammit is more lenient with his people, but his are in there as well. DeMarco is relatively new and is still working on laws for his group. Feel free to contact any of us with questions or concerns," he turned to Alex. "All that is left is the matter of the key."

Alex looked to Mason, then Monroe and Numair. Once she received their nods she straightened her arm, palm up to reveal the large, shiny and unique key in her hand. Typhon reached out and took it immediately. "I hope I don't regret that," she said softly as she stood to leave.

"I assure you, you will not," Typhon said, placing the key into a small lock box and then locking it into his briefcase. "As I said, the vault contains very little information about you. What it does contain we have never used, nor plan to use, against your people. I thank you for returning it and will not forget the trust you are placing in me. If I can be of assistance, Cornelia will have my number. It is printed on the laws Maedoc just gave you," he turned to Cornelia. "And my dear, I do look forward to working with you," he stood. "Now, if you will excuse us, we have a long journey ahead and would like to get started on our way."

Typhon, Maedoc, DeMarco and Ammit stood to leave. Ammit paused, for only a minute to speak softly to Sammael. Then he too walked out of the room. The rest of the group sat motionless as footsteps grew softer and then disappeared altogether.

Sammael stepped forward. "Martinez was planning on staying for a few days if that is alright with you." He was addressing his question to Cornelia, but also took a minute to glance at Dante. Sammael knew these two were a package deal. He intended to prove himself to both of them. He meant what he had said to Ammit. He was not cut out for the desert. He liked it in New York and wanted to stay here, indefinitely if possible.

"That is fine," Cornelia said, standing. "I will be back in a few days to see how things are going. Don't disappoint me. I'm counting on you." She still didn't trust the vampire, and she was extremely apprehensive about her new status, but she had accepted the responsibility and position of queen, she was going to do her best to make the most of it. Her biggest fear was what her mother would say.

Dante stood and pulled Cornelia to the door. She didn't know it, but they had a wedding to get to.

* * * *

Cornelia was disappointed. She thought once that nerve-racking meeting was over her and Dante could have a little alone time. That wasn't going to happen. Alex had announced they were all meeting at the Deveraux Mansion for a debriefing and food. She had made it very clear this wasn't a request, it was an order. Cornelia stepped from the cave and groaned. "Do we have to?" she asked Dante softly. "I wanted to go home and spend a romantic evening with my husband."

Dante smiled. They might not have a romantic evening, but he'd planned gobs of romance for the next two weeks. He still hadn't been able to reach his grandparents, which was a major disappointment. He was determined to keep looking, though. He was anxious for them to meet his new wife. Cornelia, unlike Shannon, was somebody he wanted to show off. He wanted to tell the world he was married and the happiest man alive. The vampire stuff was a little weird, but somehow they would find a way to make that work, too. He knew they could do anything as long as they did it together.

The instant Cornelia stepped into the foyer of Thomas and Abby's home she knew something was up. The women were all wearing formal gowns, the men in suits. She glanced at Dante and frowned. He was glowing, his excitement would have been evident a mile away. "What's going on here?"

Abby rushed in and took Cornelia by the arm. Lillie stepped to the other side and did the same. "Come with us," Abby told her, pulling her to the winding staircase. "We decided to celebrate our victory in style."

Cornelia allowed her two friends to pull her up the stairs, but continued to frown. "Abby, you do realize I would never fit into any dress of yours," she turned to Lillie, "or yours," she added for effect.

"Then it's a good thing we got you something of your own," Lillie said cheerfully as she opened a large door and pushed Cornelia inside. The door shut with a loud thud behind them. Cornelia looked up and saw the beautiful wedding gown she had picked from a magazine weeks ago. She'd been visiting with Lillie and her friend had pulled out wedding magazines. Lillie claimed she was looking for her perfect wedding dress. She couldn't decide if she should pick one, order it and have it shipped to Italy, or if she should wait and go shopping when she arrived. Zarah claimed Italy had the best shopping on the planet. Cornelia began thumbing through pictures, not really paying attention until she got to this one. Her breath had caught and she confided in Lillie. She told her that she didn't remember her wedding at all and that she wished she'd worn a gown like this one instead of old ratty jeans. Now,

Progeny

here it was. She hesitantly stepped up beside it and realized it was exactly her size.

She turned back to question Lillie, tears in her eyes when she spotted her mother. The fight was over then, tears began running in streams down Cornelia's face. "Mom!" She exclaimed as Shaylee slowly walked toward her daughter. "Why are you here?"

Shaylee smiled, at first it was a tentative, nervous smile, then a full out grin. "That husband of yours will not take no for an answer," she finally said. "And he sent two friends that are equally persuasive."

"Friends?" Cornelia asked, furrowing her brow. All of Dante's friends were here. Fighting with them in that last battle.

"Yes," Shaylee confirmed. "Tala the private detective woman that came for you so long ago and a man, a handsome man named Atticus."

Cornelia turned to Abby, narrowing her eyes at the woman. "You are such a liar. They did not follow Megan and Tony to Ireland."

Abby shrugged, not at all ashamed of the fib she'd told. "Whatever I have to do to make my friend happy."

Then it hit her. Dante had arranged a wedding. She told him she hadn't remembered the first one, so he had planned all of this just for her. And he had arranged for her mother to be there. She was practically blubbering now. The tears were coming so fast.

628

"Okay, that's enough," Shaylee finally said. "It just won't do to have my only daughter getting married with swollen, red eyes. Let's get this gown on you and get started on your makeup. If you stop now, I might be able to hide the evidence."

"Mom," Cornelia said, pulling her into another big hug. "You have no idea how much it means to me that you are here." She still couldn't believe her mother was actually in New York.

Now Shaylee's eyes began to water. "I'm sorry I'm such a burden, sweetheart." She cleared her throat. "I'll try to do better. I heard that awful vampire is dead. I think I can do better now knowing I don't have to fear him anymore."

"That's not what I meant," Cornelia corrected. "I am so glad Tala and Atticus got you to come. My wedding is going to be perfect now that you are here." And she truly believed that.

Dante walked around the large back yard and tried to picture what it would look like at dawn. He was determined to give Cornelia the perfect wedding, which meant exchanging vows right at sunrise, with the vibrant colors behind them. He just hoped Mother Nature would cooperate. He turned at the sound of the door shutting, assuming it would be Nick or Thomas then froze. It took him about two seconds to cross the lawn and pull his grandmother into his arms. "Nick?" He asked, knowing the answer.

Progeny

Jasmine Waterson held her grandson tightly against her. She was so proud of him. A tear escaped and rolled down her cheek as she thought of her daughter, Dante's mother. Chelsea would have loved to be here today, loved to give her son away to this wonderful woman. Jasmine couldn't wait to meet the bride. Nick had told them so much about her. Jasmine hoped he was right. She couldn't bear to see her boy go through another awful breakup. She couldn't bear to have him fall for another awful woman like that Shannon character. She wasn't going to think about that. Nick said Cornelia was special, Jasmine just had to trust the boy's assessment. Nick was even more protective of Dante than she and her dear Richard were. If Nick approved, she was sure they would, too.

"You're crying," Dante said taking a step back. "What's wrong?"

"I'm so happy to see you," Jasmine told him, patting his cheek. "And I was just thinking how proud your mother would be to see you now," she paused. "I guess I'm just a little sad that Chelsea can't be here to see her boy all grown up and so happy. Yes, I can see this girl makes you happy. That alone makes her precious in my eyes. I can't wait to meet her."

Richard Waterson stepped forward and pulled Dante into a big bear hug. "Son," he said, a little choked up himself. Dante was so dashing in his dark tux and that smile was enough to light up the entire back yard. "Where is this woman of yours anyway?"

"She's getting ready," Dante smiled. "I've been trying to reach you for weeks. Now I know you've been

630

avoiding my calls," he feigned heartbreak. "I always knew you loved Nick more than me."

"Yeah," Stephano said casually moving through the back door. "That's what Nick says about you, too," he stepped forward and pulled Dante into a hug, lifting him off the ground. "It's so good to see my boy again," he said softly in Dante's ear. "And this will be a good practice run for Nick and Lillie."

"Get out of the way old man," Zarah said, pushing her husband aside. "I want to see my boy," she too pulled Dante into a big hug. "You are truly happy, yes?"

"Yes," Dante said pressing a kiss to Zarah's temple. "I am finally happy and I owe it all to Cornelia. She is one of a kind."

"I agree," Zarah said with a nod. "Almost as special as my Nick's Lillie."

"I see the two of you have finally bonded," Dante said innocently. "I told you she was perfect for him."

"And you were right," Zarah said as she patted Dante's hand. "So I will believe Nick when he says that this girl is perfect for you."

Nick and Thomas stepped through the back door and the greetings began again. Once Nick escaped his parents, he moved in to stand beside Dante. "You still holding up?"

Dante turned and pulled Nick in for a hug. It was unusual for him to show his friend this kind of affection,

Progeny

but he couldn't help it. "Thank you," he choked. "Thank you so much for bringing Grams and Pops here. I had resigned myself, knowing I had to go ahead with the wedding without them, but having them here..." he paused.

Nick swung an arm around Dante's shoulder and pulled him to his side. "I know," he told his friend. "I know. You did that for me when I changed Lillie. You brought my parents here so they could meet the wonderful woman I am going to marry. How could I do any less for you?"

Dante nodded. "Well, thank you," he glanced at his grandparents then back to Nick. "I have missed them so much. I hadn't realized just how much until I turned around and saw them standing there. This trip of theirs, the war, it has taken us away from each other for far too long."

"I agree," Nick said soberly, looking at his own parents. "I guess that's another reason I am looking forward to my wedding. I miss my family, the vineyard, the peace."

Dante clapped a hand on Nick's shoulder. "I hear you, I'm all for peace."

The guests filed in and took their seats, waiting for the bride to be escorted down by her mother. All of their friends were in attendance. Alex and Dimitri held hands, Alex trying to envision her own wedding just a couple months away. Ariel sat next to Victor, remembering the amazing double wedding this group had thrown together for her, Victor, Atticus and Tala. Ty draped an arm around Sam, thinking about his wedding and the amazing time

632

they'd had at the ranch, Bastian and Kylee were lost in thoughts of their wedding and the trip to Ireland that had followed. Thomas glanced at Abby, worried this wedding was going to make her even more upset at him for his lack of proposal. Little did she know after the bride and groom left tonight, he was going to whisk her away on his jet to his private island resort in the Solomon Islands. The place was all ready for them and after a week in paradise, he was sure she would forgive him for making her wait. He could just imagine her swimming out to sea in the form of a dolphin and lounging by the natural pool with one of her favorite strawberry daiquiris. He couldn't wait. It was going to be perfect.

Nick draped an arm around Lillie's shoulder as the music started and Cornelia and Shaylee stepped out into the cool morning air. Dante had timed this perfectly. He looked so happy and a little nervous standing at the front of the room, next to Oberon, with the bright yellows and oranges of the sunrise behind him. The instant Cornelia saw him, her eyes never left his. Nick knew it was going to be like that for him and Lillie. His mother had been planning his wedding all of his life. He just hoped she got it right. He wanted his day to be just as perfect as this one was for Dante. He blinked back the moisture forming in his eyes, must be the dust. The two of them had certainly had a wild ride so far. But watching Dante take Cornelia's hand and press it to his lips made something inside Nick settle for the first time in two hundred and nineteen years. Nick somehow knew that whatever came next for them, it couldn't be as turbulent as the past had been.

Progeny

He smiled and linked hands with his mother's as she reached out to him. Life was perfect, he had the love of his life on one side and his amazing mother on the other. And his best friend was marrying the woman of his dreams. What more could a guy ask for?

Epilogue

Five Years Later

The sun was shining on the large deck of the yacht as Alex and Dimitri stepped from their luxurious room to join their friends. "This was such a good idea," Alex said to Dimitri as she lowered herself onto the padded lounge chair. "It seems like we've been traveling non-stop since our honeymoon but all of it was business. I was in desperate need of a break. I am so glad Dante and Cornelia invited the group to join them. And look at this yacht, it's amazing."

"Me too," Dimitri said as he handed Alex a freshly made Pina Colada. He couldn't remember the last time he was in the same place as all his warriors. The change was still strange to him. They took shifts patrolling each night, but they were patrolling for violators, vampires breaking

Progeny

Corrie's laws, not vampires out killing. Cornelia was now Corrie to all her friends but she was still Queen Cornelia to the vampires. The only exception to this was Sammael. Once Dante started calling her by the shortened name, it caught on with the rest of the group. Nobody even thought of her as Cornelia these days. She and Dante were now coordinating the patrol schedule. Mostly because of all the travel he and Alex had been doing the past few years. They both felt it was important to meet all the other fae royalty and their councils in person. While they were traveling the world, each of them stopped in and dealt with problems in their businesses as well. It was something that needed to be done but, like Alex said, it was all business. The two of them were exhausted and happy to be back home with friends.

Dimitri thought of the changes that had occurred since they'd left. Especially in the vampire world. The other vampires in the new alliance had been skeptical at first. Corrie had made so many changes right away. The most important one was the law sentencing any vampire to death that drained, rather than drank from a human. They were all surprised to learn that a vampire could feed on a human then wipe their memory of the event. The vampires had just gotten lazy under Balthazar's rule and then Radek's. Sammael had advised them of this ability. That vampire was proving to be a valuable asset. He was small, but extremely fierce and more intolerant of violators than the warriors were. Strange how things worked out sometimes. They all knew Sammael was still loyal to Ammit, but Corrie had become a close second for him. That was the only reason they felt comfortable leaving the city with all the warriors on board. That and the growing friendship Dante had with Canada's King, DeMarco. DeMarco had promised to be available to Sammael if there were problems. Canada had recently adopted Corrie's law regarding killing humans when feeding, as well. DeMarco had been more than skeptical at first; in fact, he'd been downright rude in his criticism. Once he realized how many problems Corrie's law had eliminated in New York, he had passed the same law for his own people. They were still getting used to it, but it seemed to be working. And, for some reason, the guy admired Dante, which only helped elevate Dante's status among the New York vampires. It had been a tough five years, but Corrie and Dante were now liked and respected among the local vampire coven.

The biggest change was the new compound Nick and Dante had built. They'd purchased a large plot of land out near the vampire caves and had developed a huge underground city where vampires could live in apartment like structures, but underground. They had just finished construction on the second structure and would be starting a larger third building within the year. There were strict rules if a vampire wanted to live there, similar to the way the two of them had set up Waterson House. Any vampire that lived there had to contribute in some way. Maedoc learned of the compound and flew out to tour the facility several months ago. He was now building his own compound in Ireland. Slowly the vampires were emerging into a more civilized society. Dimitri believed that could only lead to good things down the road.

Alex settled back in the comfortable chair and thought about the past five years. She and Dimitri had been traveling non-stop. After their wedding in April, they had

Progeny

gone to Ireland to visit Elizabeth and fill Tony and Megan in on the battle. Tony was disappointed he hadn't been there to meet Maedoc but he was sure Victor had handled things just fine. Then, it was back to New York for a short visit before they headed to Nick and Lillie's wedding in Italy. During the short time Alex had been home, she'd hired Nebi as her personal assistant. That girl was amazing and made Alex's job at Deveraux Industries a hundred times easier. Alex wondered how she was going to make it without her while Nebi took time out for maternity leave. "I didn't have a chance to tell you guys," Alex announced to the group sunning on the deck. "Nebi had the babies early this morning. Twin boys, Zeke and Nathaniel. Both healthy and the kids are so happy. I think Dusty is going to burst with joy over his new sons."

The group broke into talk of the happy couple and the wonderful asset they had become during the war and afterward. "Ty's a little worried about the company," Sam admitted. "I mean with us on vacation and Dusty taking time off with his family, he thinks the guys are going to run amok."

Ty wrapped an arm around Sam and covered her mouth. "Not worried," he corrected as Sam tried to mumble something under his hand. Nobody understood a thing she said. "It's just that I have come to rely on Dusty so heavily. Having the main office shut down makes me a little nervous. I can't believe that kid. Dusty loves everything I hate about that place. We're a good team, something I never in a million years thought I would have. I trust him explicitly and the guy is a natural with games and admin problems. He said he learned most of it from his father." Ty removed his hand from Sam's mouth and brushed a light kiss across her lips. "Another upside is the amount of time Sam and I can spend at the ranch. Making Dusty my CEO was the best business decision I've ever made."

"I agree," Sam said leaning over the side of her chair to snuggle closer to her husband. "Ty and I have so much more time to spend with the dogs and the horses. I absolutely love it when we go to the ranch. It reminds me of my childhood," she glanced at Alex. "Now that the war is over and Radek is dead, I've allowed myself to think about my family. The good times and the bad. Staying on the ranch makes me feel like I'm honoring them in a way. And it's so peaceful out there. Ty and I have come up with some amazing new gadgets. Business is booming for D-Tech and Tyson Electronics," she glanced at Alex, "So no talk from you of not working me hard enough."

Alex laughed and gave Sam a nod. "My lips are sealed."

"I heard your brother has a steady girl, is that true," Ariel asked Ty. "Any chance they're going to settle down soon?"

"I hope so," Ty said with a grin. "The sooner the better. Once that boy is married, mom will stop hounding me for grandkids. She'll have my brother and his new wife to torment."

"So, no children in the immediate future?" Kylee asked, picking up her daughter. "I was hoping little Charlie might have a friend sometime soon."

Progeny

"Sorry," Sam said, not in the least bit apologetic. "We have our hands full with the animals," she smiled at Ty as he pulled her arm, a silent request to move to his lap. She complied. "Someday we'll have one or two of the little tykes but right now it's all we can do to manage the ranch and the business. When we have kids, we want to be settled enough to actually have time with them."

"That makes sense," Kylee said, removing Charlie's blanket and setting her upright on her knee. "I decided the same. Bastian still works, hard enough for both of us most of the time. But I decided once I got pregnant I was going to quit the hospital and be a mom. Between my girl and the warrior blood project, we're busy enough."

"Did you guys hear about old man Ferguson?" Nick asked.

"You mean Pete Ferguson from Australia?" Victor inquired.

"Yeah," Nick said, "He was out four wheeling with his boys and crashed head first into a tree. He lost a lot of blood and the only thing that saved him was that contraption you two and Caleb put together. He had enough blood stored up to replace what he lost and help him heal. Word has spread. I bet AC Pharmaceuticals is hopping."

"It is, and so am I," Bastian admitted. "Our family needed this vacation. As you know I'm rarely available to patrol with the warriors nowadays. Between the installs and my women I'm a busy man," he smiled at Kylee as she placed Charlie in his lap.

"I'm still wondering how that happened," Victor said with a grin as he watched Bastian kiss Charlie's ear until she giggled. "Not the conceiving part, I'm well versed on that. But the little girl part. When was the last time a warrior had a daughter for a first born?"

"Oh, about four months ago," Dimitri chimed in. "Let me introduce you. This is Charlotte Amanda Carrigan, but her friend's call her Charlie."

Victor threw a lime at Dimitri's face, but the warrior was too fast. He batted it away with the flick of his hand. Victor gave him the middle finger and smiled as Ariel lowered herself onto his lap. "Hey babe," he greeted her as he shifted to get more comfortable. "How was the nap?" He asked softly into her ear. They had both gotten up early this morning out of habit. After coffee, Victor had headed for the deck but Ariel had gone back to bed. She said she was on vacation and intended to catch up on her sleep while they were here.

"Wonderful," Ariel answered settling in, loving the feel of Victor's arms around her. She was sure she would never get tired of their closeness. "Speaking of little Charlie, did you two ever decide if she was going to be able to shift like Luke?" Where was Abby's rug rat anyway?

"We don't know," Kylee said, frowning a little. "I hope so. My childhood was so confusing; I don't want Charlie to have to deal with that. But either way, I don't care as long as she's healthy and happy. Whether she's more warrior or shifter, it's all a natural part of life. I won't try to make her into something she's not like my mother did with me. And, with Rand and my father in her life,

Progeny

she's bound to find out at a young age. They not only spoil her rotten but thoroughly enjoy shifting for her entertainment. I think at only four months she'd already join them if she could."

"How's Rand doing anyway?" Lillie asked. "He hasn't been in New York much lately."

"Good, I think," Kylee said with a grin. "He seems happy in sunny California, and dad loves having him out there. I know dad enjoys visiting New York, but he will always be happiest in the west. Rand has settled in nicely as Security Director for Bastian's branch out there. Dad still enjoys tinkering, as he puts it, so he and Rand spend a lot of time together. We still haven't been able to convince him to work for Bastian full time. He is so amazing though. I learn something new from him every time we go out there. Anyway, I think Rand has a new girlfriend. He won't talk about it and I still can't get him to tell me who she is, which is why I think it might be serious. I hope so. He's such a great guy, I can't understand why he hasn't found someone special before now."

"His sister probably scares them all away," Dante said joining the group.

"Very funny," Kylee said, narrowing her eyes at their host. "Glad you could make it by the way."

Dante lowered himself into a lounge chair. "Late night," he explained. "We had to make an unexpected trip to Kazakhstan after Ethiopia."

"How'd it go?" Dimitri asked.

"As well as can be expected," Dante said, lowering his voice. "The alliance is working better than any of us hoped. Word is getting out that if you threaten our safety, you will pay. Martinez had to miss this trip, he's dealing with a problem down in Mexico. Things have gotten ugly since El Toro was killed. Too many drug lords, not enough customers or something like that."

"Martinez had to take him out, though," Nick said soberly. "The guy was a menace and he never had a chance once he tried to kidnap Martinez's younger sister. Francesca means the world to that man. But you're right, the place has become a mess. Too many lower level cartel members vying for the top spot."

"Anyway," Dante continued. "We held court on the vamps in Kazakhstan and the entire group had to be executed. That one was tough on Corrie. The one in Ethiopia was better. The violators were put on probation because of the circumstances. Corrie's still sleeping. We were up all night so the second we boarded, I had Charles push out then we went to our room and crashed. Sorry about the late start and not being here when you arrived. I was planning on greeting you myself and giving the grand tour. I gather you figured out sleeping arrangements okay?"

"Nick stepped in as host in your absence. Apparently, he's traveled on this ship before," Ariel assured him. "And what a ship it is. When you invited us to take a trip on your boat I had no idea, my man. You've been holding out on us."

Progeny

Dante grinned. "Not really, my grandparents bought it and decided it was too big for just the two of them. They decided to give it me and Corrie as a belated wedding gift. Not that they hadn't already given us enough. Anyway, Corrie fell in love with it the moment she saw it, I couldn't say no."

"And we are all very thankful for that decision," Lillie said, smiling. "Nick and I had the pleasure of spending the weekend on the good ship lollipop a couple weeks back. That's when we came up with the idea of a group getaway. We missed all you guys and wanted our friends back."

Dante grabbed Lillie around the neck and rubbed the top of her hair. "My ship is not called Lollipop and I don't care how many times you say it, I will not paint that ridiculous name on the side of my yacht. Let me go get Corrie and we can decide what to do with the afternoon."

"Let her sleep," Lillie said, worried about her friend. She was one of the few in the group that knew Corrie's secret. "She needs the rest."

Dante flashed Lillie a grateful smile then turned to Victor. "I heard you two expanded the shelter. How's that coming?"

"Finally finished," Victor said with a sigh. "We needed the extra room, but construction is always a pain, especially when we can't evac the place and let the workers have at it. The shelter had to continue to operate full time around the noise."

644

"Which is why I'm so happy for the peace and quiet," Ariel said stretching. "Thank you for putting this wonderful getaway together. I needed the rest more than you know."

An hour later Cornelia joined them. The group was loud, boisterous and happy to be back together again. She glanced around and spotted Luke, Thomas and Abby's three-year-old, standing with Dante on the ships deck. Dante was pointing out the various types of large fish as schools of them swam by. She settled into a comfortable chair happy to be among friends again.

"Uncle Nick," Luke said, pulling on Nick's arm.

"Yeah, squirt?" Nick asked pushing back his chair to make room for his favorite munchkin as he lifted the boy onto his lap.

"Can we swim now?" He begged. "You promised we could swim."

Nick glanced around the deck, "Yes I did, didn't I?" He pinched the boy's nose. "Ask mom if it's okay."

"Yay!" He said pumping his arms in the air as he landed on the wooden deck with a thud. "Mom can we? Pleaaase?"

Abby laughed. "Go downstairs and get dad. We'll all go for a swim."

Progeny

Moments later Luke resurfaced, Thomas in tow. He was literally dragging his father up the stairs. Thomas was laughing, holding back just to tease his son.

"Come on, dad," Luke urged impatiently. "You're too slow."

Thomas plucked Luke off the ground and threw him in the air. Luke laughed as Thomas caught him. "Do it again," he begged. Then giggled harder when Thomas threw him even higher.

Abby just shook her head. "And you wonder why the kid is such a dare devil."

Dante laughed. "Yeah, it's all Thomas. The kid doesn't have an ounce of his mother in there anywhere."

Abby grinned. "I'm glad you agree," she said, standing to join her boys. "You guys going to veg here all day or do you want to have a little fun?" She challenged.

"I'm all for fun, baby," Dante said, standing and pulling Cornelia to her feet. "What exactly did you have in mind?"

Abby leaned in and whispered something in Luke's ear. The boy giggled with delight then jumped into his mother's arms bobbing his head in agreement.

Thomas laughed. "You two go. I'm gonna help Dante unload the jet Skis then I expect you to come back for me," he pulled Abby in for a long, deep kiss. "Be careful."

646

Abby took Luke's hand and led him to the back stairs. "You ready honey?" She asked, taking his hand in hers.

Luke bobbed his head again. "Ready." He said, gazing up at his mother.

"Okay," Abby nodded. "Ready, set, go!" Mother and son jumped from the back of the yacht, shifting into dolphins before they hit the water.

Thomas watched, grinning until they swam a few yards out. Then he turned to Dante, still smiling. "You ready to unload the monsters? You and Nick can try to keep up, but my money's on my wife."

Dante turned, leaning in to give Cornelia a quick kiss. "You gonna join us, babe?"

"Not now," Cornelia said shaking her head. "Maybe later. Go have fun with the guys. I'm too content lounging here in the sun." She settled back in the large chair and closed her eyes.

Dante gave her a longer, more intense kiss then straightened and headed for the rear of the boat. "You coming old man?" He asked, shooting a glance at Nick over his shoulder.

Nick nuzzled Lillie's neck then pushed her forward to climb off the comfortable lounge chair. "You gonna stay with Corrie or you want to ride with the big boys?"

Progeny

Lillie laughed. "I'm with Corrie. It's just too comfortable here to move. And with you gone, I'll have this spacious chair all to myself. What more could a woman ask for?"

Nick leaned down and gave Lillie one more quick kiss then jogged off to join Thomas and Dante. "I'll come back and check on you in an hour," he promised.

"I'll be here," she said, shooing him away. She settled back in the chair and sighed, perfectly content.

* * * *

Hours later, the men had finished playing and had gone to their rooms to shower and change. Luke insisted on joining his father for a man's shower. Abby had laughed, then easily agreed. It was getting harder to keep up with her boys. They still hadn't told anyone they were having another baby. She secretly hoped for a girl and watching Kylee with Charlie only made that desire run deeper. She sank into a chair and wondered if she was ever going to get up again.

Kylee silently got to her feet and motioned to the baby. "She's out cold. I'm going to put her in the room and hope she can sleep a couple hours. We'll all be happier if she does," she smiled as she wandered off.

Abby leaned back and put up her feet. They were a little swollen, typical. That had happened to her with Luke, so this time around she wasn't worried about the changes to her body. She knew exactly what to expect and so far, this one seemed easier than it had been with Luke. Her eyes fluttered open when Alex sat down next to her. "How far along?" She asked in a whisper.

"What?" Abby asked, surprised Alex had noticed the signs.

"Don't be coy," Alex chided. "I know when my sister is pregnant. So, how long?"

"Three months," Abby admitted. "We weren't hiding it, not really. We just haven't announced it yet. We actually wanted to wait for you to get home so you and Dimitri would be the first to know."

"Know what?" Ariel asked sitting down next to her friends.

"We're expecting," Abby admitted.

"Really? That's great," Ariel said pulling Abby into a hug.

"So, what about you?" Ariel asked Alex. "When are you going to get started? Your brother's getting a pretty good head start."

"Now that Dimitri and I are done traveling for a while, we might. But then again we might not," Alex said cryptically.

"What exactly does that mean?" Abby asked.

Progeny

"It means we are not trying, but we're not trying to prevent it either. We're going to let nature take its course," Alex admitted, pushing back the pain this topic always caused her. "You know how it is for the fae. It could take decades before we get pregnant. I'm fine with whatever. I know eventually we'll have kids, so I'm not in any hurry. Our life has been so hectic, it's nice to just sit back, relax and enjoy each other for a while."

"I hear you," Ariel said in agreement. "Caden can be a handful. The first time I babysat him for Bree, I cried for over an hour when he left. I was so sure I could never be a good mom. Victor, of course, came to the rescue. I don't know how that man always knows when I need him, but he does. He came home early and found me blubbering in the bathroom. Anyway, we are way too busy right now but someday I know we'll start trying. Thanks to Alex we actually have that option. I can never thank you enough for that," she said soberly as she gave Alex a grateful smile. "Like you said, it could take a long time once we decide to try but we're patient enough to wait."

Corrie and Lillie joined the group. "We were thinking of docking at this secluded cove Dante and I found a while ago," Corrie announced. "You guys want to relax in the sand and sit by a fire while the men show us how manly they are and roast red meat over the hot coals?" Corrie asked.

"Love to," Sam said sitting down beside them. "I always love it when my man cooks. Red meat, mac and cheese, cold cereal, it's all the same. It's just nice to have him take care of me sometimes."

650

"We all got lucky there," Lillie admitted. "My man is aces when it comes to pampering me. Especially lately," she shot a subtle glance at Corrie then leaned back and settled into the chair.

"Why lately?" Abby asked, could Lillie be pregnant, too?

Kylee joined them, wondering what the conversation was all about.

"Because I'm having his baby," Lillie said, grinning from ear to ear.

"It's about time," Kylee said softly, glancing at Corrie in encouragement.

"You knew," Alex said accusingly.

"Of course I knew," Kylee said, not an ounce of apology in her tone. "I'm her doctor."

"Any other secrets you need to share?" Ariel asked, glaring at Kylee.

"I don't need to share anything. It's doctor-patient privilege. Even if I wanted to, I couldn't tell you guys. You know that," Kylee said defensively. "And it's unfair to be mad at me just because of my profession."

Lillie glanced at Corrie again, hoping she would share her news with the others. It was so hard keeping the secret, especially from Abby.

Progeny

"Well, I guess it's my turn for confessions," Corrie said with a sigh. "I'm pregnant, too," she absently placed her hands over her stomach to rub her baby bump.

"That is so cool," Sam said, jumping up to give Corrie a hug. "All three of you having a baby at the same time. Wouldn't it be cool if they got along as well as Dante, Nick and Thomas? Who cares what they are, they are going to be such close friends. I just know it. And Auntie Sam and Uncle Ty will show them all how to ride horses and the dogs, the dogs are going to love having kids to play with," she glanced at Alex. "How is Cane anyway? Has he settled in okay now that the traveling has ended?"

Alex smiled. Her dog was her baby. At first, she worried it would be too hard on him, moving from place to place, but he had the most wonderful time exploring each new location. Every new country was another adventure for him. Now she feared he was going to get bored being home all the time. So far, he was doing okay, though. "He's getting used to it, same as us. He's going to love having Luke around to play with, though. The two of them are so wonderful together. Luke loves to shift into a dog and go out romping and wrestling. It's adorable to watch."

"That's my boy," Abby smiled. "Wild animal by day, holy terror at night." Right on cue, Luke jumped into Abby's lap. She laughed and began showering kisses all over his face. "You smell much better. Are you wearing dad's cologne?"

"Yep," Luke said proudly. "He said I'm a man now and I need to start smelling like one."

"A man, huh?" Abby frowned. "I'm kind of partial to my little boy."

Luke kissed his mom then stood. "I'll be your little boy when we get home. Right now, I need to hang with the men," he pushed himself off her lap and ran to join his idols.

The men strolled to the lounge area and studied their women. "I'd say the cat's out of the bag," Dante said softly to Nick.

"I think you're right," Nick agreed.

"Now what are you two hiding?" Dimitri asked sliding in behind Alex.

Dante and Nick didn't say a word; they didn't want to spoil the surprise if they were wrong.

Thomas didn't have any such reservations. He knew Abby had told Alex. They'd agreed to share the secret as soon as possible. He leaned over with Luke perched on his shoulders and planted a hard, seductive kiss on Abby's lips. Luke squealed in delight as he held on tight. "Looks like you told them about the baby," he said, winking at her as he swung Luke off his shoulders and placed him on the floor.

"Aunt Corrie," Luke said, frowning. "You said that was a secret."

"I did," Corrie admitted. "But you can't keep secrets forever."

Progeny

The women laughed, the men stared.

"You too?" Dimitri asked, surprised. Dante had shared his concerns about Cornelia being able to conceive with Dimitri a few years ago. He was surprised she was willing to announce the pregnancy to the whole group just in case she lost it.

"And me," Lillie chimed in. "We're having triplets," she laughed at the horrified look on Nick's face. "Not us baby, I mean Abby, Corrie and me. We're all having babies at the same time, triplets. A new generation of bouncing baby boys. They probably will be boys. Maybe not Abs, she already has the little tyke, but Corrie and me for sure."

Nick laughed and snuggled into the chair next to his wife. "Thanks for telling," he whispered. "I had to tell Thomas and Dante earlier today. I just couldn't hold it in any longer."

"I know," Lillie admitted. "I couldn't keep the secret from Abby any longer either and with Corrie entering her twentieth week, I think it's safe to say her baby is going to make it. I know we're only two months along but I'm so excited already."

"Me too, baby," Nick said. "Me, too."

"You okay?" Dante asked Corrie as he pulled her into his arms.

She smiled up at him and snuggled close. "Everything is perfect. I'm glad we decided to do this. It's nice having everyone here again. We've all been so busy since..," she hesitated. It was always awkward discussing Radek and his death.

"Since the war ended," Dante provided. "Since things returned to normal. Since that huge weight was lifted from all of our shoulders. Yes, I know."

Cornelia smiled. Dante always did know exactly what to say to pull her out of a funk. She was still worried about her baby, but her last appointment with Kylee was encouraging. The baby was doing fine. He was healthy and active and growing like normal. They hadn't told anyone they were having a boy. The warriors would make assumptions, and that was okay. For a little while, she and Dante would be the only two who really knew the baby's gender. It would give them time to settle on a name. She knew this might be her only child, so the name was important. It had to have meaning. She and Dante had agreed, instantly, that the kid would not be named after either one of their fathers. So, they were on their own to figure it out. She wasn't worried, they had plenty of time. In fact, for once they had nothing but time.

* * * *

Alex smiled when Dimitri took her hand and led her away from the fire. He stopped in a secluded alcove and sat casually on a large rock, pulling her onto his lap. "You are so beautiful, sweetheart," he whispered. "I just had to get you alone for a while."

Progeny

Alex wrapped her arms around Dimitri's neck. "Is that what this is about? Or did you think I needed a break from all the baby talk?"

Dimitri pressed his lips to hers. He never could pull a fast one on her. "Maybe a little," he admitted. "I just wanted to make sure you were okay. They've talked about nothing but babies for hours."

"It still makes me sad," Alex admitted. "I know it happened almost four years ago, but it still makes me sad sometimes."

"You know it wasn't you, right?" He asked, pressing his lips to hers. "You know there was nothing you could have done to prevent what happened?"

"I keep telling myself that," Alex sighed. "But once again, my gift had limitations. Why can I heal myself, heal my friends, but I couldn't heal our baby?"

Dimitri ran his hand softly across her cheek then funneled his fingers through her hair. "Because the timing wasn't right," he finally said. "We were traveling and still had so much to do. I have to believe fate knew the timing was all wrong for us. I've come to terms with it, I hope you finally have, too."

"I have," she whispered, brushing a tear from her cheek. "I really have. I just look at Luke and think our boy would be about his age. I can't help but think of all we lost. But you're right. The timing was all wrong. I know that. I waited so long after my mother's death to enter this world. Once the war with Radek was over, the other kings and queens needed to meet us. I also think they needed to see just how strong we are together. We are pretty intimidating, you and me," she smiled, knowing Dimitri would agree.

"And we will have our own child one day," he assured her. "Did I tell you my mother had three miscarriages before she was able to carry me full term?" he asked. "I guess that means it's my fault, my genes not yours."

Alex knew he was just trying to make her feel better, but he didn't need to. She had accepted the loss long ago. "Neither one of us is to blame," she insisted. "Like you said, fate knew what was best," she paused. "I talked to Elizabeth about our miscarriage. Shortly after I lost our baby, I needed to know why it happened. Do you know what she told me?" At the time, Alex felt responsible for the loss. She thought she must have done something wrong to lose the baby so late in the pregnancy.

Dimitri shook his head. He thought about his talk with Richard. None of the warriors would have understood, but Richard did. That's why he had confided in him. Richard had understood the feeling of loss and the feelings of relief that made Dimitri feel guilty. He was just so thankful his wife had come away from the horrible experience alive. So many fae mothers died from similar experiences. If their bodies waited too long to miscarry the child, they became too weak and dehydrated to survive when the miscarriage finally occurred. Breena's tea was helping their people, but it hadn't eradicated the problem completely. Just thinking back to that time and all he may

Progeny

have lost brought the grief and sense of panic back to him. He swallowed the lump forming in his throat. He couldn't speak so he just pulled Alex in a little closer. He hadn't known Alex had confided in Elizabeth, but he should have. That's how she dealt with things, by gathering knowledge. Elizabeth had two adorable children, but she had also told them she had lost a baby once. Of course, Alex would turn to her when she suffered the same tragedy.

"Elizabeth told me in most cases, the fae mother miscarriages because there is a problem with the baby, not the mother. The child has some kind of serious physical defect that can't be overcome as the fetus develops. Elizabeth said they believe it's something major. It is so hard for fae to have children in the first place. Miscarriages are the body's way of protecting the mother while at the same time preserving her body for the next healthy baby. As much as I would have loved to have that baby, I am also grateful our first child wasn't born with an insurmountable defect. I don't think I could have survived carrying the baby full term only to lose him to a missing heart valve or some other disease I couldn't cure. Somehow that would have been even more difficult than losing him halfway through the pregnancy."

"You amaze me," Dimitri said, pulling her closer. "You are the most level headed, amazing woman I have ever met. Have I told you today how much I love and adore you?" He meant it. He had come to terms with the loss long ago, but he always worried that Alex was still privately struggling. Just like she'd struggled with the losses they had endured in the war with Radek. He'd been wrong. Alex had found a way to accept their loss and move